Apprehension and Desire

by
Ola Wegner

Ola Wegner

to my parents
moim rodzicom

Ola Wegner

Chapter One

Elizabeth Bennet stepped out of the carriage, supporting herself lightly on Sir William Lucas' arm. Together with Sir William and his younger daughter, Maria, she was on her way to Kent, in order to pay a long promised visit to her friend Charlotte. The eldest Lucas daughter had left Hertfordshire shortly after Christmas when she had married Mr. Collins. Her husband was the Bennets' cousin, and he held the position of the parson at Hunsford, a village presided over by Lady Catherine de Bourgh of Rosings Park.

"Miss Elizabeth, it will take some time to change the horses; perhaps you and Maria would like to have some tea at the inn?" Sir William suggested, his usual good humoured expression written on his face.

Both young ladies agreed readily, and Sir William escorted them inside the inn. He ordered the refreshments and excused himself to see to the change of the horses. The tea, little sandwiches and biscuits were promptly delivered. Elizabeth took advantage of Maria's preoccupation with the meal to remain silent and allowed her own thoughts to drift to her upcoming visit in Kent.

Although Elizabeth's feelings concerning the visit were rather mixed, she more anticipated than dreaded it. One would think the situation to be rather awkward, as Mr. Collins once courted her and even proposed to her, though he had been rejected, of course. However, Charlotte obviously did not see the awkwardness to it, as she repeated her warm invitation in every single letter that she had sent to Elizabeth since her departure.

Elizabeth had to admit to herself that last winter had been a very lonely time for her. Her elder sister, Jane, who was her dearest friend as well, had been away from Longbourn staying since January in London with their Aunt and Uncle Gardiner, at their house in Gracechurch Street. Without Jane and Charlotte's company, especially with her father becoming more and more secluded in the privacy of his library, she had literally no one to speak to and share her thoughts. The weather had been unusually cold for the south of England, which effectively discouraged her habit of taking long walks. Moreover, her mother seemed to have made a resolution to remind her daily, or at least every second day of her rejection of Mr. Collins' suit and what tragic consequences would it bring for the entire family. Elizabeth did her best not to take those remarks to her heart. She knew she could not have done otherwise as far as Mr. Collins was concerned.

There was a matter though, which worried her much more than Mr. Collins and her mother's unpleasant remarks. It was the situation with her sister Jane. Despite being almost three months in London, she had not met Mr. Bingley even once. Jane was not one to wear her heart on her sleeve, but reading between the lines of her letters, Elizabeth easily guessed that her dearest sister was heartbroken with Mr. Bingley's neglect and ignorance of her person. Elizabeth's heart bled for her sister, almost as much as if it had been she and not Jane, who had been rejected and abandoned by the man to whom she had given her heart.

Suddenly, Elizabeth's attention was drawn by a child's scream. She lifted her eyes to see the family who occupied a nearby table. There were several children of various ages, and a rather elaborately dressed woman, who obviously had to be their mother. The woman seemed to be seriously displeased with something, a permanent scowl appeared to alter her already rather unattractive features. She wore a bright dress, in a very fresh shade of green, and a few large feathers' adorned her turban hat. It momentarily crossed Elizabeth's mind that she had to share the same dressmaker as Miss Bingley.

The child, perhaps a five year-old boy, screamed again, tugging at his mother's dress impatiently.

"I want cookies," the child pronounced with a steely expression on its heavily freckled little face.

"You will not get any cookies," the woman answered coldly, pushing her son from her.

As a consequence of this action, the child started a prolonged cry, making his mother even more angry.

"Where is that girl when I need her?" the woman cried impatiently, her voice raised. "She is never with the children, always disappearing somewhere."

The boy kept wailing steadily, and Elizabeth was about to propose to Maria to move elsewhere, to a more quite place, when she saw a young woman leaving the small side room, and hastily approaching the noisy family.

"There you are! Where have you been?" the elaborately dressed woman exclaimed in a harsh tone.

The young woman bowed her head and answered politely. "I had to refresh myself, madam."

"You should have stayed with the children. I do not pay you for disappearing when you are most needed. I must take my rest before the remainder of the journey, and your responsibility is to take care of the children and allow me a moment of peace." The woman kept her voice raised high, in order to speak louder than her son's wailing. "Now, calm down Master Anthony."

The young woman took the boy's hand, but he only turned redder in the face, and kicked his governess' leg, hard enough to make her face contort in pain.

"Lizzy, is it not...? Maria asked Elizabeth in a lowered voice.

Elizabeth looked compassionately at the young woman, who appeared to be close to her own age. "Yes, it is she. It is Anne Parker."

"Perhaps we should greet her," Maria spoke hesitantly after a moment. "I remember that she and Charlotte were good friends."

Elizabeth lifted herself from her place and looked directly at the young woman, with a friendly smile on her face. Miss Parker had to feel Elizabeth's gaze on her, because she lifted her eyes. Elizabeth smiled and nodded her head, but the other woman averted her face quickly, without any acknowledgment of Elizabeth. She bent down to pick up the kicking and screaming Master Anthony, carrying him out of the inn.

"Did she not recognize you, Lizzy?" Maria asked, her curious eyes following Miss Parker when Elizabeth sat back on her chair.

Elizabeth stayed silent for a moment before answering. "I think she recognized me, and you as well, Maria, but it was her wish not to speak with us."

Maria leaned towards Elizabeth and whispered. "Poor Anne, that woman is so horrible." She glanced at the mother, who at that very moment had her mouth full of muffins. "And those children are like little monsters."

"Yes," was Elizabeth's only reply, her expression clouded.

***

"Elizabeth, my dear!" Charlotte cried, catching Elizabeth's hand and kissing her cheek. "I am so pleased to see you."

"As am I, Charlotte." Elizabeth kissed her friend's cheek back and hugged her.

Charlotte smiled at her one more time, her eyes promising a longer talk later, and moved to greet her father and her sister. Elizabeth turned to look at her friend's new home. The cottage was simply charming. It looked almost cheerful, with the tress and bushes around it, neat gravelled path leading to it, flowery curtains in the windows and a freshly painted, light blue door. Instantly, the view of the house put her into a much better mood, as her spirits had been considerably diminished with the scene she had witnessed at the inn.

"My dear cousin Elizabeth." Mr. Collins approached her with a smile. "How do you like our little home?" There was much pride in his voice when he darted his head up to look at the building.

"It is very pleasant indeed, cousin," Elizabeth said sincerely with a smile. "So happily situated and so well kept."

"Ah, yes," Mr. Collins let out a sigh of satisfaction. "We are perfectly happy here, me and my dearest Charlotte."

"And I am happy to hear it, Mr. Collins," Elizabeth said evenly, and she knew she meant it. When she had first heard that Charlotte accepted Mr. Collins, she could not imagine how her intelligent and sensible friend could be happy with such a man. But Charlotte seemed to be perfectly content, even blooming, when she was showing her father and sister her new home.

Soon Charlotte insisted all of them to walk inside the cottage while Mr. Collins stayed by the carriage to instruct the servants how to carry in the luggage.

To Elizabeth the inside of the cottage made an even better impression than the outside. The rooms, though small, looked spacious due to the light colours of very tastefully matched wallpapers. There were fresh flowers on the tables, and everything looked pristinely clean.

Elizabeth exclaimed about how much she liked the house, and she noticed how much her words of praise pleased Charlotte, who nearly beamed in pride about her household.

***

As they had arrived on Saturday, it was only on Monday morning that Elizabeth was able to talk more privately with her friend. Sir William, together with Mr. Collins and Maria, had gone to the village, and they were due to return in a few hours.

"Tell me, Elizabeth, what is your impression of Kent, Rosings Park and Hunsford?" Charlotte asked with a smile, handing Elizabeth a cup of fragrant tea.

"You know how much I like your house, Charlotte." Elizabeth took a sip of a tea, inhaling the pleasant aroma. "I had no idea you possessed such a talent for house decorating." She took another sip. "Excellent tea."

"Lady Catherine shared some of her tea with us. It is a very expensive blend, I assure you," Charlotte confided. "As for the house, I have been imagining for years how I would like my house to look like if I was ever fortunate enough to have a home of my own," she spoke with obvious enthusiasm. "There are many more things I want to change here." She looked around the room.

"It really gives you pleasure, does it not?" Elizabeth asked with a warm smile.

"Yes, it does." Charlotte lifted her cup to her lips. " However, you still have not answered my question, what do you think about Rosings Park, the manor, the gardens?"

"The gardens and the park are marvellous, from what I have managed to see. I cannot wait to explore the grounds fully. The manor itself is very grand, but perhaps too fancy and overly embellished to match my taste exactly." Elizabeth reached for a biscuit. "I was surprised that Lady Catherine insisted on our visiting there only the second day of our stay."

"She likes the company, I think." Charlotte pushed the plate with sweets closer to her friend. "We are often invited to dine at the manor. Lady Catherine likes to listen to Mr. Collins' reports on what is currently happening in the village."

Elizabeth raised her brow, munching the biscuit in her mouth. "Lady Catherine voices her opinions very decidedly, I would say."

Charlotte smiled, shaking her head a little. "The same as you, Elizabeth. I think that Lady Catherine was quite astonished with how outspoken you are."

"I hope that my behaviour will not harm your relations with Lady Catherine," Elizabeth said worriedly as she swallowed her cookie.

"No, I do not think so." Charlotte put a calming hand on Elizabeth's arm. "I think that she was quite diverted with you. Now, help yourself to another biscuit. I know you like them, I ordered the cook to prepare them especially for you."

Elizabeth let out a soft sigh, and her eyes rested longingly on the plate full of goodies. The ones covered with lemon icing were her favourite. "Oh, I really should not. I would not be able to tie my stays later."

"It is not that bad. You have a very pleasant figure, the kind that most gentlemen feel instantly attracted to." Charlotte glanced meaningfully at the low cut of Elizabeth dress, where her rather prominent bosom swelled.

"Charlotte, please," Elizabeth murmured, blushing. "You always embarrass me with such remarks."

"I am sorry." Charlotte gave her friend an apologetic look. "It was not my intention to make you uncomfortable, but simply to give you a compliment."

The friends were silent for a moment, occupied with their cups, before Elizabeth spoke again.

"I have wanted to tell you about something since I arrived, but there has not been an appropriate time alone with you so far. You will not guess who we saw when we were changing horses on our way here."

The older woman nodded. "I know. Maria mentioned that you saw Anne Parker, and described what you had witnessed at the inn."

"Oh, if you could have seen poor Anne there," Elizabeth cried. "It was so humiliating. Those people she works for are so horrible; the children she cares for are little monsters and their mother so vulgar, so unkind."

"Yes, sadly it is quite a common fate for a governess," Charlotte stated.

"A life of loneliness and humiliation." Elizabeth shook her head. "Anne does not deserve it." You remember what a brilliant, vibrant creature she was; she and her sister, Amy."

"Yes, but mind you that it was before their father's death," Charlotte pointed out. "Mr. Parker left his daughters with so little money that they had no other choice than to take employment."

"I just cannot forget what I witnessed." Elizabeth walked to the window and stared outside at the lush and green garden at the back of the house, biting her lower lip and furrowing her forehead. "Charlotte, I smiled at her, I wanted to greet her, but she pretended not to recognize me, though I am sure that she did."

"You should not be surprised," Charlotte said. "It must have been a terribly awkward situation for her. Once we were all equals, and now the situation has changed so very much for her."

"Yes, it did change." Elizabeth turned back to her friend. "But the worst is that... I cannot stop thinking that one day, and very easily too, I could become her. Oh, Charlotte, it is horrible. I am afraid."

Charlotte stood up and stepped to her. "I know how you feel about it Lizzy. Believe me, I am familiar with that fear, and I know how it feels. It might have been my future as well, had I not married Mr. Collins."

Elizabeth looked at her friend for a moment before saying. "Forgive me, Charlotte, for even mentioning that matter now, but you found me unrealistic when I rejected Mr. Collins?"

"I do understand why you acted that way." Charlotte smiled kindly. "You know, it is easy to be romantic at the age of twenty. Your youth makes you fearless of the future; but in the course of time, more and more fears tend to invade. I am happy about my decision to marry Mr. Collins."

"You look happy," Elizabeth said with conviction.

"I practically buried the hope of ever getting married." Charlotte admitted, "I should thank you for rejecting Mr. Collins' suit."

Elizabeth said nothing to this, and Charlotte continued in a soft voice. "It is not that bad. I hardly see him all day long. I have my own home, and I know that my future is safe. That is most important in life, financial security. I will always have my own home, and not be a servant to anyone like poor Anne Parker. Mr. Collins is not the smartest of people, to be sure, but he is not intentionally cruel, never that, and he is quite... I would say, manageable. As for the more private side of the marriage, you know what I mean, it is pretty disgusting and loathsome, but bearable. And you can reduce it to a minimum quite easily."

Elizabeth took her seat again, and after a long moment spoke again with a wistfulness in her voice. "I always hoped to have a marriage like my Aunt and Uncle Gardiner."

"But such marriages are so very rare," Charlotte stressed the last words. "Waiting your whole life for something, which may very well never come, cannot be good or sensible. It can only make you become bitter and disappointed. I agree that Mr. and Mrs. Gardiner are an extremely well matched couple, but to tell you the truth, they are the only married couple like such I know."

"Me too," Elizabeth agreed quietly.

"Life is not a fairy tale, and it is not like some romantic novel," Charlotte continued in a sure voice as she sat down. "Forgive me saying this, but look at your sister, Jane. She has everything a woman can desire, a rare beauty, sweetness and kindness, and what? And what? Mr. Bingley paid her much attention, but then in reality left her. In the last letter from my mother, I read that he probably has no intention of ever coming back to Netherfield. Do you think it is fair to be treated like that?"

"No." Elizabeth dropped her eyes to her lap. "My heart bleeds for Jane."

"That is why we have to take the situations that life creates to our advantage whenever we can," Charlotte spoke with great conviction. "We cannot count on men or society to help us with it."

"I must admit, I am more prone to agree with you than I have ever thought to be before," Elizabeth agreed quietly.

"You will agree even more with me when I tell you about the fate of Amy Parker, Anne's sister," Charlotte said gravely.

"What happened to her? Did she take a position as well?"

"Yes, you can say so," Charlotte lowered her voice. "She took a position, of sorts."

"Of sorts...?" Elizabeth creased her dark brows.

Charlotte leaned in confidentially. "My mother told me that she became a mistress to a rich aristocrat. The man is a viscount, the eldest son of an earl, and he is already married to some equally titled lady."

"Oh, Charlotte." Elizabeth's eyes widened. "Poor Amy, she was always such a nice person, and now her fate is even worse than Anne's."

"I am not so sure of that." Charlotte pursed her lips. "From what I have heard, she was given a small house in the country and a good living. She is very well provided for by that man. In a sense, she is more independent than a legally married wife in many cases. If she economizes and invests the money she receives from that man well, she may live comfortably on it in the future, when the whole affair ends. I dare say that the only thing she lacks now in life is respectability."

The maid entered, asking whether she could clean after tea.

Elizabeth did not say anything, lost deep in her thoughts, as the servant took the dishes away. Charlotte left the parlour as well to give instructions about dinner.

A quarter of an hour later, Elizabeth found her friend in the kitchen. "I think I need to go for a long walk. There is much indeed that I have to think about.

Chapter Two

Elizabeth, ran down the stairs at the parsonage, her bonnet, which she held dismissively by its blue ribbons, dangling by her knees.

She was already by the front door, reaching for the doorknob when she heard Charlotte's voice.

"Lizzy, you are going out?" Mrs. Collins came out from the back of the house, wearing a large, flowery apron, which protectively hugged her elegant day dress. "You have already walked before breakfast today."

"I know, Charlotte, but it is such a glorious day today," Elizabeth cried happily, her eyes sparkling. "There is only a week of my stay here left, and I want to make the most of it."

"We are expected at Rosings Park today," Charlotte reminded.

"I shall be back before four o'clock. Do not fret, my dear!" Elizabeth cried, already on the path outside the house.

"Put your bonnet on at least!" Charlotte called from the threshold. "Elizabeth, the sun is strong today. You do not want to get tanned like a gypsy, do you!?"

Mrs. Collins shook her head at her spirited friend, who only waved her hand at her, running towards the nearby grove, putting on her bonnet hastily in the process. Sometimes she truly understood why Mrs. Bennet's nerves were so affected, having such a lively daughter as Elizabeth. Sometimes she behaved like a ten year-old.

As for Elizabeth, she felt herself in high spirits today. It had been over three months now since she last had seen her dearest sister, Jane. Exactly a week from today, the manservant from her Uncle Gardiner's was to arrive at Hunsford to accompany her and Maria to London. It was planned they would stay for another week in town with the Gardiners, before returning to Longbourn. She stopped for a moment, took a deep breath and looked around, taking in the beauty of nature around her. She would miss the countryside here in Kent to be sure; but there was little chance she would visit this part of the country again.

Her stay here had proved to be very educational in more than one respect. For the last six weeks, Elizabeth had keenly observed Charlotte's life, and it seemed to her that her friend's life was truly happy. It even presented itself as attractive. Mr. Collins played such an unimportant role there. He was easily directed and easily disposed of. All day long, he was in the village, in the church, or at the manor being at every beck and call of Lady Catherine. When he happened to actually be at the parsonage, Charlotte always found a way to make sure he was occupied. She encouraged him to devote his time to preparing his sermon for the upcoming Sunday, or to work in the garden for his health.

Mr. Collins, on his part, seemed to be perfectly content with such swift management of his person and daily schedule by his wife. He was always ready, and happy to fulfil the wishes of his dearest Charlotte, as he constantly called her. The marriage had not added to his general sensibility however, and Elizabeth often barely contained herself from rolling her eyes at the nonsense Mr. Collins spoke daily at dinner. At those moments, Elizabeth looked at her friend to notice that Charlotte had not even registered her husband's stupid remarks at all. Her most typical comment in such cases was: '*Yes, yes, my dear, that is very interesting. Would you like more pudding?*'

For the first time in her life, Elizabeth doubted whether her resolution of marrying for love only, not simply for convenience, was the right one. On the other hand, she knew that whether she was given a chance to respond to Mr. Collins' proposal again, she would undoubtedly have said no again. She began to allow the thought of sharing her life with a man she did not love perhaps, but esteemed enough for his mind and intelligence to marry him. Her imagination started to create the figure of some as yet unknown gentleman, whom she would marry, without the deepest affection perhaps, but with due liking and respect, as a means of ensuring herself a safe future.

She had known for sure that the life which the Parker sisters lived was something she wanted to avoid at any cost. There was no doubt that Charlotte's life with Mr. Collins was ten times a better solution than the situation in which Anne Parker, or even worse, her sister, Amy, had been placed. For now Elizabeth was convinced, or rather she was telling herself that should there ~~would~~ be a man who could ensure her a safe, comfortable life, she would ~~reconsider~~ his offer, even without affection.

It had been in the second week of her stay at Hunsford that the guests had arrived at Rosings Park. They were Lady Catherine's nephews, Mr. Darcy and Colonel Fitzwilliam. Elizabeth had not anticipated meeting Mr. Darcy, remembering him only as the prideful, disagreeable, arrogant man who considered her not attractive enough to even tolerate dancing with. In her eyes, he was one of those haughty aristocrats, like the man who had brought poor Amy Parker to such a shameful situation.

However, his cousin Colonel Fitzwilliam proved himself to be a very different kind of man. Elizabeth had to admit that she had not ever met such an amiable, charming man since meeting Mr. Wickham and Mr. Bingley last autumn. Elizabeth was flattered that Colonel Fitzwilliam paid her attention, and she enjoyed his company. She knew that his intentions were nothing more than a light flirtation, he made himself clear enough on this, but it did not stop Elizabeth from anticipating their meetings.

Unfortunately, whenever she had a chance of carrying on a pleasant conversation with the colonel, his haughty cousin, Mr. Darcy, had to appear as well. He was always staring at her and making some odd unconnected remarks. Every time Colonel Fitzwilliam called at the parsonage, Mr. Darcy, to Elizabeth's great irritation, had to come as well. He spoke very little, and just stared at her and his cousin chatting together with a sort of disapprobation in his dark eyes, if Elizabeth could read him properly. Perhaps he was afraid that she wanted to make a catch of his precious cousin, and decided to watch and make sure that nothing improper would happen between her and Colonel Fitzwilliam.

It amused her when Charlotte suggested that Mr. Darcy was in love with her. Her friend concluded that it was the only explanation for Mr. Darcy's unusual behaviour, his staring, his seeking Elizabeth's company, his daily visits at the parsonage, even the fact that Elizabeth quite often happened to meet Mr. Darcy during her solitary walks. Elizabeth laughed off Charlotte's suspicions. She, on her part, was convinced that Mr. Darcy was the last man in the world who could have romantic feelings for her. He acted odd, that was true, but it was not Elizabeth's intention to waste her time trying to find the explanation to Mr. Darcy's idiosyncrasies.

"Miss Bennet," she heard, and turning around, she saw Colonel Fitzwilliam. Elizabeth waited with a pleasant smile till he caught up with her, and accepted the offer of his arm. The colonel started his usual amiable chit-chat, and Elizabeth relaxed in his company. Suddenly, it crossed her mind that the colonel might have heard something about Mr. Bingley's whereabouts, probably from Mr. Darcy himself. Jane had not mentioned Mr. Bingley in her letters for a very long time, and Elizabeth wondered what he was doing now.

"Do you know Mr. Bingley and his sisters?" she asked, making sure her voice had a light tone.

Colonel Fitzwilliam did not seem to be surprised with her enquiry and spoke easily. "Yes, I met them a few times. We attend the same club with Mr. Bingley, but he is more of my cousin Darcy's good friend than mine. I can even say that Darcy is very protective of him as his friend. He cares for him like a younger brother. I know for example that last autumn he saved Bingley from entering into a very unfortunate marriage."

Elizabeth's heart sank, but she managed to reply indifferently. "Oh, really?"

"Yes, as far as I understand, the lady was quite beautiful and charming, but her family proved to be entirely unsuitable. Darcy suggested to me that Bingley was simply caught by a pretty face, and not for the first time, I dare say."

Elizabeth stopped and her face went pale. It screamed in her head that the lady in question that the colonel talked about had to be Jane. Mr. Bingley had spent the entire autumn in Hertfordshire after all, and the only lady he courted there was Jane. So it was all Mr. Darcy's fault! He had to have been the one to convince Mr. Bingley to leave the country and abandon Jane without even a word of explanation or proper farewell. So far Elizabeth had only a suspicion that it had been Mr. Bingley's sisters who had opposed his interest in Jane, but apparently from the colonel's allusions, it had been Mr. Darcy as well, surely plotting together with them. What a hateful, cruel man he was; destroying the lives of people around him at his whim, first Mr. Wickham's and now her sister's. And these were only two cases of his misconduct that she was aware of – she wondered how many other lives Mr Darcy had ruined.

"Miss Bennet, Miss Bennet, are you quite well?" Colonel Fitzwilliam's concerned voice rang in her ears.

She looked up at the sincere face of the man beside her. "I..." She swallowed and her eyebrows creased. "I am afraid I must go back. I promised Mrs. Collins that I would return early."

"Yes, of course." Colonel Fitzwilliam gave her a careful look and added. "Forgive me, Miss Bennet, but you do look unwell."

"It is a sudden headache. I think I walked too far today." Elizabeth explained in a weak voice.

Colonel Fitzwilliam proposed, and even insisted on walking her back to the parsonage, but she refused, preferring to be left alone. She thanked the colonel for his company, and walked away from him, without looking back even once.

She did not remember how she reached the parsonage, but went straight to her room, and laid down on the bed, without even removing her spencer.

Soon there was a soft knock at the door and Charlotte entered. "Lizzy, I did not hear you come back. It is time for us to go to Rosings. Lady Catherine has sent a carriage for us."

"Forgive me, Charlotte, but I will not attend tonight," Elizabeth whispered, slowly lifting to a sitting position and unbuttoning her spencer.

"What is the matter, Lizzy?" Charlotte enquired with obvious concern in her voice, leaning over her friend.

"Nothing serious, Charlotte." Elizabeth shook her head. "I believe I simply walked too far. You were right, the sun has been strong today."

Mrs. Collins stroked Elizabeth's hair. "I shall explain your absence to Lady Catherine. I am sure she will understand your indisposition. Now, do rest. I shall order some herbal tea for you in the parlour in half an hour. It is a special blend I brought from home which aided my mother many times when she suffered from headaches."

"I thank you, Charlotte," Elizabeth murmured, lying back on the bed, closing her eyes.

She must have fallen asleep for some time, but it felt like only a moment when the maid knocked, informing her that her tea was being served downstairs. Elizabeth let out a weary sigh, eventually rejecting the thought of asking to bring the tea to her room.

She refreshed her face with some cool water before walking downstairs. In the parlour, she took a sip of tea, which had a pleasant scent, but tasted horrible. Still, she obediently drank the entire cup, aware of Charlotte's efforts to make her feel better. But suddenly, her surprise could not have been greater, when the maid entered, announcing Mr. Darcy. He all but stormed into the room, breathless and somehow agitated, starting immediately to ask about her well-being. Elizabeth answered shortly that she was feeling better and then stayed silent. It was not her intention to speak with that man. She did not care whether he considered her rude or unsocial. She wanted him to go away, still having no idea why he had come here alone in the first place.

Elizabeth did not lift her eyes from her lap to look at Mr. Darcy, but she was well aware of him pacing the room in a restless manner.

She felt shivers run down her spine when he walked close to the chair where she sat. He was standing so close that she imagined she could sense his warmth and smell his manly scent. His eyes were on her, and at last she gathered her courage and looked up.

Mr. Darcy stared at her for a moment or two before reaching for her hand. The next moment, a most astonished Elizabeth could feel the hot, moist kisses on the top of her hand.

"I cannot carry on like this any more. God be my witness, I cannot," Mr. Darcy whispered fervently.

To Elizabeth's relief, he freed her hand, putting it gently back on her lap. "In vain I have struggled, it will not do. My feelings will not be repressed. You must allow me to tell you how ardently I admire and love you."

For the next few minutes, the most astonished Elizabeth had the opportunity to hear about Mr. Darcy's deep admiration and most passionate regard for her; but she also heard how unsuitable he had found her family and her connections, and how much it had cost him to convince himself he could allow himself to love her. For a short moment, remembering the story of poor Amy Parker, it crossed her mind that he would propose to her the position of his mistress. But nothing like that happened; after his speech of his great affection and even greater sacrifice, he took her hand gently again, closing it into both of his, and said. "I beg you to relieve my struggles and agree to become my wife."

Her first reaction was to say no, to refuse outwardly, this prideful and selfish man. She was about to say the biting words of refusal, when the scene from the inn again stood in front of her eyes. She remembered her resolution, made only recently, that she would accept the man who would be able to ensure her a comfortable life.

Now, the situation which she had imagined herself to be in one day, was happening. Here was a rich man, with such a position in the world, who wanted to marry her. This was a chance for her to ensure a safe future. She could not fool herself that another man like Mr. Darcy would cross her path again. It was not very likely. He was not Mr. Collins either. He might be arrogant and disdainful to the feelings of others, but he was educated, worldly and intelligent. She could never have objections to his sensibility, tastes and reasoning.

Elizabeth removed her hand from his grip, stood up and walked to the window. Could she accept him? But what about all those things he had done to Jane and to Mr. Wickham? Was Mr. Darcy's behaviour towards them simply the result of his indifference to the lives of others, or some more deeply rooted general cruelty of his character? Lastly, how could she accept him when she did not know him?

She trembled when she sensed him coming behind her. She closed her eyes, hearing him softly saying her name and turning her gently to him.

"Elizabeth," he repeated very softly. "Are you well?"

She lifted her eyes and stared into his handsome face. Yes, he was handsome and tall, well built, his chest broad, his face with a noble look to it. He was nothing like Mr. Collins where his outward appearance was concerned. She had to admit he was much more than a reasonably attractive man.

And Jane, she should think of Jane. As Mrs. Darcy, she would be in a position to see to it that Jane and Mr. Bingley would meet again. If Mr. Darcy, despite all the objections concerning her family and her position in the world, which he so elaborately had laid down just a few minutes ago, had eventually decided to propose to her, he would not prevent his best friend from doing the same with her sister.

Elizabeth stared into his eyes, feeling his big, warm hands resting lightly on her shoulders. There seemed to be a truth in his eyes; his gaze was warm and genuine, as if concerned about her. She reminded herself that though he had offended her family and upbringing, he had to care, or at least imagined himself to care, for her if he had decided to propose marriage to her. He clearly found her desirable, he wanted her, but still despite her low connections and lack of fortune, he was honourable enough to ask her to be his wife and not a mistress.

"Sweetheart," she heard, and blinked her eyes at him. "Elizabeth." He leaned forward, his hands resting more heavily on her arms now. She shut her eyes tightly for a short moment and concentrated to say the words.

"I thank you, Mr. Darcy. I do accept." It came out so quietly that it was barely heard, even to herself. She averted her eyes from him, resting them stubbornly on the ornament of the mantelpiece.

She thought the silence between them lasted an eternity. Perhaps she should not have agreed so quickly, she thought in panic. She should have asked him for a day or two to think about his proposal. Her body stiffened involuntarily when she sensed him stepping closer. Her heart stopped when she felt his hot breath against her temple.

"There is no need to be shy with me, Elizabeth." He tilted her chin making her look at him.

His eyes were kind and his voice gentle, but she barely registered that. All she wanted was to be left alone now. She desperately craved a moment alone to think everything through.

Her eyes widened in shock when he began leaning further towards her, his gaze focused on her lips. He wanted to kiss her! At the last moment, she turned her face from him, offering him instead her cheek.

"Forgive me," she heard, and he stepped back from her.

"I will go to Longbourn first thing in the morning to ask your father's permission." His voice sounded more formal now. "Perhaps you would wish to write a letter to your father, explaining the situation."

"I... yes."

He walked to her again. "Could you meet me early tomorrow in the grove, before my departure? Will seven o'clock not be too early?"

"No, I am used to rising early." She felt his gaze on her, but she refused to return it. He stood by her side for some time before walking in the direction of the door.

At length, Elizabeth looked up at Mr. Darcy, standing by the door, but not reaching for the doorknob, as if he could not decide whether to go or stay. He was looking at her, and Elizabeth forced herself to smile at him. It was barely a shadow of a smile, which did not even reach her eyes; but Mr. Darcy had to take it for incentive, as he smiled back at her, widely, which completely changed his whole countenance. Before she knew it, he was beside her again, pulling her into his embrace.

One of his hands was placed firmly around her waist, the other cradled her cheek. "I would wish to stay here with you longer, but I have to go. My Aunt may have noticed my absence and guessed I am with you. It will be better for us not to mention about our understanding to her for now. You can tell Mrs. Collins of our engagement; she seems to be a sensible woman who can be trusted."

"Yes, she is," Elizabeth whispered, her eyes stubbornly focused on his elaborately tied neck cloth, wishing him to simply go and leave her alone.

"What is the matter, Lizzy?" Elizabeth's eyes lifted up to him in surprise, her eyelashes fluttering. Had Mr. Darcy just called her Lizzy?

"You look so shocked," he chuckled, his whole face beaming at her. "I know that you did not expect my proposal. I understand you are still in awe and cannot believe your own good fortune."

"Where is my impertinent little lady?" he asked laughingly, and when she did not answer, still staring at him as if spellbound, he sighed, shaking his head with a smile, and pressed her very tightly to himself.

Elizabeth froze, feeling for the first time in her life, a hard male body next to hers. She had always known that he was tall, but in such close contact, she was more aware of how he was so very large. Her face was pressed sideways on his chest, one of his arms around her shoulders, his fingers stroking the nape of her neck, the other arm placed lower around her waist.

"I really must go," he whispered into her ear.

Then go! It screamed in her head. But he did not make the smallest move to separate from her, instead she felt hot, wet kisses on her neck.

"Mr. Darcy," she choked at last, taking a decided step back from him.

He let her go finally, however, obviously very reluctantly, and sighed again. "You will have to get used to me in this respect, Elizabeth."

She gaped at him, astounded with his arrogance. His warm hands cupped her cheeks and slowly smoothed down her shoulders and arms. "I told you that my regard for you has been passionate from the first moments. Now you should go upstairs and take an early night. A good night's sleep is the best for a headache. I only hope you will be able to fall asleep with such exciting news." He smiled in satisfaction.

"I shall be waiting for you tomorrow morning in the grove," he added, placing a soft kiss on her temple and leaving the room.

Chapter Three

Mr. and Mrs. Collins returned home late, as after tea they had been invited to dine at the manor. It did not escape Charlotte's attention how agitated Mr. Darcy had appeared to be that afternoon; his behaviour had been rather unusual. First, when they had just arrived, he had disappeared somewhere for well over two hours at least. He had been back at dinner, and when his aunt enquired where he had been, he had explained himself that there had been unexpected and urgent business which he had been forced to attend to immediately. During the dinner itself, Mr. Darcy had seemed to be quite oblivious to what was happening at the table. Even Lady Catherine had been forced to repeat herself when she had addressed him, as he had not paid attention to her words whatsoever. Charlotte had observed him discreetly, conveniently sitting opposite him. It struck her that Mr. Darcy had clearly smiled to himself a few times, even though the tone of the conversation at the table had not been of a kind to sparkle any amusement.

Mrs. Collins' surprise was even greater when on returning home in one of Lady Catherine's carriages, that her ladyship had been kind enough to offer them. She was informed by the servant that during their absence, Mr. Darcy had called, and conversed for a long time in the parlour with Miss Bennet. Later Miss Bennet had gone straight to her room, refusing to take any dinner. Charlotte put all these facts together quickly, both Mr. Darcy's and Elizabeth's odd behaviour that day, Mr. Darcy's absentmindedness during dinner, and his so unusual secret smiling. Dared she hope that Mr. Darcy had actually proposed to her dearest friend?

Without delay, she sent her husband to his room, ordering him to wait there for her, as she had some business yet to attend, and she rushed to Elizabeth's room. She knocked softly at the door, but nobody answered for a moment. Knocking again, the thought crossed her mind that Eliza had probably already gone to bed, but a then soft voice was heard.

"Enter."

Elizabeth was sitting in the window seat ledge in her nightclothes, her knees hugged to her chest.

"Elizabeth," Charlotte spoke cautiously, approaching the window. "How is your headache?"

Elizabeth gave her dumbfounded look. "My headache...?" Her dark brows furrowed. "It is better... I mean, I am well. I have forgotten about it."

Charlotte put her hand on her friend's arm gently. "Are you certain you are well?" she asked, but Elizabeth only nodded her head absently in response. There was a moment of silence before Charlotte spoke slowly. "The servant said Mr. Darcy called during our absence. Did he talk with you?"

Elizabeth looked up at her, biting her lip, her eyes wide. "You cannot imagine what I have done," she whispered in distress.

"Let me try," Charlotte spoke slowly. "Mr. Darcy proposed to you, and you accepted."

"How do you know?" Elizabeth cried, her eyes wide. "Did he talk with you about this?"

"No, he did not. I simply guessed. I have been telling you that he admires you. That is wonderful, Elizabeth" Charlotte smiled warmly at her friend. "I congratulate you."

But Elizabeth sprang to her feet as if not listening to her friend, and started pacing the room in an agitated manner. "Charlotte, what have I done?" Her hands went to her head. "I dislike him so."

Charlotte walked to her, taking Elizabeth's hands into hers, she spoke in a firm voice. "Elizabeth Bennet, look at me." She waited till Elizabeth met her eyes. "Accepting Mr. Darcy's proposal of marriage was the wisest thing that you have done in all your life. Do not dare to try to deny him now."

"I do not love him," Elizabeth pleaded miserably, her face a picture of anguish. "I thought I could do it. I was remembering what you said about Jane, and what we learned about the Parker girls... I was telling myself that I could do this, that I could accept him, and I said yes."

Charlotte squeezed her hands and looked straight into her eyes with determination. "It was a very good decision," she said evenly, stressing every word.

"But…" Elizabeth started again, but her friend interrupted her decidedly. "No doubts, no hesitations, please. It is done. Think about your family; what opportunities it creates for your younger sisters; think about Jane. Mr. Bingley, as Mr. Darcy's best friend, will surely be asked to attend your wedding. He and Jane will meet again. Perhaps even both of them will stand for you and Mr. Darcy at the ceremony. Can you imagine a better opportunity to unite them? Moreover, your marriage to Mr. Darcy will ensure security for your entire family."

Elizabeth shook her head, her hands coming to her face. "I know, Charlotte I am aware of all these circumstances, but something inside me is telling me that I should not have accepted him. That it is wrong to accept a man who thinks to love me, when I do not feel the same for him."

Charlotte took a deep breath and spoke gently. "You cannot know that you will not come to love him in time."

"But he is such an arrogant, selfish, haughty man; and when I think about poor Mr. Wickham and my…" Elizabeth started, but was again abruptly interrupted by her friend.

"Elizabeth, listen to me carefully. George Wickham is nobody! Do you hear me?" Mrs. Collins placed her hands on Elizabeth's shoulders, shaking her. "He is no one of consequence to you, and you must forget about him and about his tales. As for Mr. Darcy and his unfavourable qualities, I am sure that they can be diminished if you will influence him. Clearly, he is ready to do a lot for you, to sacrifice a lot for you. You can change him for the better. It is in your power. I am sure he will be willing to please you in any respect. Remember, as well, about his intelligence, his education and knowledge of the world. I think we can safely state that he is the only man of your acquaintance apart from your father who is your intellectual equal."

Elizabeth did not contradict these words, but she did not look convinced at all by her friend's arguments. Charlotte continued more calmly. "Did he ask you for a meeting tomorrow?"

Elizabeth nodded. "Yes, he did. He wants to meet me early in the morning in the grove. I am to bring a letter to my father, informing him of our attachment. He is to deliver it to Longbourn yet the same day, and ask for my father's consent."

"Have you written the letter?"

"No." Elizabeth shook her head. "How can I lie to my father, trying to convince him that I suddenly like Mr. Darcy!" Elizabeth cried fiercely. "Papa knows how I hate him."

"You do not hate your betrothed," Charlotte scolded her sharply. "You talked yourself into hating him, because he once said you were not attractive enough for him to dance with. Now, what time are you to meet him tomorrow?"

"Seven o'clock," Elizabeth murmured.

"I will get up earlier tomorrow and help you with your dress and hair. You must look your best. It would be best to write the letter now." Charlotte, seeing that Elizabeth was standing in place, without the slightest intention of moving, she took her by the hand and sat her by the small desk. "Come, I shall help you to write a convincing letter to Mr. Bennet. He should not have any suspicions about your doubts."

***

Fitzwilliam Darcy rolled on the other side of the huge four poster bed in his chamber at Rosings Park. The night was cloudless, and the moon shone through the open curtains, allowing him to see through the darkness. He reached for the pocket watch resting on his bedside to read it was past two o'clock. In little more than four hours, he would see Elizabeth again. He had known he would not get any sleep this night. He felt funny, all giddy inside, knowing that after all the inner struggle of months, she was at last his.

She had seemed to be entirely surprised with his proposals, he smiled to himself. She had looked so adorably shocked when he had called her Lizzy. Darcy closed his eyes, concentrating again on the sensation of having her in his arms. She had been so small and warm, her body soft, and she smelt so sweetly. The skin on her graceful neck, where he had managed to kiss her, was so soft, so delicate. He was a bit disappointed that she had not let him do anything more. He would not have gone too far, of course – he respected her virtue – but he longed for a kiss. She was a true genteel lady, and an innocent, and being in a man's arms was surely very new to her. He had felt how she stiffened when he pressed her to him. Good Lord, he craved her touch and caresses so much, but he was neither stupid nor blind. He doubted that her affections matched his, not yet at least. He knew though that soon he would win her over completely, and then she would not hesitate to allow him some liberties.

Tomorrow he would procure her father's consent, and then return to Kent as soon as possible, to escort her to her family in London. He had heard her speaking to his aunt about her plans to travel by post, accompanied just by the man servant her uncle was to send. It would not be borne that his future wife travel alone by post. He would have to bear those relatives of hers in trade, whatever their name was... Gardiner. It would not be pleasant, but there was no way to avoid it. Thankfully, Elizabeth was sensible enough, and she would surely agree to sever the relations with her family after the wedding. But he would not think about her unfortunate connections now. He felt a warm sensation in the pit of his stomach at the thought of the wedding. How soon could it be? A few weeks perhaps, if all could be prepared that soon. They would spend their first summer at Pemberley this year.

He looked at the empty space beside him. How would it feel to have her there, in his bed at night? To be able to always touch her, reach for her. He would at last learn how she looked under her clothes. So far he had been well acquainted with every part of her uncovered by her dresses. She had small hands, feet and ears. Her hair was thick, and probably very long, judging by the great mass of curls pinned on top of her head. And those dark eyes, eyes in which he was lost every time she directed them at him; though at first sight, they seemed to be black, in truth they were very dark green. He loved to observe her long eyelashes, charmingly curled in the corners. Even the imperfections of her face, like too short an upper lip, an imperfectly shaped nose, with far too many freckles on it, or that slightly crooked front tooth, seemed lovely to him.

As for her body... Darcy felt himself shivering, his arousal growing. His hand moved under the bed covers and he started touching himself leisurely. She was perfect in that respect. Perfect for him. During their mutual walks across the Rosings grounds, he had many an opportunity to observe her graceful form. Her breasts were a full handful for sure; he could barely wait to see them. Judging by her reserved behaviour today, he would have to wait for the wedding night to have a look at them. Somewhere at the back of his mind, he knew it was perhaps not exactly gentlemanlike to concentrate so on his betrothed's assets, but for the first time in his life, perhaps he did not care. He had seen many loveless marriages, so cold and entirely deprived of passion, in which the woman and man met in bed only to ensure themselves an heir.

His marriage would be entirely different. It was his reward for all the sacrifices he had been forced to make to marry her. Elizabeth was his gratification for all the hardships, all the blows and sorrows he had received from life. First his mother's death, which made his father entirely indifferent to everything around him, then the years of hard work when he had to pull Pemberley out of collapse, at the same time bringing up a little girl almost alone. And lastly, the matter of that cad, Wickham, his lies, his deception and the fact that he had almost lost Georgiana to him last summer. But now, better times would come. Now he would indulge himself for the first time in his life with a lovely wife; he would love, cherish and spend every hour of the day with her, the delight of his life. Elizabeth was kind, her heart tender, and she would be good for Georgiana, the same as she had been for her own sister, Jane, when she had nursed her at Netherfield. The thought of Jane prickled his conscience for a moment, but he quickly pushed the thought aside.

Ah, Elizabeth, how good it had felt to have her in his arms today. Darcy had found himself astonished in the early days of their acquaintance, even terrified, with this violent physical reaction he had always had for Elizabeth. Before her, he had been with a few women, but perhaps apart from his first time when he had been boyishly curious of how the naked woman looked, he had never been interested in how the women he had been with looked like under their clothing. He had felt no need to disrobe them completely or to disrobe himself for that matter. But with Elizabeth… the movement of his hand below the bed sheets became more urgent.

He remembered once when he had met her on one of her walks. She had said then she had planned a very long walk, across the fields. Darcy had been aware that the ground was more uneven than in the park. He could not allow her to hurt her foot, so he had insisted on accompanying her, of course. It had been the first truly warm day of the year, and she had not worn her spenser, only a light shawl thrown on her arms. He had walked slightly behind her, staring hungrily at the back of her neck, fighting the temptation to draw her to him and kiss her there, just at the place where her hair started to form in tiny curls. Then his eyes had lowered, and he noticed that her dress had been looser at the back. Clearly Elizabeth had not been wearing stays that day, as he could not see the edge of the corset starting under her dress. She had likely anticipated the physical exertion on walking on the uneven path, and she had probably resigned from putting on such a restricting garment. They had been about to cross another field border, and he was helping her to climb over the stone fence. She had barely supported herself on his hand, practically jumping lightly down on her own. However, as he had stood in front of her, he had caught the perfect view of her front. He had observed as her breasts swayed heavily, as she had been descending down. Moreover, as the wind had blown more strongly, her nipples had protruded through the thin cotton of her dress.

Darcy's breathing grew harsher, and he scrambled awkwardly out of the bed, going hastily straight to the chamber pot in the dressing room. He returned to bed calmed down a bit, and again reached for his pocket watch. Only three hours more and he would see her. Lying on his side, he took the pillow and brought it to himself. Soon he reached for the other one, and put them together by his side, imagining that it was she with him in his bed. He closed his eyes with a blissful smile on his lips.

***

The next morning, when Elizabeth reached the grove, he was already there, pacing restlessly from place to place. She stopped before he could notice her, and took a deep breath. Charlotte was right, she had done well yesterday in accepting him. She must think about Jane and her family.

"Miss Bennet!" she heard, and he was approaching her hastily, smiling at her.

Elizabeth smiled back meekly, and was instantly surprised again that instead of his usual serious bow, he reached directly for her hands, lifting them to his lips.

"Your hands are cold." He rubbed her hands in his. "Where are your gloves?" Only then did she notice she had forgotten to put on her gloves.

"I have forgotten them," she murmured, avoiding his searching eyes.

"Elizabeth, what were you thinking? What if you catch a cold?" he scolded her, but keeping the tone of his voice gentle. "The mornings are still chilly."

"I do not feel cold, sir," she whispered. "I shall be fine."

He did not stop rubbing her hands, till he reached with his right hand to touch her nose. "You are definitely cold." He frowned.

Before she could protest, she was in his embrace like yesterday, his hands rubbing her back and arms. "Here you go," he murmured, pulling her to himself, enveloping her into his great coat.

"What am I to do with you?" he demanded, closing his coat around her. "Sporting out of the house without gloves on such a cold morning?" He tightened the lapels of his greatcoat more securely around her. "Are you feeling warmer now? The climate in Derbyshire is much more severe than in the south of the country. I will have to see that you dress properly when going for a walk."

She managed to put a small space between them and looked up into his eyes that even to her were full of desire and longing.

"You smell so good," he murmured, pressing her again to him, his face dipping into her neck.

"Mr. Darcy," she tried to stop him, her eyes widening in apprehension.

"Please," he rasped thickly. "Let me." He bent his head down and caught her lower lip between both of his. "Let me, Lizzy. Just one kiss," he murmured and cupped her face with trembling fingers, deepening the kiss.

"No!" she tore away from him after a short moment. "I cannot." She walked to the other end of the grove. "I cannot do it," she repeated, her voice stronger.

"Elizabeth?" Mr. Darcy's confused eyes followed her. "What is the meaning of this?"

Everything in her screamed to tell him that she had made a mistake yesterday saying yes, that she could not marry him. It was not too late yet to back away. What should she do? She did not want a life like that of Parker sisters, but marrying a man for whom she had no feelings, nor any respect, whose character she doubted? Could she do that?

"It is all too fast for me." She shook her head, standing with her back to him. "I barely know you. Perhaps we... should wait ... we know each other so little... not enough to take on such a serious commitment."

He strode to her and turned her to look at him. "Elizabeth, I do not understand. We are engaged. You agreed to marry me."

"I know but... I am not sure whether it was a good decision." She looked to the side, avoiding his eyes. "I have doubts."

She stiffened when he pulled her to him, but more gently this time, keeping a safe space between them. "Forgive me. I should not have..." he sighed. "You are so bright, self confident, so lively, that I tend to forget how young and innocent you really are." He reached for her hand and gave it a squeeze. "I promise to try to restrain myself from touching you till you feel more comfortable in my company. Though is will not be easy for me."

"It is not only that..." she whispered.

"I can understand that this situation is very new for you," he spoke, his voice patient. "You simply must accustom yourself to it."

Elizabeth searched the dark brown eyes; they were honest, concerned, warm, as if he truly cared for her.

"I do not know what to do," she whispered helplessly, more to herself than to him.

There was a long silence. She felt his eyes on her the entire time.

"Have you written a letter to your father?" Darcy asked abruptly.

She gave him a surprised look. His expression changed, he wore his usual unreadable mask. "Yes, I have."

"Do you have it now?" he prompted.

Slowly, hesitantly, she reached to the hidden pocket of her dress and took out the letter.

Darcy nearly snatched it from her hand. "Do not fret. It is expected you may be apprehensive, marriage to me will alter your life completely, after all," he said in a voice of cold superiority. You will be Mistress of a great estate now, not just a country miss with no consequence in the world, scampering around the fields."

Elizabeth went pale and then scarlet at his arrogance and this new insult. She was about to retort sharply, but was taken aback when he stepped to her and placed a soft kiss on the side of her neck, just below her bonnet ribbon.

"I will return to you as soon as possible," he whispered into her neck, squeezed her hand and was gone.

"Wait!" she cried after his retreating figure, but he did not stop.

"What I have done?" she whispered, covering her burning face with her hands. "He is so ruthless... so arrogant. How can I bear such a man, share my life with him? Oh, Good God!"

Chapter Four

Darcy pounded the pillow with his fist repeatedly before he buried his head deeply into it and closed his eyes with determination. The sooner he fell asleep, the quicker the morning would come and he would be able to leave the place. It was nearly eleven, but the house was far from quiet. Every few minutes, someone was running down the corridor and the doors were open and closed many times. There were muffled voices and laughs coming every few minutes from the adjacent room. Did this family never retire? What a wild family the Bennets were! How could his lovely, intelligent Elizabeth abide living in such a household?

His thoughts returned to his dark haired Lizzy, and a shadow of worry tugged his heart. She had been so retreated, unwelcoming this morning. He was ever afraid she would want to call off their understanding. He could not allow it. She was the only one for him, and they were perfect for one another. He just needed some time to make her see it.

She had some doubts, he could feel her reluctant attitude, her apprehension, though honestly, he failed to understand why she was so hesitant. His offer was the best that could ever happen to her. She was a reasonable and intelligent creature. She must have seen that. She would lack nothing as his wife, he would love and cherish her as long as he lived. Most importantly she would be many miles away from her insufferable family.

He rolled on his stomach. He had planned the day in detail, and it certainly had not gone as he had expected. He was to meet Elizabeth in the morning, fervently hoping to steal a kiss or two, then reach Meryton by the afternoon, pay a quick call to Longbourn to ascertain Mr. Bennet's consent, spend the night at the inn, and return to Kent by the afternoon the next day.

However, so far, he had no reason to be pleased. Elizabeth had been shy and unresponsive in the morning. Her father had treated him harshly, as some villain wanting to deprive him of his favourite daughter (which truth to be told was exactly what Darcy wanted to do).

Mr. Bennet, as a supposedly intelligent person, should have perceived what an honour Darcy had bestowed on his second daughter with his offer. However, the older man had not only refused him Elizabeth's hand, but ridiculed him and exposed him to the unwanted attentions of Mrs. Bennet as well. Darcy groaned, thinking how it was possible that such a silly woman could have birthed his Elizabeth. What was even worse, Mr. Bennet had proved to be not much better than his wife, almost openly laughing at his expense during the dinner when Mrs. Bennet had attempted to force Darcy to eat every dish which had been served, stating he had been in need of feeding up.

No, indeed, the day had not gone well at all for Darcy.

Some minutes later, when he was on the verge of sleep, calmed with the thoughts of seeing his Elizabeth tomorrow, being close to her, having her fine eyes looking at him, he heard a sort of scraping.

"Mice?" he frowned.

The scraping repeated, and next the prolonged, stifled giggling came from the corridor.

"What the hell?" he murmured, got out of bed and strode across the room.

He shoved the door open with one wide move of his arm, only to see the two youngest Bennet girls just in their nightclothes, long blonde hanging hair loose around the shoulders, squatted on the floor at his feet.

For a long moment, Lydia and Kitty only gaped, with round, blue, unblinking eyes at his imposing figure clad in a nightshirt, but then Lydia glanced down at his hairy, bare legs. She nudged her sister with her elbow to look down, and both girls erupted into a new wave of wild laughter at the sight of his calves and feet.

Darcy shut the door, turned the key in the lock and checked again whether it was definitely closed.

"If you knew what I suffer for you, Elizabeth," he murmured into the pillow as he got back under the covers.

Earlier that day

Darcy sat in the dusty, darkish library, cluttered with the books from the floor to the ceiling.

Mr. Bennet sat in the overstuffed armchair, his dark eyes, Elizabeth' eyes, concentrated on the letter in his hand, which Darcy had handed to him, reading it with the most ⬛ incredible expression on his face.

For the first time, perhaps, Darcy had the opportunity to take a good look at the older gentleman, and was stricken with the great resemblance between his beloved and her father. They had the same eyes, framed with feminine, extremely long curled at the ends thick eyelashes, thin nose, and high intelligent forehead. Even what little was left of Mr. Bennet's silver hair had a decided curl to it.

Mr. Bennet arched an eyebrow, imitating Elizabeth's expression to perfection. "Mr. Darcy, I congratulate you."

Darcy gave him a cautious look. "You do?" he cleared his throat. "Thank you, sir."

"Yes, I do, I do." Mr. Bennet smiled. "You surprised me today, and I can tell you that there is very little in this world that can surprise me."

"There is?"

"Yes, indeed. Your visit was a surprise itself, to be sure, but this..." he waved the paper, "I am reading this letter, and I see that my daughter's hand penned it, though I still cannot believe that she wrote it."

Darcy frowned. "I assure you that I received it from her this very morning."

"Still, it definitely sounds as if it had been written by someone else, and not my Lizzy. Listen to this, Mr. Darcy. Mr Bennet reopened the letter and quoted. *The gentleman has done me an honour to propose marriage to me, and you can be sure of my full consent to his kind offer.*

Darcy smiled.

Mr. Bennet folded the letter, put it into a thick volume, which he placed on the top of one shaky book heap beside him.

"Forgive me, Mr. Darcy, but I simply cannot understand why she wants to accept the man she always called most disagreeable, whom she professed to dislike most of all the gentlemen of her acquaintance."

Darcy's smile fell flat. "I know nothing of that," he murmured.

The other man gave him a long, inquisitive, assessing look. "Mr. Darcy, may I ask how it happened that you developed such an affection for my daughter, Elizabeth? I understand that you indeed have some feelings for her if you want to marry her."

Darcy tried to square his shoulders even more than he already had. "From the very beginning of our acquaintance, I have held Miss Elizabeth in the highest esteem...."

"You have?" Mr. Bennet interrupted him, both his eyebrows arched. "Oh, come now, Mr. Darcy, we both know that is a lie," he stated good humouredly.

"We do?" Darcy asked stupidly, then shook his head with a frown. " I am afraid I do not understand your meaning, sir."

Mr. Bennet sighed, and spoke with little patience in his voice. "Let us be truthful, Mr. Darcy, shall we? As far as I remember, you refused to even dance with her, finding her not tolerable enough, if I recall correctly, not handsome enough to tempt a man such as you."

Darcy closed and opened his mouth several times before he stammered. "I... I was not aware that she heard..."

"She did."

"I must apologize to her then," he said quietly. "Mr Bennet, I was in bad mood that evening. Bingley insisted that I attend that Assembly, and in general, I dislike such gatherings... I usually prefer to stay home in my own company or with the people dear to me, like my sister."

"I can understand your dislike for large gatherings, believe me, Mr Darcy. I feel the same about it. Still I do not know why you decided to slight my daughter without even knowing her."

Darcy squirmed in his chair. "I thought that Bingley was trying to force another dull young lady into my company," he admitted "The remark was not directed against your daughter but rather against all the ladies present at the Assembly that evening, and the other women in Hertfordshire, London, and in fact the entire of England."

"I see, very interesting, young man, very interesting..." Mr. Bennet pinched the bridge of his nose, his eyes twinkling in amusement. "You dislike all females, I gather."

"No, not all, there are some women whom I hold in high esteem, perhaps not many of them... my sister is one of them, my late mother, my housekeeper and now your daughter. You must believe me that very early in our acquaintance, I started to discover and admire all the admirable qualities of Miss Elizabeth..."

"Such as?"

Darcy smiled and spoke more confidently, "Not only her beauty, but everything about her, her kind, compassionate heart, her lively disposition, her intelligence and so rare nowadays integrity and self respect, her grace, her manners, her voice, the way she expresses her opinions and defends them even when she is wrong. The passion in her eyes when she speaks about something. I have never met a woman like her, never thought that someone like her existed. When met again in Kent, I understood that there was no point in fighting my feelings for her."

"Well, Mr. Darcy that was perhaps the longest speech I have ever heard from you," Mr. Bennet noted.

"Thank you, sir," Darcy murmured.

Mr. Bennet did not say more, and looked out of the window.

Darcy stared at him without comprehension. Then he stood up abruptly.

"May I have the honour to ask for your daughter's hand in marriage?" he asked loudly.

"Sit down, young man." Mr. Bennet waved him down. "Are you aware that my daughter has no dowry to speak of?"

Darcy sat as ordered. "I am aware of that."

"It does not bother you?"

Darcy shook his head. "I am in a fortunate position to marry where I wish. I am fully able to support her so she would lack nothing. My income estimates at..."

He did not finish, because the older man interrupted him again. "Mr. Darcy I will be sincere with you. I am not willing to give my favourite daughter to a man I know so little about, nor without speaking with Elizabeth directly."

"You refuse," Darcy mumbled incredibly.

"Not exactly," Mr. Bennet said slowly. "I can agree to a courtship. You may stay in the neighbourhood as long as you wish, come here every day, accompany her on walks, and to parties, assemblies and church. If after... let us say six months, she still wants you, I will not oppose."

Darcy gave him a heavy look. "Is it your last word, sir?"

"Yes, you do not like it?"

"Not particularly," he murmured.

Mr. Bennet's eyes narrowed into black slits. "So we have a problem."

Darcy shook his head and stood up. "No, there is no problem." He spoke evenly, "I hardly have any other choice but to agree to your conditions. I respect your decision, and understand it, though I am hardly pleased with this unexpected delay. However, I have a sixteen year-old sister under my care, and I would like to know the man I will one day give her to."

Mr. Bennet rose as well and held out his hand. Darcy instantly accepted it. Mr. Bennet was nearly as tall as him, and their eyes were at the same level. Height, seemed to be the only thing that Elizabeth had not inherited from her father.

"Mrs. Bennet! Wife!" the older gentleman cried in a raised voice when he released Darcy's hand. "Mrs. Bennet, would you come here, please!"

The very next moment, the door opened, and Mrs. Bennet's blond curls and a white lacy cap popped in.

Mr. Bennet extended his hand. "My dear."

The woman walked to them, looking from her husband to Darcy.

"Imagine, my dear, that Mr. Darcy paid us a visit today to ask me permission to court Lizzy."

Mrs. Bennet gave her husband a most incredible look, " Lizzy? Our Lizzy?" she wanted to make sure.

Mr. Bennet smiled, nodding his bald head. "Yes, my dear, our Lizzy."

"Mr. Darcy... our Lizzy." Mrs. Bennet repeated slowly.

"What are your plans for the rest of day, Mr. Darcy?" Mr. Bennet asked, turning to the guest, and ignoring his wife for a moment as she digested the news.

"I will spend the night at the inn at Meryton before heading back to Kent tomorrow morning."

"At the inn? We cannot allow that!" Mr. Bennet cried almost theatrically, "Mrs. Bennet, do you agree with me that we cannot let Mr. Darcy stay at the inn?"

The woman shook her head eagerly. "No, indeed, Mr. Bennet. Mr. Darcy should be our guest."

Mr. Bennet smiled wildly, his eyes twinkling with mischief as he looked at the younger man. "Of course he should." He turned to his wife. "I hope you have a good dinner planned for today, Mrs. Bennet. Our guest travelled many miles to pay us a visit."

Mrs. Bennet gave a loud gasp. "Dinner." She turned on her feet and running to the door cried. "Excuse me, gentlemen. I must speak with Hill directly."

When Mrs. Bennet was gone, Darcy spoke hastily. "It is not necessary, sir. I will gladly stay at the inn."

"You will not disappoint us, Mr. Darcy. We may be a family one day, after all. I am sure Lizzy will like to visit us very often as your wife."

***

Darcy ordered the driver to stop the carriage on the outskirts of Rosings Park. He sent his people to the manor, while he decided to take a short walk to the parsonage. He had left Longbourn at first light, when the whole house had been yet in deep sleep, avoiding unwanted farewells.

Elizabeth. He would see her soon, talk with her, touch her. He hastened his pace. He had never thought that such an occurrence could happen to him, that he would fall for any woman so deeply. One her smile directed at him, one glance at her comely figure and a sort of balmy feeling instantly overpowered him. He felt content, peaceful and perfectly happy simply being in the same room with her. He lived for the next time he would see her. He had been alone as his own Master for so long, but not any more. He was a true fool in love. It was like an addiction, an illness which had afflicted him.

He reached the parsonage from the back gate, sincerely hoping not to meet Collins working in the garden. Thankfully, there was no sign of the parson, and the cottage seemed very quiet. As he darted his eyes to the façade of the building, his heart squeezed pleasantly at the sight of Elizabeth seated in the window, reading.

The back door stood wide open, and he entered, passing by the kitchen and the pantry. From the corner of his eye, he noticed Mrs. Collins talking with the cook. They did not see him, so undisturbed, he reached the staircase. Once upstairs, he counted the doors, trying to guess which one belonged to Elizabeth's room.

To his relief, his estimation proved right, and when he knocked lightly at the white, wooden surface, her sweet voice was heard. "Enter."

As he had expected, she was seated on the cushioned window seat ledge, her small, stocking clad feet resting neatly in front of her.

"Mr. Darcy," she whispered, her eyes widening at the sight. "What are you doing here?"

He closed the door. God, she was lovely. Her hair was only partially pinned up, and the cascade of rich chocolate curls was falling gracefully down her shoulders and back. Never before had he seen her so domestic, so intimate in her appearance.

With grace, she lifted herself from her place, her feet looking for pale green house slippers abandoned nearby.

He could not stop himself. He had to put his hands on her as he walked closer.

"I did not expect you today, sir," she said, as he toyed with a lock of her hair.

He stared at her mouth, distracted. "You did not."

She shook her head. "You did not go to Herefordshire?"

"I did. I talked with your father yesterday afternoon."

"You returned so soon?"

He smiled down at her. "I told you that I wanted to be back with you as soon as possible."

She allowed their eyes to meet at last, only to cast them down again. "Let us go downstairs," she tried to walk past him but he caught her hand, stopping her.

He shook his head.

"You should not be here, sir," she said nervously, her colour high. "Let us go to the parlour. We shall have some tea with Charlotte."

"No, please. Let us stay here." He pulled her to him, draping an arm around her back "Nobody saw me coming here. I want some privacy."

She stiffened and her eyes widened. Was she afraid of him? "It is not proper for you to be here, in my room," she said.

"Come," he whispered.

He sat in the only armchair present in the small room, and without a word of warning, pulled her onto his lap.

"Mr. Darcy!" she gasped, trying to lift herself.

"Do you have to be so formal with me, Elizabeth?" he tightened his embrace around her, ignoring her struggles to free herself. "Could you call me by my given name?"

When she did not do what he asked for immediately, he prompted. "It is Fitzwilliam."

She glared at him, slightly offended. "I do remember. Rather unusual first name, I dare say, like your cousin's surname."

"Yes, it was my mother's idea, I guess. She always shortened it though, and called me, William."

He noticed that she slowly relaxed in his arms, she was less tense and allowed her back to rest against his chest.

He took one wisp of dark hair, straightened it and then let it curl naturally around his finger. His gaze rested on the simple garnet cross placed in the dip of her throat, then lowered to the swell of her bosom, uncovered by the rather daring cut of her dress. She had a small dark mole on the left breast, visible just above the lace of her bodice. He swallowed and his manhood hardened. How would he able to survive those long months of courtship without even a small gratification.

She was affected, too, by their proximity, he realised. Her breasts started to heave, her lovely face flushed pink. It was so easy to reach for her lips, kiss and caress her. But he had promised her that he would try to restrain himself. He needed to control his urges. She deserved better.

He took her small hand and lifted it to his lips. "You did not want to know what your father said?" he asked as he nudged her off his lap, and stood up.

She nodded. "I do. Of course, I do."

Darcy walked away from her, raking his hand through his hair. "He agreed to courtship only. He wants to speak with you first before giving his consent to the marriage."

"I see."

"Perhaps you could try to convince him that the courting period is not necessary in our case?" he asked with hope.

She was silent for a moment. "In your opinion, I do not deserve to be courted in front of my family and friends?"she asked with the edge to her voice, not looking at him.

"No, of course not." He stepped to her again, catching her eyes. "You deserve everything, all the best in the world, but I had hoped that we could be together sooner."

She looked to the side. "We will spend a lot of time together during the courtship."

"I meant to spend time together as a man and a wife," he stroked her cheek, "Days and nights together," he whispered.

She blushed, as he pronounced the word nights. "I must be honest. I do not think I am ready for this. I am glad with my father's condition."

There was a pause. "We shall do as you wish then," he agreed. "I want you to be happy, content. We shall wait to be married."

"Thank you... William."

He did not like that her voice sounded so relieved, so he added more firmly. "I still want to be married before the end of the year."

She nodded only, standing in front of him, her eyes downcast, her whole posture uninviting, distant.

"When do you plan to return home?" he asked, stepping very close to her, so their bodies almost touched, making her look at him.

She looked up. "The beginning of next week. My uncle will send a man servant for Miss Lucas and me. We will travel by post to London in his company."

Darcy scowled. "I do not like that idea," he announced. "It is highly improper for a young gentle woman to travel by post with common strangers."

"It is but a few hours journey to London. I shall be fine," she answered calmly, stepping from him.

"I want you and Miss Lucas to travel in my carriage," he spoke in the commanding tone, he often used with Georgiana. "I will escort you to your uncle's home."

"I cannot do that!" she protested. "You know very well that would not be proper."

"You think that travelling with strangers is proper?" he cried, exasperated.

Elizabeth pressed her lips in a thin line. "I will not go to London alone with you in a carriage. My reputation will be ruined, you know it very well."

"Elizabeth, be reasonable, we are about to be married, surely before the end of the year. You will travel with me in a carriage all your future life. Besides Miss Lucas will be there too, and the manservant from your uncle that you mentioned. I may even go in another carriage after yours."

Elizabeth lifted her chin up. "I will go by post as was planned before."

"I cannot agree to that. I will not allow it!" he snapped.

She squared her shoulders. "You are not my husband yet, sir. To be precise, you are not even my betrothed. You are not my father or uncle to decide about me, and if they think that I can safely travel by post with Miss Lucas, I do not see the reason to do otherwise!"

"Do you not understand that I am worried for you! Something may happen to you!" He hovered over her. "Why are you so obstinate about this?"

She raised one finely drawn eyebrow. "I can ask you exactly the same question."

Darcy walked from her, pacing the restricted space of the small room. Why was she so stubborn? He was not used to such behaviour. His sister, Georgiana, would have never wanted to oppose him in such a way. He only wanted the very best for her. It was his right, his responsibility. He wanted her safe and protected. What was wrong with that? Why could she not see that?

He strived to calm himself. "Well then...would you consider using one of my aunt's carriages?"

"I am not sure whether Lady Catherine will be willing to..."

"She will," he interrupted her. "I will take care of that."

"As you wish," she said quietly after a moment.

He smiled, pleased that she had agreed with him. He walked to her. "I will go now."

"Yes, you must be tired after the long journey."

He took her hand. "We shall see each other tomorrow."

She shook her head. "No, yet today. Your aunt invited us to dinner."

He leaned into her, and whispered in low, soft voice. It was so natural to use such tones when speaking to her. "Then I will have the pleasure of seeing you again tonight."

"Yes."

He wanted to say something more, touch her again, but her expression did not invite that. She had withdrawn into herself, and did not look at him. He walked to the door, and with a final glance at her, left the room.

He had not imagined it like that. He had always thought her to be more responsive.

"I must be patient with her," he whispered.

Chapter Five

Elizabeth did not go for a walk that day, as she preferred to stay in her room. She could not concentrate on reading, or on anything else. Her father had offered her a safe escape, a rescue from the situation she had put herself in. She was grateful for that, but she did not know whether she would use it.

She was torn, she was afraid. Was she ruining her life or attempting to make it better? The more she thought about her situation, about her decision, the more undecided and confused she was. The only bright point that she had no doubts about was Jane. She wanted to help her sister, and now it was in her power.

She could not forget about what had induced her into accepting Mr. Darcy's proposal in the first place. The fate of the Parker sisters was the last thing she desired. The life of humiliation and loneliness, as a governess, or a mistress of some wealthy man, was something she wanted to avoid not only for herself, but for her sisters as well. She felt depressed only thinking of it. Mr. Darcy was her only chance to rescue herself. Who could guarantee her that another man of means would come her way in the future?

As Mrs. Darcy, she would have social standing and respect; the distress and humiliation would certainly accompany her existence daily, but at least she would have her own family, surely children. Mr. Darcy would make sure to visit her bedchamber often enough to have his heir. She would have someone to love. Perhaps she would have more than one child.

At least Jane would be happy. With their new connections to Mr. Darcy, Mr. Bingley, as his best friend, would reappear in their lives. Jane would be given another chance with Mr. Bingley - a chance for true happiness and a true love match.

Her father gave her time to think, to change her mind, but was it wise? After all, she had decided to marry him. A long courtship would only fuel her doubts, weaken her resolve. Perhaps it was more prudent to tell her father that she was ready to accept Mr. Darcy's offer, to announce a formal engagement, and set a wedding before the summer.

A soft knock at the door drew her attention back to the present moment.

"Elizabeth?" Charlotte appeared in the open door. "May I come in?"

"Of course." Elizabeth smiled, noting that her friend had her second best evening dress on.

"We are invited to dine with Lady Catherine's tonight. Have you forgotten?" Mrs. Collins enquired.

"Yes, I have forgotten. But only for a moment."

Charlotte sat next to her on the narrow bed. "Have you got a headache again? Do you wish to stay at home?" she examined her friend's pale face. "I am worried. It is so unlike you to feel unwell so often."

Elizabeth shook her head. "I do not feel unwell. I am truly well. I only worry about Mr. Darcy. I cannot stop thinking about it, back and forth, wondering whether it was a good decision."

Charlotte touched her hand reassuringly. "You did well. You will have your own home, security, and one day, children."

Elizabeth nodded. "Yes, I know; but it does not feel right. I feel guilty. Mr. Darcy, despite his faults, seems to love me. He acts like a man in love, and he thinks I love him too. I am deceiving him, it is unfair."

"You think about it too much." Charlotte patted her hand. "Do not worry so much about Mr. Darcy. He is his own man, he knows what he wants and gets it. I will risk saying that he knows you better than you think, and is aware of your true feelings for him. All will be well."

Elizabeth lifted and dropped her shoulders. "At least he knows." She stood up from the bed. "Give me a quarter of an hour, and I shall be ready for the evening."

Charlotte stood up as well, smoothing the bed. "Good, because Mr. Collins dislikes when we are not exactly on time."

"I have noticed," Elizabeth murmured dryly as she walked to her friend, looking into her face. "You are truly glowing today."

"It is because..." Charlotte's pale eyes sparkled. "I have been to the village to visit a midwife," she paused, "and she confirmed my suspicions."

"A baby?" Elizabeth whispered, a big smile appearing on her face.

Charlotte nodded.

"That is so wonderful! I am so happy for you! Have you told Mr. Collins?"

Charlotte shook her head. "No, and I want to keep the news to myself as long as possible. You are the first and the only person to know for the time being."

"Your secret is safe with me."

Charlotte squeezed her hands. "Oh, Elizabeth. I will have someone to love."

Elizabeth gave her a hug and whispered. "Yes, you will."

***

For the evening, Elizabeth donned her most favourite, in her opinion most flattering gown she had brought with herself to Kent; a very fine pale yellow muslin, with a green front, matching her dark green eyes. She put special effort to her hair as well, with the help of Charlotte pulling her curls tightly at the top of her head, with a few loose locks falling back on her neck. She thought this coiffure a bit extravagant, so unlike her usual, simpler style, but Charlotte convinced her that it suited her very well, making her eyes look even bigger and wider, and revealing her high forehead.

Lady Catherine welcomed them as usual, and acted her own self in the course of the evening, speaking nonsense, remarking on every subject, interfering and giving her advice, requested or not. Elizabeth preferred to be silent for most of the time. She felt Mr. Darcy's eyes on her constantly, but she refused to look back at him.

"Miss Bennet!"

Lady Catherine's sharp voice rang in her ears, when they were taking tea after dinner. "I hear that you and Miss Lucas intend to travel by post."

"Yes, your ladyship." Elizabeth confirmed.

"I cannot allow that. You were under my care for nearly two months. I cannot allow you to go alone with common strangers. You will go in one of my carriages."

Elizabeth lifted her eyes and saw Darcy's piercing gaze on her. He had obviously no trouble with convincing his aunt to his ideas. "Thank you, your ladyship." she said quietly, "It is very kind of you."

The lady narrowed her eyes at Elizabeth and spoke. "You are unusually quiet, Miss Bennet. But this is not surprising, you are leaving in a few days, this must be very disappointing to you."

Mr. Collins, as it was expected, began to praise Lady Catherine's thoughtfulness, angelic heart and her unmistakable sense of propriety, ending his paeans by mentioning the excellent state of the stables. As the company was engaged in a discussion over the grandness of Rosings' carriages and horses, Elizabeth stood up and walked to the window to look in the garden which was nearly black, due to the late hour and moonless night, no shapes visible.

"I think my aunt is right, Miss Bennet."

She looked up to see Colonel Fitzwilliam standing by her side. She turned to him with a polite expression. "She is?"

"Yes, you are not yourself tonight, indeed you are very quiet."

"There are matters which have occupied my mind of late, but they are not good material for a drawing room conversation, I am afraid." she explained apologetically.

The colonel looked into her eyes, his expression one of sincere care. "I hope it is nothing very upsetting."

Elizabeth smiled at him. "I am very happy that I will see my family soon, my sister Jane especially. We have not seen each other since January."

"You are close, you and your sister."

"Very. Jane is the eldest, and I am the second daughter. We have three other younger sisters, but though I care for other girls and love them, only Jane is my true confidant and friend."

Mr. Darcy walked to them then, putting an end to their conversation. Soon Colonel Fitzwilliam returned to his place near Lady Catherine, and they were left alone.

"What have you been talking about with my cousin?" he asked with an unpleasant scowl on his face, deforming his handsome features. Was she to watch this charming expression for the rest of her life?

"I think he was concerned about my low spirits tonight."

Darcy stepped closer and blocked her view of the room. "He is a second son, he cannot marry as he wishes, Elizabeth."

She lifted her chin high and spoke with cold dignity. "I fail to understand why you tell me this."

He gave her a dark, unreadable, serious look, his lips pressed in a thin line. She could feel his breath on her cheek, he was so close.

"I am afraid we shall not see each other before your journey back home."

She looked up at him. His voice was cold, angry.

"My uncle, the Earl of Matlock, has asked me to come to Matlock as soon as possible." he explained. "I must go tomorrow, together with Colonel Fitzwilliam."

"Has something happened?" she asked tentatively.

"Yes, but it is not the time or place to speak of it now. I will tell you everything when we meet again."

"I hope that all the matters concerning your family will be resolved..." she began, but Lady Catherine's voice interrupted her words.

"Nephew, what are you telling Miss Bennet? I must have my share in the conversation."

Elizabeth glanced up at Darcy to see him rolling his eyes. She smiled at him, and he returned it, his eyes glowing with warmth, his bad mood miraculously wiped away with her smile.

"We have just been discussing the state of the roads from here to London, Aunt," he lied without blinking, as he stepped after Elizabeth who returned to her previous place.

The rest of the evening went uneventfully, till the carriage was called for the Hunsford party. Everyone seemed astonished when Mr Darcy, without a word of warning or any sort of explanation to his actions, walked them to the carriage, something he had never done before.

After Mr. Collins shakily stepped into one of the grand vehicles of his noble patroness, Darcy handed in Mrs. Collins.

Elizabeth was the last to get in. He stepped to her.

"Can you come to the grove in the morning?" he whispered and she felt his gentle grasp on her elbow, the other hand intimately rested on the side of her hip.

"I will be waiting," she heard as he lifted her into the box.

***

Elizabeth was both surprised and relieved to fall asleep easily, almost the moment her head touched the pillow, after the dinner at

Rosings. She expected another sleepless night, full of disturbing thoughts and fears. Instead she slept like a babe. She must have been very exhausted.

When she woke up, her first thought was that it had to be very early as there was very little light seeping through the closed curtains. Shivering, she stalked to the window and saw gray skies, and the drops of water on the glass.

She drew the curtains wide to let in more light, and glanced at the clock on the small mantelpiece.

A few minutes after six, Mr. Darcy was probably already waiting for her. Should she go? She could not decide what to do. The weather was hardly inviting. This was one of the days she wanted to crawl back into a warm bed. Eventually, with a sigh, she walked to the water stand and began her toilette, shivering repeatedly at the cold water touching her still flushed from sleep skin.

The clock struck half past while, on her tiptoes, she walked downstairs. Noise coming from the kitchen told her that the servants had already begun their day, and the back door was open. She pulled her shawl over her head and slipped from the house unnoticed.

The rain was not heavy, merely a persistent drizzle, but the feeling of cold was magnified with the strong, biting wind. Elizabeth usually liked when it blew, but not today.

"You came."

She heard his voice before she saw him. She did not have a bonnet, because she was afraid to ruin it in the rain. She had found it especially hard to pin her hair up in a reasonable fashion this morning, because the wet weather curled it into numerous, tiny locks, sticking in all directions. She had left it in a simple braid.

She could not stop shivering.

"You are cold." He pulled her to him. "You should not have come."

"Yes." she agreed, and watched as the puff of air came out of her mouth.

He rubbed her arms. "I will be worrying now whether you got ill, coming here to see me. Come, I will walk you back to the parsonage."

She shook her head. "No, you should not. Someone might see us."

He enveloped her completely into his embrace, and like once before, opened his great coat, wrapping it about her.

"Better?" he asked after a moment, rubbing her back.

She nodded, relishing his warmth, her eyes closed, sudden sleepiness overpowering her. He smelt nice, spicy and clean, and something else she could not define.

"We will not see each other for a week at least. I think that the family business I must deal with will take at least that long."

She stifled a yawn, still sleepy, which made him grin, exposing large white teeth. It was so strange, the thought of Mr. Darcy having teeth. He had never smiled wide enough before, allowing only infrequent half smiles.

"We shall see you at Longbourn then," she spoke, once again amazed how a simple smile changed his entire countenance. "I wish you a safe trip," she added formally, taking a small step back from him.

He pulled her back to him, lowered his head and spoke in a quiet voice. "There is one more thing... Since I came back, I have wanted to apologize to you, but there was no opportunity for that."

Her eyelashes fluttered, and she titled her head. "Apologize?"

He gazed into her eyes. "Yes, for what I said about you the evening when we were introduced. I know you overheard my remark."

Elizabeth gaped at him, completely taken aback with the turn of the conversation. "How do you know about it?"

"From your father, he told me." His arms tightened around her. "Forgive me for what I said, I was in a foul mood unhappy that Bingley dragged me to that Assembly. I knew I was lying, even when I uttered that nonsense. You were not meant to overhear it."

She did not speak for a moment, but then her lips curled into a smile, eyes sparkling. "Should I now understand that you consider me tolerable enough to tempt you?"

Darcy laughed out loud, picked her up into the air, and twirled her around. "You know very well that I consider you a most tempting creature," he said as he put her down, "much too tempting for my peace of mind, " he murmured against her lips.

"What has happened which requires you go to Matlock so suddenly?" Elizabeth asked abruptly, putting an end to the tender moment, afraid he would kiss her. She realized that she should be more careful in the future; her usual teasing had a very definite effect on him.

"Such a shameful, sordid affair." Darcy shook his head, frowning again. "My cousin's mistress, Colonel Fitzwilliam's elder brother, expects a child."

Elizabeth's eyes widened. "It is serious indeed. Is he married?"

"Yes, he is married, but refuses to send the woman away."

"Do you think he should?"

"We cannot be sure that the child is his."

"This is very sad."

"Yes, it is. He should not have taken a mistress in the first place. But let us not talk about others these last minutes." He pulled her closer. "I will miss you, and think about you every single day till we meet again."

She knew he expected her to say something similar, but she did not want to lie, and she certainly could not return his sentiments. If she had been truthful, she would have had to say that she was more than relieved with the prospect of his absence from her side.

Because the right words, the ones he surely wished to hear could not be uttered, she reached her gloved hand and stroked his cheek. It seemed such a natural thing to do. He closed his eyes for a moment as she caressed the side of his face.

"Oh, sweetheart," he murmured, and before she knew it, she was in his arms again.

Elizabeth accepted the embrace, not feeling alarmed with it any more. She was more embarrassed with his tenderness, astonished with his caring attitude. She had always thought him to be so cold, so unfeeling. Not even a week ago, she would have never considered Mr. Darcy to be so... demonstrative when in private. He seemed to like to hold her, touch her, be close.

"I should go." He pulled away from her after a long moment, the regret obvious in his voice. "It is high time. Colonel Fitzwilliam is surely waiting for me, wondering where I am."

"Have a safe trip," she repeated, smiling.

"Do not worry about me, but promise you will take a good care of yourself."

She nodded, pulled the shawl over her head and ran from the spot.

Chapter Six

Lady Catherine's carriage brought Elizabeth to Longbourn late afternoon one day, almost a week after she had seen Mr. Darcy the last time. They first stopped at Lucas Lodge to deliver Maria, where Elizabeth learned from Lady Lucas that her sister Jane had returned from London the day before.

Mrs. Bennet was very much impressed with the grand way her daughter travelled back home.

"Oh, Lizzy, my dearest child, is it Mr. Darcy's carriage?" she questioned, before Elizabeth managed to step out. "When we heard from your uncle that you and Maria would not travel by post, I was sure you would use one of Mr. Darcy's carriages.

"No, Mama. It is Lady Catherine's carriage," Elizabeth explained, kissing her mother's smooth, pink cheek.

Elizabeth walked to greet Jane and her younger sisters as Mrs. Bennet walked around the vehicle, and even peeked inside. "Surely, Mr. Darcy convinced his aunt to offer it to you for your journey home."

"I believe so, Mama," Elizabeth agreed quietly as she walked to her father.

She kissed her father's cheek. "Papa, it is good to be home."

Mr. Bennet gave her a long, dubious look, and then unexpectedly pulled her to him, giving her a rough hug, something he very rarely did.

"We must talk, child," he said.

"Yes, Papa."

He smiled. "Not now though, there will be time. You must be exhausted, and your mother surely has many questions for you that you will not escape today."

True to Mr. Bennet's word, Mrs. Bennet allowed her second daughter to have a warm meal first, before asking dozens of questions concerning Mr. Darcy, starting from why he was not here yet, and ending on what his favourite dish was. Elizabeth tried to dutifully answer all the enquiries, being aware how curious her mother had to be about the whole affair.

"I am tired, Mama." she confessed at last. "We got up very early in the morning, and I would like to retire."

"Of course, Lizzy," Mrs. Bennet agreed promptly. "It is natural you must be exhausted. I ordered Lady Catherine's people a good dinner and comfortable beds for the night's rest, so do not worry, they will not complain about anything to Mr. Darcy's aunt."

"Thank you, Mama." Elizabeth stood up, her eyes meeting Jane's.

Her sister took the hint immediately. "I think I will go with Lizzy, Mama, in case she needs anything." Jane left her embroidery and followed Elizabeth.

"Go, Janie, go." Mrs. Bennet nodded, but then cried out after her retreating daughters. "Lizzy, but you must tell me everything tomorrow!"

"Yes, Mama," Elizabeth agreed tiredly.

The sisters were silent on their way upstairs.

"You must be tired indeed, Lizzy, " Jane said when the door to their shared bedroom closed.

Without a word or a warning, Elizabeth rushed into her sister's arms. "I am so happy to see you, Jane."

They hugged, and Elizabeth sensed that her sister wanted to ask more, but restrained herself, thinking her to be truly exhausted.

"You are surprised, Jane," Elizabeth said as they sat together on Elizabeth's bed.

"I confess that I am," Jane said with a light frown of her smooth forehead. "You and Mr. Darcy? Lizzy dear, as far as I recall, you wrote to me yourself that he was engaged to his cousin, Lady Catherine's daughter."

Elizabeth shook her head. "No, he is not, Janie. I do not think that he would make me an offer being engaged to another. In my opinion, his aunt desires this union, and Mr. Collins feels it is his duty to spread such rumour as a well established fact."

"But how did it happen?" Jane questioned, her eyes wide. "You never liked him. And Mr. Darcy of all people? He seems so cold, so detached!"

Elizabeth slipped from the bed and walked to the window, her arms folded in front of her. Should she tell her everything? What would Jane think of her, hearing that her sister was mercenary.

"Do you remember how I wrote to you about the Parker sisters?" she asked after a long moment.

Jane nodded.

"I thought a lot about their lives now, after their father's death, and what happened to them. God forbid, but if anything happened to Papa, all of us, you, me, Mary, Kitty and Lydia would share their fate."

"We cannot think about the worst possible situation, Elizabeth," Jane said slowly. "Papa is in good health, and we have uncles..."

"Jane," Elizabeth interrupted her, "I saw Anne Parker in that inn, with the family she works for. You cannot imagine how horribly they treated her. Her sister's fate is even worse, you know that she became a mistress to some wealthy man."

Jane did not say anything, only looked at her sister with great concern.

"Once I thought that marriage without love was the worst thing that could happen in a woman's life." Elizabeth continued. "Today, my perspective is altered. Now, I truly understand Charlotte's decision to marry Mr. Collins. Do not think for a moment that I regret rejecting him! But while I stayed with them for those weeks, I started to think differently. I decided that I would accept the next man who would be willing to make me an offer, even if I had not loved him. I know it was an act of cowardice on my part, but I was afraid of poverty and loneliness. I thought that in a marriage, I would have at least the children who I could love."

"You did not think that Mr. Darcy would prove to be that man," Jane whispered.

"Exactly." Elizabeth returned to the bed, to sit next to her sister. "Oh, Jane, I was so astonished when he came to me!"

"You said yes to him. It makes sense now."

Elizabeth lowered her head. "Jane, you are disappointed with me."

"Why Lizzy?"

"For accepting Mr. Darcy."

"No, Lizzy, never that. I am only worried for you, I want you to be happy."

Elizabeth bit her lower lip. "Oh, Jane, I have become a true mercenary."

Jane touched her arm. "You are too harsh on yourself."

"No, Jane, I know I am deceiving him. I agreed because of his wealth, when he thinks himself to be in love with me."

"I am sure he truly loves you, Lizzy, and very much too if he wants to marry you."

"He says that he does."

"It is good, Lizzy; he will treat you well, take care of you. Perhaps you will fall in love with him in the future. He cannot be that bad."

Elizabeth stood up again, and started pacing the length of the room, waving her arms in an agitated manner. "Oh, Jane, I do not know what to think of him! Sometimes he is so haughty, and arrogant, insults our family and upbringing, then the next moment he can be so nice. He even apologized to me for what he said at the assembly when we were introduced. You remember the tolerable, but not handsome enough comment?"

Jane nodded.

"He explained that he was in a bad mood that day, and he was sorry that I overhead that."

"You see yourself, Lizzy, he is not that bad, he may be a bit antisocial, but there is no doubt he cares for you deeply. All will be well, sister."

Elizabeth stared desperately into Jane's blue eyes. "Do you really believe in that?"

"Yes, Lizzy, I feel that all will be well. He loves you, so there is something to begin with. Perhaps, in the course of time, when you know him better, you will start to like him too."

Elizabeth sighed. "Perhaps. But what about Mr. Wickham? Mr. Darcy did him a great harm, I do not find it encouraging that my future husband is able to act so abominably."

Jane was silent for a while, her delicate eyebrows frowned, her shapely nose slightly wrinkled, her usual expression when she was thinking over something. "We know only Mr. Wickham's version of this story, do we not?"

"Yes."

"I think that you should, at the first opportunity, tell Mr. Darcy what Mr. Wickham told you, and then see how he acts and if he can explain it. We should not judge him, knowing only Mr. Wickham's version. What is more, to our knowledge, there was no one who could confirm the truthfulness of Mr. Wickham's words. Mr. Darcy should have a chance to speak for himself on this matter."

Elizabeth looked at her sister in awe. Jane was so good, so understanding. She defended Mr. Darcy, even though he was the man who had ruined her chances for happiness with Mr. Bingley. I will do everything to reunite you with Mr. Bingley, dear sister, Elizabeth promised herself in her thoughts.

"Oh, Jane," she leaned forward to hug her sister. "You are too good. What would I do without you? You always keep my spirits up."

"Give it a chance, Lizzy." Jane patted her back. "I have a feeling that all will be well. Trust me."

***

Despite the long day of travel from Kent, and late night talk with Jane, Elizabeth woke up early the next morning, before her sister. She finished her toilette quietly, so as not to disturb Jane's sleep, and walked downstairs, hoping to manage a short walk before breakfast. She was putting on her bonnet in front of the old looking glass hanging in the foyer, when she heard her father's voice.

"Elizabeth, can you come here, please?"

Mr. Bennet stood in the open door to the library, his face unreadable, and lacking his usual warm, teasing look in his eyes. Elizabeth took a deep breath, and removed her bonnet. She had expected her father would want to talk to her, sooner or later. She preferred later, but was surprised he had not done it yesterday just as she had arrived. He had called her Elizabeth too, which was not a good sign. She was always Lizzy to him, unless he was displeased with her, which happened very rarely. The last time, some ten years ago, was when she had fallen off the tree and broken her arm.

"Yes, Papa," she said politely as she entered the library.

He gestured to the chair opposite his armchair. "Sit down, child."

Elizabeth did as she was asked.

After a long moment of mutual silence, Mr. Bennet asked. "What were you thinking, Lizzy, accepting this man?"

"Papa, I..."

"How do you imagine your life with someone whom you cannot respect? As far as I know, someone you dislike."

"Papa, I have doubts too, but... I have given a lot of thought to it, and there are many other reasons which speak in favour of Mr. Darcy."

"May I know those reasons?"

Elizabeth lowered her head. "He is wealthy," she acknowledged very quietly.

There was a sharp intake of air on Mr. Bennet's side. "Lizzy, wealth is not the most important matter. I thought that I taught you that."

"Father, it is easy to say for you, Longbourn will always provide you with a comfortable life. Have you ever thought about us, me, Jane, Mary, Kitty, Lydia, and Mama?" she asked grudgingly.

Mr. Bennet seemed surprised with her outburst, and said nothing for a moment. "I am not dying yet, child. Surely some man would come along in the right time for you, who will give you security."

"You cannot know that, Papa. You cannot be sure of that," she protested. "Have you ever given a second thought to what will happen with us in the future? There is no financial safety for us. The only work we could do is to be a governess, and it is a life of insecurity and humiliation. I do not want such a life."

"You exaggerate, Elizabeth. We are well to do."

"Today, yes, but what about tomorrow?" she cried.

"It is not your responsibility to think about it," he dismissed her worry.

"Perhaps I should think about it if you choose not to!" she blurted out, and then covered her mouth with a hand, realizing what she had just said.

Mr. Bennet's jaws set in tight lines, and he ordered. "Elizabeth, I will not allow you to speak to me like this."

"I am sorry, Papa. I said too much, I should not have," she apologized quietly, but then added more firmly. "However, I still do not think that you should hold it against me that I am afraid of the future, and I am trying to find some solution."

She stood up and stalked out of the library, running straight to the garden. She needed to be alone for a while, and she walked farther than she had intended, fighting tears the entire time. She hated quarrelling with her father. They had understood each other so well in the past, what had happened? Why could he not understand her now, her fears and apprehension?

When she returned home, from the doorstep, she heard her mother's voice.

"Lizzy, where have you been for so long?" Mrs. Bennet cried, looking at her second daughter, bonnet pulled down and hanging by the ribbons on her back, hair in disarray, the edge of her petticoats edged in mud.

"Look at yourself! Where have you been?" she demanded. "We finished breakfast over an hour ago."

"I went for a walk, Mama," Elizabeth answered listlessly, dragging her feet as she stepped upstairs. "I needed some time alone, and I forgot about breakfast. I am not hungry."

Mrs. Bennet blinked her blue eyes, staring at her second daughter. In all twenty years of Elizabeth's life, or at least since the girl had learned to stand on her own feet, she had never been upset after her favourite activity, a long walk.

The lady stood in the hallway for a long moment, before she hurried after Elizabeth.

"Lizzy." Mrs. Bennet knocked, and without waiting for an invitation, stepped into the large bedroom with two identical beds, which her two eldest daughters had shared for years.

Elizabeth lay on the bed, the woollen blanket draped over her. Her bonnet and spencer were abandoned on the chair, her shoes kicked under it.

Mrs. Bennet picked up the spencer and put it neatly on a hanger, and then arranged the abandoned shoes next to the door, for the maid to take for cleaning later. Then she sat on the edge of the bed, and reached her hand to touch the dark curls.

Elizabeth glanced at her in surprise, not accustomed to such affectionate gestures on her part.

"Is this about Mr. Darcy?" Mrs. Bennet asked fretfully. "Did you have a misunderstanding? Is he angry with you, about something, Lizzy? Is that the reason he did not come here after you?"

Elizabeth sat up.

"No, Mama. Mr. Darcy needed to go to Matlock, as I told you. His uncle asked his help on some urgent family matter. He promised to be back to see me as soon as possible."

"What is the matter then?"

Elizabeth looked at the woman who was her mother. Mrs. Bennet looked sincerely concerned.

"It is about, Papa," Elizabeth sighed. "He is upset with me."

"Your father is upset with you?" Mrs. Bennet cried. "You never do anything wrong in his eyes."

"He thinks me a mercenary."

Mrs. Bennet frowned. "How?"

Elizabeth bit her lower lip and two large tears rolled down her cheeks. "He thinks I agreed to marry Mr. Darcy just because of his wealth."

Mrs. Bennet blinked her blue eyes. "What? Mr. Darcy actually asked you to marry you?"

"Yes, he did, back in Kent."

"Your father told us that Mr. Darcy asked only for the permission to court you."

Elizabeth shook her head. "No, Mr. Darcy came one day, unexpectedly, to the parsonage when I was all alone and proposed. I agreed, and he decided to come to Longbourn the very next day to ask Papa for my hand. Papa agreed to courtship only. He said six months at least."

"What a fool!" Mrs. Bennet cried angrily. "I will go talk with him right away!"

Elizabeth grabbed her hand, stopping her. "Mama, please do not! Do not talk to Papa about it!"

"But, Lizzy, Mr. Darcy may very well not want to wait that long."

"He will, Mama. Mr. Darcy is willing to wait, he said that to me."

"Are you sure?"

"Yes, Mama. I think he is rather fond of me."

"My smart girl, to catch such a man." Mrs. Bennet patted her cheek, calming down with Elizabeth's assurance. "I am so proud of you. I still do not understand why your father did not agree at once to the engagement."

"I think that Papa wanted to give me time to think, a chance to change my mind."

Mrs. Bennet gasped loudly. "Heaven forbid."

"What if Papa is right? Mama, I know I agreed to Mr. Darcy's proposal for security reasons only. Papa thinks I will not be happy marrying a man I do not care for and respect, I do not love."

"Elizabeth, child, you cannot think like that. I truly loved your father when I married him, but he never respected me, and tired of me quickly. He thinks I failed him, not giving him a son."

"Mama, I am not convinced whether Mr. Darcy has any true respect for me. He wants to have me."

"Lizzy, you are too smart for anyone not to respect you! Do not be so childish," Mrs. Bennet chided her. "Use your head this time, girl, for something different than reading books in foreign languages, or discussing politics from your father's newspapers. Mr. Darcy is smart too. I heard him speaking a few times to other people, and I always failed to catch his meaning. You are so bright, Lizzy, you can make him listen to you, and respect your opinions."

"I do not love him, Mama," Elizabeth murmured weakly.

Mrs. Bennet lifted her chin. "Lizzy, if love is so important to you, who says that you cannot learn to love Mr. Darcy?"

Elizabeth scrambled from the bed with energy. "Oh, Mama, he is so rude, haughty and unsociable! He thinks himself above us all, you said it yourself more than once. If you heard the tone of his proposal." She threw her arms in the air. "He insulted all of us! What is more, I am sure he put his hand to separating Jane and Mr. Bingley. What about Mr. Wickham, how Mr. Darcy mistreated him, denying him the promised living?"

"Mr. Wickham!" Mrs. Bennet shrugged. "He is nobody. People of no consequence to the world often weave such stories about rich people because they are jealous. I must tell you Lizzy, from the very beginning, I thought that Mr. Wickham's story about Mr. Darcy was untrue."

Elizabeth stood in the middle of the room, her whole posture tense.

Mrs. Bennet walked to her, placing a gentle hand on her arm. "As for Jane, I think that your marriage to Mr. Darcy is an excellent way to bring her and Mr. Bingley together."

Elizabeth relaxed. "I thought about the same, Mama," she agreed in a much calmer voice. "Jane deserves to be happy. She is the best person in the world. I know she hasn't forgotten Mr. Bingley, even though she insists that she has."

Mrs. Bennet turned her daughter to her. "You are a good child, Lizzy. I know that I was harsh on you when you rejected Mr. Collins, but understand me, I want you all to have secure futures. I wish all my girls to have their own home, be respectable, and never suffer from poverty. I made a good match, and I want the same for you and all your sisters."

"I know, Mama. I understand you better now."

Mrs. Bennet pulled Elizabeth closer, and patted her back. "Do not worry about your father, Lizzy. I will deal with him, and he will not bother you any more. He does not understand some things. He is a man, and he is jealous."

Elizabeth blinked her eyes. "Jealous?"

Mrs. Bennet shrugged her arms. "Of course. You were always his favourite, he cannot bear that such an intelligent and powerful man wants you, and will take you away from him, or even worse that you could care for Mr. Darcy more than for him. Poor old fool."

Elizabeth swallowed away new tears. "You think so."

"Yes, child, all fathers are in love with their daughters, and do not want to give them away. You fret too much about everything, child, always seeing the worst thing to happen, and sometimes I think it is the only thing that you have taken after me." Mrs. Bennet patted her cheek. "Now, have some rest, I will send you a warm breakfast to your room, and later, perhaps we could take an open carriage and go to Meryton for a little shopping with the girls?"

Elizabeth smiled through her tears. "Yes, Mama." then she stepped forwards and wrapped her arms around the older woman. "Thank you."

Chapter Seven

A few days had passed, and Elizabeth's spirits began to gradually improve, despite the fact that Mr. Bennet barely spoke to her. It was not only to her though, for he appeared only during meals, spending the rest of the day in the library or on horseback in the field. The fact that her father disapproved of her hurt very much, causing almost physical pain deep inside her. She had offended him, and she regretted that, but she could not make herself apologize to him one more time.

Surprisingly, her mother became much kinder to her these days than ever before. Elizabeth felt that her mother's new attitude had not only been caused by the fact that she managed to bring to the family a wealthy man. Mrs. Bennet, as a woman, understood her decision better than her father, and was more sympathetic to her feelings.

One afternoon, almost a week after her return from Kent, Elizabeth was curled on the sofa in the parlour with a~~the~~ new book. Jane was sewing, Kitty remodelling her old bonnet, Mary studying new music sheets, their mother dozing on her favourite chair, and Lydia sitting in the window ledge, observing the drive to the house.

"Someone is coming," the youngest Bennet noted in a dull voice, and after a moment added more excitedly. "A man."

Mrs. Bennet bolted from her place. "Mr. Darcy! It must be Mr. Darcy." She rushed to the window. "Yes, it is he! How handsome he is on that black horse!" She turned from the window and ran to Elizabeth. "Oh, Lizzy, leave that book and show me your dress." She grabbed the book from Elizabeth's hands, and pulled her to her feet. "This dress is no good at all. You should have picked something newer, in a brighter colour, and most importantly, cut lower."

Elizabeth blushed. "Mama!"

"Oh, child, do not be so naive! You will not tell me he always looks only into your eyes."

"I will not change into another dress," Elizabeth argued, her teeth clenched. "This dress is perfectly suitable, and it is too late for that anyway."

Soon there was a knock on the door. All the ladies arranged themselves in decorous positions, and Mrs. Bennet spoke loudly, blinking at Elizabeth.

"Enter."

The door opened and the servant announced. "Mr. Darcy to see Miss Elizabeth."

Mr. Darcy entered, and his eyes scanned the room, stopping on Elizabeth, who stood in the farthest corner of the room. She met his eyes bravely, and smiled, before dropping a curtesy. He instantly smiled back, but his face went emotionless again when he stepped to greet the lady of the house.

Mr. Darcy sat down on the indicated chair, but said nothing. Mrs. Bennet found herself responsible for carrying the conversation, which was limited to numerous questions on her part. She enquired of the guest about his journey, about the business which detained him for so long, about the state of the roads, and ended on the question whether he was hungry.

Darcy answered in monosyllables, his eyes not leaving Elizabeth's person most of the time. The object of his attention said little, answering only his general questions about her health and well-being.

Elizabeth lowered her eyes to her hands, placed on her lap, blushing furiously at her mother's rude questioning of the guest, but at the same time, angry at Mr. Darcy's neglectful answers.

Fifteen minutes into the visit, it came to the point when Mrs. Bennet had nothing more to ask Mr. Darcy, unless she wanted to enquire at what age he went to university or stopped wearing nappies. She noticed him looking steadily at Elizabeth, and at last, she figured out what he truly wanted.

"Lizzy, would you like to show the garden to Mr. Darcy? We have introduced quite a few changes this spring, Mr. Darcy. We have a new gardener and he is very progressive. I am sure that you will be happy to see them."

"Indeed, ma'am." Darcy stood up, bowed to the lady of the house, and walked to the door, where he waited for Elizabeth.

Elizabeth forced a smiled and silently walked to join Darcy, who opened the door for her.

"Lizzy, just make sure to bring Mr. Darcy back for tea," Mrs. Bennet said when Elizabeth walked past her. "We have a cake today that he enjoyed so much the last time he was at Longbourn."

Elizabeth did not bother with fetching her spenser and bonnet or changing her shoes; the day was warm, and they did not intend to walk far.

She accepted his arm as they stepped outside. He kept her close to him, but did not try to speak, and Elizabeth decided not to start the conversation first. She was curious how long it would take for him to say something.

To her surprise, he directed them away from the house, towards the small park at the back, which was separated by a low brick wall from the main garden.

"At last," she heard, when they walked between the trees, their branches hiding them completely from view from the house.

"Mr. Darcy," she managed to say before she was pulled into his arms.

"William, please."

He was whispering into her ear, kissing the sensitive skin on her neck.

"William!" She pushed away from him, "We should not," she murmured.

He was not displeased with her resistance; he smiled. "As you wish." He took her hand and asked. "Is there a quiet place where we can sit down ?"

Elizabeth nodded and led them to a stone bench nearby.

Darcy did not wait for her to sit first, as she expected him to do, but took his place and then pulled her down so she sat close to him in the crook of his arm, his right hand casually draped over her back. Once again, she was astounded with his casual attitude when they were in private, in contrast with his usual very proper manners when in company.

"How have you been for the last fortnight, Lizzy?" he asked softly.

Elizabeth shivered at his baritone voice resonating near her ear.

"Are you cold?" his arm wrapped protectively around her, his hand rubbing her bare forearm.

"No, it is just..." she turned her head to look up at him.

He smiled, his eyes warm. "What, love?"

Elizabeth bit her lower lip. What was she to say to him? Was she to admit that she felt a warm feeling pulling at the pit of her stomach every time he lowered his voice, called her an endearment or looked at her like he was at this very moment?

"How was your trip?" she asked, trying to give her voice a normal tone, and ignore the goose bumps prickling on her skin as he stroked her arm with the pads of his fingertips.

Darcy sighed, and she felt his body tense. "My cousin refuses to make that woman go. He says he loves her and wants to take care of her and their child."

Elizabeth turned to him completely, placing her hand lightly on his thigh for a moment. "Do you find his decision wrong?" she asked and took her hand away because he stiffened visibly when she touched him.

"He is married," he paused. "His marriage was arranged though. His wife comes from a very wealthy family, and it was a very good match for our family as far as connections and fortune are concerned but..."

"Yes."

He looked in front of himself. "His wife is not someone who could be recognised as amiable. She is like Caroline Bingley, only ten times worse. Her past, before she entered our family, is questionable to say the least, and she has conducted herself not like the lady should do. I do not blame George that he escaped home in the past. I think he really loves this other woman. She is not a harlot, I understand. She had never had such an arrangement with a man before she met my cousin."

"What is your uncle's reaction?"

"As expected in such a situation, he is furious. He insists on sending the woman away, but I think that after the babe is born, in a month or two, I believe, and he and my aunt see it, he will change his mind. This will be their first grandchild. They cannot count on one from Richard, I mean Colonel Fitzwilliam, any time soon."

Elizabeth allowed herself to relax against his solid frame again, supporting her back against his chest. "I understand that your uncle expected you to try to persuade your cousin out of his decision to stay with his mistress and their child."

"Yes, and I went there thinking that I should do just that, convince him to abandon his mistress and go back to his wife. I must confess that I was surprised that George had ever decided on such an arrangement - he never had been what could be called a rake. He is rather shy with women, like me, a family trait, I dare say."

She turned her head to look into his face. "You shy?"

He laughed softly. "Yes, have you not noticed? It took me half a year to tell you about how I felt for you."

Elizabeth frowned and said nothing to this, allowing him again to arrange her in the crook of his arm.

"When I listened to George, talked with him in private, I could not do it," Darcy continued. "I thought how I would have acted in his position. What if I had married, pressured by the family and society, to a woman I could not abide, had no children with her, and then met you. Would I be able to stay away from you?"

"I think that your cousin's situation is very difficult."

"Yes, it is, but surprisingly, he is happier than I have seen him since the beginning of his marriage. He is very excited about becoming a father. He told me that it elated him that the woman he truly loved would bear his child."

He shifted sideways so he could look into her face. "I do understand him, Elizabeth, to think that one day you will tell me that I will become a father... makes me feel, I cannot explain it."

Elizabeth gaped at him, full of wonder, feeling both hot and cold, blushing rosily, her heart rapidly beating in her chest. She would have never suspected Mr. Darcy to be so... sympathetic, so sensitive about such delicate matters.

"In the end, I gave him my full support, and even invited him to come with that woman to Pemberley after the baby is born, and old enough to travel. This invitation was an impulsive act that I have since then started to regret."

"Why?"

"Because..." he hesitated, "Perhaps you would not like to admit someone like her under your roof, such a woman."

"No, not at all," Elizabeth contradicted quickly, "I imagine that I would have nothing against it, taking everything into consideration. I would welcome her as your relative, I guess, who she is now when there will be a baby."

"There is Georgiana to consider too, but..." Darcy frowned. "Since last year..." he sighed, "I have started to believe that young girls should not be so sheltered from the realities of life. Being too naive about certain matters does not always help them."

He was absent with his thoughts for a moment, his expression distant, and Elizabeth was about to ask what the reason for this, when he stood up and offered his arm.

"Let us not discuss this sad matter any more," he proposed as she stood up.

Elizabeth smiled and nodded, accepting his arm again as they resumed their walk.

"You did not tell me how your time has been spent since your return from Kent."

"It was very nice to see all my sisters, Mama, Jane especially." She smiled. "You cannot imagine how surprised she was when I told her how you proposed to me. She cried, 'Mr. Darcy... that cannot be, Lizzy, the man is so cold!" she laughed and looked at him, only then realizing what she had said.

"I am sorry..." she whispered.

He shrugged. "I do not mind people seeing me thus, or in other words, I do not care how others perceive me. However, I hope you know that indeed, I am not cold." His dark brown eyes bore into hers, and those hot, cold, trembling sensations came back to her with magnified force.

He lowered his head, and Elizabeth was sure that he wanted to kiss her, but then he lifted his head, looked around with a frown, and directed them energetically towards the stables, which were on the left from the small park.

At first Elizabeth did not quite capture why he chose that place. He strode confidently in, and seeing no one in sight, pulled her inside one of the empty stalls.

The stable was not a place which Elizabeth visited often, or ever. At first she was disturbed by its particular smells, and the idea that she could stamp on something unexpected with her slippered foot. To her relief, the stall looked reasonably clean, and the hay, it was strewn with, was fresh.

Soon she forgot about those fears, when he supported himself against one wall, hooked an arm about her waist and brought her to him, between his spread thighs.

"Now..." he leaned forward and his lips touched hers.

Elizabeth closed her eyes, and allowed him to do what he wanted, half curious, half apprehensive about what would happen.

Her very first sensation was that he was very gentle, and what he did felt good, safe, very right and exciting at the same time. His hands were at ▓▓ both sides of her face, as he teased her mouth, tugging at her lower and upper lip interchangeably. She stiffened when she felt him trying to push his tongue inside. He took the hint, retreated at once, and concentrated on kissing her neck, which felt even better than what he had done earlier.

Elizabeth allowed herself to lean into his body with more trust, which enticed him to take her hands, so far securely resting on his shoulders, and wind them around his neck.

He was so much taller, that she needed to stand on tiptoe, pressing into his body even more. His arms wrapped around her with force, and pinned her to him. His breathing suddenly became harsh and laboured. He was becoming hard and swelling down there, his manhood poking into her belly.

He let her go abruptly.

Elizabeth stepped back from him tentatively, and for a very short moment allowed her eyes to rest at the front of his beige coloured britches. He was definitely affected by what had happened, by their close proximity.

Blushing furiously, she turned her back to him, allowing him the needed time to compose himself.

When a long moment later she felt a tap on her shoulder and turned around, he looked his normal self again.

"Forgive me," he said.

She shook her head hard, so her locks bobbed up. "No... I should not..."

"No, Elizabeth, I am the experienced one here, and I should be responsible so things will not go too far too soon."

He took her hand in his, gave it a squeeze, and leaned forward to kiss her cheek.

"Do not stress over what happened, love." He smiled at her, his eyes warm. "It was perfectly natural, and bodes well for the future, only as I said, it happened too soon."

She smiled, still unsure, and shy about what had just trespassed.

Holding her hand in his, he led her out of the stall. "I want to give you something. That is why I brought you here."

They walked to the next stall, where what seemed was Mr. Darcy's horse was kept.

Elizabeth gave him an unsure look. He did not want to give her a horse? Surely not.

He walked inside the stall, and opened the satchel at the saddle, taking a parcel wrapped in elegant paper out of it.

"For me?" Elizabeth asked.

"I stopped in London for a few days to see Georgiana, and bought it for you."

"You should not have..." she tried to protest, but he pushed the parcel into her hands.

"Of course I should. I wanted to."

She weighed the parcel in her hands. "I am not certain whether I should accept it."

She looked at him and saw that she would give him a great deal of disappointment if she refused the gift. Slowly, she unwrapped the paper, and a silk material fell into her hands. It was a beautiful shawl, in a stunning, rich deep colour of red wine.

"How beautiful," she gasped.

With the tips of her fingers she touched the material. The silk was of the highest quality. She assumed it had cost a small fortune, certainly more than any piece of clothing she had ever owned, including her very best yellow ball gown. She was not sure how she felt about him giving her such an expensive gifts.

"Do you like it?" he asked, as excited as a child.

"Yes," she admitted reluctantly.

"May I?" he draped the shawl around her shoulders. "The colour suits you very well."

"I did not know you were an expert in women's fashions, sir." she teased.

He grinned. "I am not. I went to the shop where my sister usually makes her purchases. I told the owner I was looking for something for a young lady. I described your looks, and she assured me that this colour would match well with your chocolate curls, dark eyes and pale skin. I am very pleased to see that she was right."

"Thank you." She lifted on her toes, and kissed his cheek. "I will wear it with pleasure."

***

"Oh, Jane I think that he wants to buy me." Elizabeth complained later when she was alone with Jane in their room upstairs. Mr. Darcy bade her goodbye in front of the house, saying he had to deal with some matters in Meryton before dark.

"Lizzy, I think he just wanted to buy you something nice, you read too much into it. Imagine the situation when you are in London with all the wonderful shops around you and with unlimited resources. Would you not want buy something for me, Mama, Papa, Mary, Kitty and Lydia?"

"Of course I would."

"He has a much younger sister, am I right?"

"Yes."

"We can safely assume then that he likes to spoil her, buy her nice things. He sees nothing wrong with doing the same when it comes to you. I know your independent spirit, Lizzy, and your pride, but think about all the time and thought which he had to devote to the idea of buying you this. He chose it by himself, thinking only of you."

"It must have been frightfully expensive. It will stand out against my plainer gowns."

"I am sure he did not want to embarrass you. He is simply used to buying the very best."

Elizabeth wrapped the shawl around herself and touched the soft material to her face. Then she took it off, spread it on her bed and folded it neatly. There was a knock on the door and Mrs Bennet appeared.

"Lizzy, I came to ask how your walk with Mr. Darcy was. He did not want to stay for tea with us? Was he displeased?"

Elizabeth looked at her mother, her compassionate heart tugging at the woman's worried expression. She could not tell her that her future son-in-law considered himself above them all.

"No, Mama. He came here straight from London. He did not want to be rude, but I think he was tired after the journey, and needed to see to some matters in Meryton yet today."

"Oh," Mrs. Bennet said, her expression still unsure.

Jane wanted to turn her mother's attention, so she pointed to a shawl. "Look, Mama, what Lizzy got from Mr. Darcy."

Mrs. Bennet came closer to the bed and saw the silk shawl. "What is that?" She took the shawl and started to admire it from every side. "How beautiful!" she exclaimed, "Surely very expensive!"

"I think that too expensive, Mama." Elizabeth pointed. "I am not certain whether I should accept it."

"Of course you should! Silly girl. Such a generous man." She put the shawl to Lizzy's face. "Look how it suits your complexion, he must have picked it up by himself, thinking of you. You should appreciate it, such caring. Your father never in his life thought about buying me anything as beautiful as this gift."

"Mama we are not even officially engaged."

"Just because of your father's stubbornness."

"Nevertheless, I think people should not be aware he gave me such an expensive gift."

"Lizzy is right, Mama." Jane said in her most serious tone. "I am sure that Mr. Darcy would not wish any improper gossip to circulate about him or his future wife."

Mrs. Bennet thought for a moment. "You are right, Jane. No one should know for the time being how generous towards Lizzy he is. Everyone is already green with envy that you secured such a man for yourself. You will wear it, of course, to make him happy, but no one needs to know it is a gift from Mr. Darcy."

"What about Kitty and Lydia, Mama?" Elizabeth asked apprehensively. "I doubt they could keep it to themselves."

"Leave them to me. I will tell them... I will think what to tell them so they will stay quiet about it."

She reached her hand to squeeze Elizabeth's cheek. "Such a generous man, Lizzy," she repeated, and left the room.

Chapter Eight

The other day after breakfast, Jane and Elizabeth, enveloped in large aprons, started on the long postponed task of preparing baskets for the tenants' families. They hoped to distribute them later in the afternoon. Concentrating on their work, in quiet tones, they spoke about the man who had been the main subject of their conversations recently, Mr. Darcy.

"You shall see yourself, Lizzy, he is not that bad at all," Jane said after Elizabeth had told her what she had heard from Mr. Darcy yesterday. "The fact that Mr. Darcy does not condemn his cousin, only tries to understand his difficult situation, proves that he cares deeply about his relatives and can be very sympathetic."

"I must say I was truly astonished with his attitude on this matter. I always thought him to be a man who sees everything only as black or white, without any doubt," Elizabeth said as she wrapped the hocks of ham into the white clean rugs so Jane could put them into baskets. "He seemed so human."

"Lizzy," Jane laughed. "You talk about him as if he was of some different species."

Elizabeth finished with the ham, and went to wash her hands. Mr. Darcy was a human, of course; a warm, strong, living man, with a deep voice, who affected her more than she was ready to acknowledge. Every time she had closed her eyes last evening, determined to fall asleep, she had memories of how he held and kissed her. Only a month ago, she had hated the man. Hatred was too strong a word perhaps, but she had sincerely disliked him and now...

"What I cannot understand is why he treated Mr. Wickham so poorly," she cried in frustration, lathering her hands with energy.

"I have already told you that we know only one side of the story," Jane reminded her. "I think that you should ask Mr. Darcy about this matter. He should have an opportunity to defend himself, explain what happened from his perspective."

Before Elizabeth could answer, the voice of their mother was heard, speaking loudly.

"After me, Mr. Darcy! She will be a most excellent wife to you! She knows everything about running a house. I taught her myself!"

Mrs. Bennet hurried into the room with a very sober looking Mr. Darcy behind her.

"Here she is, Mr. Darcy." Mrs. Bennet made a wide gesture in the direction of Elizabeth, who was drying her hands with a clean cloth. "As you see, sir, she is making the baskets for the tenants."

"Miss Bennet, Miss Elizabeth," Darcy bowed.

The girls curtseyed in response. Elizabeth's face turned beetroot red at her mother's crassness.

Mrs. Bennet, standing next to her second daughter, winked at her. "Mr. Darcy wants to take you for a walk again, Lizzy," she announced in a theatrical whisper.

"Mama..." Elizabeth murmured, not knowing where to hide her eyes.

Seeing her sister's discomposure, Jane spoke. "Mama, we were to distribute the baskets today."

"Lydia and Mary will go with you, Jane." Mrs. Bennet dismissed her worry, untying Elizabeth's apron. "Kitty will accompany Mr. Darcy and Lizzy on their walk. Now, Lizzy, run upstairs to prepare yourself, and do remember to wear the shawl Mr. Darcy was so kind to give you."

The matron walked to Darcy. "I think that the walk to Oakham Mount is an excellent idea, do you not think so, sir? A nice, long walk."

Darcy nodded. "I agree, madam. I have heard that the view from that spot is spectacular, and I have not yet had the opportunity to admire it."

"Excellent, excellent!" Mrs. Bennet smiled widely at the man, receiving only a severe frown in return.

Elizabeth came to the conclusion that it was a high time to separate her mother from her intended.

"Mr. Darcy." She approached him with smile. "Let us go to the foyer. I will call Kitty and go upstairs to change into more appropriate attire."

Darcy smiled down at her, bowed in front of Mrs. Bennet and Jane, and turned to the entrance.

Mrs. Bennet gave Elizabeth a worried look, whispering, "Is he displeased with something?"

"I do not think so, Mama." Elizabeth whispered back. She felt sorry for her mother who, she knew, had tried hard to please the man. Mrs. Bennet's intentions were the best, and despite her faults, she did not deserve such rude, cold treatment from Darcy.

She glanced at Darcy, who was waiting for her in the doorway. Taking a deep breath, she walked to him with a polite smile.

Darcy let her go first as they walked through the narrow, darkened hall leading from the kitchens area to the main part of the house. At one moment, she felt his hand on her hip, later her waist, and his mouth at the back of her neck.

She stopped, and in semi darkness turned her head to look up into his face. She did not manage to say anything, because his mouth captured hers, as he pushed her against the wall.

At first she did not know how to react, astonished with his unexpected act. His kisses were gentle and tentative, so after a moment she responded in kind, tilting her face to give him better access.

"Lizzy," she heard him groan her name, and he pushed his body against hers more aggressively.

Her eyes popped open as he pushed his tongue inside her mouth. It happened so quickly, without warning, that she was not prepared for the invasion, and broke the kiss, turning her face away to the side.

"Sweet," he murmured, as his face dipped into her throat, sucking there.

Elizabeth began to take deep breaths, not a bit concerned that he was losing his control, and she could do little to stop him. She was torn, what he did to her gave her wonderful sensations, his body next to hers, so hard and warm, rubbing against her and pushing her against the wall. She did not want to stop, but at the same time, she was afraid of the unknown.

His mouth once again covered hers, in one long, deep, drugging kiss, which she accepted more graciously this time. When one large hand cupped her breast and squeezed, she tore away from him.

"Stop," she exclaimed in a croaked whisper, "Please."

She rushed away from him, trying to compose herself. It was too much, too fast. She knew that something happened, and they had gone too far, because she felt uncomfortable all over, her breasts tingling, the wetness pooling between her thighs.

It took her a long moment to take her courage and look at him. He was leaning against the wall, his breathing still laboured, and then unexpectedly, hit the wall with his fist, muffled words escaping him. She thought she heard - *I am no better than Wickham.*

She eyed him wearily as he walked to her.

"Forgive me, Elizabeth, I have nothing to defend myself. You deserve so much better."

"You scared me," she said, still unsure of him.

"I know," he reached for her hand and clasped it as if it was made of the finest China. "I swear it will never happen again."

Elizabeth nodded only, and then pulled her hand away from him.

"Let us go," she whispered and stepped forward, without looking back.

***

Darcy paced the foyer, waiting for Elizabeth, who was taking ages in her room. He would have not been surprised if she had refused to go with him anywhere today. He had treated her worse than... *You are an idiot and a rake! Like a bull in heat!* It screamed in his mind. His father would be rolling in his grave if he could see him now. Elizabeth was his future wife, an innocent, a lady; she deserved respect, patience, caring – and he had nearly taken her against the wall in her parents' home. The desire he felt for her, and the long years of abstinence could not justify his scandalous behaviour.

At last he saw her on the landing of the staircase with her younger sister Kitty. Her face looked as if it was freshly scrubbed, and she had on another dress. She did not wear the shawl he had given her, only her pale blue spencer. Definitely not a good sign.

Darcy tried to read her face, gaze into her eyes, but she avoided looking at him, her posture stiff and unwelcoming.

"May we go?" he asked.

Elizabeth nodded, her eyes lowered, as she put on her gloves. "We may."

Kitty said nothing at all, her eyes pointed to the limestone tiled floor. Darcy suspected that the girl was, as she should be, embarrassed with the night's escapade to his bedroom door at his last visit.

Darcy wanted to offer his arm to Elizabeth, but decided to postpone it for a while, not being quite sure whether she would accept it. They were about to go out, the butler opening the door for them, when Mrs. Bennet fled down the stairs.

"Lizzy, Lizzy child, you forgot your shawl!" she cried, out of breath as she approached them.

"Thank you, Mama." Elizabeth stared at the shawl for a moment, then took it and wrapped it around herself tightly, stepping out of the house.

Elizabeth set off at such a brisk pace, that Darcy and Kitty needed to jog a few yards to catch up on her.

Darcy wished to talk to her, apologize, assure himself that she was not afraid of him, but the presence of the younger sister close behind them made it all impossible. He understood that Elizabeth preferred not to be alone with him after what had transpired. She still refused to look in his direction, her head pointed to the fields on the opposite side of the road.

"Lizzy," Darcy heard the small voice from behind his back. "Can I stop at the Lucases to visit Maria? It is such a long walk to Oakham Mount. You know it tires me to walk so far."

Elizabeth glanced at Darcy. He was sure she would refuse to be left alone with him.

"Of course, Kitty." She smiled at the younger girl. "We will stop to pick you on our way back."

"Thank you, Lizzy." Kitty cried and sprinted down the path on the right leading to Lucas Lodge.

Darcy and Elizabeth resumed their walk without a word. After five minutes of silence, Darcy touched her arm, stopping them.

"Please, Lizzy, say you have forgiven me."

At last she looked up at him from the rim of her straw bonnet.

"You should have not done that. What if my father had come, or one of my sisters, or a servant was passing by?" she cried in earnest, "How would I be able to look in their eyes later on?"

"I know, love. You are perfectly right." His hands rested on her shoulders, and then moved down her arms to her palms, stroking the uncovered skin of her wrist between her glove and the sleeve. "I want you so much, Lizzy. I... forgot myself."

"I am not your wife, sir, not yet," Elizabeth reminded him in a firm voice, "You cannot do whatever you want, whenever you wish to. I do not know much about these matters... and cannot guess what you will do next. I know you too little to..." She blushed. "I am not ready to..." She took a deep breath, lifted her chin, and spoke with dignity. "I do not want to be treated like this."

Darcy had a gulp growing in his throat. In front of him stood the woman he loved, asking him to respect her. What Darcy felt could be only compared to the last time his father had disciplined him for some misbehaviour when he had been yet a lad, only it was much worse this time.

He swallowed. "Elizabeth, I swear on my honour, on the memory of my parents, on Georgiana, that I will never try to touch you in an intimate way, kiss you unless you tell me so directly or show me that you desire it."

Her pretty face covered with a lovely blush as he was speaking about touching her intimately. She took a long moment to look into his eyes, as if checking whether he was serious.

She smiled at last, her usual, easy smile. "Let us forget about it then."

As if the stone was thrown off his heart, the relief at her forgiveness was great.

"Thank you, dear," he reached for her hand, and squeezed it.

"If you are not afraid of the mud, Mr. Darcy, I suggest taking a shortcut across the pastures." she proposed. "I dare say it is much more picturesque."

Darcy agreed readily, stepping after her off the main road they had walked so far. He noticed, of course, that he had become 'Mr. Darcy' again, but decided not to comment on that. He did not want to test his good luck. She would surely start using his given name when she felt ready, and not pressured into it.

On their way, they needed to cross several fences separating the fields. Darcy insisted on going first, like once in Kent, to help her down on the other side. At first she tried to argue that she was perfectly capable of climbing over the fence on her own, as she had done it all her life. Eventually she grudgingly – and with a discreet roll of her eyes – allowed herself to be helped.

He had never met a more stubborn and independent female to be sure.

When they were crossing the first border, Darcy limited himself to supporting her arm as she jumped down, but at the next ones, he simply chose to put his hands on her waist and lift her down. He thought it safer and easier, not to mention more painfully pleasurable for him. Having her in his hands for a moment or two, so warm and soft, her sweet scent mixed with her sweat; it was a sheer torture. She gave him a sharp look when he placed his hands on her middle the first time. But when he did not try to do anything more, and his hands did not linger on her body longer than necessary as he put her on the ground, she calmed down and did not protest the procedure at the next obstacle.

As they finally reached their destination, Darcy needed to turn his eyes away from her so as not to be tempted to take her in his arms again, so attractive was she to him; cheeks flushed, bosom heaving from the exertion, dark, chocolate curls escaping the pins because she had removed her bonnet much earlier.

"Pleasant view," Darcy noted as she walked to the edge.

"Surely, it cannot be compared to the views of Derbyshire. My Aunt, Mrs. Gardiner, was born and brought up there, and she always praises the wild beauty of that county."

"I cannot deny it. Where exactly did your aunt live in Derbyshire?"

Elizabeth turned to him. "Lambton."

Darcy's eyebrows shot up. "But it is only five miles from Pemberely."

"I know, Aunt mentioned it, when Mr. Wickham was introduced to her last December."

The scowl altered Darcy's features at hearing Wickham's name. He hated the thought of this bastard anywhere near his Elizabeth. "I have heard that the militia is about to leave Meryton... within days," he tried to keep his voice calm and detached.

"Yes, they are moving to Brighton for the summer," she confirmed.

As the memories of July last year returned to him, how Wickham had nearly succeeded in ruining his sister, he did not register that Elizabeth stepped close to him, touching his arm to bring his attention.

"For a long time now, I have wanted to ask you about one matter."

He gave her a warm look. "Yes."

"It is about Mr. Wickham. He told me some things about you..." she hesitated, "Very unfavourable ones."

"What did he tell you?" Darcy barked, his voice losing all its soft tones.

Her eyes widened at his tone. "He complained that you unfairly refused him the living in the church that your late father had promised to him." she explained quietly.

Darcy clenched his fists. "It is a gross untruth. I paid him off, three thousand pounds, and he never intended to become a parson in the first place. Wickham a clergyman, Good Lord!" he exclaimed, "He was more interested in gambling and womanizing."

Elizabeth's dark eyebrows frowned as she stared at him. Could it be possible that she did not believe his words? Did she think Wickham a victim?

"Elizabeth, I have a proof, the documents he signed. I do not have them on me, but I can send for them."

Her expression was still uncertain. "I just do not understand," she searched his face, "Why did he say such things about you to strangers, to me?"

"Elizabeth, I am not surprised. Wickham hates me. He was always jealous of me because *I* was the heir to Pemberley, and he only the steward's son, though due to my father's generosity, brought up as a gentleman."

"He told me that your father loved him more than you, and it was you who were jealous of him."

Darcy began pacing, clenching and unclenching his fists. "He did tell you that, the bastard." He grunted under his breath. "Did he also tell that last summer he attempted to ruin my sister? He talked her into elopement, convinced her of his love, and all because of her dowry. He wanted her thirty thousand pounds!"

Elizabeth gaped at him in shock. "But your sister is very young, a child."

Darcy nodded. "She was barely fifteen then."

"He should be prosecuted for it!" Elizabeth cried fiercely.

"No, I do not want anyone to know. You must understand that I want to keep it secret for Georgiana's sake. I want her to forget, and protect her reputation."

"You can trust my secrecy," she assured.

Darcy nodded. "Thank you. You are the only person who knows about it, apart from Colonel Fitzwilliam, who is her second guardian."

"How is she now?" Elizabeth asked after a moment, her expression of true concern.

Darcy answered in a calmer voice. "She is a bit better, but still not how she used to be. Georgiana is shy by nature, we both are, but after what happened last summer, she became worse. I have hoped that you, with all your liveliness, will help her to open herself."

"I would wish to meet her."

"I would wish that too, but you must see that I cannot bring her here while Wickham is in Meryton."

"Of course." Elizabeth agreed as she walked to sit on the fallen tree trunk. "I am still shocked with what you have told me." She shook her head, "What a cad he is! And he pretends to be so agreeable, so charming."

Darcy came closer, hovering over her. "Charm was something Wickham never lacked."

She looked up at him. "I cannot imagine what you felt when you discovered his intentions."

"It was one of the worst moments in my life, to say the least."

Elizabeth took his hand and made him sit down next to her.

"I am so sorry that it happened to your sister and to you."

Darcy looked into her dark, big eyes. He knew that Georgiana's history had moved her tender heart, but did she really care?

"It is behind us," he said curtly.

She squeezed his hand in both of her smaller ones.

"I just want Wickham forever out of our lives." He cupped her cheek, "Promise you will be careful when you see him. It would be best to not talk to him at all. I fear that he will try to hurt you somehow, now that he has surely learned about us."

She nodded. "I promise. I shall do my best to avoid him."

Chapter Nine

"Lizzy, Lizzy, come here." Mrs. Bennet hissed, widening her large blue eyes even more as she stood on the doorstep to her bedroom.

Elizabeth, already dressed in her nightclothes, was on her way to Mary's room to retrieve her book. She had no idea what her mother wanted from her that she could have not told her before. Elizabeth frowned. "Mama?"

"Come here." Her mother mouthed, making a wide, inviting gesture with her hand.

Elizabeth pulled her shawl tighter over her arms and stepped across the hall. "Yes, Mama."

Mrs. Bennet shoved her inside the room and closed the door, "I did not want to talk about it in the presence of Jane. Poor, poor Janie."

Elizabeth's heart fluttered in worry. "What has happened?"

Mrs. Bennet settled in her favourite armchair in front of the fireplace. "I paid a visit to my sister Phillips today while you were walking with Mr. Darcy."

"Yes, I know. You have told us about it already, Mama, at dinner."

"What I did not tell you is what I heard there about Mr. Darcy."

Elizabeth stared down at her mother with a frown. "Mr. Darcy? What would that have to do with Jane?"

"Mr. Darcy is not staying at Netherfield." Mrs. Bennet announced.

"He is not? Then where?" Elizabeth's eyebrows shot up. "Are you sure, Mama?"

"Yes, Lizzy. It is certain."

Elizabeth's frown deepened. "But..." She sat down on the opposite chair.

"Has he ever mentioned to you that he was staying at Netherfield?" Mrs. Bennet asked.

Elizabeth hesitated. "No, he has not, although I took it for granted. It seemed logical - Mr. Bingley is his friend - so I thought that Mr. Darcy asked his permission to use his house during his visit in the neighbourhood."

"Nothing like that has happened, it seems. Mr. Darcy has been staying at the inn in Meryton since he arrived."

Elizabeth stared at her mother. "I had no idea."

"There is more, child. He is buying Purvis Lodge."

Elizabeth blinked her eyes. "Who?"

"Mr. Darcy, of course," the older woman cried impatiently.

"Mr. Darcy, Purvis Lodge?" Elizabeth questioned unbelievingly. Purvis Lodge was a spacious cottage with a large garden, stables and even a small park, just outside Meryton. It had been uninhabited for the last couple of years.

"Are you sure, Mama?"

"Yes, Mr. Darcy came to your uncle yesterday to ask him if he would care to deal with all the legal papers concerning the sale."

"I know nothing about it," Elizabeth said. "Mr. Darcy never mentioned it to me."

Mrs. Bennet leaned forward. "Lizzy, child, you must ask Mr. Darcy about it. If he is buying Purvis Lodge, it can only mean that Mr. Bingley does not intend to ever come back to Netherfield, and Mr. Darcy, as his friend, knows that. Perhaps Mr. Bingley already decided to give up the lease of Netherfield. You must talk with Mr. Darcy about it, and question him whether his friend intends to ever return here. You must do it as soon as possible, tomorrow."

Elizabeth gave her a worried look. "But Mama... Mr. Darcy told me today that he will be away for the next two days. Tomorrow morning he goes to London to see to some important business there."

Mrs. Bennet clasped her hands together. "He needs to bring money to pay for Purvis Lodge," she exclaimed. "It is the only explanation."

"I think you are correct on this, Mama."

Mrs. Bennet was shaking her head. "Lizzy, I do not like it. I do not like it at all. What if Mr. Darcy had an argument with Mr. Bingley! Perhaps they are not friends any more? Mr. Bingley will never come here to be the groomsman at your wedding, and he and Jane will never have another chance. Oh, my poor nerves!"

"Mama, we cannot know that."

"Did Mr. Darcy speak to you about Mr. Bingley?"

"No, he did not."

"You see yourself! Poor, poor Jane. I have thought that all will be well now, but no, all is lost."

"No, Mama, it is not," Elizabeth spoke with force. "I will ask Mr. Darcy about his friend at the first opportunity. I promise you. I am sure it is just a misunderstanding of sorts."

"I hope so, Lizzy. I do hope so," Mrs. Bennet said in a weak voice.

Elizabeth leaned to kiss her cheek and quietly left the room.

***

On the day when Mr. Darcy was to come back from London, Elizabeth impatiently awaited his visit since midday. She sat near the window, to see who was coming, calmly bearing the teasing of her younger sisters, who joked that she awaited her admirer. The sale of Purvis Lodge seemed to be a fact. Elizabeth had walked by the place earlier in the morning, and had seen that the doors and windows had been opened wide, servants working, putting the house into order.

The more she thought about the matter, the more she was convinced that Mr. Darcy had not told Mr. Bingley about their courtship, about his intentions toward her. Her suspicion was that Mr. Darcy still considered Jane not good enough for his friend, and tried to keep Mr. Bingley away, not informing him of his stay in Hertfordshire. Such reasoning on Mr. Darcy's part did not make much sense to Elizabeth. After all, he had decided to marry her, and she was Jane's sister, they belonged to the same family. If she was good enough for Mr. Darcy of Pemberley, her sister should be considered an appropriate match for his friend. For certain, not all of Mr. Darcy's actions could have been easily explained.

The sun began lowering on the skyline, but Mr. Darcy had not arrived. Elizabeth began to wonder what could have kept him away, because she was sure he would pay her a visit the same day he returned to the neighbourhood.

Closer to dinner time, a man came, whom Elizabeth recognised as one of Mr. Darcy's servants, bringing a small parcel for her.

She ran upstairs to her room, and tore the wrapping with impatient hands. There was a book inside, and a note, with *Elizabeth* written in a strong hand.

She sat close to the window, opened the seal and began to read.

My dearest, loveliest Elizabeth,

I dearly hope you are in good health, the same as when I last saw you. When we spoke, I said that I would return to you in two days' time, but some unexpected circumstances have detained me in London. My sister, Georgiana, insists on meeting you, and wants to travel with me to Hertfordshire. I know for certain that the Militia is to leave by the end of the week, so we will probably arrive on Monday afternoon, as there will be no risk of her meeting W.

I think about you every day, my love. I passed by a bookshop today, and I noticed this book, thinking you would like to read those poems. I saw you reading Wordsworth in the past, and this is the newest selection of his poetry. I hope you will enjoy it.

Yours,

F. Darcy.

There was a knock on the door and Mrs. Bennet came in.

"Lizzy?"

Elizabeth turned to her. "Yes, Mama."

The woman walked closer. "What does he write?"

"He is coming back on Monday."

"What has he sent you?"

"A book of poems."

"Does he write anything about Mr. Bingley, about Purvis Lodge?" Mrs. Bennet asked in a whisper.

Elizabeth folded the note. "No, Mama, he does not. "

"He does not," Mrs. Bennet sighed fretfully.

"No, but he says that he will bring his sister with him so I could meet her."

"His sister, that is good. The girls will have a new company," she said listlessly. "Come, Lizzy. We have fish for dinner, the way you like it."

***

On Thursday evening, there was a farewell party thrown in honour of the Militia by Aunt Phillips at her house in Meryton. The Bennets came, as expected, sans Mr. Bennet, who rarely attended such gatherings. The two youngest girls were in despair, which fact they thought necessary to announce every hour of the day, beginning at breakfast, because the officers were leaving the neighbourhood. Together with their mother, they had already started pressing Mr. Bennet to take them to Brighton for the summer, which, not surprisingly, Mr. Bennet had no intention of doing. Elizabeth could not imagine her father at such a crowded place, away from his beloved books and the peace of his library.

In usual circumstances, Elizabeth would have rejoiced at the opportunity to spend the evening in pleasant company, but this time she was much less eager to go. She never doubted what Mr. Darcy had told her about Wickham. There had been real pain in his voice and expression as he had spoken about what had happened to his sister.

As for her so-called friendship with Mr. Wickham, she had learned once and for all not to believe so easily in people who liked to tell unfavourable stories about others to strangers.

The gathering at her aunt's house was not planned as a ball, but Elizabeth was not surprised that it had eventually evolved into one. It was, after all, the last opportunity to engage the officers in dancing.

Elizabeth was asked to dance the first, but refused, doubting whether she would be able to behave with ease and politeness passing by Mr.Wickham for half an hour as he danced the same set with Lydia.

She sat next to Jane, and they began to talk in quiet voices about the matter which had emerged with the arrival of today's post. Elizabeth had received a letter from the Gardiners, inviting her to accompany them on their planned on July trip to the Lakes. It was Elizabeth's long time dream to see the place, and she was decided to thank kindly the Aunt and Uncle for their invitation and accept.

"You must first ask Mr. Darcy before you accept their invitation, Lizzy." Jane noted.

Elizabeth bristled immediately. "Why should I? Papa has agreed. I have already asked him."

"Sister, you know you should consult Mr. Darcy as well, not only with Papa."

Elizabeth folded her arms on her chest, in a childlike gesture. "He cannot forbid my going."

"No, of course not." Jane soothed, "He will be your husband one day though. You need to discuss such trips with him."

"He did not tell me he intended to buy Purvis Lodge," Elizabeth argued, "Why I should consult him?"

"Lizzy, you are too hasty in reaching your conclusion. I am sure he wanted to tell you, but perhaps did not have the opportunity. I think that those rare moments when you are together alone, he does not want to talk about business."

"Perhaps." Elizabeth admitted reluctantly.

"Has it not occurred to you that he would like to take you there one day, knowing it has been your wish for a long time? He seems eager to please you," Jane pointed out.

Elizabeth looked at her sister, into her kind, smiling eyes. Jane was right as always. She should discuss the matter with Mr. Darcy.

"Miss Elizabeth, may I ask you for the next set?" Mr. Wickham's rich, pleasant voice caught her attention.

"No, thank you," she answered briskly.

Wickham looked surprised, but there was something more in his expression as he glanced down at her.

"Are you unwell tonight?"

Elizabeth forced a smile. "I am very well, Mr. Wickham, simply not inclined to dance."

Wickham's eyes did not leave her. "I hear of major changes in your life. Darcy is a happy man, I dare say. Some people are given all the best in life, while others are not so lucky."

Elizabeth barely stopped herself from rolling her eyes. Mr. Wickham stepped into his plaintive melody one more time. She glanced at Jane, whose corners of her mouth lifted in the slightest of smiles. Jane, of course, knew of everything Mr. Darcy had told her.

"I think that Mama, needs me," Jane stood up. "Excuse me, Mr. Wickham."

Wickham bowed as Jane walked away with her usual grace.

"May I?" he pointed to an abandoned chair.

"Please," Elizabeth said unsmilingly, and turned her face towards the dancing couples, as the next set had just started.

"We were good friends once, Miss Bennet," Wickham noted after a while.

"Were we?" she laughed, not looking at him. "I have always considered that people could be referred to as friends only if they are perfectly sincere with one another."

It silenced Wickham for a while, but some minutes later, he tried to begin conversation again.

"I hear that you will know Pemberley very well in the future, and even live there."

"Yes, it seems so," she agreed in a calm voice.

"I must congratulate you then. It is a beautiful place, and I am sure you will like it there. I am jealous because I will never be able to return there."

Elizabeth turned her whole person to him at last. "Oh, come now, Mr. Wickham, do not pretend to be the one harmed. I know exactly what happened between you and the Darcys, and whose fault it is that you will never be ever admitted at Pemberley. I wish you more luck in Brighton, Mr. Wickham, with your tales of misfortune." She stood up, "Excuse me."

She was astonished when she felt Wickham's fingers clench on her forearm.

"You are mistaken, Miss Elizabeth," he murmured.

"Let me go," she said, stressing each word.

He took his hand off her, but leaned forward. "Let me explain myself, you do not know..."

Elizabeth cut in, "I do not intend to listen to you or speak to you any more. After what you have done, you should not be admitted into the homes of decent people like my aunt and uncle. I ask you not to bother me any more, or I will have to relate this to Mr. Darcy."

Without a second glance at the man, she walked away. Thankfully, he did not seek her company any more that evening.

***

"What is she like, Brother?" Georgiana Darcy asked eagerly as she observed the passing scenery, their carriage just entering the Meryton outskirts.

Darcy smiled. "I have already told you about her."

"I want to learn more. I already know that she likes walking, reading and plays the piano forte very well, and has a very sweet voice when she sings. She has dark hair, and very beautiful, expressive dark eyes." Georgiana counted on her slim fingers.

Darcy's smile grew wider. His sister had not yet met Elizabeth, and already seemed happier and more animated.

"Is that not enough?" he asked.

Georgiana shook her head. "No, it is not."

"You will meet her tomorrow, and will be able to see for yourself what she is like."

The girl frowned. "Tomorrow? Why not today?"

"It is quite late today, and I thought that you wanted to refresh yourself after the journey."

"I am not tired, Brother. I want to go to Longbourn now."

Because it was Darcy's desire as well, he smiled. "As you wish." He opened the window to get the attention of the driver to take them directly to Longbourn.

They had only been separated a week, and he had missed her so. He had read perhaps twenty times, the note which she had sent him back through his man, thanking him for the book. He doubted whether he would be separate from her for more than a day when they would at last be married.

He doubted whether the Bennets expected them to visit the same day they returned to the neighbourhood. He only hoped Elizabeth was home.

When they stopped in front of the manor, he noticed that the house was unusually quiet. There were no tortured sounds of an ill used pianoforte, or the shrieks over the ownership of a bonnet.

"What a pleasant house." Georgiana said, looking curiously around, her blue eyes stopping at the manicured bed flowers, green lawns, and sparkling large windows.

His sister was clearly determined to like everything connected with his intended. He glanced around with frown of his own; perhaps she was right. The house did not look half that bad, quite affluent indeed, and well taken care of. Collins would inherit a very good estate one day.

They were asked into the smaller parlour, occupied only by the two members of the family, Elizabeth and Miss Bennet.

Darcy wished to walk straight to Elizabeth, kiss and hug her, talk with her and many things more, which understandably, he could not do in front of their sisters.

"Miss Elizabeth, Miss Bennet, this is my sister, Georgiana," he spoke with pleasure, and observed as Elizabeth walked closer. "Georgiana, this is Miss Elizabeth Bennet, the future Mrs. Darcy" he finished the introduction with pride, noticing the intense blush steadily covering Elizabeth's lovely face, down her neck, and lower. Were there more places she blushed?

As they sat down and Jane rang for the refreshments, Darcy watched with pleasure as Elizabeth talked with Georgiana, working her usual charm on the girl. His sister smiled a lot, answered all the enquiries and even asked her own. He preferred to be silent, allowing his women to get better acquainted.

"We are all alone at home today, Mr. Darcy. We expected your visit tomorrow," Jane voice brought his attention.

Darcy went tense all over. "That was the initial plan, but Georgiana was eager to meet Elizabeth yet today." he murmured. He did not like interacting directly with Jane, and tried to avoid it. Deep in his heart, he felt guilty about what he had done, separating Bingley from her.

"Our father went to London for a few days this morning on business, while our mother and younger sisters went to visit Aunt Philips." Jane explained.

"I see." Darcy said only.

Jane kept smiling at him kindly, and in response, he managed a half smile on his own.

"Miss Darcy," Jane said, some time later, glancing at Darcy, who at the same moment was contentedly staring at Elizabeth. "Would you like to see the garden? It will be my pleasure to show it to you."

Georgiana looked to her brother for approval and then at Elizabeth, guessing Jane's intentions to leave the couple alone. "Yes, I would, Miss Bennet." She stood up, "I admired the bed flowers in front of the house as we came."

As their sisters departed, and they were left alone, Elizabeth walked to him. "It seems we are at our sisters' mercy. They are determined to leave us in each other's company.'

"I cannot complain about that. On the contrary I am grateful."

He took her hand and kissed it. He wanted more, but after what had happened last time, he now needed to prove to her that he could control himself and that she could trust him.

She gazed into his eyes for a long minute, then closed her own, lifted up on her feet, and tilted her face. It was the exact invitation he needed.

She was sweet and willing in his arms, and he strived to be gentle to keep the exchange innocent.

"I missed you," he said as he lifted his lips from hers. Her eyes were closed and she seemed dazed.

"It was only a week." she whispered, as she opened her now misty eyes.

He walked back and sat back blindly on the nearest seat, pulling her onto his lap. "On my way here, I was thinking that I will not be able to part from you more than for a day once we are married."

He tugged the edge of her sleeve away and kissed the newly exposed skin of her smooth, creamy shoulder, then rubbed his cheek against it. "Now I think that one hour would be too long."

She pulled from him. "You are scratchy."

He kissed the reddened spot and pulled the sleeve back in place. "I am sorry, love, I should shave twice a day, so as not to leave whisker burns on your skin."

She leaned against him more comfortably, and he tightened his hold on her. He was happy to be silent, simply holding her, relishing in her presence so close to him.

A while later, she spoke at last, with hesitation, "You bought Purvis Lodge."

"Yes, I came to the conclusion that a house in the neighbourhood would be useful." he explained, "I imagined you would wish to visit your family in the future. We will need a comfortable place to stay."

In his personal opinion, Longbourn was not a household where a man could spend even one night in peace and quiet, with those wild girls running from room to room till late in night. He restrained himself from saying this aloud; it was not necessary, and she would probably become upset with such a remark.

"We could stay at Longbourn at such times."

"What about when we have children? There will not always be just the two of us," he pointed out. "Longbourn is too small, I dare say, to admit that many guests."

Elizabeth frowned, and released herself from his hold, standing up.

He caught her hand.

"We must talk in earnest," she said, looking down at him.

His heart tugged in worry. She sounded exactly like that morning in the grove in Kent, when she had acted as if she had been about to break off their engagement. "Has something happened?"

She nodded. "Yes, two matters actually; one much less serious than the other, but we must discuss both of them."

He enclosed her hand in both of his. "As you wish. I will listen to you."

Elizabeth freed her palm and stepped to the window, "I see our sisters coming back. We must postpone it."

He walked to stand behind her. "I will find the opportunity so we could talk in private."

She turned to him with a smile. "That may not be that easy. We were lucky today."

Chapter Ten

Elizabeth stood in the corner of the spacious drawing room at Lucas Lodge, watching her sisters dance a Scottish dance while Mary accompanied them on the pianoforte. The evening had begun as a simple dinner party, but like every large gathering in the neighbourhood, had evloved into a small ball.

Her feet itched to partake in the entertainment, but no one had asked her. She looked up at the tall man standing close beside her. Mr. Darcy could have asked her, but he had not, though she loved fast dances. He must have known how much she enjoyed them; he had stared at her often enough last autumn to notice. She was guessing that no other man dared approach her and ask her, when she had a dark, brooding shadow beside her for the entire evening.

Elizabeth knew that she still had to speak with Darcy about Mr. Bingley, and the role he had played in the separation of his friend and Jane. Unlike the matter of Wickham, in this case, there could be no misjudgement on her part. Colonel Fitzwilliam had accidentally testified to Darcy's involvement in the whole affair.

In the course of the last few days she had lacked the opportunity to have a serious conversation with Darcy. It required some time alone, so no one could interrupt or hear them. However, as she was putting much effort into becoming better acquainted with Georgiana, she had little time left to spend with her brother.

Elizabeth had to admit that Miss Darcy was a lovely girl, sweet and unspoiled, adoring her brother, and wanting to please him. At the same time, Georgiana was shy, unsure of herself, and doubting her beauty and accomplishments. The way she spoke about Darcy was always with love and respect, as if he was the most important person in the world for her. Such great affection and attachment for her brother, turned out to not be surprising at all, when Elizabeth heard from the girl more of the family history.

Georgiana did not remember her mother, who had died when she had been just a year and a half old. Judging from what Georgiana said about her father, he had never recovered from his wife's death, and passed away himself when she was eleven. It seemed that the girl had been mostly brought up by a housekeeper, Mrs. Reynolds, and a very busy brother, who had to compromise his own education to take care of the girl twelve years his junior and run the large estate, plus attend other family business from a very early age.

After a few walks across the countryside with Georgiana, listening to her and asking questions, Elizabeth had developed a healthy dose of respect for Fitzwilliam Darcy. In some ways, it even began to flatter her that he had chosen her, Elizabeth Bennet, as his wife. Moreover, she understood better now why he was often so hard on the edges, serious and sober.

There were still two matters which she held against him; Jane and Bingley was one, and his general attitude towards her family and neighbours the other. His behaviour could be called at best as unsocial, but in truth, he was plain rude most of the time; this evening being a prime example. Even when he did talk to someone, he found it necessary to show his condescending superiority at every word and gesture. He was kind only when he spoke to her.

Elizabeth was determined not to delay their conversation about Jane any longer, though she was aware it would not be a pleasant talk. As they were never truly alone these days, Elizabeth thought the best way to find some privacy would be ask him to meet her early in the morning in some secluded place.

The sound of Kitty and Lydia's laughter drew her attention; the girls had missed their steps and bumped into one another. A loud, longing sigh escaped her.

Instantly, she felt his warm, big hand on the small of her back. "Tired, love?" he asked, so quietly that only she could hear.

"I wanted to dance this dance."

There was a long silence, and his hand on her back stilled. "Do you not find it a bit childish?"

"No, I do not. I like to dance," she argued. "You do not want to ask me, and no other men will do it because you are standing here like a hawk," she added grudgingly.

His warm hand began stroking her back, up and down, from the uncovered skin of her shoulder blades to the base of her spine. "You might have told me you wanted to dance."

She shrugged and said nothing.

Without a word, Darcy wrapped her hand around his arm and led them across the room to the corner where Mrs. Bennet sat together with her sister, Mrs. Philips.

He bowed. "Miss Elizabeth is in a need of fresh air. We will walk out on the terrace for a moment." he announced, and without waiting for an answer, walked away.

"Will you tell me what is bothering you tonight?" he asked when they were outside.

She set her lips in a tight line, afraid to say too much at once, knowing it was neither the time, nor place for it.

He waited for her to answer, and when she did not, he pulled her to him, wrapping his arms tightly around her. She relaxed after a moment, and allowed him to cradle her.

When she felt calmed enough, she raised her head from his chest. "Will you come tomorrow to the grove by the pond, the one I showed to Georgiana the other day?"

He searched her eyes. "Ah, yes." he frowned, "You wanted to discuss something, but there has been no opportunity so far."

She nodded. "At dawn?"

"As you wish, I will be there."

He lowered his head, and kissed her gently, a light caress. She closed her eyes and allowed her head rest back on his solid chest. It felt good to stand here, in his embrace, breathing the clear night air.

A few short minutes later, she heard her mother's voice. "Lizzy? Where are you? Lizzy?"

Elizabeth stiffened instantly and stepped away. She hoped her mother had not seen too much, as it was dark on the terrace.

"Yes, Mama." She cleared her throat, "We are here."

"Ah," Mrs. Bennet came from the shadows. "Here you are, Lizzy."

The woman glanced at Darcy wearily, before placing her eyes on her daughter. "I think we should go now." she said slowly.

"So early, Mama?" It was unusual of Mrs. Bennet to want to leave any party before others.

"Yeees." the woman drawled, "I think that we are all tired tonight."

"I will go call the carriage," Darcy said formally and left the terrace.

Mrs. Bennet waited till he was gone and whispered. "Lizzy, are you well?"

Elizabeth was more than taken aback by the question. "Yes, Mama."

The older woman hesitated. "I know he is rich, daughter but so... unwelcoming at the same time. Does he treat you right?"

Elizabeth's heart melted. She knew how much her mother desired this match, and still she worried about her happiness. "Yes, Mama. You cannot imagine how kind he is when we are all alone. He does not enjoy large gatherings, like this, that is all."

The woman nodded. "Yes, of course, your father does not like them either. Well, let us return, it is getting cold here."

As they stepped inside, Mrs. Bennet added. "Perhaps Mr. Collins would have been better for you, Lizzy. Not so smart, perhaps, or rich, but certainly less... less..." the woman could not find the word.

Rude, condescending, arrogant. Elizabeth finished in her thoughts.

"All is well, Mama," Elizabeth ensured. "Do not worry."

Mrs. Bennet shook her head. "I do not, Lizzy. I do not."

***

Darcy endured a mostly sleepless night. Elizabeth was so determined to talk with him in private. He knew that something was bothering her, and he was becoming more and more apprehensive about the reason for her anxiety.

He chose to go on horseback, and saw her long before she could see him, already waiting for him.

She stood with her back to him, staring into the mirror of the water, the early morning mist surrounding her. He tried to approach her very quietly, but she turned as she heard the horse's neigh.

Her eyes widened and she took a step back.

"Come," he held out his hand, "let us go from here."

Her eyes widened. "On horseback?"

"Yes."

She stared at the horse. "I do not ride."

"I will ride. You will sit in front of me."

She shook her head. "I prefer to stay here. *On my feet.*" She stressed.

He smirked. "You are afraid."

"No, I am not." She glanced at the animal who was interested in her person and tried to sniff her. "I just do not see the reason why..."

She did not finish, as he moved the horse a few steps forward, leaned down and picked her up by the waist, in one swift move, putting her before him.

"No!" she cried, her eyes terrified for a moment as she looked down.

She clung to him, her hands wrapped around his neck with such force that she might strangle him.

"Easy," he crooned.

He kicked the horse into the slowest of gaits, and gradually she relaxed.

"Do you always have to do as you wish?" she asked grudgingly after a moment. He helped her arrange herself with her back to his chest, holding her securely to him with his arm around her middle so she could feel safe.

"I only think that you can admire the countryside much better from the top of the horse rather than from a five foot perspective."

As he expected, she gasped in offended dignity, "I am five foot two inches."

"Just enjoy," he said, and put the horse into faster motion, "Look around."

She listened to him, and for the rest of the ride, she was quiet, her bonnet in front of him, moving in all directions. They reached the top of the Oakham Mount soon. Darcy dismounted first and reached for her.

"It was not that bad, was it?" he asked when her feet touched the steady ground.

"No, it was not," she admitted.

He walked the horse to a grassy spot and left him there to feed.

She turned to him and spoke without preamble. "I received a letter from my aunt, Mrs. Gardiner."

"The one who was brought up in Lambton?"

"Yes, the same one. She and my uncle plan a trip to the lakes this summer, and they invited me to join them."

Darcy felt as if a great weight was lifted off his chest. *That is all?* From her previous tone and her pleas for an earnest conversation, he had thought that the matter was serious indeed, not just a summer trip with the relatives.

"Would you like to go?" he asked smilingly, pleased that she found it necessary to consult with him regarding her future plans, asking *his* permission.

"Very much, it has been my dream for a long time to see that part of the country."

He pulled her closer, "I will take you there once we are married then. Understandably, you should accept the invitation, on one condition though..." he paused, "You must convince your aunt and uncle to stay at Pemberley for at least a week."

She looked shocked. "You would invite them?"

Darcy nodded, thinking that those Gardiners could not be entirely bad. Elizabeth often mentioned them with admiration, praised their good taste and their love for books and the theatre. Yes, Pemberley would have to survive the tradesmen if it meant having Elizabeth there too. "I will write a letter with a personal invitation for them, which you can enclose with your correspondence."

Her mouth curled in a smile, her eyes sparkling. "Oh, thank you!" she jumped up into his arms, her arms wrapping around his neck. "Thank you so much!"

He picked her up, holding her tightly, her feet dangling in the air. From all the gifts he had given her so far, he had never received such an enthusiastic reaction like now, inviting her relatives to his home.

"I would have to return to Pemberley for the summer anyway," he said as he put her down, "So this trip is very accommodating to all of us."

"I will write yet today," she promised.

"Good." he leaned forward, hoping for a kiss, but she pushed away from him. "There is another matter we need to discuss."

He put a welcoming expression on his face. "Yes."

She took a deep breath and spoke solemnly. "Have you told Mr. Bingley about our understanding? Does he know you are here?"

All the pleasantness was wiped away from Darcy's face. "No, he does not know."

She searched his face for a long moment. "I know it was you who separated Jane and Mr. Bingley."

Darcy froze. "How do you know about that?"

"Last autumn, I noticed the disapproving looks you directed many times at Jane when she danced or talked with Mr. Bingley. When the entire company left Netherfield so abruptly, I suspected that you had intervened in some way, but I was not entirely sure. In Kent, Colonel Fitzwilliam confirmed my suspicions accidentally. He did not know he was speaking of my sister when he mentioned to me how good a friend of Mr. Bingley you were by rescuing him from a most unfortunate marriage to a woman from a most unsuitable family."

Darcy felt his throat tighten. He knew how much Elizabeth loved and cared for her elder sister. Damn Richard and his big mouth.

"Do you deny it?" she asked.

Darcy braced himself inside. "No, I cannot deny it. I observed you sister most carefully, and she seemed to welcome his advances but stayed indifferent and demure, not showing any real affection, which convinced me she did not love Bingley. I did everything in my power to separate them, and at the time I rejoiced in my success. Towards him I have been kinder than towards myself." he murmured the last sentence.

Only as he spoke the last sentence, did he realize how it must have sounded to her ears.

She lowered her eyes to the ground for a long minute, and when she eventually did look at him with all the hurt and pain, he wished she had not. Her beautiful eyes were full of tears, her pale face washed out, as if someone had slapped her.

She turned from him and started to walk.

"No, Elizabeth, wait!" he cried. "I did not mean it the way that sounded." He caught her arm, stopping her in place for a moment, but she freed herself from his embrace and started to run. His height and long legs gave him an advantage, and he caught up to her soon. "Please, I did not mean to say that." He grounded her in place, "I am ready to overlook your low connections, the impropriety of your family's behaviour, everything. You are worth it. I know you are not like your family. You are so much better." He was breathing harshly, his hands on her, trying to bring her closer to him.

"Do not touch me." she said evenly, and waited till he took his hands off her. "Who do you think you are?" she called, "You consider your family better than mine. They have more money, and that is the only difference between our families. My cousins do not keep mistresses, and neither of my aunts is so stupid, egocentric and ill behaved like Lady Catherine." she paused, striving to calm herself. "My sister loved Mr. Bingley, and has been heartbroken for months because of your selfishness and disdain for the feelings of others." She took a step closer and cried into his face, her hands clenched into fists, "You are rude, conceited and arrogant! Certainly, you are not the gentleman you think yourself to be."

As Darcy was digesting the assessment of his character, Elizabeth turned on her feet, and in her agitated state, she mistook a step, hooked her foot around a protruding root, and fell flat on the ground.

He was beside her before she could manage to lift herself to her arms and knees. "Elizabeth, are you well?"

"Fine." she muttered, as he turned her on her back.

His eyes crawled over her body, hands touching, checking for injuries.

She sat up and touched her head. Then she attempted to stand up, but when her right foot touched the ground, she hissed. "My ankle!" She moved her weight on the other side and hissed again. "My knee..."

His arm went around here waist, keeping her in a standing position. Her face was twisted in pain, so he picked her up into his arms and carried her to the fallen trunk.

"Thoughtless, stupid..." she was murmuring under her breath.

"Who me?" Darcy asked, as he sat her down.

"No, I!" she cried angrily, "To fall down like that, to trip over my own feet."

"Now, now, it could happen to anyone," he soothed, lifting the hem of her dress.

"Which ankle is it?" he asked.

Elizabeth pointed to the injured one, and he removed her sturdy leather shoe to examine it.

"Ouch!" she cried out when he pressed harder.

"It is twisted, I am afraid."

"My knee hurts more..." she betrayed.

He tried to push the mass of petticoats higher, but she stopped him. "You cannot..."

He glanced at her. "What?"

"You should not... look there," she glanced down at her lap.

"Should not see your legs? Has it not occurred to you that I will see them eventually one day?" he flipped her petticoats over her knees, exposing white stockings, and a few inches of naked thighs, visible above the garters. There was a bloody mark on the left knee.

He loosened the garter and pushed the stocking down. There was a tiny stream of blood coming from the small cut. He was so concentrated on checking the degree of her injury, that he did not even feel excited with the fact he had his hands under her skirts for the first time.

"When you tripped, twisting your ankle, you must have hit your knee over a stone here, hard enough that it broke the skin even through the layers of your clothing." He touched the skin around the cut, which was slowly changing colour into deep purple. "I do not like the sight of it. Knee injuries can be nasty and difficult to heal completely."

Elizabeth pushed his hands away and covered herself. "I shall be fine."

"I doubt it."

He stood up and reached to pick her up, but she slapped his hands.

She frowned. "I do not want your help."

"Elizabeth, do not be childish," he tried to sound patient. "You cannot walk on your own."

She lifted her chin high in the air and announced. "I will wait till someone comes passing by."

Darcy did not reply, only walked to his horse and brought it closer.

"I am taking you to Longbourn, and then I will fetch a doctor." He picked her up unceremoniously.

She attempted to struggle out of his iron embrace. "I do not need one."

He ignored her, and lifted her up on the horseback, which as he expected, silencing her instantly. A second later, he was in the saddle behind her.

"Now, hold on," he said, bringing her closer to himself and kicking the horse into a fast gait.

Chapter Eleven

"Good morning, Miss Elizabeth," the old doctor said as he entered Elizabeth and Jane's bedroom.

"Good morning, Doctor," Elizabeth smiled, propped against the pillows, sitting on her bed.

Darcy stood on the left side of her bed, the spot he had not left since he had carried her upstairs.

"Doctor, what must I do with this girl?" Mrs. Bennet exclaimed from behind the man's back. "I had thought that she would calm herself now, when she is almost engaged, but no! She wants to put me into an early grave. She is to become a wife and mother, the mistress of a grand estate, not climbing the trees like a naughty boy."

"I was not climbing anything today, Mama," Elizabeth protested.

"Oh, do be quiet, you wild girl!" Mrs. Bennet cried in anger, "What will Mr. Darcy think of you now? What if he does not take you, knowing your wild, wild ways? What if you killed yourself falling off that tree?" she took a calming breath, and added weakly, "You have no compassion for my poor nerves."

"It was not a tree, Mama!" Elizabeth spoke, her voice rapidly losing its patient tone.

The doctor turned to the older woman. "Now, now, Mrs. Bennet. No, need to exert yourself so." He walked her to the chair. "I can already see that there is no danger to Miss Elizabeth's life."

He returned to Elizabeth, leaving Mrs. Bennet fanning herself with her handkerchief, and asked good humouredly, "What did you break this time, Miss Lizzy?"

Elizabeth presented a toothy smile at the doctor's expression and then murmured. "I just twisted my ankle."

"Just the ankle," the doctor sat on the chair which Jane pushed over for him. "Well, well, it is not that bad then. We have seen worse things on your part, have we not?" He looked around the room full of people, including all the Bennets (sans Mr. Bennet, who was expected to return from London any day) and Darcy, who still stood firmly by the bedside.

"May I be alone with the patient?" the doctor asked.

Mrs. Bennet began pushing everyone out, when the doctor glanced at Jane. "Miss Bennet will stay to help me, if necessary."

Stubbornly, Darcy did not move from his post by Elizabeth's side, eyeing the greying man somehow suspiciously.

The doctor raised his bushy eyebrows. "This gentleman?"

As Darcy did not react, Jane walked up to him, "Mr. Darcy, I think it would be better if you waited outside, or perhaps took tea in the parlour with all of us." She took his arm and attempted to pull him decidedly towards the door.

Elizabeth looked at him. "Please, go with Jane."

Darcy allowed himself to be walked out, while the doctor lifted Elizabeth's skirts and slowly examined the bruised, though no longer bleeding, knee, and ankle. He tried to bend the leg, and when Elizabeth hissed in pain, he said, "Aha."

He dressed the small wound on the knee and said. "Four weeks in bed."

Elizabeth's eyes widened. "No!" she cried.

"Yes." the doctor nodded. "And I will have to stabilize the knee, put the left leg into a brace to lessen movement. I do not like this swelling."

"But four weeks?" Elizabeth pleaded.

The doctor's face turned sober and he asked very seriously, "You do not want to become a cripple, do you?"

Elizabeth shook her head.

"We shall see to it, she does not walk, Doctor." Jane assured, giving her sister a meaningful stare.

"Good." He closed his bag and moved to the door. "I will be back shortly, and no moving from that bed." He wagged his finger at Elizabeth.

When the doctor opened the door, he found Darcy was waiting outside in the corridor.

Jane found it to be the appropriate time to introduce both men. "Doctor, this is Mr. Darcy, my sister's intended. Mr. Darcy, this is

Doctor Sharp. He has treated our family as long as I can remember."

Darcy bowed his head with respect. "Doctor, my pleasure. How is she?"

The doctor glanced at the tall, sober looking young man. "Her ankle should heal within few days, but as for the knee, I will have to stabilize the left leg. It may be nothing, but contrary to the bones in the calves or arms, I cannot really feel whether something is broken, or dislodged inside the knee. As precaution, she should not walk or move it for about a month, or at least till the swelling goes down and she has no pain in it.

Darcy listened intently, and then bowed again. "Thank you, Doctor."

"I will return with the braces," Doctor Sharp added, and moved down the corridor, with Jane following him.

Darcy walked inside the room and closed the door. Elizabeth did not look at him; she only stared out of the window. He sat on the edge of her bed.

"I am so sorry you are hurt and in pain," he started. "I feel guilty..."

She turned her face to look at him. "The fault is entirely mine," she interrupted him. "I cannot walk properly without hurting myself, it seems. Silly, silly me," she murmured, exasperated, "Now, I will have to spend four weeks closed up in at home. I do not know how I will stand this," she sighed miserably as she looked out the window again at the sunny day.

Darcy took her hand in both of his. Surprised, she gave him a long look, "Are you not angry with me?"

He shifted closer, his eyes serious. "I could ask you the same question."

She shrugged, "I am usually angry... or rather irritated with you for this reason or another. For example, when you are so rude towards my mother." She looked straight into his eyes, "I know that Mama is silly, and perhaps not the most intelligent woman in England, but she has a good heart, and always means well. She is never purposely hurtful or cruel, never that. She is a good mother, and would do everything for my sisters and me, and I think that she deserves some respect if only for that. When *you* most of the time simply ignore her, and do not even bother to answer her questions civilly."

Elizabeth glanced out the window again, and she did not see how Darcy lowered his head, his forehead furrowed.

After a moment, she added quietly, "I wonder sometimes whether your parents taught you such behaviour towards people. Perhaps things are different with the aristocracy."

He did not say anything to her words, and she understood his reactions in her own way.

"You have every right to be displeased with me now, after I have criticized you so... and all that I said about your family."

"You have given me a lot of to think about, to be sure," he said at last.

Elizabeth lowered herself onto the bed from a sitting position to lying one, and turned on her side, careful not to bend the injured knee. "I am tired after getting up so early. I will try to nap till the doctor returns," she whispered.

Darcy looked around, and found a knitted blanket folded on Jane's bed. He reached for it, and draped it over her.

She closed her eyes, pretending to sleep, but relaxed only when she heard his steps on the wooden floor, as he left the room.

***

Elizabeth sighed, her eyes wide open, staring into the dark night.

"Lizzy, are you all well?" she heard her sister's sleepy voice coming from the nearby bed.

"I am well, Jane," she whispered back.

"You sighed several times. I have thought perhaps your leg may be getting worse," Jane murmured.

"No, no, I am sorry I have disturbed you. Go back to sleep."

Jane rolled onto her other side.

Elizabeth could not sleep, but not so much because of the slight lingering pain in her knee, but all the thoughts which had invaded her mind and refused to go away and let her rest. She was furious with herself. Her mother was right, she had behaved like a child, injuring herself in such a stupid way, not looking where she was going. Her punishment was acute indeed, and she deserved it, forced to stay at home for a month, not being able to even move on her own.

There was Darcy too. She had told him everything she had against him. At first she had felt relieved, and even, in a way, proud of herself. However, very soon, the feelings of guilt came to her. She felt that she had said too much and had been unkind. She knew that he cared for her; her words must have pained him. She acted like Caroline Bingley's sort would have, spiteful and harsh. He had been wrong about Jane, but she should not have reacted so strongly. She might have attempted to resolve it in a gentler way. Even after she fell down, he had been only kind and caring, when she was cold and aloof, pushing him away.

That was what she had been doing for the last weeks, keeping him at distance, pushing him away. She had to admit that for most of the time, especially when they were alone, he was very good to her, and tried so hard to please her. He had even agreed to invite the Gardiners to Pemberley, though he had never met them before.

She had allowed him to believe that she cared for him when she accepted him. Consequently, she should be treating him accordingly, even if she felt less. She was responsible for him now, not only for hurting his feelings, but first of all, for his happiness.

***

Due all the late night's thinking, Elizabeth overslept the next day. When she woke up at nearly ten in the morning, Jane told her that the Darcys were already waiting to see her.

She did her best to hurry with her toilette and breakfast, which went twice as long as usual. It was only after eleven when she was ready to admit her guests, sitting on top of her made bed, covered with pretty lace coverlet.

Georgiana came in, but there was no sign of her brother.

The girl walked near her bed. "Miss Elizabeth, I was so distressed when my brother told me what happened to you yesterday." She spoke with genuine compassion.

"I am well, but please, I thought we had agreed to use our first names." Elizabeth patted the place beside her.

Georgiana sat down on the edge of the bed. "Are you in pain?"

"No, not now, when the leg is in these braces." Elizabeth uncovered her leg so Georgiana could see a stocking clad leg clasped in wooden boards. "It pains me only when I try to bend the leg."

The girl touched the braces with gentle fingers. "I am so sorry it happened to you."

"It was my own fault, I am afraid. It only serves me right though. I will be looking under my feet now."

Georgiana leaned forward confidentially. "Brother was so worried yesterday. I have not seen him so concerned for a very..." Georgiana paused, her expression even more clouded, "very long time now. He closed himself in his room for the entire evening. I doubt whether he slept much either."

Elizabeth swallowed. "Has he come with you?"

Georgiana nodded. "Yes, he is waiting outside in the corridor. I think that he was reluctant to invade the privacy of your bedroom, because he did not want to walk in with me when Miss Jane invited us upstairs."

"Could you please ask him to come here?"

Jane stood up from her chair. "I will go."

Elizabeth thanked her with her eyes. Then she looked at Georgiana and smiled, at the same time twisting her hands nervously.

Darcy walked in soon, with Jane following him, sober looking to say the least.

He bowed, walked to the bed and asked, "Are you feeling better today?"

Elizabeth managed a weak smile. "Much better, thank you."

Darcy said nothing more, and walked to the window to stare out of it, turning his back to the company. All three ladies looked at him, before Elizabeth turned to Georgiana and spoke in lowered voice, "Would you be so kind to leave us alone for a moment?" She gave the girl a pleading look. "Jane could you please...?"

"We will go to Mary's room." Jane proposed in a decided, but kind voice, "She has wanted to show Miss Darcy her collection of music sheets for a long time now, I believe."

As they were left alone, just two of them, Darcy turned from the window.

"Are you truly better?" he asked, standing some distance from her bed.

"I am truly well, only angry with myself for this." She pointed to her leg. "I cannot imagine how I will be able to stay like this for four weeks."

Darcy nodded. "I am pleased you are not in pain."

Elizabeth shook her head, and whispered. "No, I am not." she gave him a long look. Her heart squeezed, he looked terrible, so pale, his face drawn.

Ola Wegner

She reached out her hand. "Please, come and be seated here."

He seemed reluctant to do as she asked, but he stepped to her bed, and sat down on the edge, his back straight.

Elizabeth did not know what to say, what words to use, so she leaned forward and hooked her arms around his neck tightly. "I am sorry. Please, forgive me for being unkind yesterday, and for the last days. I am not proud of my behaviour." she whispered into his neck.

She did not wait long when he returned the embrace, bringing her to him.

"I cannot bear when you hate me," he murmured, his voice cracking.

"I do not, I do not." she assured, and pulled away from him to see his face; his eyes dark brown eyes were suspiciously misty.

She ran her fingers from his dark, mussed hair, to his temple and down his cheek, and then placed gentle kisses on the places that she had just touched.

He closed his eyes, allowing himself to be caressed for a moment, but soon he sought her lips. Elizabeth accepted the kiss, and once again wound her hand around his neck. He kissed her gently, just lightly tugging at her lower and upper lip. Determined to show him her new, changed attitude, she closed her eyes tight, and what felt to her very awkwardly, she attempted to push her tongue between his lips.

He stiffened for a short moment, then to her great embarrassment, she heard him chuckle. She broke the kiss, blushing, hiding her eyes from his, her face turned to the side. He did not allow it, and taking the initiative, caught her lips with his and deepened the kiss. She was aware how important it was now not to push him away this time. He should feel her willingness to be convinced that she was sincere in her assertions.

She barely noticed when he pushed her down on the bed, she was so overwhelmed with the deep, passionate kisses. At one moment she finally tore her lips away, needing some air.

She was breathing deeply, staring at the white painted ceiling as he sucked on the skin of her neck, his hand in her hair, combing through her locks, loosening hairpins. When his hand rested heavily on her breast, she whimpered at the shocking pleasure it caused within her. She gasped, panted and strained against his hand as he squeezed her bosom. She had no stays on today, so

108

there was only her dress, and the thin chemise underneath, separating his warm hand from her flesh.

She felt that she desperately needed something, needed more, and tried to lift her lower body against him in a silent plea. She wanted him closer.

The next moment she was all alone on the bed, his weight suddenly taken off her, as he jumped from her as if she had been made of hot iron.

Slowly, she sat up, trying to compose herself. She touched her swollen lips.

"Damn, I should have known better by this time," Darcy murmured, as he paced the room.

"I hurt all over," she complained, touching her aching breasts.

He laughed shortly. "I know what you mean."

He walked to the washstand and wet the towel. Then sat next to her and put the cool material against her hot face.

"You should not trust me," he said.

"But I d,." she protested.

"Elizabeth, this must stop." His voice was so harsh that she startled, "The fault is entirely mine, but we cannot carry on like this," he added more gently as he put the towel away, and reached to her loosened locks, deftly pushing the hairpins into the right places. "One of our sisters might have come upon us at any moment."

"I just wanted to show you that I..." she looked at him, troubled, "I wanted to be close."

"I know, but we do not even have a wedding date settled, and I cannot allow you to be round with babe at our wedding. You deserve better."

Her soft mouth fell open, "But we have not..."

"We certainly have." He cut her in. "Had it not been your leg, and the fact the door is open..." he raked his hand through his hair. "You must promise me, that next time I try touch your breasts, you will slap my hand."

She looked up at him docilely, "I liked how you touched me," she admitted.

He groaned. "Elizabeth, you are not making it easier for me." He placed his hands on her shoulders. "I am trying to protect you, do you understand?" He shook her gently.

She stared at him, wide eyed, and slowly shook her head, and mouthed. *No.*

He laughed, kissed the top of her head, and marched to the door. "I am going to fetch our sisters. We are safe with them."

She plopped on the bed with a loud sigh when he left. She touched her breast and then her hand moved low on her belly and she shivered. She was so relieved he was not angry with her. She preferred not to think what she would do if he took offence and simply walked away from her life forever. She certainly did not like the idea.

Chapter Twelve

"No, Lizzy, not like that," Jane said as she pointed to the seam that Elizabeth was working on. "Look, the material is all wrinkled around the letter '*F.*' You need to undo it and start from the beginning."

"I will never have it right," Elizabeth sighed in frustration.

"You are doing well; just a bit of patience is necessary on such a task," Jane soothed.

Elizabeth began to unravel the '*FD*' monogram embroidered in the fine cotton with the help of her small scissors, murmuring to herself. "I hate needlework. I hate it."

"Ever more reason for Mr. Darcy will be very pleased with his present," her sister noted.

"I doubt it, Jane, I truly do." Elizabeth looked critically at the now partially destroyed initials. "He is always so neat, and surely will not like to use such uneven, poorly trimmed handkerchiefs."

"Nonsense," Jane dismissed her worry. "He would wear a potato sack if you told him you sewed it especially for him."

Elizabeth laughed. "You are making fun of me!" she accused.

Jane only glanced at her from behind her long, dark blond eyelashes, her expression completely serious. "Want to make a wager on that?"

Elizabeth shook her head at her sister's teasing, and with a new found energy, cleared the area of cloth completely to start embroidering the FD initials anew.

A few days ago, she had mentioned to her mother and Jane, that she had felt embarrassed with all the gifts Mr. Darcy brought her almost daily, from books to chocolates, flowers and other small trinkets. Understandably, she could not repay his generosity, as trips to Meryton were impossible for her due to her still healing ankle and knee. Then Jane had proposed that Elizabeth could make a set of embroidered handkerchiefs for Mr. Darcy. Mrs. Bennet had acclaimed the idea, and the same day, together with Jane, they had taken a carriage and gone to Meryton to shop for the cloth. They had returned with two yards of expensive white cotton, and Elizabeth had no excuse now but to start working on the project.

There was a noise in the corridor, a door smacked loudly and someone ran down the corridor. A second later, her door flew wide open, and Kitty Bennet, red faced and in teary eyed, stepped in.

"Jane, Jane tell Mama that it is so unfair!" the girl cried from the doorstep.

"What happened, Kitty? What is unfair?" Jane stood up from her place by the window beside Elizabeth.

Kitty sniffed as she walked inside. "Lydia is going to Brighton for the summer, and I am to stay at home."

"What are you saying, Kitty?" Elizabeth questioned. "There is no possibility she would go alone."

"Papa would never allow that." Jane supported.

Kitty plopped on the nearby chair. "She received an invitation from the wife of Colonel Forster to stay with them, as Mrs. Forster's particular friend. They should have invited me as well! I am two years older! It is so unfair."

"Kitty, Papa will never agree to such a scheme." Elizabeth assured in a calm voice.

"He already has, Lizzy," Kitty said, pouting.

The older sisters glanced at one another.

Elizabeth shook her head. "That cannot be."

Kitty lifted her handkerchief to her already red eyes. "Mama said that Lydia would get two new dresses and a new bonnet and..." she hiccupped, "...a spencer just for the occasion of this trip."

The last words slurred as she began to weep.

Jane walked to the younger girl and wrapped an arm around Kitty's shaking arms in a compassionate gesture. "Now, now. It will not be that bad."

Kitty lifted her heart shaped face. "It is so unfair, Jane. Lizzy is going to the Lake country, Lydia to Brighton, and we will stay all summer at home with Mary!" She hid her face into her already completely soaked handkerchief, and only quiet sobs were heard.

Jane did her best to soothe the girl. She walked her to her room, promising to send a cup of strong tea and a piece of cake from the kitchen.

When Jane returned to her and Elizabeth's room, she found her other sister staring intently out of the window, her needlework abandoned in the basket.

"How is Kitty?" Elizabeth asked.

"I think that a healthy chunk of chocolate cake and the promise I will give her my last year's bonnet for remodelling has vastly improved her spirits," Jane said, and gave Elizabeth a long look. "I see that you are not pleased, sister."

Elizabeth turned to her, lifting from the chaise lounge (which to her comfort was brought from Mrs. Bennet's room) as far as her stabilized leg allowed. "Jane, you know very well that Papa should not allow it. I can hardly believe that he gave his consent to that. Lydia in Brighton, alone, with all the officers around? Such a trip can only be a complete disaster. She will compromise herself and all of us."

Jane hesitated, drawing her delicate eyebrows together. "She has always wanted so much to go to Brighton, and she will be under Mrs. Forster's care, after all."

"Mrs. Forster!" Elizabeth cried in anger. "You know very well that she is the silliest woman of our acquaintance. Lydia's behaviour is scandalous already. She will be forever lost to any sense after a few months' stay in Brighton."

Jane bit on her pink lower lip, glancing at her sister uncertainly.

"You know that I am right, Jane," Elizabeth pressed further. "Our family is already looked down upon because of Lydia's wild behaviour, her general lack of manners, and any kind of self restraint."

"Saying that our family is looked down upon, you mean, by Mr. Darcy, do you not?" Jane asked quietly.

"Yes." Elizabeth answered after a moment, lowering her head, "It pains me to admit it, but he is right on that score." She sighed, "Try to compare Lydia's or even Kitty's conduct and manners to those displayed by Georgiana Darcy, or even Maria Lucas. I know it is not yet too late to improve them, but sending Lydia alone to Brighton is certainly not a good way to accomplish that."

"Mama surely supports the idea," Jane noted.

"I must talk with Papa," Elizabeth tried to move her stabilized leg to the floor. "He cannot allow Lydia to go. He must say no to her. I will talk with Papa. I must go downstairs."

Jane pushed her back on the chaise lounge as Elizabeth attempted to stand up. "No, you cannot, Lizzy. It has barely been a week since the doctor put the braces on, it is too early for you to walk. I will go to the library and ask Papa to come here."

Calmed, Elizabeth rested against the back of the chaise. "Thank you, Jane."

As Jane left, Elizabeth tried to return to her needlework, but she found it hard to focus. Lydia in Brighton alone, without a family to look upon her was a catastrophe. Unguarded, she would only indulge in her open flirtations with men.

Soon there was a knock on the door, and Mr. Bennet appeared in the doorway. "Jane told me you wanted to talk with me."

Elizabeth put a smile on her face. "Yes, Papa. Please, come in."

She looked up at the tall man with dark eyes. For the first time, it struck her how in posture and bearing, he reminded her of Darcy. Her father was nearly as tall as William.

"Are you feeling worse today?" Mr. Bennet asked as he sat on the chair closest to her.

"No, Papa, I feel very well," she assured.

Mr. Bennet reached his hand to stroke her dark curls. "I was so worried when I found you injured on my return from London." The scowl appeared on this face, "That Darcy..."

"Papa," she interrupted him quickly. "I told you that the fault was entirely mine. Did Mr. Darcy not bring me home so promptly? And he immediately fetched the doctor; it could have been much worse."

"You should not have been alone with him in the first place, Elizabeth!" Mr. Bennet cried sharply. "Did he talk you into that? Meeting with him at dawn in a secluded place?"

She shook her head. "No, it was I who asked him. We needed a private moment to talk."

"Lizzy, child," Mr. Bennet leaned toward her, "You do not know what men think of when they are alone with women. You are so small and delicate, you would not be able to protect yourself if he had wanted to..." concerned, now almost black eyes bore sternly into her face. "You know what I mean, have his way with you, hurt you."

"Papa, Mr. Darcy is a gentleman!" Elizabeth exclaimed. "He would never do anything against my will. Do you really think that he agreed to all your conditions, agreed to a half year courtship period, because he wanted to force himself on me during this time?"

Mr. Bennet grunted something incomprehensible under his breath, but said nothing.

Elizabeth took a calming breath, and touched her father's arm to bring back his attention. "Papa, I asked you here because I wanted to talk with you about Lydia. I have heard that you have agreed to her trip to Brighton."

Mr. Bennet nodded. "Yes, I think that it is the cheapest way to give her the entertainment that she craves so much; and we all will gain a few months of peace and quiet in return," he said that as a jest, smiling.

"Papa, is this the only matter you can think of, peace?" she asked quietly. "She will be lost if she goes there, cannot you see that? You are perhaps not aware of what people think about our family precisely because of Lydia's improper behaviour."

Instantly, all the merriness wiped out from Mr. Bennet's face. "By people you mean Mr. Darcy?" he grunted.

Elizabeth lowered her head and did not contradict him.

Mr. Bennet stood up, walked to the window, standing there for a long minute, before he returned to his previous place. "Lizzy, child, there is something I want to tell you."

Elizabeth gave him a curious look. "Yes, Papa."

"You do not have to marry Darcy any more." Mr. Bennet announced proudly.

She frowned. "I do not understand."

"While in London, I talked with my brother-in-law," he said with unusual in his tone excitement. "He listened to me, my concerns about your future, and advised me to invest a quarter of the income from Longbourn into one of his businesses. To be sure, we cannot expect profits for a while, but I am in good health, and I expect to live long years. Perhaps it is not too late to start saving after all. You and your sisters will be protected when my times comes."

Elizabeth stared at her father in astonishment before her face beamed in bright smile. "Papa, it is so thoughtful of you! How wonderful! Have you told of this to Mama?"

"No."

"Why, Papa? She would be so pleased to hear what you did for us."

Mr. Bennet shrugged his shoulders with indifference. "I do not want to hear her raptures. I am tired of them," he spoke flatly, without any feeling. "She will learn in due time."

Elizabeth lowered her head. She felt sorry for her mother. Mr. Bennet talked about his wife as if she were complete stranger who accidentally lived with him under the same roof. She could not imagine William treating her like that; ever, not now not in twenty years.

"What about Lydia, Papa?" she pleaded. "I truly think it would be far better for our family keep her home, forbid her this trip."

Mr. Bennet squared his shoulders, "Elizabeth, I made my decision about Lydia." His voice gained an impatient note to it, "I have had quite enough of your lecturing. I know what is good for the family, contrary to what you or Mr. Darcy may think. Now, I ask you, daughter, will you dissolve your associations with that man?"

"What do you have against him, Papa?" she questioned softly. "Why do you oppose him so?"

"I told you once. I do not want you to be unhappy in a marriage, to regret your decision one day when it is too late to go back."

"I will not regret, Papa," she said with conviction. "I care for him, more and more every day. I truly do. He has his faults, to be sure, but he is a good man, and he loves me."

Mr. Bennet stood up. "Do as you wish then. Tell him you have my approval to announce the official engagement. You can settle the date, and your mother may start with preparations."

Elizabeth caught his hand, trying to stop him from walking away. "Papa, please do not be angry with me." Her eyes pleaded him.

Mr. Bennet freed his hand. "You made your decision, Elizabeth." he said dryly, and left the room hurriedly.

When Jane walked in with tea a few minutes later, she found her sister in tears.

"What happened?" she asked, as she put the tray on the small table.

"Oh, Jane," Elizabeth sighed and dried her cheeks with the back of her hands. In short words she related the conversation with Mr. Bennet.

"I think that Papa is having a difficult time parting with you, sister," Jane said slowly, handling Elizabeth a cup of aromatic tea. "You have always been his favourite. I am sure that he will come to terms with the situation, but needs some time. You cannot expect him to be happy when you are about to leave us. We shall all miss you," she sighed, "Derbyshire is so far away."

***

Later that day, the house grew quiet. Mr. Bennet closed himself in the library, announcing to the housekeeper that he was not to be disturbed until dinner time. Mrs. Bennet took the younger girls to Meryton, having bribed Kitty with the promise of getting a new bonnet. Elizabeth, after having tea with Jane, with determination began to work on her embroidery again; still sad about the situation with her father, but decided not to weep more over it. Jane told her that she needed some fresh air and excused herself for the stroll in the gardens. Elizabeth thought her elder sister would return soon, as Jane was not a great walker.

She found it odd when Jane did not return within an hour, but she became even more astonished when instead of her sister, Mr. Darcy appeared in the door to their room.

"William?" she cried softly, hiding the unfinished handkerchief in the sewing basket.

He seemed slightly out of breath. "Forgive me the intrusion, but Miss Bennet had just paid a visit to Georgiana, and she told me that something had upset you, and you needed me."

"Papa would not be happy at finding you here," she said nervously.

"Miss Jane said that we should not be disturbed. I walked in through the back door, and nobody saw me."

Elizabeth reached out her hand to him. In a second, he was beside her.

"You've been crying." He touched her face as he sat on the edge of her chaise.

"I had a serious conversation with my father."

Darcy frowned. "And?"

She lowered her head and murmured. "He agreed to announce the official engagement and setting the wedding date."

"Good Lord, tell me it is not the reason you wept."

She looked at him in shock. She could not believe that such a thought could have come to his mind. "No, of course not! No! I am pleased he gave his permission at last. Still, he disapproves of me, and it is difficult for me to come to terms with the fact."

"You wanted to say he disapproves of me," he said matter of factly.

She shook her head. "No, not exactly, but... Mama said once that he was jealous of you, that I am leaving him for you. Every time we talk nowadays, Papa and me, we disagree. Today he was so cold and indifferent. It was not a pleasant conversation for me to say the least. We understood each other well once, I was his favourite, and now..." she sighed, "Perhaps, it is I who has changed."

Darcy listened to her intently, and when she finished he pulled her closer. "I wish I could do something to..." he paused.

She scooted closer. "Just hold me."

Not releasing her from his embrace, he shifted, supporting himself against the back of the chaise lounge, then he pulled her to him, with her back to his chest.

She stared out of the window as he cradled her, kissing her neck from time to time.

"Did your parents love one another?" she asked unexpectedly.

He seemed taken aback by the question, but soon answered, "Very much so, sometimes I think too much."

"How so?"

"My mother died when I was twelve years old, and Georgiana was just a babe. Father closed himself in with her body for two days, and did not want to open the door."

Elizabeth turned in his arms to look up at him. "Good God. What happened next?"

"They had to force the door to bury her. He went completely grey over a few days, looking ten years older."

She lacked the words, not knowing what to say, cold shivers running down her back.

"From today's perspective, I think that it was worse for Georgiana," Darcy continued calmly, looking straight ahead. "I was at school most of the time, away from home, busy with my studies. Father became so indifferent to everything and everyone, including Pemberley and his own children. He saw Georgiana once a week at best, and could not look at her for very long, as she resembles my mother greatly. You will see my mother's portrait when you visit. I think that it is the reason why Georgiana is so attached to me and why she believed Wickham last year. She craves for people to love her. When she was a child, she was so clingy, she was able to climb on the lap of a complete stranger just to be cuddled."

Elizabeth stared at him. Was he not aware how 'clingy' he was himself? "It is so sad, I cannot imagine how you survived this." she whispered.

He shrugged. "Everyone has their own hardship in life, it seems." he smiled at her, "I swore to myself once I would not give myself so completely to any woman like my father had, that I would be more controlled and reasonable about these matters. But I failed completely when I met you."

She reached her hand to stroke his cheek.

He squeezed her to him. "Now, good times had come for me at last. I have nothing to complain about because I have you."

Her arms locked around his neck and she held tight. After a moment, she heard his soft laugh, and he gently disentangled herself from him. "Do you want to strangle me?"

She shook her head, her eyes full of tears.

He frowned. "Weeping again?"

He dried the moisture from her cheeks with his fingers.

She shook her head. "What about a wedding date?" she asked, blinking her tears away. "September or October perhaps? Three months should be enough for my mother to see to all the preparations."

"Elizabeth," he whispered with raw intensity.

"You wish to wait?"

He pulled her back to him. "What do you think?" he kissed her neck, making her giggle, because he tickled her sensitive skin. "September sounds perfect, though I would wish we could be married at Pemberely when you will come there with your aunt and uncle, so you could stay with me forever."

"But..."

"I know you want it here with your family."

She smiled, pleased that he understood.

"I will go tomorrow to London to post announcement to the newspaper about our engagement and bring you my mother's ring. I know it is not always a custom, but I want you to wear it, so I know you are mine."

"I will be honoured."

"I gave it to the jeweller for refreshing when I was last time in London and I think it should be ready by now."

There was a soft knock on the door, and Jane's muffled voice was heard. "Lizzy, Mama should return soon."

"It is a sign for me to go."

He stood up from her and helped her to arrange herself comfortably, putting several pillows behind her back.

He leaned for a kiss, and she hooked her arms around his neck again, pursing her lips. He smiled and kissed her, but chastely. She was disappointed but not surprised, as since their last interlude when they had lost control sitting on her bed, he had visibly restrained himself in the short times when they were alone, allowing only short pecks on her lips, or kisses on the cheeks.

"Do not stay long in London."

He kissed her again. "I will not."

He was about to walk away, when she whispered.

"I have almost forgotten. Have you received a response from Mr. Bingley?"

Darcy's face clouded. "Not yet," he let out a heavy sigh. "I pray he will wish to speak to me again after what I have confessed to him in my last letter."

Chapter Thirteen

Darcy was on his way to Longbourn, the same as every single day for the last three weeks. Elizabeth was to have the braces removed from her leg tomorrow, and as soon as he made sure that she was well, he would set off north. Pemberley needed his attention. He could hardly wait to have Elizabeth there, if only for a few days, on her way to the Lake District with her aunt and uncle.

Despite Elizabeth's accident and their prior argument, he thought of the last week as of the best since he had met her, and the happiest in his life for a very long time. Understandably, he felt compassionate, and not a bit responsible about the fact that she had hurt herself and had been forced to bed rest. On the other hand though, the relationship between them had changed, and was now better than ever before.

When he had met her, he had been drawn to her instantly; to her looks, eyes, smiles, her teasing, the sound of her voice, her laugh. At that time, they had been mere acquaintances, not even friends. He had been honest enough with himself to admit that he had been falling for her. However, as he had convinced himself not to pursue her, the only honourable way then had been to step aside and torture himself watching her from the distance.

In Kent, when he had decided to court her, she had continued sharpening her wit on him and teasing him. However, she had often seemed to overlook his presence, paying more attention to his cousin than to him, which as his future mother in law would have said, had vexed him greatly.

When he had proposed, she seemed so stunned, that he had to believe that it had not been only an act on her part, but that she had truly not expected his offer. Even though she had agreed, she had not opened herself completely to him. He could feel it, that she had resisted him at every step, keeping her distance both physically and mentally. It had taken him some time and effort to one by one force her defences.

Since their discussion over Jane and Charles, everything had changed completely. After their argument and her consequent accident, he had been terrified, in utter despair almost, that she would break their understanding. Her father would have supported her decision. He had expected the worst to happen, but to his astonishment, relief, and heart melting joy, she had opened herself completely to him and embraced him with her whole self. His days had been measured to the next visit at Longbourn when he would see her and talk to her, hold her hand, have her listen to him attentively when he talked about his plans, concerns, doubts. She had let him in, accepted him. It made him smile wide every single day from the moment he awoke.

He did not quite know how he reached Longbourn, but soon his horse stopped in front of the house. Shaking his head at his own absentmindedness, he dismounted and gave the reins to a stable hand. The servant led him to the parlour, where he expected the ladies of the house to be gathered, as every day. He put a pleasant expression on his face, reminding himself to be as amiable as possible to Mrs. Bennet. For Elizabeth, he had made a resolution to be more open and polite to the people around him.

He was more than taken aback to see Bingley sitting there among the ladies, taking tea. He had written a letter to him over two weeks ago, where he had confessed that he had been wrong in his assessment of Jane Bennet's feelings last autumn, admitting that the lady in question had not been as indifferent as he had claimed her to be. He had showed the letter to Elizabeth, wanting to prove to her that he had truly wanted to repair his mistake.

"Mr. Darcy." Mrs. Bennet rushed to him. "How good to see you, we did not expect you today."

Darcy bowed, "I hope my visit is not an untimely one, madam."

"No, of course not, although Lizzy has mentioned that she expects you tomorrow. However, you are, of course, most welcome at any time," Mrs. Bennet stressed. "You see that Mr. Bingley has called. Why did you not tell us about his return to the neighbourhood?"

Darcy glanced at Bingley, who, for once, did not smile; but neither did he look displeased. "I assure you that I had no prior knowledge of it."

Mrs. Bennet opened her mouth, her brow creased. "You did not?"

Bingley stood up. "Darcy, how are you?"

"I am very well, thank you. Thank you," Darcy murmured, not knowing what to make of Bingley's expression and behaviour.

"I congratulate you on your engagement," Bingley said, holding out his right hand. "I must admit that I was quite surprised when I read the announcement in the newspaper."

"Yes, yes... We kept our understanding to ourselves for some time," Darcy said and then looked at Jane. He tried to guess whether she was pleased, but like last autumn, her expression was hard to read. Elizabeth wanted her sister to be happy, and Darcy wanted Elizabeth to be happy. He hoped that bringing Bingley back would ensure it. He could hardly do more; he had confessed his misgivings to Bingley, and the rest depended on him.

"I believe that my sister is still in the gardens," Jane mentioned in her usual sweet voice. "The doctor visited today and removed her braces a day earlier than we expected."

Darcy blinked repeatedly in surprise, "Today? Is she well?"

"Oh yes, quite well," Jane assured. "We could hardly keep her home as soon as she could walk freely on her own."

Darcy walked to the window, hoping to see her.

"Perhaps you could look for her, Mr. Darcy, and bring her home for tea," Mrs. Bennet suggested.

At that moment, he felt that he almost liked the woman. "Ah, yes, excellent thought, madam, excellent..." he murmured, already retreating towards the door.

Outside, he scanned the area, to see Elizabeth sitting on the bench not far from the house. She was staring at the blue skies, her whole face smiling. She did not see him till he walked closer.

"William!" she exclaimed and ran to him.

"Easy." He caught her by her arms. "You should not run. Your braces have been just removed."

She shook her head. "I have no pain in my leg. It felt a bit stiff at first, but it was gone quickly."

She hopped.

"No jumping," he laughed, trying to stop her from bouncing.

"I am so thrilled to be able to move on my own," she grinned. "I want to dance!"

He laughed at her enthusiasm and inability to stay still. He still found it hard to believe that this dark haired spitfire was a part of his life now. How could he live without her, realizing how sour his life had been before he had met her?

She lifted up on her toes and gave him a peck on the cheek. "Wait here for me, I will be back soon," she whispered, smiling, and sprinted to the house.

Darcy opened his mouth to cry so she would not run, but then thought there was no use trying to stop her.

She returned within minutes, out of breath and beautifully flushed, her chest heaving. His eyes travelled from her sparkling eyes to her lips, creamy neck and lower, and he felt himself growing hard again. This instant reaction he had for her was troubling and uncomfortable, especially when they were in company. After the wedding, he would keep her in their bedroom for a week at least, until his hunger would ease and he could think straight again and act normally around her. He would have himself under good regulation like before.

She took his arm and led him where the small park started, and where they could not be seen from the windows. She sat on the bench, and with a gesture of her hand, invited him to take a place next to her.

He sat close, inhaling her sweet scent, fighting the temptation to kiss her neck. Then he noticed the package in her hands, a flat box wrapped in lavender coloured paper.

"What is that?"

She placed the thing on his lap. "I made these for you," she said, her voice shy.

He gave her a questioning look. He had not expected any gifts. His fingers touched the bluish ribbon that it was tied with.

"Please open..." she hesitated, "I know that they are nothing special, but I wanted to repay you for your generosity; all the gifts I have received from you."

With careful fingers, he untied the bow, pushed the wrapping away, and opened the box. Inside there were neatly arranged white handkerchiefs with his initials embroidered in the corners.

"I know that the embroidery is a bit uneven and the material wrinkles here and there, but I never had patience for sewing the way Jane does," she said after a moment, her voice unsure.

His throat squeezed; he could hardly remember receiving any gifts for years now. Apart from Georgiana's drawings, or the new songs she had learned to play for him, nobody had thought to do something like that.

"They are beautiful," his voice cracked. She must have made them especially for him during the time she had been convalescing.

Elizabeth gave him a doubtful look, "You do not have to pretend that they are something exceptional for my sake. I know that they a far cry from what you could buy in London."

He took a calming breath, feeling once again in control of himself, his sudden emotions over her gift safely repressed. He hated to be so touched with things, and it happened quite often when he was in Elizabeth's company. Good Lord, a moment ago he had been on the verge of crying over the fact that his betrothed had hand made a set of handkerchiefs.

"I meant what I said." He looked at her, implying his most serious voice.

"Will you use them?" she asked hopefully.

"Till they are completely worn out."

"Seven." A small finger pointed to the box. "One for every day of the week."

He covered the box and put it aside, then wrapped her tightly in his arms. "Thank you so much, sweetheart." He kissed her neck. "I will treasure them."

"I want you to use them."

"I will, I promise."

He kissed her briefly, and then crushed her to him again.

He felt her pushing away from him.

"Have you seen Mr. Bingley?"

"Yes, I have." He pushed an escaped lock of hair behind her ear. "I was surprised to see him sitting in the parlour with your mother and sisters. He has not replied to my letter; I had no idea he would return."

"Do you think he is offended?" she asked, placing her small hand on his thigh, her tone concerned.

"I do not know. It was hard to read his expression," he said, his blood running faster again. Did she know what he felt when she touched him like that?

Her hand on his leg pressed harder. "I do not wish for Mr. Bingley to be angry with you. I do not want you losing a friend," she said, her expression earnest.

At this very moment, Darcy could not care less whether Bingley would ever speak to him or not. He wanted her fingers to move higher, inside his thigh; it was all he was able to think about.

"I am so pleased he is back though," she continued, "Perhaps he and Jane will come to an understanding now. I think that he still likes her. He called yesterday in the afternoon, and again today in the morning. Had it not been for your letter...You know how grateful I am that you wrote..." At some point in her speech, he stopped listening, concentrating entirely on the sensation of her being so close to him, her small hand settled on his thigh. He started to listen again when her fingers brushed a few inches higher.

"I have almost forgotten. I received a letter from Aunt Gardiner yesterday. She writes about our trip, it seems that she and uncle have certain concerns."

He frowned. "Concerns?"

He did not want to hear that her relatives wanted to postpone the trip or, even worse, call it off.

"Yes. My uncle's business will not allow him to travel as far as the lake district this summer. They will only have time to tour Derbyshire."

He relaxed instantly. "That is even better. I will have you at Pemberley for a longer time, not just a few short days. That is excellent news. I will take you to the lakes next spring, I promise."

"My aunt wants to know whether you are willing to host us for the entire period of the stay, or should they look for accommodations at the inn in Lambton."

"The inn!" he snorted. "Certainly not. You must stay at Pemberley. It is a best place for taking trips about the area."

She looked up at him with smile. "Thank you. I will write to my aunt yet today."

He leaned and whispered into her ear, his voice needy, even to his own ears. "Love, could we go somewhere where no one could see us?"

She gave him a quizzical look, biting her lower lip.

He nuzzled her temple. "Please, I will go away tomorrow. We will not see each other for weeks."

She blushed and lowered her head. "You said I should not trust you."

He kissed her neck, breathing into her ear. "Please."

She stood up and extended her hand. He was about to reach for his gift, but she shook her head.

"Leave it here. We cannot be away for a long time anyway. No one will take it."

She took his arm and led him towards the tall hedgerow. When they were close to it, she looked around and quickly stepped inside, between the thick branches. He stared for a moment before he felt her grabbing his hand and pulling him inside.

On the other side there was a small clearing with fresh grass, enclosed by a high brick wall, approximately his height.

She stepped to him. "No one will see us here. I used to hide in here as a child when I did not want anyone to find me."

"I will not... go too far. " He touched her arm. "I just want to hold and kiss you."

"I know," she whispered, and pulled him close, her arms wrapped around his waist.

They began kissing, his heart melting at how sweetly and willingly she responded to him.

"I want to see your breasts," he murmured, before he could think what he asked her for.

She stiffened instantly, removed her hands from his middle and stepped away. *Idiot!* he thought. Now he had offended her, and she would walk away from him, or worse, slap him.

Slowly, looking into his eyes, her hands went to the front of her spencer, and she opened it. She removed the garment and placed it neatly on the ground. Then she reached to her back and began unbuttoning her dress. As the yellow muslin loosened, she pushed the short sleeves aside, lowering the top of her dress.

Darcy stared at the newly uncovered flesh. Her stays pushed her breasts upward, and he could clearly see wide, dusky nipples through the nearly transparent chemise.

He took her mouth while his hand stroked down her back in slow caress till she relaxed. Then he pushed the straps of the undergarment and bared her. She was... he lacked the right words, perfect, beautiful. He had so many times wondered what her bosom looked like, but the reality exceeded his imagination. She was so lovely, and he was one lucky gent to have her.

He forced himself to tear his eyes away from her breasts and move them up to her face. She was flushed, her face so unsure. At last she covered herself with her hands.

"No, please." He pushed her hands away. "You are beautiful."

She stepped closer, hiding her face and body from his view. "I am not."

He kissed the top of her head. "You are to me."

Keeping her close, his hand moved down to touch one plump, warm mound. He stroked her breast lightly, till she sighed and shivered. He felt her warm mouth on his jaw, as she strained against him.

Darcy wrapped his arms around her, crushing her to himself, wondering what he could do here, behind the hedgerow, for this short amount of time they had.

He looked into her eyes. "Trust me?"

She nodded without hesitation. He stepped back from her to remove his coat. For a short moment she made a gesture as if she had wanted to cover herself again, but then she forced her hands to stay back along her sides.

He spread his coat on the grass and quickly pulled her down with him.

"Comfortable?" he asked, reclining by her side. She smiled, her dark green eyes staring trustingly into his.

His lips suckled on the soft skin of her neck, but gently, so as not to mark her. He would do that after the wedding, and then he would not care whether someone would see it or not. Her breasts lured him down, and he began kissing, suckling and stroking. She strained against his hands and mouth, eyes closed, making sweet, little, clipped noises at the back of her throat. She must have liked it; he had already noticed before that she reacted passionately when he touched her breasts. He tried to envelop one mound in his hand; she was quite a handful to be sure.

He kissed the path back to her jaw line and whispered. "You must be quiet so nobody can hear us."

She nodded, wrapping her arms around him and bringing him closer. As they kissed, with one move of his hand, he hitched up her skirt, his hand stroking his way inside her thigh. She gasped into his mouth as he slid his fingers between her soft, warm thighs. Her legs parted, allowing him better access. He felt the soft, moist curls, and then the delicate flesh. He stroked and petted her for a moment only, but it was enough. Her pelvis pushed against his hand, her teeth bit her lower lip, her eyes squeezed tight, and she moaned. The next moment she was all relaxed, her hot creamy essence flowing over his fingers.

Recalling his earlier encounters with the opposite sex, he did not think that a woman could be so responsive, become aroused so quickly. He had not truly tried hard to please Elizabeth. He was a blessed man that she was so passionate. He knew that not all wives behaved in such a way. He remembered how his cousin had once confessed to him that his wife used to lie flat on the bed, and say to him to just do it and leave her.

He lifted higher on his arm, gazing at her prone body next to him. She seemed to be sleeping, her eyes closed, her face turned into his waistcoat. He knew he could do everything now, and she would not protest. He crouched in front of her and lifted her skirt together with the mass of petticoats, piling everything around her waist. His hands rested on her knees and he spread her thighs wider. He combed the wet curls away from her centre to see better; her flesh was deeply pink, her small slit glistened with moisture. He tore at the opening of his breeches, and pulled out his manhood, directing it straight to her opening. He teased himself for a moment, touching the tip of his member against her flesh, at the same time knowing very well that he could not do it to her now. She deserved better than losing her virginity on the hard ground, without any real comfort or even complete privacy.

Heavily, he laid down on her body and slowly started rubbing himself against her. It was heaven to have her under him, even with their clothes as a barrier between them. She held on to him, cradling him to her. As he had been almost aroused since the moment he had seen her today, it did not take him long to reach his own release. He emptied his seed on her belly and dropped on the ground beside her.

She scooted to his side, rubbing her nose against his waistcoat. "Have we...?"

"No, we have not." He pulled her to him, kissing her head.

"But I felt you," she whispered.

"No, I only rubbed against you." He stretched lazily. "You will see how different it is when I enter you on our wedding night."

He wanted to cuddle with her, place his hand on her breast, her plump, warm thigh wrapped around him, and take a nap. It was hardly a place or time for such a pleasure. Gathering all his strength, his self discipline, he sat up and righted his breeches. Reaching to the pocket, he took out his handkerchief, and carefully wiped clean her soft, rounded belly.

She was still groggy as he pulled her to her feet, adjusted her chemise and buttoned up her dress.

"Was I... Have I done everything right?" she asked, as he helped her into the spencer.

He cupped her face, making sure their eyes met. "Do you regret what we have done?"

"No, but... I know so little. I do not wish to disappoint you."

He laughed, "Lizzy, I could swear you were born to be loved like that."

"I have never... no other man has ever," she stuttered, her face red to the roots of her hair.

"God Elizabeth, I did not want to imply that..." He shook his head. "I do not want to offend you, love. I feel that sometimes I should not speak, and only keep my mouth shut. I am lucky that you responded to me in such a way."

She still looked troubled, so he wrapped her into his embrace, moulding her into his frame. "We have done nothing wrong," he whispered, "You are mine, we are engaged and about to be married in less than three months. Promise you will not think less of yourself because of what happened here. Promise?" he prompted her.

She nodded.

"Yes?" he did not give up till he heard it.

"I promise."

"Good."

He pulled away from her to collect his coat from the ground.

They checked each other's attire carefully, making sure it did not give hints as to their recent activities, and returned on the main path of the garden.

Chapter Fourteen

Darcy finished arranging the mail on his desk, as he intended to spend the rest of the day answering letters. His long absence from Pemberley had allowed several urgent matters to accumulate, and he needed to address them without further delay. After his wedding, he planned to spend most of the year at Pemberley, using the Darcy townhouse in London only occasionally. He had not yet spoken about this with Elizabeth, but he had little doubt that she shared his attitude, being raised in the country, enjoying long walks and fresh air.

There was a knock on the door as he was in the middle of reading the first letter. He scowled at the disturbance, having specifically asked not to be interrupted.

The knock repeated.

"Enter," he said in clipped voice.

The butler walked in. "New mail has just arrived."

"Thank you. Leave it there." He pointed to the small side table, without taking his eyes from the letter.

He did not hear the servant leave, so he lifted his gaze. "Yes? Something else?"

"A letter from Hertfordshire is on the top, Master. Miss Darcy suggested I bring it to you without delay."

Darcy nearly leaped from behind his desk. "Why did you not say so from the start?" He grabbed the first letter, recognising Elizabeth's neat handwriting. "Remember to always notify me immediately whenever a letter from Miss Bennet comes."

The servant bowed, "Yes, Master."

"You may go now, and thank you," he smiled at the older man, who had served his parents, before he had even been born.

The servant hesitated for a moment before speaking again. "May I also add how we are all very glad that soon there will be a new Mistress at Pemberley."

Darcy's smile grew wider. "I hope you will welcome her warmly. Miss Bennet is young, and may feel apprehensive about her new role."

"Yes, Master. We will do everything to make her feel at home." The man bowed again and left the room.

Alone again, Darcy stretched in a chair next to the window and tore the seal. He was surprised to receive the letter so soon, and he hoped dearly that nothing bad had happened.

He took a calming breath and began to scan a tightly written single page.

Dear William,

I imagine your surprise at receiving a letter from me only a few days after your departure. However, what has happened here today induces me to write it. I want to assure you that I am in good health, much as I hope you and Georgiana are.

We had a most unexpected guest today. Your aunt, Lady Catherine de Bourgh of Rosings Park, paid us an unannounced visit. She came with her daughter, and wanted to know whether the news of our engagement was true. When I confirmed it, showing her your mother's ring, she became extremely vexed. She claimed that you had been engaged to Anne from your earliest years, and that our understanding could not be in such case respected or valid.

She demanded I promise to break any relations with you, and swear never to approach you again. When I refused, stating that you would have never proposed marriage to me, while being engaged to someone else, she left Longbourn, extremely angry, and without saying goodbye to any of us. She also said that it was not the end, and that she would not leave this matter alone, unfinished. I think it is probable that she may pay a visit to you as well.

I must end now, because the servant awaits to post this letter yet today. I fear only that I was not as polite towards your relative as I should have been. I think that I insulted her; at some point of her visit, losing any sense of decorum when addressing her. You know only too well that I am capable of saying things in a manner which a proper lady should not practise.

Yours,

E. B.

Darcy read the letter twice more. He could only imagine how his aunt had acted at Longbourn, and shame burned within him. What a hypocrite he was; criticizing Elizabeth's family, when his own aunt was capable to behave in such a way. The situation was his own fault to a large degree. He had written to Matlock, informing his uncle, the earl, about his engagement, but purposely ignored Lady Catherine in this duty. He had feared her reaction, and he had been right. Now Elizabeth and the Bennets had paid the consequences, having been exposed to his aunt's ire. Elizabeth was right that Catherine might come to Pemberley any day, demanding he call off his engagement to Elizabeth and marry Anne.

He returned to his desk, and pulled out a fresh sheet of paper. First he needed to write to Elizabeth, to assure her of his love and devotion, and apologize for this shameful incident.

***

The following day, after long hours spent on horseback, monitoring the summer works on the estate, Darcy relaxed in the comfort of the smaller drawing room, nursing a glass of wine. Georgiana played a new song that she had learned recently, and the only thing he missed now, which would make this evening perfect, was Elizabeth, snuggled against his side. *Just two months*, he reminded himself. Nine weeks exactly, and he would have her here, next to him.

The music stopped in the middle of the passage. "Cousin, Richard!" Georgiana exclaimed and ran towards a man who had just entered.

Darcy stood up and walked to the guest who was hugging his sister and placing a brotherly kiss on the top of her head.

"Richard, we did not expect to see you," he smiled. "Welcome."

The men shook hands.

"I was granted a short leave, and decided to use it to visit my parents," Colonel Fitzwilliam said as he sat down.

"Have you been to Matlock already?" Darcy wanted to know.

"Yes, I have been visiting my parents for the last week or so."

Darcy patted his back. "We are glad you came to us. We have not yet sat to dinner. You must eat with us and stay as long as you can," he turned to Georgiana, "Dearest, please tell Mrs. Reynolds to prepare an additional setting at the table, and make sure that Colonel Fitzwilliam's usual room is ready."

"Yes, brother." Georgiana dropped a curtesy and fled from the room.

"I came with a purpose," the colonel said when Georgiana left. "To warn you."

Darcy stood up to pour a drink for the guest. "Warn me?"

"Lady Catherine paid an unexpected visit to my parents, arriving yesterday, quite late in the evening. I must say that she is quite put out with the news about your engagement to Miss Bennet."

Darcy returned to the sofa, handing his cousin a tall glass of brandy.

The colonel raised an eyebrow as he took the drink. "You do not seem in the least surprised."

Darcy sat back in his chair. "I expected it. I received a letter from Elizabeth yesterday. She wrote that our aunt paid, let us say, her respects to her family."

"Ouch." Colonel Fitzwilliam twisted his face as if in pain, "Miss Bennet's parents must have thought that their daughter was about to enter rather an interesting family."

Darcy gave him a heavy look. "I prefer not to think how our dear aunt acted there. The tone of Elizabeth's letter was very tactful, but there is no doubt that Lady Catherine made quite a scene at Longbourn. She insisted that I was engaged to Anne in front of Elizabeth's parents. Can you imagine that?"

The other man nodded. "Yes, she spoke the same to my parents."

Darcy leaned forward. "What was their reaction?"

Fitzwilliam took a hearty sip. "Do not worry, Darcy, they have no intention of supporting her on this. Father told her that you were an adult, your own master and he would not interfere in your decision concerning the choice of a wife."

Darcy's eyebrows raised. "I did not expect that."

"I think he learned something after Edward's arranged marriage."

"And how is Edward?" Darcy changed the subject. "Has something changed in his situation?"

"Oh, yes," the colonel smiled. "He is very well, happy being a father."

"So soon? When did it happen?"

"Ten days ago. The mother and the child feel well, and my brother is over the moon."

"And the earl? What was his reaction?"

"He pretended not to acknowledge the news, not to hear it even, but I think that it is just a matter of time before he will wish to see the boy. My mother openly said she wanted to see her only grandchild. She bought out half the store with toys and children's clothes, and we went together to pay our respects."

"And?"

"That woman... surprised me. She is very charming and pretty, not in the least resembling a harlot... Seems very sensible too."

"And the baby?"

"My mother swears he looks exactly like Edward and me when we were born, but I failed to find resemblance. The infant looks healthy and strong, to be sure, a rather big boy, like any other newborn baby, I imagine."

"Last time we saw each other, Edward mentioned they lived at Harwood Hall."

"Yes, the estate he inherited from our late aunt. You did not know her, I believe. Edward signed it to the child's mother, so if anything happened to him, they would be secured."

"That is very wise. What is the child's surname?"

"James Fitzwilliam."

"Indeed? I must say that I thought it would bear its mother's name."

"No." The colonel shook his head, "I think that Edward would not have it any different. He was very serious about it. "

"What about his wife?" Darcy asked. "Will she not try to do something against his new family?"

"No, believe me, she will sit quietly in London. Edward has in his possession a letter compromising her in a way that... would ruin her family's reputation. Perhaps you have heard that her brother, Lord X, is in politics, and they do not wish for any scandals."

"I know that she has had lovers, but is there something more...?" Darcy's voice traced.

His cousin hesitated. "You must keep it to yourself."

Darcy nodded. "Of course."

Colonel leaned forward. "She took part in... let us say, very private parties for the chosen ones. She all alone and some twenty men, each of them... having a special time with her. I think that I do not have to finish, you can imagine the rest."

The repulsion was obvious on Darcy's face. "Good God... That is a blessing indeed she never became with child. Edward would have to give his name to no one knows whose son."

"My father does not know anything about it. My brother thought it would be too much for him. You remember how he pressed him to this marriage."

Darcy raked his hand through his hair. "It sounds like some nightmare, his own wife, I am speechless... poor Edward."

"You can see now why I do not blame him that he left her and started a new life with someone else."

"Neither do I," Darcy agreed. "I should send something for the baby. I will wait for Elizabeth, and perhaps she would advise me on the right thing. She will be here in two weeks' time."

Colonel Fitzwilliam smiled. "I see that you are pleased with her visit."

Darcy tried not to grin like a fool. "She is travelling the country with her aunt and uncle, and they will stop here. The wedding is in Hertfordshire the last Saturday of September. You are invited."

"Thank you, but I will not be able to participate, I am afraid."

"You must visit us then on your next leave."

"I will, certainly. Thank you for the invitation. I will not miss the pleasure of talking again with the delectable Miss Bennet."

Darcy scowled. "She will be Mrs. Darcy by that time. Please remember it."

"Come now, Darcy!" Colonel Fitzwilliam laughed. "Do not glare at me like that. I will not try to sway her from you. I only acclaim your choice. I would do exactly the same in your position, could I afford to marry her."

***

Darcy woke to the sound of the rain drumming against the windows. Today was the day of Elizabeth and the Gardiners's arrival. He dragged himself out of bed. A beautiful, balmy, weather had held for the last days, but this very morning, when he wanted everything to be perfect for her, dark, low clouds covered the sky completely, and strong winds tore at the trees. He had so wished that she could see Pemberley in ~~its all~~ glory, and all in vain.

The guests were expected in the early afternoon, around one o'clock. He had planned many tasks to occupy himself till midday, so the time would pass quicker for him.

When no carriage came by two o'clock, he began to worry. In such weather, it was possible an accident had occurred. At last, at half past two, they came.

There was no opportunity to welcome the guests outside, so they were rushed inside the great hall.

From the first look at her, Darcy knew that Elizabeth was not at her best. She was polite and welcoming towards everyone, and she smiled at the servants who came to have a peek at their future Mistress. However, her complexion was unusually pale, lacking its usual healthy glow. Her eyes did not sparkle, but had a hollow look to them. Even her lips, usually a vivid pink, now almost matched the whiteness of her face.

Concentrated on Elizabeth, he paid little attention to her relatives. Understandably, he greeted them graciously, having in mind how Elizabeth favoured them, and how sensitive she was about his polite performance in front of her friends, relatives and newly acquainted people in general. Firstly, he was surprised with their age as he had expected a middle aged couple, not people just a few years his seniors. He noticed that they spoke in low, pleasantly modulated voices, not at all similar to his future mother-in-law's shrieks. From what he remembered, Mr. Gardiner was Mrs. Bennet's brother, which was surprising, because he seemed nothing like his sister, and even his facial features were different. He was still a young man in his middle thirties, while his wife was a pleasant looking, handsome blonde around thirty years old. The couple was dressed well, even in a refined way, especially Mrs. Gardiner, who carried herself with grace.

Convinced that the Gardiners were worldly enough, and should not cause any shame to Pemberley, he brought all his attention to his beloved.

They sat in the drawing room, taking tea in small sips. Elizabeth smiled at Georgiana, who talked about the plans that had been made for their stay.

"Mr. Darcy." Mrs. Gardiner's voice made him look away from the only true object of his interest.

He bowed his head, "Yes, madam."

"I think that my niece is tired."

Darcy's eyes went to Elizabeth, "Are you well?"

"Just a slight headache," she admitted.

"We had a taxing journey," Mr. Gardiner noted, looking at his wife.

"Yes, of course. I will ask Mrs. Reynolds to show you to your apartments."

Mr. Gardiner stood up and offered an arm to his wife. Before Elizabeth managed to lift herself, Darcy was beside her. She leaned against him heavily, and as he covered her small hand with his, he discovered it was icy cold. Had she caught a cold?

He was not relieved when Elizabeth disappeared in her rooms. She looked ill. Perhaps she needed a doctor.

He managed to stay away for three quarters of an hour before storming the stairs. Seeing no one in the corridor, he knocked at her door. Silence. He knocked again.

"Enter," a hoarse voice was heard.

He walked inside and closed the door quickly. He swallowed. She sat in the middle of the big bed, wearing what seemed to be only her robe and undergarments, a heavy looking mass of dark curls hanging down her back, her big eyes staring at him.

"Forgive me," he managed to say. "I was worried."

She held her hand out to him.

"I am sorry, it is not the best day for me," she said as he sat on the edge of the bed. "I will be myself by dinner time, I promise."

He cupped her face. "I will call a doctor."

She shook her head. "No, a doctor cannot help me. It will pass tomorrow."

"How can you know?"

"William, you are a man of the world, educated. You brought up your sister almost all by yourself. You must know that women may feel unwell once a month."

He stared at her for a moment, before he got her meaning. "Oh."

He was relieved. He had thought it something worse, and it was only her monthly, as he had heard his sister once refer to it. He frowned. "It never puts Georgiana to bed."

"Everyone is different. I have always had it worse than my sisters."

His frown did not disappear. "Can I help you in any way?"

She smiled, her eyes twinkling for the first since her arrival. "Actually, yes. Mama said to me once that she had it the same until the first baby, so..." she grinned.

He let out the sigh of relief. She could not feel that bad if she teased him. "I meant what I could do *now* to ease your discomfort."

She scooted closer. "Just stay with me till I fall asleep."

Darcy looked down at her with hunger he did not care to disguise, his eyes focusing at the gaping opening in her rope. She must have only her chemise and petticoats under it, her plump breasts, unrestrained by the cut of the dress and stays, spilled freely on her chest.

He stood up and kicked off his half shoes, at the same time removing his coat and unbuttoning the waistcoat. He was not sure how close she wanted to be, so he laid on the bed beside her. She reached for the blanket from the bottom of the bed and then handed it to him, positioning herself on her side.

Gently he moulded his body to hers, her back to his chest, draping a blanket around her. She sighed, her eyes closed and reached for his hand, pulling it over her middle. Darcy squeezed her to him. She answered, murmuring something.

As if of its own, his hand moved higher from the safe place on her waist, right inside of her robe. As she had no stays, it was easy to feel one warm, heavy mound through the thin chemise. He could not do anything more than this, but what a sweet torture it was to touch her.

Small fingers wrapped around his wrist and pulled the hand down back on its previous place.

"Not today," she whispered sleepily, not opening her eyes. "They are too tender."

He kissed her ear and temple, and watched as her breathing slowed, and he thought she had drifted to sleep completely. But then she opened her eyes, and turned to him.

"What about Lady Catherine? Was she here?"

"Yes, here and at Matlock. She tried to convince my uncle to support her, and convince me to marry Anne."

The cloud crossed her face, "I do not wish you to alienate yourself from your family because of me."

"You cannot even think so, love. Lady Catherine is nothing to me. Nothing, compared to you. I only kept relations with her because it seemed the right thing to do, because she was my late mother's only sister. If she cannot accept you, apologize to you, and respect you, I will not see her any more. As for my uncle, the earl, he said that he would not interfere into my affairs, and that it was my decision who I wanted to marry."

She snuggled closer, burying her face into his chest.

"Do you remember how I told you about my other cousin, Colonel Fitzwilliam's older brother, Edward?"

She looked up. "Yes."

"He has a son with that woman now."

"What was his parents' reaction?"

"Richard, Colonel Fitzwilliam, told me that the earl still did not acknowledge the fact that he had become a grandfather, but he thinks that it is just a matter of time. My aunt went to see the baby already. They live in a small estate, only twenty miles from Pemberley. I thought that we could send a present for the baby to show our support."

"I am sure that your cousin will appreciate such gesture very much."

"I do not know what it could be though. Perhaps you will have some idea."

She nodded. "I will think about it."

"Thank you," he kissed her lips gently. "Apart from my aunt's unfortunate visit, how has your time at Longbourn been since I left?"

She started to play with his neck cloth. "Busy. My mother could talk only about the new gowns I would need as a married woman, so I spent most of the time choosing the patterns and materials. We even travelled to London to order a wedding dress there. My father seems to be less angry with me though. I asked him to teach me horse riding, and he gave me a few lessons."

He gaped at her in surprise. "Horse riding? You dislike the activity, and are afraid to..."

"I am not afraid," she cut in, "And I do not dislike it. I only never cared enough for it to learn."

He grinned."You did that for me?"

She rolled her eyes, "No, for myself. You are far too conceited thinking that I do everything for you, Mr. Darcy." She pointed with a small finger into his chest. "Simply, the fact is that you ride so well, as does Georgiana, and I do not want people here to look down at me because I lack the ability."

"We must buy you a horse and a new saddle."

"Oh, you do not have to," she assured quickly. "I am sure that there is some old docile horse here I could ride."

"I doubt it, all the horses are rather too spirited for a beginner. Besides, you deserve your own mount. One of my neighbours is an excellent breeder. We will go one day when you feel better, and you will chose a nice mare for your own use."

"If you insist," she complied. He smiled again; he liked when she agreed with him so sweetly, especially that such situation happened rarely.

"I do." He stretched on his back, bringing her to his side. "Close your eyes, love. You are tired, and need the rest before dinner."

She yawned. "I know, but when we are alone, I want to talk with you, especially after we have not seen each other for so long."

"There will be time to talk. Now it is time to rest."

She snuggled closer, placing her arm over his chest and her leg over his.

Darcy intended to stay with her till she fell asleep, and leave quietly without waking her. When he awoke though, the room was darkened, indicating that a few hours had passed. Elizabeth slept, stretched on top of him.

He blinked, seeing a woman standing next to the bed. It was Mrs. Gardiner.

Carefully, he pushed Elizabeth, who was still soundly sleeping, off him, and scrambled from the bed. As he found his shoes and collected his coat, Mrs. Gardiner tiptoed to the door, waiting there for him.

They were outside in the corridor, when he spoke in lowered voice. "Mrs. Gardiner, what you have seen... nothing happened. I was worried that she was unwell, and stayed with her for a moment." He ran a hand over his face, "I must have fallen asleep."

"I do not intend to lecture you, Mr. Darcy." The woman spoke in a calm, but decided voice. "I was once engaged as well, and I do understand that you are in love and want to spend time alone. Nevertheless I still find such behaviour not acceptable especially when the maid may enter any time to help Elizabeth with her bath and dressing for dinner."

"I do not know how it happened, I truly intended to stay with her briefly and then leave," he tried to explain.

The woman looked straight into his eyes. "Mr. Darcy, you and my niece are both adults, and about to be married in a few weeks. It is your personal matter what you do in private, but I know that Elizabeth would be very uncomfortable, and distressed, if it was not I, but a servant, who found you together."

"You are perfectly right, Mrs. Gardiner," Darcy agreed, embarrassed, not knowing where to turn his eyes, "I will make sure that nothing like this happens in the future."

Mrs. Gardiner nodded, smiling. "I think that I will go now to wake her up." She said kindly and walked away.

Chapter Fifteen

"Elizabeth, be careful!" Mrs. Gardiner cried, turning up her head to look at her niece who stood on the highest point of the hilltop. "Step back from the edge at once! What would I say to your family if you took a fall?"

"I am fine, Aunt," Elizabeth cried back in a strong voice, "It is so beautiful here. I can see the entire valley from this very spot."

Mrs. Gardiner shook her head and turned to see Darcy approaching with her husband.

"Mr. Darcy, pray help me." She pointed to the hilltop. "Only look where she has got herself."

"Do not worry, madam." Darcy walked past the Gardiners with energy. "I will get her down."

As Darcy began climbing the rocky path, Mr. Gardiner spoke, standing close to his wife, "He is very much in love with her."

His wife smiled. "Yes, he is. He is completely enamoured, a pleasure to watch how he treats her. He sees only her."

"Do you think she is equally engaged with her feelings?" Mr. Gardiner asked as he looked up, observing as Darcy literally dragged Elizabeth a safe distance from the edge.

"I am not so sure," Mrs. Gardiner said slowly. "She claimed to almost hate him last December, when we visited at Longbourn."

"A short route from hatred to love, they say."

"Yes, I think this is the case. I am not aware of the details, but it must have been a very interesting courtship, a stormy one."

Mr. Gardiner smirked. "He strikes me as a steady, serious, even sober type of fellow."

"She will change him."

"I only hope he knows what he is getting himself into."

"What do you mean?" Mrs. Gardiner questioned, her voice defensive in tone, "Elizabeth is a sweet girl, with a good heart, principles and morals."

"As well as stubborn, opinionated, too quick to judge people, and she has a temper," he pointed out.

"I think he knows that already, and it does not bother him. On the contrary, her liveliness allures him. They will have to learn how to reach a compromise."

Mr. Gardiner pulled her tightly to his side, his arm wrapped around her shoulders. "My romantic wife," he smiled down at the woman in his arms, "you are so pleased because you will be able to visit Derbyshire often now."

Mrs. Gardiner looked up at him, smiling. "I must admit that as a girl I never imagined that my niece would one day become the Mistress of Pemberley."

***

The day was hot and sunny, the air still, without even the gentlest of breeze. Darcy readied the small boat and held out his hand to Elizabeth. She walked closer, and he helped her into it, sitting her on a small bench.

He rowed to the middle of the lake and, put the paddles away, allowing the boat to float on the water.

Elizabeth tilted her face to the sun and closed her eyes, her body stretched in a most comfortable position.

Darcy did not look at the sky, only at her. She wore a thin, white cotton dress, and appeared there were no stays underneath it. He could see not only the natural shape of her plump bosom resting on her chest without support, but the visible curve of her lower belly, as well not disguised with a constricting corset. He recalled how he first saw her, he had thought her figure pleasant but imperfect, too full in comparison with what a fashionable woman in town should look like, tall and willowy. Very soon though, he had discovered that he much preferred Elizabeth's soft curves to Caroline Bingley's flat chest, narrow bottom, and protruding collar bones. What a pleasure to snuggle up to such a well cushioned form on a cold night.

He tore his eyes from her body and took the paddles in his hands and concentrated on rowing again, trying not to think about the sudden flow of blood into his groin. Perhaps he could find some private place and opportunity to repeat what they had done the day before his departure from Hertfordshire, behind the hedgerow, and relieve himself to a degree. She had been here for six days, surely her courses had ended.

"What do you think of Pemberley?" he asked to distract himself from other thoughts.

She opened her eyes, "It is wonderful," she said warmly, "but you must know that. Everything here seems so grand, yet still familiar and homey. I cannot blame you that you are so proud of it," she shook her head, "I still cannot believe I will live here one day, it is so... unrealistic."

"Not one day, but yet this autumn," he corrected her.

She reached her hands to her head to remove her bonnet. "It is such a hot day."

"Yes," he murmured, his eyes on her. "Perhaps the hottest day of this summer."

She leaned to the side and dipped her fingers in the water. "The water is so cool. Would you mind if I removed my shoes?"

He shook his head.

Happily, she untied the ribbons of her flat, light green shoes from around her ankles, and pulled down the thin, sheer silk stockings. She wiggled her toes, and with one swift move, turned on the narrow bench, and before he could say anything, stretched her legs over the side, dipping the soles of her feet into the water.

Darcy swallowed; was she torturing him like that on purpose?

"Look, a fish!" she splashed her foot against the water mirror, laughing merrily.

She glanced at him. "Why are you so sober? Are you worrying about something?"

"I have to direct the boat, and cannot be as comfortable as you are," he grunted, clenching his fingers on the paddles.

Her feet returned inside the boat and she crouched in front of him. "You are dressed way too formally." She reached to the lapels of his coat. "Let us remove that."

Without protest, he helped her to remove his coat, waistcoat and, in the end, his neck cloth.

"Is that not better?" she asked, undoing the first buttons of his shirt.

"Yes, it is," he admitted, inhaling her sweat mixed with her perfume, and her natural scent.

He stilled when he felt her mouth on his throat. "I like your neck... I want to kiss it every time I see it."

He grabbed her arms, and made an effort to push her away. "Stop... it. It is not the time or place, we may overturn the boat."

"Would it be so bad?" She moved closer, kneeling between his thighs. "I can swim, and it would be nice to take a cooling swim in the lake on such a hot day."

"Love, be serious, you would drown yourself."

She pushed back from him," You do not believe that I can swim?"

"Women cannot swim," he said matter of factly.

"I can," she protested. "Papa taught Jane and me when we were little girls. Our friend fell into the lake and drowned herself, so he decided to teach us one summer just in case."

He gave her an understanding smile, and spoke in gentle voice. "Love, I do believe you can move your hands and legs about in the water, I truly do, or even float on the surface, but..."

"I can do much more!" she cried. "I can even dive."

He only stared at her indulgently.

Her eyes narrowed. "You do not believe me, do you?"

"I do, love, I do," he said, wanting to placate her.

"How deep is it in here?" she asked.

"Quite deep, ten feet in places."

"Very well." She turned from him, stepped on the bench she had previously occupied, and jumped head first into the water in one fluid movement.

***

Mrs. Reynolds, the housekeeper at Pemberley, was keeping her eye on the new maid, who was tidying the drawing room, wanting to be sure of the quality of her work. She walked to the window, to see whether the glass was sparkling clean as it should be, when she saw the Master and Miss Bennet, soaking wet, walking towards the house.

"They must have had an accident on the boat." she cried out. Hurrying through the assembly of rooms, she reached the great hall just as the couple was entering.

"Master, what happened?" she asked, looking at Miss Bennet's dress, soiled with mud and seaweeds, her bare feet and loosened dark locks.

"We had a small accident." Darcy, not in much better condition, with the exception that he had his shoes on, answered in his usual calm voice. "Miss Bennet needs a bath and a change of clothes. I am afraid that I lost control of the ship." he explained, glaring at the lady beside him, who at that moment was innocently admiring the painting on the wall.

The housekeeper looked at him incredibly; how could he lose control on the lake on such a windless day?

"Come, my dear," Darcy pulled at Miss Bennet's arm, and they began to climb the staircase, leaving wet footprints on the carpet.

Mrs. Reynolds kept staring after the couple, till someone's steps on the marble floor finally caught her attention.

"Peters!" She rushed to the butler. "Have you heard about the accident? Thank heavens they are alive, that lake is very deep in places."

"Yes, and I think that I know exactly what happened there, " the man murmured dryly.

Only then did she notice the pile of clothes he was bearing in his arms. "I see you have their things..." she frowned. "I do not understand. "She touched the straw bonnet which looked immaculate, as if freshly taken from the window shop display. "All dry and ironed."

Peters gave the pile to a maid who just approached, and led Mrs. Reynolds to the side. "It was not an accident, " he said in a lowered voice, "We found their clothes in the boat."

"Are you saying that they first removed their outer clothes, and then took a swim in that muddy lake, leaving the boat aside?"

Peters nodded. "And I am also pretty sure whose idea it was," he added gravely. "Master would have never done anything that reckless, even as a small boy."

"Oh, come now," she protested, "I will not have you say a word against Miss Bennet. She is kind, merry and cares for him, and Miss Georgiana, not at all like that snooty Miss Bingley who has shillings in her eyes and sees only how much money everything cost. The boy needs some joy in his life!" she cried with conviction. "She makes him smile."

Peters exhaled a long dramatic breath. "We shall see what you will say when these two have children. They will tear the house apart, mind my words."

"Oh, be gone!" Mrs. Reynolds huffed, "They will be good, sweet, if not a bit lively, children I am sure of that. You always see everything in dark colours. This house needs some life and laughter after so many years of sorrow."

***

"How far is Mr. Cowlishaw's estate?" Elizabeth asked.

They were on their way to Darcy's neighbour, where Elizabeth was to choose a horse for herself. Georgiana sat next to her, and Darcy on the opposite seat in the open carriage. The Gardiners had declined the trip because they wanted to visit friends in Lambton.

"It is not so much of an estate, but rather a large farm about ten miles from Pemberley," Darcy explained. "Cowlishaws were once our tenants, but then enriched themselves on horse breeding, and bought some land, joining together several small farms."

"Mr. Cowlishaw has three daughters." Georgian added. "I have small presents for them."

"Do they have a son as well?" Elizabeth wanted to know.

Darcy shook his head, "Mrs. Cowlishaw died in childbirth a couple of years ago."

Elizabeth gasped. "What a tragedy. What ages are the girls?"

"The youngest is three, I believe." Darcy looked at Georgiana who nodded.

"Yes, three, while the older ones are five and seven."

Elizabeth heart tugged at the image of three small girls being brought up without a mother. "Poor   little ones. Does Mr. Cowlishaw have any help?"

"There is a housekeeper, I believe," Darcy answered, "For a while an aunt lived with them but she died too."

"The farm is quite secluded, away from the nearest village, so the girls do not even have friends to play with," Georgiana mentioned. "They are very sweet and unspoiled, and love their father very much."

"No wonder," Darcy mused. "They have only him."

The ten mile drive passed quickly for Elizabeth as she was admiring the passing countryside, still new to her. Soon a large farm house could be seen at the bend of the road. The house was newly built, and very solid, but designed more for comfort than for fashion, with small windows and brightly painted red doors.

The carriage came to a halt and three little girls ran out of the house. As Darcy helped them out of the carriage, Elizabeth looked carefully at the children. They had fiery red hair, heavily freckled round faces, and wide green eyes. All three, including the youngest one, were dressed in identical, utilitarian brown dresses, solid, heavy leather boots, and even their thick red braids were tied with dark, plain ribbons. Elizabeth's first thought was that who would have dressed a child in such dour, sad colours, but then she remembered that they had no mother. Probably whoever had bought those clothes had not given much consideration to what is suitable and pretty for little girls.

Georgiana took a basket from a driver and stepped to the girls with a wide smile. "Hello." She greeted them.

Two elder smiled back, while the youngest one hid behind them, peeking with one green eye at the guests. "Do you remember me?" Georgiana asked.

The eldest nodded. "Yes, Miss Darcy. Papa asked me to say that he would come in a moment, and to invite you into the house."

"Then let us go," Georgiana kept smiling.

The girls showed the guests to the what seemed to be a sizeable family room. Georgiana and Elizabeth sat down on the sofa, while Darcy walked to the window. Elizabeth was surprised that no servant came to greet them. The room looked as if it had not been cleaned properly for a considerable time.

"Will you not come closer?" Georgiana asked, and the girls stepped to the sofa. "This is Miss Bennet. She will marry my brother, Mr. Darcy."

Elizabeth put the warmest of smiles on her face. "It is very nice to meet you. Will you tell me your names?"

"I am Abigail," the eldest pointed to herself, "This is Becky, and Mary." She introduced her sisters.

Elizabeth pulled the youngest girl closer, "I have a sister and her name is Mary too."

"Do you have a brother, Miss Bennet?" the middle one asked.

Elizabeth shook her head, smiling. "No, but I have four sisters back at home in Hertfordshire where I come from."

The girls gaped at her and then started to laugh, starting with Mary, who scooted close to Elizabeth.

"Hertfordshire is in the south of England," Abigail announced.

"Very good, Abigail, I see that you know a lot about England for such a young lady," Elizabeth praised.

Becky shook her head. "No, she doesn't know. Papa told us yesterday that you would visit us, that you would marry Mr. Darcy and that you are from Her... Hert..." she tried to pronounce the word.

"Hertfordshire," Abigail finished for her.

"I have something for you," Georgiana reached for the basket she had brought with herself, and uncovered it. The girls did not move from their places, but glanced towards it.

She took out three small dolls, with identical porcelain faces, but dressed differently, and three colourful little bags with candies.

"Oh, thank you, Miss Darcy!" the girls exclaimed all at once as Georgiana distributed the gifts.

Georgiana and Elizabeth watched with wide smiles as girls sat together in one large chair, each of them clenching the doll to her chest, mouth full of sweets, chewing faithfully.

Soon Abigail stepped to them again."Would you like some?" she offered the last of her candies to Elizabeth.

Elizabeth shook her head. "No, thank you, dear."

Georgiana stood up and walked into the corner of the room, where a brand new pianoforte stood.

The elder girls ran to her. "Papa bought it so we could learn to play." Becky explained.

"We do not have a teacher," Abigail added. "Papa says there is a teacher in Lambton, but he does not have time to take us there."

"We do not even have a cook," Becky mentioned. "Papa made today's breakfast all by himself. It was not good."

"Papa sent the cook away because she stole from us; he said so," Abigail announced in grave voice.

Georgiana and Elizabeth looked at one another. The family had problems with the servants it seemed. It explained why no tea had been offered and why the girls had devoured the sweets so quickly; they were hungry.

Darcy walked closer, and the girls stepped away from him, gaping at his imposing figure. "I will go look for Cowlishaw," he said.

"Will you play for us, Miss Darcy?" Becky pleaded, as Darcy left.

"Perhaps Miss Bennet will play for you?" Georgiana proposed, "She knows more merry songs than I."

Half an hour later, when Darcy and Mr. Cowlishaw walked into the room, Georgiana and Elizabeth were playing a duet, with Mary sitting between them and the elder girls gathered closely.

"Ladies, I am so sorry not to greet you as you came." Mr. Cowlishaw bowed deeply with visible respect, "We had a difficult birth, and I could not leave the stable for a while."

Elizabeth and Georgiana stood up from behind the instrument and walked closer.

"That is quite all right, sir. The girls have entertained us." Elizabeth glanced at the tall man. He was huge and bulky in build, heavy, and she felt like a dwarf next to him. He was even taller than Fitzwilliam, and his hair was the same fiery red as his daughters.

Darcy introduced Elizabeth formally, and it was decided that they would walk to the stables so she could see the horses.

"I have three horses that I think should be suitable for you, Miss Bennet," Mr. Cowlishaw said as they were approaching the stables which were impressive, several times bigger than the farmhouse. "Mr. Darcy mentioned to me that you have just started to learn horse riding, and require a calm and small animal."

Elizabeth nodded. "That would be the best in my case, I think."

The stable hand brought out three different horses, but Elizabeth's attention instantly was drawn to the small white mare, with long soft mane, and a black patch above her eyes, shaped like a star.

"Are you sure?" Darcy asked.

Elizabeth stroked the animal's neck. "Yes. She is beautiful."

"Good choice," Mr. Cowlishaw patted the horse's back, "She is very docile. Her name is Star, but you can rename her if you wish."

"Oh, no, Star is perfect."

"We will need a new saddle as well," Darcy said, as he checked the horse legs and later took a good look at the animal's teeth.

"I have only two good lady's saddles at the moment, but I can have more by the end of the week," Mr. Cowlishaw assured.

Elizabeth did not want to cause more trouble than she already had, so she said quickly. "I am sure that will not be necessary and one of them will be quite suitable."

The saddle was brought and put on Star.

"Will you try to ride her?" Darcy asked.

Elizabeth nodded, and Darcy lifted her up on the horse. He took the reins and led the horse around the circuit.

"Well?" He looked up at her. "What do you think?"

"I feel more sure on her than on my father's horse. She is not as tall."

Darcy stopped the mare. "Straighten your back, love. Your leg should go higher, so you can sit more firmly," he put a hand on her thigh and arranged it in the right position.

Elizabeth tried to do as he instructed, but found it hard to accomplish. "I need more lessons, I am afraid, to be confident enough," she admitted.

Darcy smiled at her as he put his hands on her waist, and brought her down. "Do not worry. We shall learn."

Mr. Cowlishaw stepped closer. "Is the saddle to your satisfaction, Miss Bennet?"

She smiled, "It is beautiful, and very comfortable."

"It is done then," Darcy said.

Mr. Cowlishaw bowed. "I will send Star to Pemberley yet today."

Elizabeth thought that they wanted to talk about the price, so she walked away, giving them some privacy.

They were on their way back to Pemberley, when Elizabeth said, "William, do you think that you could send some help for the Cowlishaws?"

Darcy looked at her in surprise. "Help?"

She nodded. "Yes, the girls told us that Mr. Cowlishaw needed to send the cook away. I doubt whether they were left with any house servant."

"The girls told us that Mr. Cowlishaw cooked their breakfast today," Georgiana added, "Poor little ones, they looked a bit hungry."

Darcy listened intently, "As you wish, Elizabeth, if you think that they need help. Address Mrs. Reynolds about this, she will know what to do."

"Me?" Elizabeth asked shyly.

"Who else?" he questioned and then smiled at her to reassure her, "You will be Mistress of Pemberley in less than two months. Such matters will be your responsibility only. You can very well start from today."

Elizabeth was not as certain as he. She felt she lacked the authority yet to give instructions to Mrs. Reynolds. The role of the Mistress of such a grand household intimidated her more than she was ready to acknowledge, but she did not want to disappoint

Darcy. She would approach Mrs. Reynolds and deal with this matter as soon as they returned, she decided.

Chapter Sixteen

Darcy wrapped his favourite dressing gown around his long, lean body and stretched in a chair in front of the fireplace. The hour was late, and he was more than usually tired. The day had been eventful, first with buying a horse for Elizabeth, and later with an estate matter requiring his full attention. Even when everyone had retired for the night, he had to yet answer two important letters that needed to be sent out tomorrow morning. He glanced at the empty bed. What would he have given to have Elizabeth there now, to be able to fall asleep in her arms after a long, tiring day.

At first when he heard a knock, he thought that he imagined it, because it was so quiet, but when it repeated, he walked to the door with a frown. Perhaps it was Georgiana. She had used to run to him at night when she had nightmares, deeply convinced that there was some scary monster living under her bed. He would then have gone with her to her room, lit the candles and made her look under the furniture to prove there was nothing there apart from some abandoned doll. It had not happened though for many years now.

"Elizabeth," he whispered as he saw a small brunette in pristine white nightclothes standing on the doorstep with a single candle in her hand. He pulled her quickly in and closed the door. "Has something happened?"

She shook her head. "I was afraid you were already asleep. You did not answer the door for so long."

"What is wrong?" he questioned.

"Nothing, I just wanted to talk with you," she murmured, staring at her feet. "I miss you... we are often together, but almost never alone."

He took the candle from her hand and put it away. "Come."

He led her to the fireplace, sat down in the chair and pulled her on his lap. She sighed, wrapped her arms around his neck, and wriggled herself for a moment till she found the most comfortable position for herself.

"Feeling better now?" he asked, kissing the top of her head.

"Mhm..." she murmured. "I have realized now that I have not yet thanked you for Star." She lifted her head from his shoulder and kissed his cheek. "Thank you."

"You are welcome. We can start riding tomorrow. Would you like that?"

"Yes," she drawled, and he could feel a hesitation in her tone.

"Are you sure everything is well?" he asked.

He felt her stiffen for a very short moment. "Can I stay with you?" she asked in one breath.

Did he hear right? "Stay...?"

"For the night," she clarified.

His hands on her stilled, "Do you understand what you are saying?"

"Yes," she answered, her voice clear.

"If you stay, it will not be only sleeping in one bed," he said, his voice blunt.

"I know."

He nudged her off his lap and stood up to his full height. They should not do it, he knew. There was always a risk of her becoming with child, even the first time. With their wedding at the end of September, the baby would be born about a month early. Such an occurrence would raise some eyebrows for sure, but it would hardly be a scandal.

Sending her away to her bed was out of question; he would have been an utter fool if he had done that.

Patience, he thought as he took her hand and led her towards his bed. She was responsive and passionate, but was still a maiden, and needed long preliminaries. Perhaps later, he would be able to simply pull her under him, open her legs and ease himself into her prone, soft body, but tonight, all the attention had to be concentrated entirely on her.

He pushed the covers aside and helped her to climb onto the tall bed. She sat in the middle, her legs curled under her, her big eyes shining with curiosity.

He was naked under his dressing gown, because that how he slept. After the wedding, he planned to start wearing a nightshirt for the sake of her sensibilities. He untied the garment and threw it aside, standing as God made him in front of her. Would she run back to her room now?

She shifted closer to the edge of the bed, her eyes scanning his form up and down, finally stopping on his abdomen and lower. She examined him like some exotic animal.

"Can I touch it?" she asked, looking up to him.

He only nodded, not being sure of his voice.

She reached out her hand and began her gentle probing.

"So smooth." She ran her small finger around his tip. "It is growing," she giggled.

"I think that is quite enough of the anatomy lesson," he murmured dryly, quickly joining her on the bed, afraid to ridicule himself.

She was still dressed, including light home slippers, a nightgown and a dressing robe, even her hair was braided. His arm wrapped around her and he pulled her under him.

He kissed her, tugging at the fuller lower lip. "Are you sure? It is not too late to stop."

She nodded. "I want to."

"You do not know how long I waited for this, longed for you." he whispered, his hand running down her body, feeling her breasts, her soft waist and lower.

"Wait!" she exclaimed, scrambling from under him, disappearing under the covers to crawl under them across the mattress. She appeared standing on the other side of the bed. "I must remove my clothes."

He moved forward. "I will help you."

"No!" she pushed her hands in front of herself. "I will do it. I do not want... anything to crumple or get damaged."

Darcy's eyebrows shot up. What did she imagine, that he would tear the nightgown off her?

She walked to the chair standing next to the wall, and began to undress. First she removed her shoes, and later her dressing gown, hanging it carefully over the furniture. She was less diligent with her nightgown, which she neglectfully flipped over her head.

For a moment she stood naked with her back to him, her thick braid hanging down her back, clearly shy to turn around. Not that he did not like the sight of her round backside. At last she did turn, after which she raced to the bed, diving under the covers. As the result of this action, he could not see much, or for a long time, but he enjoyed very much how her bosom swayed and jiggled during the run.

He shivered, feeling her naked soft body next to his as he brought her closer. Turning on his back he pulled her partially on him. "Let your hair free." he said, palming her round, soft bottom.

"It will tangle," she protested.

"Please." He tugged at the ribbon at the end of her braid.

She moved away from him, sat up, and began loosening her braid.

"You hair is beautiful..." he dipped his hands into the rich mass of curls.

She shrugged, "It is hard to arrange ...too thick and unruly, heavy to pin up, curls too tightly on rainy days. Mama says I look like a Gypsy, not like an English lady should."

Darcy bit his tongue not to say something very unpleasant about Mrs. Bennet.

"I like it." He pushed her down on her back.

Hovering over her, he kissed her till she was all relaxed and yielding, before turning his attention to her breasts. She began pronouncing those sweet noises as he suckled on her, the same as the last time behind the hedgerow.

He kissed her belly and then opened her legs, shifting between her legs, spreading them. She arched like a bow when he kissed the inside of her thigh the first time. Happy with her initial response, he lay comfortably on his stomach and placed her warm thighs over his shoulders. He looked up at her; she did not protest but covered her face with hands.

His aim was to find a place he had heard about, which should bring her pleasure. He pushed her black tight curls aside to uncover delicate, pinkish flesh. There it was, above her opening, a small button of flesh hooded for protection. He touched his mouth to the place and began to kiss it gently.

For a moment she was still, but then she began moving her hips and panting. He discovered that she reacted more violently when he did not touch the button directly, but only fleetingly; kissed and touched around it.

"Ahh... ahhh...." her moans rose in volume, her belly was trembling and she pulled at the bed sheets. Confident that he found the right way to please her, he doubled his efforts and made her have her pleasure once again.

She was limp all over after that. He could feel her heart beating wildly in her chest when he ran his hand over her body touching her right breast.

He cradled her to him for a while till she calmed down.

"I cannot believe it," she whispered, opening her eyes, smiling at him. "I thought I would die, that my heart would not bear it."

He laughed and kissed her forehead. Crouching in front of her, he reopened her thighs and not hesitating, pushed into her. He watched, fascinated as his manhood disappeared into her small opening, inch by inch. At one moment she hissed quietly, her face twisted in pain, her back arched. She placed her hands on his belly and pushed him away, her eyes wide. He pulled out at once and saw blood on his member.

She turned on her side with her back to him, bringing the sheet with her, curling into a ball.

For Darcy it was like a bucket of cold water poured over his head. He felt like a complete brute. What was he supposed to do now?

At last he moulded his body behind her, drawing the covers over both of them.

"Are you well?" he whispered, touching her arm.

Slowly, she turned her head, and looked at him, her expression troubled. "I did not expect it to feel quite like that."

"Like what? Was it that painful? Unbearable?"

She searched his eyes and then slowly shook her head. "Do it again, I think it should be better now. It was probably like that only the first time."

"I am not sure. If you could have seen your face when I..."

She turned on her back completely, "Please, do it again." She put her hand on his bottom, trying to bring him closer.

"Please, I shall be fine," she was coaxing him.

Darcy nudged himself between her thighs and she wrapped her hands and legs tightly around him. He pushed again, this time just a little bit, and stared into her face.

"Is it painful?"

She smiled. "No. I think... that I am getting used to the feeling."

He was not sure whether she was completely sincere, because she hid her face into his chest, locking her arms tightly around his shoulders. He could hardly stop himself any more and began to move. With each move, each thrust into her tight, warm, wet sheath it was getting harder and harder to be gentle. Soon, he lost himself completely in her, pushing her against the headboard, rocking the old, heavy bed.

He emptied into her, and dropped on her damp body.

After a long moment, he lifted on his arm and looked into her face. She smiled.

"You are well?"

She nodded.

He kissed the top of her breast and got out of bed, pulling on his dressing gown. He walked into a dressing room to the washstand and wetted the towel to clean himself. He returned to her with a clean one, sat on the edge and pulled the covers aside.

She stopped his hand, "I will do that."

"No, no... It is my responsibility," he pushed her on her back and opened her legs.

"God, Elizabeth..." he stared at the red, rather sizeable stain on the sheet. He touched her, she was still bleeding.

"I am sorry. I ruined the bed."

He touched the towel to her thighs, wiping her clean. Soon new blood appeared. "We must call a doctor!"

"No!" she cried. "We cannot."

"Elizabeth, do you want to bleed yourself to death?"

"I will not, it is passing."

He touched the clean part of the towel to her secret place again. There was a fresh patch of red on it.

"You hurt when I asked?" he asked angrily.

She nodded. "Yes."

"Why did you not tell me, stop me?"

"I..." she faltered, "I thought that it would lessen in time, and you... seemed to enjoy yourself so much."

He ran his hand over his face. She was sitting, curled on the bed, clenching sheets to herself, not looking at him. What was he supposed to do now? He expected some blood, but not that much. What he had done to her? Did he tear something he should not have? It could not be her monthly courses because she had just had them. He stared at the stained towel for a moment and hurried to bring a new one.

He returned in a minute, and sat on the edge of the bed and brought her to him, "I am sorry." He stroked her hair, his arm around her. "It is my fault. I am a selfish oaf." He nudged her thighs open, putting the clean, wet towel between them.

"No, it is me," she whispered against his chest, her face wet from tears. "There must be something wrong with me."

He cupped her face. "What are you saying, sweetheart? You are delicate, that is all. I heard of bleeding the first time, I am only not sure how long it should last. Perhaps we should wake Mrs. Gardiner. She should know what to do."

"William, please no, do not even think of that!" Her eyes pleaded with him, "I would die of shame. No, you can tell absolutely no one. This is such an intimate matter, please."

As she was nearly hysterical, he said nothing more and began to rock her, till she calmed down.

He took out the towel and saw the red stains again. Will it ever end?

"Are you in pain now?"

She shook her head. "No."

"Truly? You are not lying to me?" he asked sharply, frowning at her.

"Truly. I feel well."

He kissed the top of her head and went to bring another towel. As he found no clean one left, he utilized his own clean nightshirts, taken from the neat pile in the closet. When he returned and wiped her clean again there seemed not to be any fresh blood.

"I think it stopped," he said, the relief in his voice great. "Thank you, God," he whispered.

"What will you say about the bed and the towels, the blood...?"

"My valet is very discreet, he will deal with it. Do not fret."

He disentangled from her to bring her nightgown. He put it on her.

"May I sleep here?" she asked shyly.

"What kind of question is that?" He scolded gently and helped her under the covers. "You think that I will let you go before morning?"

He checked one more time whether she bled before putting out the candles. Thankfully, she did not. They moved to the other side of the bed, away from the bloody stains. As she fell asleep, snuggled against him, he decided that he needed to learn more about what had happened, ask someone knowledgeable, perhaps some trusted midwife, so he would know what to do if it repeated itself the next time. Her bleeding had nearly given him apoplexy.

When he woke up early in the morning, he was alone in bed, but there was a letter resting on the opposite pillow.

Rubbing his sleepy eyes, he took it and saw his name written on top of it, in Elizabeth's handwriting.

"Elizabeth?" he called, getting out of the bed.

He walked into the dressing room but no one was there. He pulled on his dressing gown, and sat in a chair near the window, frowning over the letter.

Then he opened it and started to read.

Dearest William

If you are reading this letter it means that I lacked the courage last night to tell you everything in person.

I know that I must say this to you so I will start without preamble.

There is one matter which has bothered me greatly since the day I accepted your proposal of marriage. I want you to know that today I can honestly say that I care for you. I have fallen in love with you over the past months when I had the opportunity to know you better and discover how wonderful a person you are. My fault is that I did not love you when I accepted your proposal back in Kent. To be perfectly sincere, I did not like you particularly back then. I blamed you not only for Jane's unhappiness but as well for Wickham's supposed misfortunes. I agreed to marry you that evening at Hunsford because I feared for my future, and knew that a marriage to you would ensure me security.

It all started at the inn we stopped for the change of horses as I travelled with Sir William and Maria to Kent. I saw there my childhood friend, Anne Parker...

** ** **

An hour later, Darcy knocked at the door to Elizabeth's room. Her maid opened and stood unmoving for a minute, her eyes round, staring at him, mouth open.

He walked inside and closed the door. The bed was empty and already neatly made.

"Is Miss Bennet in her rooms?"

She nodded. "Finishing her bath, Master."

"Leave us alone now, and you have not seen me here. Do you understand?" He glared at the servant, using his most imposing, severe tone.

"Yes, Master." The girl bowed and hurried out of the room.

Darcy turned the key in the lock so no one would interrupt them and walked farther inside the spacious chamber. The room was situated in the guest part of the house, but still placed as close to the family wing as possible.

The door leading to the dressing room opened and Elizabeth walked in, wearing a dressing gown, towelling her hair dry.

"William!" she gasped.

He stepped closer, encircled her waist with his arm and walked her to the window.

"Good morning, my love," he kissed her brow, taking in her features, which he found a bit pale, "Are you feeling well?"

"Yes, I am well."

He lowered his voice. "No more bleeding this morning?"

She shook her head.

He was not sure whether she tried to shield him from the truth, so without warning, he brought her closer, opened her dressing gown, and slid his hand inside, down her belly and between her thighs.

"William!" she scolded, blushing to the roots of her hair.

He pulled out his hand, thankfully clean of any blood, smiled and respectfully retied her dressing gown.

"You have not... found my letter?" she asked, as he sat on the chair and pulled her on his lap.

"On the contrary."

Her face reflected her astonishment, "You are not angry with me?"

He shook his head, and leaned to kiss her. "I can only be angry with myself for being a conceited and arrogant fool when I proposed to you," he whispered, looking into her eyes.

"I took you for granted, and I should not have," he continued. "Please believe me, that I cringe every time I remember the manner of my proposal. I have not yet apologized to you because I was ashamed of myself, I wanted to forget my behaviour, never return to it. You were right about all that you said to me at Ockham Mount, when you mentioned that you wondered whether my parents had taught me such behaviour towards people... You cannot imagine how these words have haunted me since then."

"What about me?" she questioned with feeling, "Do you not find the reasons why I accepted you repulsive, mercenary?"

"I was not that surprised with your confessions after reading the letter, love," he replied calmly. "I could not know the exact circumstances, of course. However, do you not think that I must have felt from the very beginning that something was wrong? You believe that it did not bother me when you kept your distance from me, stiffened in my arms, resisted my touch, even the most innocent one? I was determined to maintain our understanding knowing. I could not lose you."

She was shaking her head. "I cannot believe that you do not think badly about me. Had I not seen my childhood friend at that inn, and got frightened and upset with the reality of her current life, which very well could have been mine one day..."

He put a finger on her lips, "Then you would have refused my proposal, saying I was not a gentleman, claiming that you could not marry a man who had ruined the happiness of your sister, who destroyed Wickham's life. I would have ridden away from you, hurt, furious and probably we would have never seen each other again."

Elizabeth fell silent and supported her head on his arm.

"The most important thing now is that all that misunderstanding is behind us and that we love each other now, do we not?"

"Yes, we do," she agreed sweetly.

They held on to each other tightly for a few moments, taking mutual comfort in their embrace and the closeness.

Reluctantly, Darcy nudged her off his lap and stood up, "I should go, but there is one more matter." He frowned heavily, "You must tell me whether or not your courses have come next month. I want to be prepared if we made a baby last night."

"I do not think that it will happen," she said lightly, "It was only one time."

"You doubt my abilities, Madam," he laughed. "I assure you that one time is quite enough."

He kissed her forehead, and walked to the door, unlocking it. "We shall see each other at breakfast."

Chapter Seventeen

"You seem a bit pale, Elizabeth," Mrs. Gardiner noted as she looked at her niece over the breakfast table.

Elizabeth glanced at her aunt, and then quickly lowered her eyes. "No... I am well."

The older woman gazed intently at the girl, feeling that something was amiss; it was uncharacteristic for Elizabeth to answer one's question not looking into the enquirer's eyes. "Have you slept well?"

The hot blush bloomed on Elizabeth's face. "Yes, quite well," she answered, her voice raspy, her eyes focused on the content of her plate.

Mrs. Gardiner frowned and squinted her eyes as she stared at the undeniably pretty brunette in front of her. Could she see faint red marks on her graceful neck and around the collar bones? They must have snuck away somehow yesterday, and managed to have a private moment long enough for Mr. Darcy to apply those marks. Unless...

Mrs. Gardiner shifted her attention to Darcy. Contrary to Elizabeth, he did not avoid her eyes, but held her gaze calmly for a moment before returning it to his betrothed, who was still very much flustered.

Mrs. Gardiner looked at her husband who, she was not surprised, did not seem to notice anything, and was entirely concentrated on his scrambled eggs and bacon. *Men*, she snorted quietly under her breath.

"Excuse me," Darcy stood up, folding his napkin. "I need to deal with some urgent correspondence."

"But of course, of course." Mr. Gardiner nodded good humouredly. "We understand."

Darcy walked around the table, placed a kiss on the top of his sister's blond head, before stepping to Elizabeth.

"We shall see each other later," he said, as he took her hand and lifted it to his lips.

There was such a great deal of intimacy in this small gesture that it instantly convinced Mrs. Gardiner that indeed something had happened between these two last night, which caused Elizabeth to be so changed this morning. She could hardly wait for the opportunity to share her suspicions with her husband.

Soon after Darcy left the room, a servant entered, and walked to Elizabeth.

"Letters for Miss Bennet." He bowed, holding the silver tray in front of Elizabeth. "Mr. Darcy assumed that you would like to read them without delay."

Elizabeth glanced at the handwriting as she dabbed her lips with a napkin. "These are from Jane!" she cried out. "I wondered why she had not written." She took the letters and examined the address. "This one was misdirected..." she frowned. "No wonder, the direction is written very ill indeed. It is so strange, Jane is always so neat about her writing."

She stood up. "Will you excuse me?"

Mrs. Gardiner smiled. "Of course, my dear. Go and read your letters while your uncle and I take a turn around the park."

"We will?" Mr. Gardiner questioned, looking longingly towards the fresh newspaper, just brought by the servant.

"Yes, we will." His wife glanced at him meaningfully.

Georgiana lifted herself as well. "I think I will excuse myself to the music room." She pronounced in her usual quiet, drawled voice. "Because of our trip, I did not practice enough yesterday."

When the Gardiners were left alone, Mrs. Gardiner rose hurriedly from her place and walked to her husband.

"Come, we must talk."

"Can we not sit here for a while?" He patted his rounded belly. "You know I like to rest a while after a good meal."

"I know, and I would not ask you, but it is truly of great import, and we do need some privacy."

Mr. Gardiner sighed, pushed the chair away and allowed himself to be guided out of the room.

"Well?" he questioned, as they were outside on the path leading to the park. "What is the matter?"

"Have you not noticed anything at breakfast?"

Mr. Gardiner lifted his shoulders. "Should I have noticed anything?"

"Yes, Elizabeth has been pale and not acting her usual self."

He shook his head. "I have not noticed. She looked the same as usual to me."

"Why is it that you never see anything?" Mrs. Gardiner questioned, irritated.

"I think it will be much easier for both of us if you simply tell me what I should have seen." Mr. Gardiner said, his voice resigned.

His wife took a deep breath and announced. "I think that Mr. Darcy and Elizabeth anticipated their vows last night."

Mr. Gardiner gave her a sharp look. "They did? How do you know that?"

"She was timid, pale, and I noticed faint marks on her neck."

"That is no proof at all." Mr. Gardiner said, much calmed. "Probably they simply found some private moment for kissing and groping behind some convenient curtain and he marked her; nothing unusual between a young couple in love."

"No, there is more to it than that, I can feel it," she insisted. "When he kissed her hand on his leaving, there was such a tangible sense of belonging and intimacy in his gesture."

Mr. Gardiner rolled his eyes. "I beg you, Maddy, none of that. You read too much of those nonsensical novels, an occupation which a married woman with several children had no use for in my opinion, and now you see romance everywhere. He kissed her hand, so what? I really like Darcy, and I do not particularly fancy the idea of going to him now and questioning him on this. What am I supposed to tell him? You compromised her, so you must marry her now? He would do that tomorrow if he only could. They are already engaged. Their wedding is set in five weeks."

"You think we should do nothing? Pretend to be blind?"

"That would be most convenient. It is their private matter, after all. I will not lecture the man who is less than ten years my junior how he should carry himself. I truly think that he is the responsible one, and loves her very much. Elizabeth must trust him if she allowed anything, because neither of us believe that he in any way would force her."

Mrs. Gardiner bit her lower lip. "Perhaps I should talk with Elizabeth."

"You may. She will not lie to you about this, but I still consider it none of our business at this point. Were they not engaged, then the situation would be entirely different... besides we were not much better."

Mrs. Gardiner nodded, blushing slightly. "That is true."

He brought her to him, wrapping his arm around her. "Nobody seemed to notice that Annie was born two weeks early," he whispered, his eyes twinkling with mischief.

"My mother did notice."

"That would explain why she does not like me." Mr. Gardiner murmured, before kissing his wife.

When Mrs. Gardiner lifted her head from her husband's shoulder after a short embrace they shared, she saw her niece running towards them across the lawn.

"Elizabeth is coming." She put her hand over her eyes to see better. "Something must have happened. She seems distressed."

The Gardiners walked forward with haste, to meet Elizabeth in the middle of the great lawn.

"What has happened?" Mrs. Gardiner cried.

"Jane writes..." Elizabeth began but then her speech slurred into sobs which shook her.

Mr. Gardiner's face went white. "Good God, do not tell us it is something with the children!"

"No, they are fine. It is about Lydia."

"Lydia?" The Gardiners echoed.

Elizabeth nodded. "She left all her friends and had departed Brighton. She eloped... with Mr. Wickham."

"Are you sure?" Mrs. Gardiner questioned. "She was under Colonel Forster's care. How could she escape? There must be some misunderstanding surely."

Elizabeth was shaking her head. "No, no mistake. They left for London in the middle of the night over a week ago, and no one has heard from them since then. She is ruined, I know that." She was pacing, clenching her hands to her temples. "He will not marry her, I know he will not. She has no money, no connections, nothing to tempt him. Nothing."

"Lizzy, dear, please calm yourself." Mr. Gardiner walked to her, and reached to touch her arm, stopping her in place. "Perhaps his intentions are honest, and we will hear the news of their

168

wedding any day. Mr. Wickham seemed to be so agreeable when we were introduced to him last winter."

"No, you do not know him." Elizabeth cried, new tears gathering in her dark eyes. "Wickham is a rake and gambler, Uncle. It is not the first time he has tried to seduce a young girl like her. But why Lydia? She is nothing to him, I cannot believe he has any feeling for her. Papa cannot pay him much, he must know that."

The Gardiners looked worriedly at one another.

"Oh, please, can we go home, today?" Elizabeth pleaded.

"Of course, as soon as can be." Mr. Gardiner agreed. "We must talk with Mr. Darcy first though. Perhaps he will be able to help..."

"No!" Elizabeth interrupted. "He cannot know."

"Elizabeth, be reasonable," the man spoke gently but firmly. "It is impossible to hide what happened from Darcy. He will notice your distress."

Mr. Gardiner glanced towards the house. "He must know something already."

Elizabeth turned to see Darcy striding towards them, his long legs carrying him with fast efficiency. A heavy frown on his countenance was visible from afar. She lifted her hand to her face, trying to dry her tears with the back of her palm.

"What has happened?" Darcy asked without preamble as he reached them. He glanced down at Elizabeth. "Mrs. Reynolds told me she saw you running out of the house in tears."

As Elizabeth remained silent, biting her lip, trying to stop her tears, Mrs. Gardiner explained. "She has received bad news from home."

"Has someone died?" Darcy asked tentatively, trying to meet the girl's eyes, which she kept stubbornly downcast. "Is someone ill?"

Elizabeth shook her head only.

He touched her arm. "What happened?" he demanded in a sharper tone. "Tell me."

At last she lifted her eyes to him and before long stepped into his embrace, hiding her face into his chest, erupting in quiet sobs.

Darcy looked helplessly over her head at the Gardiners.

Mr. Gardiner pointed with his eyes to the letter which Elizabeth still held in her hand. "All is in the letter." He took his wife's arm. "Come, my dear. They need some time alone."

Darcy waited till the older couple left them alone, and led Elizabeth to the nearby bench. He sat her down and retrieved his handkerchief, one of those she had once made for him.

"There, there..." he dried her face, "It cannot be that bad if no one has died, or is seriously ill."

"You cannot even imagine..." she finally voiced. "It is even worse in a way. Our whole family is ruined."

Darcy took the crumpled letter from her cold, trembling hand. He straightened it, opened it and started to read. After a few sentences, his expression darkened, he stood up and began pacing.

"That is grave indeed," he said at last.

Elizabeth glanced at him, and then burst into a new wave of tears.

"I must go." She stood up and started walking hastily towards the manor.

He stopped her in no time. "Wait. We must think what to do now."

She looked up at him. "You do not have to do anything. We both know that Lydia is too poor to tempt Wickham and he would never marry her. My family is ruined. I understand that you will not wish to have anything to do with me now, and I do not blame you."

She tried to walk away from him, but he grounded her in place. "What are you talking about? You think I will leave you alone with that. You *are* my wife. Especially after what happened between us last night."

"I understand you may feel responsible for me after ~~the~~ last night, but it was I who initiated it..."

He interrupted her with a short laugh. "Come now, Elizabeth, you cannot tell me that you forced me into anything. I knew very well what I was doing, love."

She took a deep breath and spoke with determination, "As I have said, there may be no consequence to it so..."

"Do you hear yourself?" he shook her, not so gently, his voice getting angry. "Who do you think I am? I decided to stand by you for better and for worse that day in Kent when I proposed. I made my commitment to you that day. I will find Wickham and force him to marry your sister."

She only stared at him.

"I would have done the same, even if I had I not bedded you, and there was not the possibility of you carrying my child." She searched his eyes, as if not sure, so he added with force. "Were we not engaged, and I learned about it, I would do exactly the same. I would go to London, find them and see to it they marry."

She swallowed her tears. "You would?"

His eyes bore into hers. "Yes, because I love you, damn it, and I cannot bear to look as you cry over that bastard."

He kissed her wet lips shortly, and brought her into a tight embrace.

"Now, we will find your uncle and talk with him." He cupped her face. "Yes?"

She nodded, new tears streaming down her cheeks.

Darcy took his own handkerchief from her clenched fist. "Do not cry." He dabbed her face. "I promise that everything will be well. I dare say that Wickham, knowing of our engagement, did it on purpose to be paid off again. Your sister is quite safe, I dare say. He will not mistreat her, he is not that stupid." He kissed her wet cheek. "Please, stop crying, it breaks my heart when I see you like this."

She nodded, blinking her tears away. "I am not crying any more."

"Come." He took her hand and turned to the manor.

***

"Yes, I do think so that it is the best possible solution." Mr. Gardiner said an hour later as they were gathered in the smaller drawing room. "Mr. Darcy will depart today, and we will go tomorrow, early in the morning."

Elizabeth looked at Darcy with pleading eyes. She would have much preferred to go yet today.

Darcy seemed to guess her wish. "Your uncle is right, Elizabeth. I will go horseback yet today, and this way should be in London by tomorrow evening. I know Wickham's ways well, as well as people who could have helped him in this shameful endeavour. Finding him will not be difficult. I dare say I will already know his whereabouts by the time you and Mr. and Mrs. Gardiner reach London."

Elizabeth nodded, lowering her head. She knew that Darcy was right on this. Her going now with Darcy would only slow him down, and time was of great import. It was the only rational solution, so she and the Gardiners would set off tomorrow.

"I think we should start packing." Mrs. Gardiner stood up, eyeing her husband to follow her.

When the Gardiners left, Darcy moved to Elizabeth, sitting next to her on the sofa. "Promise you will not worry yourself over this."

She lifted her eyes at him. "How can I not worry? It is all my fault. I knew who he was. I could have prevented it somehow, warned my father so he would not let her go to Brighton. But how could anyone perceive that Wickham would take even the slightest interest in Lydia? I considered her too poor to tempt anyone. I thought that in the worst case she would ridicule herself even more."

"Elizabeth," Darcy took her hand, "There is no your fault to it. It was I who did not want to reveal his true character, fearing for Georgiana, her reputation and her spirits. I wanted her to forget about what happened last summer."

Elizabeth paled. "Georgiana... How will she react, hearing this? We cannot hide it from her for long."

"I will go and tell her." Darcy said. "Now." He stood up. "Before my departure."

She rose too. "I am going with you."

He put his hands on her shoulders, steadying her. "No, it is my responsibility. Besides, she is not aware that I told you about Ramsgate. "

Elizabeth nodded. "She may think you betrayed her trust in telling me."

Darcy shook his head. "Rather she will be worried that you may think less of her because you know what happened."

"I would never do that. She is such a lovely, selfless person."

Darcy sighed. "She doubts herself constantly."

Elizabeth stepped closer to him, their bodies touching.

"I must go." He cupped her face, "Worry not. We shall go through this, and in a few short weeks we will marry and be together forever."

She wrapped her arms around his neck tightly. "Be safe."

He stroked her cheek and kissed her lips before leaving the room.

***

That afternoon, as Elizabeth was packing her things with the help of the maid, there was a soft knock on the door. It was Georgiana.

"Leave us alone," Elizabeth asked the servant.

Georgiana walked in and looked at the open trunk placed in the middle of the room.

"You are packing."

"Yes, we must go, I am afraid," Elizabeth confirmed quietly. "You must have heard about what happened with my youngest sister."

The girl nodded. "Yes, I know. Brother told me everything. I am very sorry."

Elizabeth closed her trunk and walked to sit on the bed, her arms slumped. "I cannot imagine how she can be rescued. She has not money to tempt him. I fear she is ruined forever."

Georgiana sat next to her. "She is not lost. Brother will find them and make Wickham marry her. He told me so."

Elizabeth's troubled eyes met Georgiana's. "I hate to burden him with this." she admitted.

"Brother loves you. He will do anything for you. "

Elizabeth smiled. "And for you."

The girl smiled. "That is true. I could not wish for a better brother."

Georgiana was silent for a moment before she spoke with hesitation. "Elizabeth, you are aware about what happened last summer in Ramsgate."

Elizabeth viewed her with concern. "Yes."

"Brother told me that you knew."

"Yes, your brother did tell me some time ago, but only to protect me against Mr. Wickham, his lies and deception. But I have never told anyone about it." she assured quickly.

"Do you think less of me?" Georgiana asked very quietly.

"No, of course not. Never." She clasped the girl's slim hand, giving it a squeeze to reassure her. "I think that you are the most generous, the sweetest, kindest person in the world. You were so young when Wickham abused your trust. It was not your fault."

The girl gave her a long, sad look, before lowering her eyes. "I know how much I disappointed Brother last summer. He never said so... He was so kind after everything, but I know well what he must have thought of me."

"No, no sweetheart, no. It was not like that, I am sure." Elizabeth touched her face to make her look up. "If anything, he only worried about you, about your spirits and well being. He blamed only himself for the situation, that he failed to protect you."

Georgiana shook her head, two large tears running down her cheeks. "It was not his fault. Only mine. I did not behave the way Miss Darcy of Pemberley should have."

"No one is perfect," Elizabeth soothed. "We need to accept the fact that we make mistakes from time to time."

"Brother does only good. He is never wrong," the girl announced with conviction.

Elizabeth smiled. "There is no such person. Your brother is not perfect either."

Georgiana frowned at her in wonder.

"I did not like your brother for the first months of our acquaintance. I did not like him at all," Elizabeth confessed. "I was angry with him because of how he behaved in certain situations, things he said to me and about me."

"But he loves you so much!" Georgiana cried with feeling.

Elizabeth smiled. "I was not aware of that back then. He stared at me a great deal, but I thought he did that only to find a fault in me. It certainly took me some time to learn to appreciate him."

Georgiana looked at her as if she had not quite believed her, making Elizabeth laugh. "That is true."

The girl smiled too, but then sobered, a new cloud passing her expressive features. "I will stay here. I do not want to go to London. I cannot meet him again..." she trembled. "I cannot."

"Of course. No one would ask it of you." Elizabeth touched her arm. "You will have no need to see him ever again. I am sure William will do everything in his power so the two of you never meet in the future."

"I feel for Miss Lydia. Wickham is not a good man. She will be miserable with him."

"Yet, she has no choice now but to marry him," Elizabeth noted sadly.

Georgiana stared in front of herself . "It only makes me realize how lucky I was." She leaned over and wrapped Elizabeth in a quick embrace. "I am so happy that you will be my sister."

Chapter Eighteen

Elizabeth stared out of the window at the passing countryside. The farther south they travelled, the more the landscape reminded her of Hertfordshire. She glanced at her aunt and uncle; they were sleeping. William should have reached London yesterday afternoon at the latest. Had he been lucky in acquiring some information about Wickham and Lydia? She repeated to herself that if there was someone who could find them, it was Darcy, but that knowledge did not ease her heart. How he must suffer to be forced to deal with Wickham again after what he had done to Georgiana. He had offered his help without hesitation, and it was the same man she was so close to rejecting half a year ago. She felt humbled by him. How could she have been so blind about him once? Some good angel must have had her in his protection that evening at Hunsford when despite her doubts, and her blind apprehension, she had said yes to him.

She closed her eyes, and tried to revoke the sensation of his presence next to her; his strong arms around her, his warmth and scent. She wanted the next weeks to pass in one moment, the matter with Lydia to be resolved in a most quiet way, and forgotten. She wanted to be married to him, and never be separated again. She smiled at the memory of the night they had spent together. What had got into her to come to him? She touched her face with her fingers, feeling the hot blush spreading on her cheeks. She was shameless, but only with him, as she had never before experienced such desires. She had never wanted to be kissed by any other man. The way William touched her, held her to him, caressed her felt heavenly, but she was not so much convinced about the main part of the act. Crudely speaking, it had felt as if someone had shoved a pole right between her legs. Later when he had moved in and out, it had been less painful, but still mightily uncomfortable.

Perhaps all which occurred before, all the kisses and caresses and the after part, sleeping in the safety of his arms, was so pleasant to reward somehow the discomfort of him being inside her. *We need to practice more*, she thought with determination. She knew what to expect now. She would try to brace herself the next time, and not show any signs of uneasiness. She only hoped there would be no bleeding in the future. He had been so terrified the last time.

Four weeks only, she whispered to herself. She refused to think that Lydia's elopement might delay their wedding.

***

Elizabeth and the Gardiners reached Longbourn the third day of their journey in the early afternoon.

Only Jane, accompanied by her cousins, came out in front of the house to greet them. The little Gardiners gathered around their parents, simultaneously pulling at their sleeves, climbing up them and speaking all three at once.

"Oh, Jane." Elizabeth fell into her sister's embrace. "Any news?"

Jane shook her head. "No, Lizzy. Father went to London the day we received the letter from Brighton to look for them, but we have not heard from him since then."

"Mr. Darcy went to London as well," Elizabeth informed. "He promised to help, find them and make him marry her."

Jane let out a sigh of relief. "Then we are rescued. Mr. Darcy is a man of his word. He has the influence and means to find them."

"Jane, dear." Mrs. Gardiner walked to them, with the youngest boy cuddled in her arms. "Tell me, please, how my children behaved."

"They were perfectly well behaved. I had absolutely no trouble with them," Jane said without hesitation, smiling.

"You are the only person who says so, Jane," Mr. Gardiner said as he stepped closer with another boy in his arms and a girl wrapped tightly around his leg. "I know them far too well to believe this."

"They are sometimes too spirited," Jane acknowledged cautiously. "However, it is quite enough to take them aside and have an earnest talk with them, and they are again on their best behaviour."

Elizabeth shook her head. "No, Jane. It is you, sister. You have a way with children like no one else, so they always obey you, even the naughty ones."

"Lizzy is right." Mrs. Gardiner put the boy on the ground, taking his small hand. "You will be a wonderful mother one day."

The Gardiners, together with the children, went inside where the hot meal was already waiting for them. Elizabeth refused to eat anything, saying she was not hungry after the long hours spent in the carriage on uneven roads.

"Let us go to Mama, then," Jane proposed.

Elizabeth sighed. She could only imagine the state her mother was in.

"She is not leaving her room these days," Jane whispered as they approached Mrs. Bennet's room.

Jane knocked and entered. "Mama, Lizzy is here."

"Lizzy, my child." Mrs. Bennet opened her arms wide in an almost theatrical gesture. "You came! At last!"

"Yes, Mama." Elizabeth knelt beside her mother, who half lay on the sofa and returned her embrace.

"Did Mr. Darcy throw you out of Pemberley when he learned the truth about the ruin of our family?" Mrs. Bennet asked, her eyes wide.

Elizabeth was taken aback with her mother's presumption. "No, Mama. No, of course not."

"Mr. Darcy is currently in London now," Jane explained. "Lizzy says he promised her to find Mr. Wickham and Lydia and marry them."

Mrs. Bennet clasped her hands together. "That cannot be!" Her round eyes directed at Elizabeth for confirmation. "He said he would find them?"

Elizabeth nodded. "Yes, Mama. He assured me that he knew Wickham well, and his ways. He asked me not to worry about the entire matter as he would deal with it."

Mrs. Bennet was mute for a long moment. "Thank you, God," she breathed at last. "We are rescued. Such a good man this Mr. Darcy is! And we once all thought him to be so disagreeable. You are lucky indeed, he stood by you in such dire times, Lizzy."

"I know, Mama. I know," Elizabeth agreed quietly.

"But how could Lydia have done this to me? Did she not know what a scandal it would be?" Mrs. Bennet exclaimed after a moment, her ire rising once again. "What if Mr. Darcy does not find them, or Wickham will not want to marry her?"

"We cannot think the worst, Mama." Elizabeth patted her hand.

"Indeed Mama," Jane supported her younger sister. "We must have faith that Mr. Darcy and Papa will find them."

***

The Gardiners returned to London the very next day, and though Elizabeth wished dearly to go with them, her mother disagreed strongly. Mrs. Bennet insisted that she would be of no need in London. Elizabeth knew that she should stay and help Jane to take care of their mother, their younger sisters and the household, but she missed Darcy and wanted to see him. Waiting at home for any scrap of news was infuriating. The fact that she, as a woman, was not able to act, to do something to improve the situation, and could only sit at home drove her insane.

One day as she was working together with Jane in the garden, clearing the weeds out of the flowers beds she saw a servant running to them from the house.

"Some news must have come," she said, removing her thick gloves and raising from the ground.

"For you, Miss Elizabeth." Out of breath, the maid handed her the letter, addressed with now familiar strong, masculine handwriting.

She tore at the seal.

My dearest, loveliest Elizabeth,

We have found them. Miss Lydia is currently staying with the Gardiners. She is well and in good spirits. The wedding will take place in three days. Mr. and Mrs. Wickham will go directly to his new station in Newcastle, as Wickham has decided to join the regulars as his new life career. Understandable, unless they are going to be first invited to Longbourn. However, your father feels severely against this idea, I believe.

*I cannot wait to see you, my love, and you are always on my
mind. I will try to return to you as soon as possible, but there are
still things I need to deal with here in London. Please, take a good
care of yourself while I am absent from you. I hope that the
preparations for our wedding are running smoothly.*

Yours,

F. D.

*P.S. One more matter, it seems that my Aunt and Uncle, Lord
and Lady Matlock, will attend the ceremony of our wedding. I
wrote to them some time ago, inviting them to the wedding, but
issued the invitation pro forma only, not quite expecting they
would want to come as they rarely travel away from Matlock
these days. I am not yet aware of the details of their trip, but I ask
you to inform your mother about such possibility.*

Jane stared at her with tension. "What had happened?" she
questioned.

Elizabeth smiled and handed her the letter to read. "All is well."

Jane read greedily. "Thank you God, she is rescued," she said
with relief, handing the letter back to her sister.

Elizabeth smiled. "Yes, it seems so."

Jane gave her a long, unsure look. "Lizzy..." her voice traced.

"Yes, Jane." Elizabeth kept smiling as she folded her letter
neatly and hid it in the pocket of her apron. "We should go and tell
Mama at once."

Jane stopped her, placing a hand on her arm. "Is he always so
kind when he speaks with you? Like in this letter?"

"Yes, always."

Jane nodded slowly, her expression absent minded. "He refers
so nicely to you. I knew that he loved you, but I never imagined..."
She shook her head.

Elizabeth stepped to her, touching her arm. "Jane? What is
wrong?"

"Mr. Bingley is gone again. Have you not noticed?"

Elizabeth blinked her eyes. "No, I must say that I have not."

Jane forced a smile. "He has not visited us since the news about Lydia broke. I heard from our housekeeper that he left Netherfield."

"Perhaps, it is only a coincidence," Elizabeth suggested after a long moment of silence. She did not want to think that the amiable Mr. Bingley had abandoned her sister once again, even though the circumstances seemed to confirm that. "He must have some business in town."

Jane nodded, smiling almost brightly. "Yes, you are surely right."

"He will be back in no time," Elizabeth assured.

Jane smiled at her again, but her wide blue eyes were sad. "There is no point staying here and talking fruitlessly when we should go and tell Mama."

As they strolled back to the house, Jane asked. "Will you tell Mama now about the possibility of Lord and Lady Matlock attending the wedding?"

Elizabeth sighed with resignation. "Yes, I think that I should. I cannot imagine though how she will react. I think we can expect anything from fainting to turning absolutely speechless for some time at least.

Jane's blue eyes twinkled with mischief. "I think that she will take a carriage and start visiting all our neighbours, announcing this news to them."

Elizabeth chuckled, shaking her head. "I truly cannot guess where you have learned this teasing manner, dear sister."

***

Elizabeth's disappointment was great indeed when in four days' time, carriage stopped in front of Loungbourn but contained only Mr. Bennet and the newly wed couple.

Mrs. Bennet greeted Wickham and Lydia as if nothing had happened, and was seriously displeased that her husband insisted on them staying in the neighbourhood for two days only, before going to Newcastle.

Elizabeth could barely contain herself in the presence of Wickham. More than once, he tried to initiate conversation with her, but she pretended not to hear him. He had difficulty with taking a hint that she had no intention of speaking to him. The day of their departure, he found her alone in the breakfast room.

"We should talk, Miss Elizabeth." He spoke with a smile which Elizabeth would have once found pleasant and now seemed false and abhorrent.

She rushed to the door, but he cut her way, blocking the only door.

"Come on, Elizabeth, we are family now. Will you not invite me to the wedding?" He rudely looked into her face.

"I have not given you leave to use my Christian name," she said with cold dignity.

He smiled jovially. "Are you so rigid and formal with Darcy as well?"

"Let me pass."

He reached his hand to touch the wisp of hair, curling gracefully around her forehead. "I am curious what you did to Darcy that he was so determined and efficient in finding me and my dear Lydia, paying for everything without a blink of an eye. What charms of yours did you work on him to make his so generous?"

She looked up at him, his handsome countenance the image of ugliness for her now. "You are the lowest creature I know."

He laughed. "Do not compliment me so, Lizzy. I do not deserve it." He lowered his head, his voice rumbling next to her ear. "Lizzy, Lizzy..." he chanted. "Does he call you Lizzy when you pay him your duty in his bed? I am sure he does."

She lifted her hand with the intention of slapping him, but he grabbed her slim wrist in an iron grip before she managed anything.

She pressed her lips together. "Let me go."

"Or what?" he laughed.

"Or I will tell him about this."

"I am not afraid of Darcy." His tone was nonchalant, but Elizabeth could feel his grip on her hand loosening.

"Are you not?" She freed her hand. "In your place, I would pray this mark will disappear before he comes here." With her eyes, she pointed to her wrist. "I have no intention of lying to him about who did it."

"You would not be so bold without him," he muttered furiously, but he stepped aside, allowing her to go.

She turned once more to him as she was leaving. "I feel for my sister. She is so young, and her life is already ruined. Marrying you is the worst fate for any woman. I do not wish death to anyone, but

Lydia's only chance for happiness and normal existence is to widow young."

Mr. and Mrs. Wickham's left Longbourn a few hours later, the whole family waving them goodbye in front of the house.

"Newcastle," Mrs. Bennet sighed, bringing handkerchief to her eyes. "My baby so far away. Who knows when I will see her again."

"We should be thankful that they are married, Mama," Jane pointed out, her voice unusually severe.

"Yes, yes, Jane, but why do they have to go so far away? Could they not live somewhere closer? Purvis Lodge for example?"

"Do not talk nonsense, Fanny," Mr. Bennet's sharp voice cut the air. "It would be better for everyone if you did not speak at all. Darcy did enough. You cannot expect him to offer them one of his houses to live in. Perhaps you think that he should share a part of his income with Wickham as well."

Mrs. Bennet pressed her lips tightly, and hastily walked inside the house, Mary and Kitty following her.

Elizabeth glanced at the retreating back of her mother with compassion. Her comment was not the smartest or most sensible in the present situation, but Mr. Bennet acted wrong, silencing her in such a manner. A man should not talk like that to his wife in front of their children.

"Come with me. Elizabeth, please," Mr. Bennet said as Elizabeth and Jane passed by him.

Elizabeth nodded. "Yes, Papa."

She followed him to the library. She closed the door with care, and walked a few steps inside the room.

Mr. Bennet stood next to the window, staring out of it.

"You were right when you tried to convince me not to let Lydia go to Brighton."

"Nobody could foresee that something like that might have happened," Elizabeth said calmly. "The most important thing is that they are married, that you have found them in time."

Mr. Bennet laughed, turning to her. "You wanted to say, Darcy found them. He did everything. I did not lift a finger in the entire matter. He found Wickham, paid his debts, and bought his commission in the army. He refused to tell me how much it all cost him, but I think it was certainly not less than ten thousand pounds."

Elizabeth's eyes widened. "Ten thousand... Heaven forbid."

"At least." Mr. Bennet walked closer. "He paid for my mistakes as a father, and he never even mentioned your name."

Elizabeth lowered her eyes.

"I envy him. He is twice my junior, but already a better man that I have ever been."

She stepped closer, touched with the raw bitterness in his voice. "Papa. I..." she began, but he did not let her finish.

"I could not trust you with a more worthy man, Elizabeth." He took her hand. "I know you will always be safe with him."

Chapter Nineteen

Elizabeth ran out of the house, urgently craving not only fresh air, but some peace and quiet as well. She was about to become a married woman in five days. Her mother was shaking Longbourn in its foundations in the midst of wedding preparations. With the matter of Lydia's elopement resolved and the youngest Bennet girl being safely married and settled in the far north, newly invigorated Mrs. Bennet concentrated all her attention and efforts on the wedding of her second daughter.

Elizabeth sincerely had enough of packing, her wedding gown's alterations, the constant, endless talks about the menu and the seating arrangements at the reception.

Darcy had not yet returned from London, and she had not received any news from him since his last letter where he had revealed the news about finding her youngest sister. She could not stop herself from wondering why he was not here yet. Surely something important detained him; she only hoped that it was nothing bad.

She took her usual shortcut across the fields to Oakham Mount. As she walked, she kept glancing down at the road, hoping to see Darcy's carriage. When indeed she saw a familiar rider on a black horse, she could hardly believe her own eyes, thinking it was only her good wishing.

"William!" she exclaimed, jumping up and down, but the rider did not stop. "William!" she shouted at the top of her lungs, waving her hands. "William!"

Finally he looked up, and seeing her, instantly reined his horse.

Elizabeth waved again, and sprinted down the gentle hill towards him. By the time she reached the road, he had dismounted, and held his arms wide open, waiting for her.

"William!" she cried one more time as she leaped straight into his embrace.

"That is a welcome I like." he laughed, twirling her in the air.

She locked her hands around his neck. "What took you so long?"

He shifted her down on her feet, his hands running possessively down her back.

"Have you missed me?" he asked, his deep voice resonating warmly, making her knees weak.

She nodded. "I have wondered why you were not coming back."

"I was about to depart two days ago, when my aunt and uncle came to London, bringing Georgiana with them," he explained. "I needed to postpone my departure and take care of them."

"Will they come here?"

"Yes, tomorrow." He bent his head, and their lips met.

"I am on my way to Oakham Mount," she whispered with a soft sigh when the kiss ended. "Let us not return to Longbourn yet. Once my mother sees you, we will not even have a short moment alone till after the wedding breakfast."

Darcy smiled and led her to his horse. He lifted her up, and the next moment he was in the saddle behind her.

They spoke almost nothing on the ride to their destination, apart from his enquiries whether she was comfortable and her assurances that she was indeed well seated. Darcy was silent as usual, as it was more in his character to speak little. Elizabeth had many concerns she wished to discuss with him, mainly the matter of Lydia and all things connected with it. However, she preferred to wait till they were on the solid ground, for now enjoying the ride with him, his solid frame behind her back, his strong arm hooked around her middle.

Once atop Oakham Mount, as he dismounted and lifted her down from the horse, he did not release her from his embrace for a moment, allowing his horse to stride away to enjoy some fresh grass. He kissed her again, only this time, she felt more of his hunger. With an impatient hand, he untied the big bow beneath her chin and pulled the bonnet down, letting it fall to the ground.

"Lizzy," he murmured as his fingers slid between her tightly pinned curls, loosening a few pins. His other hand cupped her bottom, lifting her to his groin, pressing her to him.

She broke the kiss, and breathed against his mouth. "We are almost in open view."

A deep, frustrated growl escaped from Darcy's chest before he put her down. They stood quietly for a moment, calming down, their breathing returning to normal.

"Are you well?" he asked, cupping her cheek.

She blinked her eyes, focusing her gaze on him, "Do I look unwell?"

He searched her eyes. "You must know what I mean." When she did not speak immediately, he took her hand, picked up her bonnet and led her to a fallen log. "Is there anything you want to tell me?"

Elizabeth sat down, looking at him steadily. She knew what he was asking about. "I am late. About ten days."

His face broke into a rare grin as he sat next to her. "I will be a father then?"

"It is not certain yet." She gave him an earnest look. "I do not want you to blow your hopes for something that may not be. I remember when I stayed with the Gardiners in London a few years ago, keeping my aunt company when uncle was away on some extended business trip. Aunt carried her youngest at the time. She was sleepy, tired, lacked appetite, and was often sick. I have no such symptoms."

He took her hand. "I think it is too early yet for you to feel like that."

She frowned. "I am not sure what I should feel now, but I cannot quite believe that I am indeed with child. I always thought that a woman should know it somehow."

"I am sure it will come with time. I am very happy." He squeezed her hand gently. "Not only will you be my wife in less than a week, but we will have a child."

She searched his eyes. "What will people say when they see the baby comes too soon?"

"It will only be a month early," he dismissed her worry.

She shook her head. "Five weeks."

"As far as I know, babies are not always perfectly on time. It will be born at Pemberley next spring. We can wait to send the information about its birth to your family for a few weeks. In Derbyshire, no one will dare to say anything, such cases are not so uncommon there. Do not worry about a thing. It is not good in your state."

She rested her head on his arm. He seemed so happy, and she... She still could not believe in this child. Should she not feel the same as he? What was wrong with her?

"I want to thank you for everything you did for Lydia," she said, wanting to change the subject.

He frowned.

"I know it was you who found them and managed everything, bought Wickham's commission, paid his debts."

"Who told you that?" he sounded displeased.

"Papa."

He rose and strolled away from her, stopping by the edge with his back to her. "I specifically asked Mr. Bennet and the Gardiners not to tell you all the details."

She walked to him. "Why? Should I not know?"

He glanced at her over his shoulder. "Elizabeth, I do not wish for you to think that you should be indebted to me."

"But I am indebted," she pressed her hand to his arm. "All I want to do is thank you on behalf of my family and..."

"Shush." He turned to her and put a finger on her lips, silencing her. "I did it only for you, but I do not want to discuss it."

His eyes told her he was adamant about it. She had to respect his decision. "As you wish," she agreed quietly.

***

Lord and Lady Matlock proved to be much more polite than anyone at Longbourn could have perceived. They were invited to dine at Longbourn two days before the wedding.

After Lady Catherine's violent visit, the family involuntarily braced themselves for something equally intense, and very grand. What they saw was a small lady, and a gray haired gentleman, both quiet and rather unimpressive, hardly demanding, calm and very much restrained in their manners.

Mrs. Bennet was so much in awe of her noble guests, and the fact that the countess particularly praised her drawing room, that she kept mostly silent; to Elizabeth's great relief.

After dinner Lord Matlock, Darcy, Bingley and Mr. Bennet went to the library for a drink and a cigar. In the parlour, Lady Matlock invited Elizabeth to sit next to her.

"Miss Elizabeth, my younger son has spoken much you," Lady Matlock said with a warm smile. "Last spring he told me he met a most delightful young lady in Kent."

"Colonel Fitzwilliam is very good company," Elizabeth smiled, remembering Darcy's amiable cousin. "There is an honesty and sincerity about him, in his eyes, his expression. He can carry a good conversation like no one other I know."

Lady Matlock nodded. "Richard is a good boy." There was an unmistakable pride in her voice. "The same as my elder son, Edward. His life has been complicated in the
recent years, but none of it was his fault," she added ardently.

Elizabeth nodded with a compassionate smile. "Of course."

She observed as the woman's face, visibly saddened. She was not sure whether she should breach the subject of little James Fitzwilliam, the ladyship's first and only grandson.

Her dilemma was resolved by Lady Matlock herself. "My eldest son became a father not so long ago."

Elizabeth smile widened. "Yes, I am aware of that. Mr. Darcy mentioned it to me."

"My son and his...the mother of his son asked me to thank you for the crib they received. Mr. Darcy wrote in a letter to them that it was you who chose it."

"Yes, Mr. Darcy wanted me to advise him what he should sent as a gift for your grandson during my stay in Pemberley this summer. While shopping in Lambton with Miss Darcy, I saw a crib which looked similar to the one my aunt, Mrs. Gardiner, had with her two younger children. She praised it as the best she had ever used. I thought it would be a useful item for the little one and his parents."

"It was and excellent idea, my dear," Lady Matlock seconded her. "My son said that once they put the boy into it, he slept for the entire night without interruption for the first time."

"I am glad. I imagine that your grandson is a delightful infant."

Lady Matlock's face lit up. "Oh, yes, so handsome, and strong. He looks exactly like my boys when they were little."

For the next few minutes, Elizabeth listened as the woman talked about her grandson, how beautiful and smart he was, and how he smiled repeatedly at her the last time she saw him. She listened with a genuine smile on her face, and good humoured, polite expression. At the same time, she kept thinking what this

child's future would be with the stigma of a bastard following him
through life.

***

The evening before her wedding, Elizabeth and Jane packed the
last of her things into a small trunk, kneeling on the floor. They
were mostly little trifles left to the very last minute that Elizabeth
had accumulated over the years; porcelain figurines, boxes with
jewellery, hair accessories and childhood secrets, like shells and
dried flowers. The trunks with Elizabeth's books, her French
incrusted desk (a treasured gift from her grandmother), and most
of her wardrobe, had been sent to Pemberley yesterday. The sisters
were unusually quiet, too aware of the fact that it would be the last
night they slept in this room together.

"I can hardly believe that you will live so far away from us,
Lizzy. We will see you once or perhaps twice a year if we are
lucky," Jane noted wistfully after a while.

"Jane, you know you can visit me any time you wish."

Jane gave her an earnest smile. "You will have your own family
now, a husband, and surely children."

"I will always find time for you," Elizabeth spoke with
conviction.

"You will be occupied with your new life now, Lizzy. Know
that I am happy for you, but I can see how lonely I will be here
without you." The tears pooled in Jane's wide blue eyes.

Elizabeth touched her cheek. "Jane, please do not say so, or I
will cry as well. Tomorrow I will look a fright with red brimmed
eyes, and Mr. Darcy will run away from me before saying I do."
Her attempt to joke turned flat, even to her own ears.

Jane dried her eyes with the back of her hand. "I am sorry,
Lizzy, I do not want to upset you. I was thinking that perhaps I
could live with the Gardiners for some time. I heard Aunt saying
that she is considering hiring a governess for the children. I could
take that position. I know them and love them. I would not take the
money, of course. It is enough if they allow me to live with them. I
will feel needed."

Elizabeth stared at her with little comprehension for a long
moment. "Jane, what are you talking about?" she finally cried.
"What about Mr. Bingley?"

Jane shrugged. "What about him?"

The younger sister gaped at the older one in astonishment. "Well... I am quite sure that he will propose soon. Everyone expects it. Once married to him, you could convince him to terminate the lease of Netherfield. You could move north, and perhaps one day we will live close together. Surely, you do not wish to live so close to Mama forever. Convincing Mr. Bingley to buy an estate in the north seems quite rational when asking Mr. Darcy to relocate to the south is out of question, we both know that. Not everything is lost." Elizabeth touched Jane's arm. "Perhaps we shall be neighbours in the future, visiting each other almost every day."

Jane shook her head. "I do not think that this will happen, Lizzy. I mean, me marrying Mr. Bingley, not us living close by, which I would dearly wish for."

"You do not love him?"

Jane turned her gaze away. "I was in love with him once. Since then, however, my feelings have changed."

"You hold it against him that he departed when the news about Lydia broke," Elizabeth guessed. "But you told me that he explained himself, that he needed to visit his uncle in Scarborough."

Jane's delicate eyebrows knitted together on her smooth forehead. "I am not sure of him, Lizzy. I feel I cannot count on him like you can on Mr. Darcy. Marriage to a man you do not love is one thing, but marrying someone you know that you cannot rely on is even worse, I believe."

A knock on the door interrupted their conversation. Mrs. Bennet entered.

"Lizzy, you are still packing? You should go to bed, girl, there is an exhausting day before you tomorrow. You need your strength," Mrs. Bennet nagged in her usual grumpy tone.

Jane rose from the carpet. "Yes, Mama."

Mrs. Bennet cleared her throat as she looked at her eldest. "Jane, could you please leave as alone for a short time?" she asked, and then added quickly, "A quarter of an hour will be quite enough."

"Of course, Mama."

"I must talk with your sister about her marriage duties," Mrs. Bennet announced solemnly in a grave tone.

Jane turned to Elizabeth so Mrs. Bennet could not see her face, and winked at her younger sister before leaving the room.

Mrs. Bennet sat stiffly on the edge of Jane's bed, her back perfectly straight, shoulders squared. "I think you know what I want to talk about, Elizabeth."

"Yes, Mama," Elizabeth murmured.

The woman nodded curtly. "Good. I will ask you to listen and not interrupt me till I finish. It is not easy to talk about such matters with my daughter, believe me, but it is my duty as a mother, and I will abide it." She took a deep breath. "Tomorrow your husband will visit you in your bedroom, and take his rights. He will perform a similar act to what animals do to procreate. You must have seen what animals do in the farmyard to have calves, kittens and puppies. He will reach for you, lay down on you, open your legs and enter you where you secret place is. The first time it will hurt you terribly, and you will have no pleasure out of it, and you will bleed. I bled for a long time, like a slaughtered animal almost."

Elizabeth blushed heavily, remembering what had happened to her, but she tried to keep a neutral expression, not to give her mother any suspicions. Thankfully Mrs. Bennet did not look directly at her.

"I advise you to cover the bed with something so as not to ruin the mattress, and the silk sheets that Mr. Darcy surely has in his home," her mother continued. "I think it will be quite similar with you, as you have clearly inherited my body build. You should ease your husband's worry that the bleeding is a one time experience. Your father was rather terrified when it occurred. I never bled later, so I do not perceive you will. Though the first time may seem horrible, you will surely find the entire experience pleasurable after some time. As Mr. Darcy genuinely loves you, a blind one would notice that, he will take an effort to please you. Do you understand so far what I am saying, girl?" Mrs. Bennet asked sharply.

"Yes, Mama," Elizabeth said through a squeezed throat.

"You should be prepared that your husband will want you every night, and sometimes even during the daytime. As you have no dowry or great connections, we can safely assume that his desire for you was what drove him into proposing. You should not push him away." The woman stressed. "He will be happier, more content, and most importantly, kinder to you if you let him to have his way, and show him your enjoyment from the act. He will love you more and be more willing to listen to you on the matters concerning your life together, including the financial decisions, his businesses and running the estate."

Mrs. Bennet took a break then. Elizabeth walked to the small table and poured her a glass of water.

"Thank you," the woman said with a smile as she drank thirstily.

"After you bear him several children, you will feel you do not wish to be close with him so often. It is quite natural, and you should not be surprised by such a reaction. You may also want to banish him from your bedroom completely. But I will not advise that. A man's way of understanding is very simple, and he may think that you simply do not care for him any more if you do not want him in your bed. Your marriage may suffer then. Desire in men is stronger than in women, and you, as his wife, should answer it. He gives you security, respectability, children and a beautiful home, all that a woman can hope for in life, and you on your behalf, should ease his need from time to time at least. I know you too well, Lizzy, to think that you would wish for your husband to take a lover to replace you in that role. Besides, Mr. Darcy is too decent a man to do that, the same as your father. In other words, you should prepare yourself for long years spent in his arms, in his bed, making yourself available to him."

Mrs. Bennet finished and stared at Elizabeth, "Well, do you have any questions?" she asked impatiently.

"No."

"Very well." Mrs. Bennet rose and walked to her. "Good night then. Rest well." She kissed the top of Elizabeth's head and hastily left the room.

Chapter Twenty

"Lizzy, sweetheart," Darcy nudged the sleeping woman gently off his chest. "We are about to reach London."

She did not react, only buried deeper into him. He allowed her to sleep for a few minutes more. However, when they entered the busy streets of Town, he nudged her again, speaking to her softly, asking her to open her eyes. He observed as her impossibly long eyelashes batted against her rosy cheeks to reveal dark green, now misty eyes.

"We are on the outskirts of London," he repeated.

She stretched, stifling a yawn. "So soon?"

"No, right on time. Even a bit slower than usual, as it rained for the last two days, and the roads are not what they should be. You slept soundly, despite the bumps on the road."

She was still rubbing her eyes and yawning. "I am sorry. I was a poor companion."

"I felt happy enough with having you in my arms, watching you sleep. But you must be tired, love," he noted with concern.

She had fallen asleep almost the same moment he sat her beside him in his spacious carriage, wrapping his arm around her shoulders.

She reached for her bonnet, which he had removed to make her comfortable. "Those last weeks were exhausting, all the preparations, and before that worrying about Lydia. Moreover, I could not sleep at all last night. I managed two hours before dawn."

"Were you scared of the wedding day?" he asked half jestingly.

She shook her head with a smile. "No, it was not because of the wedding. I had a long conversation with Jane the evening before, which gave me a lot to think about. Moreover, Mama came to my room as well to enlighten me as to my marriage duties, you know, the part about the marriage bed."

Darcy winced. "I can only imagine what she said to you. Your mother has a tendency to exaggerate."

"To tell the truth, it was not that bad. She was honest and truly tried to help me. Her intentions were the best. However, I must say that if the situation between us was different, and I had not already known what to expect, what she said could be disturbing, even frightening."

Darcy looked at her with such an expression, both puzzled and unreadable, that she assumed that he did not want to really hear the details.

"The most important piece of information I learned for now is that there should not be any bleeding the second time."

"Was she sure of that?"

"Quite sure. She said I would probably bleed a lot the first time, but never after that."

"That is a relief indeed. I planned to postpone any further intimacy between us till we learned more about what happened the first time. Last month was so busy that I hardly had time to think where I could look for advice on such a delicate matter."

He pulled her into his arms. "I will ask to have dinner brought to our rooms, and we will go upstairs. I cannot wait to be with you."

"It is not yet evening. What will the servants say?"

"I do not care."

She smiled and snuggled closer, watching the busy streets of London through the window.

***

They were both in their night attire already, out of the restricting travelling clothes, refreshed with their separate baths they had taken after arrival at the Darcy townhouse. Dinner was served in the small sitting room next to the Mistress' bedroom. Darcy was hungry, both for food and his wife. He decided it was wise to first satisfy his empty stomach, before dealing with more carnal desires. He always had a good appetite, even as a child, not to mention a young lad when he had seemed to grow foot a year. Today was not different, he was famished, as he had eaten very little at the wedding breakfast. He had prepared himself mentally for the possibility of spending his wedding night with Elizabeth in his arms, but not being able to love her completely. Thankfully there seemed not to be such need. His mother-in-law had turned out to be quite useful for a change. While munching on his roast beef, he stared at his wife's breasts, mostly uncovered by the deep V of her robe.

"Is the food not to your satisfaction?" Darcy asked, noticing that Elizabeth was only moving the bits of meat and vegetable from one place to the other with her fork.

"No, no, it is all delicious," she assured, and put the tiniest piece of potato into her mouth, chewing slowly.

Soon she dabbed her lips with a napkin, gaining a new glare from Darcy.

"Do not tell me that you are finished? You barely touched it. Have you eaten anything today?"

She wrapped her arms around her middle. "Mama tried to force some bread and white cheese into me early in the morning, but I vomited everything when she left the room."

"Why have you not told me that you are ill?" he demanded angrily.

She smiled gently. "I am not ill. Only with child, it seems. It is rather normal in my condition, I understand, to have little appetite at the beginning of confinement."

He looked at her with concern. "Still, you need to sustain yourself and the baby. You must eat."

"But not today, please. I am not hungry, please do not force me."

Darcy gave her a stern look, but did not insist. He would have to see from tomorrow morning that she ate properly.

She did not touch more food, but she kept his company through the meal, sitting opposite him, with a smile on her face. However, every time he looked at her, she seemed more and more absent, almost dozing off. He hurried to consume the rest of his food, which was not his custom, afraid that she would fall asleep right on the chair before he managed to get her into bed. Finally, as he saw her eyelids drop several times, he pushed his plate away, leaving a good chunk of meat untouched.

"I will be back with you in a minute," he assured as he cupped her face and kissed her high forehead. "Do not move from here."

He dashed to his dressing room to clean his teeth, and relieve his bladder. When he finished refreshing, he nearly ran through his darkened bedroom back to the sitting room, afraid she had already managed to drift away into the embrace of Morpheus.

His fears doubled when he saw the sitting room empty, the rest of the food neatly covered with lids, ready to be taken away by the servant, the candles put down.

"I am here," he heard her sweet, uplifted voice from the direction of his bedroom. He stepped back blindly.

She sat in the middle of his bed, naked obviously, clenching the sheets to her bosom, her dark locks tumbling down her delicate arms.

"You have overlooked me," she complained, pouting.

"No... it is just..." he stuttered, overwhelmed with the vision of her in his bed. "I did not quite expect you here..."

She laid back and lifted the covers, inviting him in.

Darcy nearly tore at his robe and shirt, throwing them on the ground. As he sat on the edge of the bed, he felt her arms wrapping around him from behind, her warm, soft breasts mashing against his back.

His fingers were suddenly like wood, refusing to cooperate in the simple task of opening the flap on his breeches.

"Should I help you?" she murmured sleepily, her hands stroking their way down from his shoulders to his waist.

"I will manage," he grunted, finally pushing his breeches successfully down his legs.

"Now, Mrs. Darcy," he said as he joined her under the covers, pulling her close.

He simply held her in his embrace for a long moment, thinking how he had missed her constantly since the night she had come to him. Now that they were married, there would be no more separations, no lonely nights.

"I have missed you," he murmured, kissing the path from her neck down her bosom.

He touched his cheek to her breast, and closed his eyes for a moment. She felt her fingers combing through his hair.

"You are so sweet, so perfect," he cupped her breast, playing with the puffy nipple. "You have the most beautiful breasts in England, and they are all mine." He kneaded one mound.

"You are surprisingly talkative at night time, it seems," she noted teasingly.

He shifted on his arm above her to look into her smiling eyes. "I talk where there is something to discuss."

She rolled her eyes. "Like my bosom?"

"Not only that; there is also your hair." He kissed a curl over her forehead, and moved lower. "Your eyes... your neck... your ..." he shifted lower, "...your belly."

She giggled as he placed wet kisses on her waist.

He pushed her on her side, with her back to him. "Your delightful behind," he blew a noisy raspberry on the mentioned part of her body. But before she could react to that, he brought her back into the cradle of his arms, his eyes staring into hers.

"And of course..." his hand went down between her legs which parted obediently, "Your sweet, tight, little..." the rest he whispered in her ear.

Darcy observed with satisfaction as the intense blush spread from her already rosy face down her body.

"My, my, Mr. Darcy. I did not quite expect such a language coming from your lips," she said sternly, trying to somehow cover her discomposure. She hooked her thigh over his lean hips, her hand stroked down his chest, and she gazed at him from behind her eyelashes. "I must say that I am becoming rather impatient with your current lenient attitude towards your husbandly duty."

"You impertinent minx!" he cried, pinning her to the bed. "Here I am, trying to relax you, make you comfortable, and not throw myself at you like some brute, and you call my attitude lenient."

She grinned, and cocked one eyebrow up. "I only tried to induce you into some more serious action."

He captured her small wrists on both sides of her head. "You will pay for this." He frowned his most imposing scowl. "You will beg for mercy." He informed her menacingly.

To his great satisfaction, after kissing and stroking every inch of her skin, and spending a good half hour between her legs, he heard, "No more, please, no more."

She tugged at his hair with both hands, trying to dislodge him from between her open thighs, now glistening with her own juices. "Please no more, William. I beg you. I will not survive this any more."

He put his ear to her heart; it was beating wildly. He locked her in his embrace, and waited till she calmed down.

197

"Lizzy." He cupped her face when he felt that her heartbeat had returned to normal. "You must tell me whether it will pain you now."

"Do not worry, I shall be fine," she murmured, her half open eyes shining with something intensive; tenderness if he read her expression properly.

He sighed, pulled her to his chest, his hand reaching directly between her legs. He pushed one finger easily. "Does it hurt?"

"No."

He slowly pushed another finger. "And this?"

"No."

So far so good. He began slipping the third finger, but she flinched so he retreated. How was he supposed to that, if more than two fingers were too much for her? He was undoubtedly thicker, not to mention longer than that, especially when aroused.

He pulled out his hand, his fingers glistened with her moisture, but thankfully there was no blood.

He kissed her lips. "We must stretch you a bit, love."

He slipped back two fingers and started pushing them apart inside her, at the same time rubbing interchangeably with circling the tiny nub above her opening with his thumb. He did that until she had her pleasure again, her inner muscles tightening rhythmically around his fingers, soft cries coming from her parted lips.

When she quietened down, he rolled over her, careful not to give her too much of his weight. He raised himself, supported on his arm, so he could watch her face in the light coming from the fire. He bent her knee, to see better, and pushed himself slowly inside.

Her eyes opened and she smiled at him, a most beautiful smile. "Come here." She locked his hips between her legs, pushing him much deeper. Her mesmerizing eyes stared into his. "Let go," she breathed. "I am not made of glass."

With a growl of surrender, he lowered down on her, crashing her into the bed. He felt her hands, stroking down his back, and her bottom moving up to meet him.

"So good..." he murmured as he began moving slowly. He had no intention of losing control like the last time. He must have hurt her, though she had never complained. He measured his thrusts, not allowing himself to give in completely. He noticed that she flinched again when he pushed deeper, so he kept the penetration shallow.

She attempted to move with him, but it only made everything worse; multiplied his pleasure, made it harder to control himself and be gentle. When he felt his release close, his control broke and with a few last thrusts, he drove to the very end, before spilling into her.

He rolled on his back, bringing her with him, their bodies still connected.

She was completely silent as he recuperated.

"Elizabeth?" he asked, glancing down at her, taking her hair out of the way to see her face. She was sleeping, her breathing even.

Carefully, he pushed her limp body off him, regretfully slipping out of her. He would have loved to have another coupling with her, but she was clearly too tired for anything more that night. He drew the sheet over her, so she would not feel cold. He padded to his dressing room with the intention of wetting the towel to clean her. When he returned, she lay curled on her side, most of the covers taken with her, tumbling above her small body so only the peak of head was visible.

He threw the towel over the chair dismissively. He did not want to interrupt her sleep. If she was comfortable enough to fall asleep, he would not bother her with cleaning up. As he climbed back into bed, he scooted behind her, pulling at the sheet to cover himself. She was warm and soft, and he soon registered the rising of his manhood against the cleft of her plump bottom.

He was not really tired, the lovemaking had only invigorated him. It was still only eight o'clock in the evening, too early for bed. He wanted her again very much, but willing, and more importantly, participating.

When the clock struck nine, he closed his eyes, determined to fall asleep. He thought to be almost successful, when she murmured something in her sleep, and the next moment a small, very cold foot kicked him squarely on the front of his shin.

He cursed involuntarily at the piercing pain, that reminded him of the last time his cousin Richard kicked him when they fought over something as boys. She had a strong kick, probably from all the walking she performed daily, not unlike Richard's, he had to admit.

Massaging his leg, he separated from her cautiously. She had not been in a kicking mood the last time they had slept together.

Than he realized how late at night it had been then, and that she must have escaped to her room soon after he had fallen asleep, leaving the letter for him on the pillow. With the pain in his leg diminished, he laid on his back, a good two feet away from her. Surely, she could not reach him from such a distance.

He was on the verge of sleep again, when he heard her murmuring something again. She flipped on her back, and then rolled to him across the bed, scooting nearby. With a sigh, he pulled her closer, wrapping his arm around her, her head tucked on his chest.

He woke twice during that night, being kicked twice more. Fortunately she spared the most vulnerable areas.

Chapter Twenty-One

Darcy had been a married man for full three days. He remembered this period as constant bliss, and he dearly hoped it did not show on his face. The acquaintances and servants would not have recognised him, grinning like a fool. Since his wedding, he had not even once checked on his correspondence or business matters. All he concentrated on was spending time with his wife, which mostly meant making love to his wife. As Elizabeth insisted they needed to practice a lot to improve on the mechanics due to the differences in their height and sizes, he joyfully supported her on that with his whole heart. He only worried about her because she seemed uncommonly tired. She slept late in the morning, which he knew that was not her custom before, and took long naps during a day. The baby had to be the cause of such an effect on her, and he dearly hoped it was something natural and expected in her condition..

After three days spent entirely at home, the newlywed couple decided to take an open carriage to the park, and take a walk to admire the autumn colours in full bloom. Next, Darcy wanted to stop in a familiar bookshop to collect some previously ordered book on sheep husbandry.

On their way to the bookshop, they stopped in front of an elegant store with all sorts of lady's accessories.

"We must think about buying something for Georgiana," Elizabeth said as she stared with enchanted eyes at the window display.

Darcy smirked as he glanced at her beaming face, her eyes devouring the articles in front of them. He had once thought that

Elizabeth was above all the temptations of shops full of most fashionable attire, but seeing her present expression, he knew he had been wrong. She might have been a bit more subtle about it, she did not pull at his arm like Georgiana, bouncing up and down, pointing with her little finger, *Oh, Brother can we go there, can we see that, it is so pretty...*

"I do not know what else we could possibly get her. She has everything, I dare say," he noted severely. Georgiana had returned to Derbyshire together with the Matlocks, the day after the wedding.

"William, she will feel neglected if we do not remember her," Elizabeth said with feeling.

"Then what do you suggest we could buy for her?" he asked, resigned.

"A new bonnet or a reticule always improved the girl's spirits."

Darcy glared at her without much comprehension.

"Does your mood not improve when you buy yourself a new top hat?" she asked.

He gave her an offended look. "No, it does not. It is just a head covering. I buy a new one when the previous one is worn down," he grunted.

She burst into a short laugh, followed by another and another.

He narrowed his eyes at her. "You are such a tease, making sport of me all the time."

She rolled her eyes. "You are still far too serious. I am going to teach you out of it."

He opened his mouth to respond when he heard his name cried from not far.

"Darcy!"

He looked up to see an old university acquaintance with his younger brother, if he was correct, marching towards them. He was not delighted with that; he had no desire to introduce Elizabeth to strangers at the moment, sharing her attention with them.

"What are doing in London, Darcy?" Marcus Livingstone cried. "We see you in town so rarely, and I dare say never this time of the year."

"You are quite right, Livingstone," Darcy responded sternly. "We are just passing through, and permanently relocating to Pemberley next week."

The man seemed not to listen him, only staring, down at Elizabeth.

"Will you not introduce, us? I guess this is Mrs. Darcy. We read about your wedding in the newspaper. You have no idea how many young, and quite mature ladies too, cried themselves to sleep after hearing such news. Fitzwilliam Darcy swept out of the marriage market. What a tragedy!"

Darcy gave him a hard look, before moving his eyes to Elizabeth, his expression softening.

"Elizabeth, this is Sir Marcus Livingstone, and his younger brother, Percival."

Elizabeth performed a perfect curtsey.

Livingstone bowed deeply. "We are enchanted, madam."

"*Enchante,*" the younger Mr. Livingstone murmured.

"I know Sir Marcus from university." Darcy explained, not at all liking the rude way the both men stared at his wife.

Elizabeth smiled, her most lovely smile, her eyes sparkling, and instantly, both men smiled back. "Indeed, from Oxford? Then you must know Mr. Charles Bingley."

Livingstone nodded. "Of course we know Bingley. Are you well acquainted with him, Mrs. Darcy?"

"Bingley is currently courting one of Mrs. Darcy's sisters." Darcy answered for her.

Livingstone glanced back at Elizabeth. "I cannot blame him," he murmured.

"How many sisters do you have, Mrs. Darcy?" Percival wanted to know.

"Four, but one is married, the other almost engaged, and the two left are still very young," Darcy barked.

Livingstone laughed. "Does your husband always answer for you, Mrs. Darcy?"

Elizabeth smiled, looking up at Darcy warmly. "Only when he feels protective about me."

Livingstone did not quite know what to answer to that, so he changed the subject. "By the end of the next week, my wife is planning a small private ball in our townhouse. You must come. She will be delighted to host the new Mrs. Darcy."

"We thank you for the invitation, Livingstone, but we will be on our way north by the end of the next week." Darcy said quickly, but then felt Elizabeth pulling at his arm. He looked down at her.

She stared at him, her big eyes pleading.

"Do you want to go?" he asked gently.

She bit her lower lip and smiled at him.

Darcy sighed and returned his attention to the men. "I think we can postpone our journey a couple of days to attend."

"Excellent, excellent!" Livingstone cried. "I will talk with Lady Livingstone to send the formal invitation for you yet today."

"If it is no trouble, of course." Elizabeth added sweetly.

Livingstone bowed again. "We shall be delighted to have you, Mrs. Darcy."

Elizabeth smiled at him, before looking up at her husband. "I dare say you wish to talk with your friends without female company. I will look for a gift for Georgiana and wait for you there." She pointed with her eyes at the store nearby. "Gentlemen." She curtseyed again, before releasing Darcy's arm and walking away.

Three pairs of eyes followed her, especially Darcy's, as he looked after her till she safely entered the shop.

"Where did you find her?" Livingstone asked when Elizabeth was out of earshot.

"I heard Hertfordshire," his brother answered.

"That is correct. Mrs. Darcy's father's estate is in Hertfordshire," Darcy confirmed formally.

"I congratulate you," Livingstone said. "She is very pretty, not a classical beauty perhaps, but those eyes, remarkable."

"And intelligent," Percival added. "She looked as if she was laughing at us secretly the entire time."

Darcy pushed his chest up. "Mrs. Darcy is quite unique," he agreed proudly.

"The way she looks at you, Darce. She appears besotted with you," Livingstone noted, giving the other man a kind look.

Darcy fought the temptation not to hug the other man after hearing his welcoming observation of his wife's attachment to himself.

He cleared his throat, changing the subject, speaking in his usual controlled voice. "On exactly what day does Lady Livingstone plan this ball?

***

Darcy was on his way home from meeting with his solicitor. He had decided to walk today in order to have the possibility to think everything through once again.

He was certain he had made a good decision today. He had invested some of his savings into Mr. Gardiner's company. Pemberley provided a good income, but he had to think about the future. Everyone seemed to take an interest in the colonies these days, the West Indies especially, and though he knew little about overseas trade, and found it rather risky due to the constant wars, he trusted Elizabeth's uncle enough not to be afraid of losing his money. The Gardiners might live in Cheapside, close to their warehouses but when he had visited them for the first time because of the unfortunate matter with Lydia, he had been convinced they were considerably well to do people. Mr. Gardiner guaranteed fifteen percent from his investment, but he assured that it could be even doubled.

Darcy did not want one day to find himself in his father-in-law's position, not being able to secure all his children, daughters especially. Boys always had an easier way in life,- he could learn a profession, and undoubtedly have more opportunities than a girl. Mrs. Bennet had borne five healthy children in the short span of eight years. He had to admit one thing, that the woman was physically very fit, and looked youthful for her age. Elizabeth might have favoured her father's dark colouring, and his personality, but she had inherited her mother's constitution and body build. He needed to take into consideration that they would have more children than his parents. De facto, Elizabeth was already expecting a baby. The possibility of having daughters, even as many as five, did not fret him at all; he could always pass Pemberley to one of his grandsons, or a nephew. The vision of several little girls with curls and bright green eyes, running the halls of Pemberley, little copies of Elizabeth, delighted him.

As he entered the Darcy townhouse, he found it very quiet. Perhaps Elizabeth was napping again.

"Where is my wife?" he asked the butler. He felt such an inflow of pride saying the words, *my wife*. He had a wife.

"Mrs. Darcy ordered a carriage shortly after you left this morning," the servant explained.

Darcy frowned. Elizabeth did not mention she had any particular plans for today when they talked over late breakfast. He preferred to know about her trips in town.

"Did Mrs. Darcy mention where she was going?"

The man nodded. "Yes, Master. She received a note from her aunt, I believe. She asked me to tell you that she went to visit Mrs. Gardiner."

"Ah, good. I will be in my study if she returns."

"Should I send tea?"

"No, thank you."

In his study, Darcy sat near the window. He had little desire for dealing with all the correspondence piling on his desk, that he had neglected for the last few days. If Elizabeth had been here, he would have had an excuse not to work today. After all, he was a newlywed, and he should be paying a lot of attention to his wife. She should not feel neglected.

Soon there was a knock on the door.

"Enter," cried almost cheerfully, thinking that Elizabeth had returned.

It was not Elizabeth though, but the housekeeper. "Master, I wish a word if you have time."

Darcy was surprised. He did not expect to need to talk with the housekeeper now that he had a wife. He could not imagine what the woman could want from him that Elizabeth was not able to answer.

Even so, he put a pleasant expression on his face. His father had taught him to treat servants kindly and respectfully. "Yes, please, Mrs. Robertson." He gestured to a chair in front of his large mahogany desk. "Is there a problem?"

The woman sat down. "Yes, Master. I must say it is about Mrs. Darcy."

Darcy's expression clouded. "I do not understand."

"Yesterday, when you were out, she asked me to show her the household account books."

Darcy's frown deepened.

The housekeeper, as if encouraged with his expression, continued, her voice more confident. "She ordered me to change a butcher, calling the one we used too expensive. Then she took away the keys to the cabinet where we keep tea, chocolate and coffee. She went down to the kitchen and talked with cook..."

Darcy lifted his hand. "That is quite enough. Mrs. Robertson."

"But Master," the woman tried again. "We have used the butcher for the last fifteen years at least. Your late mother approved him. The new Mrs. Darcy seems so young, and she is all too... uhm...confident ..."

"How dare you to criticize my wife?" Darcy hissed.

He stood up from his desk and paced the room, trying to control his ire.

"Mrs. Robertson, I always had a high opinion of you, but now I am most amazed with your attitude." His voice was calm, but cold. "My wife has full control over the household and all the home servants, both here in London and in the country. She has my full support and trust. I have enough matters to deal with, and I do not want to be bothered because she changed a butcher. What she says is the same as if I said it. Do we understand each other?"

Mrs. Robertson stared at him for a moment, before lowering her head and murmuring. "Yes, Master."

When the woman was gone, he found it hard to return to his former pleasant mood. He had complete faith in Elizabeth's abilities. Mrs. Bennet had taught her well, he had no doubt of that. She had not even mentioned to him that she had looked through the books. She must have thought it a natural thing to do in her position, not even worth mentioning. He was content and proud that his young wife was confident enough to take a rein over the household without even the smallest hint from him that she should.

Another knock at the door, brought his attention. "What?" he cried impatiently.

Elizabeth stood in the open door, her expression concerned. "William?" She watched him cautiously with her big eyes. He realized he rarely, perhaps never, had spoken to her in his less pleasant voice.

"It is you." His smile returned.

She closed the door and walked to him. "Is something wrong?"

He pulled her in his embrace. "No, love."

Her eyes searched his face. "I can see that something upset you."

"Yes, but it is not important."

"Is it about your meeting with the solicitor? The business with my uncle proved not what you expected, perhaps?"

"No, on the contrary. It is only..."

She walked him to the armchair, pushed him to sit in it, and then settled on his lap.

"Tell me."

"I had a surprising talk with the housekeeper," he relented at last.

Her eyebrows lifted on her high forehead. "Mrs. Robertson?"

"I am not sure whether I should tell you this."

Elizabeth looked at him expectantly.

"She came to complain that you demanded to look through the books."

"You think that I should not do that?" she asked slowly.

"No, of course you should. I am glad that you feel responsible for the household, and appreciate your effort. I am only surprised with Mrs. Roberston. I always had a high opinion of her, and now I am not sure whether we should not look for someone different."

Elizabeth shook her head. "I do not think that would be necessary. She has ruled this house for so many years, she needs some time to get used to this new situation. I am sure that she is not happy that a twenty year old tells her what to do."

Darcy sobered, his voice stern. "You are Mrs. Darcy; her job is to follow your orders and aid you when you ask it. She is the servant – you are the *mistress* of our home."

"William, there is no point in blowing this out of proportion." She tried to soothe him, slipping her hand under his coat to stroke his chest through his shirt. "Nothing bad happened, truly. You settled the matter, and I am sure Mrs. Robertson understood your point, and what happened will not recur."

"But you will tell me if she disobeys you."

"I am sure it will not be necessary. I can deal with it."

He took her hand, and lifted it to his lips. "I have no doubt that you can." He looked at her with enamoured eyes.

His eyes darkened, and he cupped her cheek, but before their lips met, she said.

"You cannot guess what news I bring from Gracechurch Street."

"What news?" he asked distractedly, hooking his arm more securely around her waist, bringing her closer.

"My aunt expect a child. It seems it will be born around the same time as ours."

"They have not wasted their time at Pemberley."

She nodded with sweet smile. "No, they have not."

"Does she know about ...?" he placed his hand on her middle, his face buried into her neck.

She sighed at the sensation of his lips nuzzling her neck. "I have not told her anything, but I think she suspects something."

"Such a perceptive woman your aunt is," Darcy murmured, reaching to the back of her dress.

"Wait," she whispered when he opened the first buttons and the material around her arms began loosening. She slipped from his lap and ran to the door, turning the key in the lock.

As she walked back to him, she opened her dress and took it off, placing it neatly on a nearby chair. Then with a few swift movements, she unsnapped the front clasps of her corset.

His eyes crawled over her body, stopping at her breasts, clearly visible under the near transparent chemise. With an impatient gesture, he reached for her, pulling her back to him. He was surprised when she started wriggling on his lap, till she settled herself astride, in front of him, her legs bent on both sides. Her fingers began fighting with the knots at his cravat. When his neck was uncovered, she attached her lips to it, sucking there. He was surprised, because usually she was not so forward. But his shock was even greater when one small hand moved down to his trousers, stroking him through the material. She had avoided this area so far in their encounters, apart from their very first night at Pemberley.

She looked down between them, and with quick fingers opened the falls. He sprang fully aroused into her small, capable hands, and she stroked him.

"God," he grunted, his head falling back on the headrest of the chair.

He closed his eyes, allowing her hand to caress him. Soon he felt her warm thigh and glanced back at her. Her petticoats gathered up over one arm, she tried to insert the tip into her with a determined expression painted on her face.

"Stop, love," he groaned. "You will hurt yourself."

She bit her lower lip. "I will manage." She put the tip in and slowly lowered herself.

He stroked her hip with concern. "Are you in pain?"

She wiggled her bottom. "No, just stretched," she breathed a sigh of relief. "I think I am slowly getting used to you and how very *tall* you are."

Darcy actually blushed. He brought her closer, and guided her to move up and down him. Soon the ferocity of their ride was too much for the old armchair, his grandfather had bought when he had been furnishing the house, so they moved down to the carpet.

***

"Darcy." Livingstone patted his back, approaching him. "Join us in the library. We are looking for one more partner for cards."

Darcy did not even bother to look at him, his eyes on Elizabeth. "No, thank you," he said distractedly.

Livingstone followed his gaze to the dancing area, where Elizabeth stood with his brother.

"Come on, Darcy. She will be quite safe here. No one will take her from you." He laughed at his own joke.

Darcy honoured him with a heavy glare. "I simply detest cards. You know that."

"You can sit with us then, and have a cigar. You do look kind of silly standing here amongst the women, mothers and widows, watching her like a hawk. They will say she wrapped you around her finger already."

"I never cared what others say about me."

"That is true."

This time Elizabeth walked close by them, giving her husband a beautiful smile.

"Not classical beauty perhaps, but undeniably very pretty, and that figure ..." His voice traced, his gaze resting on Elizabeth's rounded bottom.

Livingstone laughed again at Darcy's scowl directed at him. "If you could see yourself, you have daggers in your eyes, man."

"I would be grateful if you took your attention off my wife's posterior," Darcy grunted coldly.

"Will you warn all the other men dancing with her like that?" Livingstone smirked, before walking away to his wife.

Darcy's eyes glued back to the dancing Elizabeth. No wonder she drew attention, she looked absolutely stunning tonight, with her dark curls shining, eyes sparkling, cheeks rosy. His old habit of staring at her was hard to resist, and now he could give himself to it completely, without guilt. He did not care what others were thinking.

His only doubts were about her dress. It was a new gown, and he had not seen it on her before they had arrived here and he was helping her out of her coat. His mouth had fallen wide open, and all he could do was to stare. The cut was daring indeed, showing her lovely neck and breasts, additionally pushed up by the stays. He was more than sure that Mrs. Bennet had chosen it for Elizabeth. He could not remember if she had ever worn anything cut that low. He liked it on her, how she looked in it, the way it showed her figure to the very best advantage, but certainly he was not so pleased when the other men's eyes stopped too long, not on her face, but lower. He felt pride, and sort of excitement that they could only look, while he was in right to touch wherever he wanted when in private, and most important, see in all glory once they returned home. On the other hand, his inborn possessiveness preferred her to wear such dresses only for him, while for the outside world she would put on something more covered up.

The dance ended, and Percival Livingstone walked Elizabeth back to his side.

"Mrs. Darcy is a most wonderful dancer," the boy exclaimed enthusiastically.

Darcy gave him a cold look through narrowed eyes. "Yes, I am aware of that."

The youth stepped from one foot to another, and then murmuring something, walked away.

"You scared him." Elizabeth complained. "He was good company, and so polite."

Darcy's hand sneaked around her back, stroking her shoulder blade. "Are you having fun?"

"Oh, yes!" she beamed.

"Are you not tired?" he asked, mindful of her state.

"Oh, no. Remember that I slept a good few hours in the afternoon. I do not recall the last time I danced to such well performed music. It had to be at the Netherfield ball."

He smiled. "When we danced together for the first time."

"Yes, and though I did not like you at all back then, I had to admit how well you danced. I do not understand why you danced only once tonight."

"I do not like the activity in particular," he said simply. "I danced the one only because I had such a tempting partner, with dark green eyes and black curls."

"My hair is dark brown, not black." She inclined her head, decorated in ribbons matching her gown, towards his arm. "I thought you would join other gentlemen in the library. I saw our host speaking with you. You must be bored standing here all alone the entire evening."

"I developed a bit of a headache. The smoke from cigars will only worsen it. I preferred to stay here."

He was not exactly lying to her. As a rule, he had a headache whenever he had to attend a ball.

"You do look pale." Her concerned eyes rested on his face. "Do you want to return home?"

He shook his head. "The evening is far from over, and you surely want to dance a couple more dances."

"I danced enough, and I cannot allow you to suffer. It is well past midnight, our hosts will not be offended if we leave now."

"Are you sure?"

She nodded. "I will go and tell Lady Livingstone that we are leaving."

Once outside, as they waited for the carriage, he proposed. "Let us walk. It is only one block away."

He sent the carriage home and made sure she was well bundled up. "Where is your shawl?" he asked.

"I left it in the carriage."

He sighed, took off his own white scarf, and wound it around her neck several times. "It is October," he explained, "The nights are cold."

"Will you not be cold?" she asked.

He only snorted at such assumption.

Once home, they walked straight upstairs. Elizabeth sent Darcy's valet away. She sat him on the bed and helped to remove his clothes.

When he was dressed down to his breeches and shirt, she touched her lips to his forehead. "It is cool, you have no fever."

"But I am still not feeling well," he complained. "Though I do know one way to ease my suffering," he murmured, and before she could utter a sound, he pulled her on the bed right under him.

"I thought you felt unwell!" she cried when he released her lips from a deep kiss.

"I am much better now," he murmured into her neck.

"You tricked me!" She pounded his back with a small fist. "I was worried about you."

"Do not be angry." He kissed her lips. "I wanted to be alone with you."

He made a puppy face.

"You could have said the truth, not making me think you were sick!"

"I am sorry. Next time I will tell you straightforwardly that I want to bed you." He gazed into her face. "You are so pretty when you are angry. Do you know that?"

"Insufferable man!" she cried, but allowed his kisses.

Darcy hooked his fingers on the edge of her bodice, and with one easy move, tore it down. He smiled with satisfaction, now she would never wear it again.

"What have you done?" she cried, as she pushed him off her and sat up. "You ruined it." She stared at the tattered silk, embroidered in gold with tiny flowers. "It is beyond repair now! My very best gown. What will Mama say when she knows about that? She chose it for me herself."

"Elizabeth, you are married, and your mother will not learn about it," Darcy pointed out reasonably. "I will buy you two nicer ones in place of this one." *Only not so low cut,* he added in his thoughts.

She made a grumpy face. "I liked this very well, thank you."

He began unsnapping her stays. "Lizzy, I want you."

"You could have waited till I removed my dress," she cried angrily.

"No, I could not have waited." He kissed her again, taking her hand and moving it down to his groin.

She sighed with resignation, rolling her eyes. "When you put something into this thick head of yours..." she murmured.

"Shush." He closed her mouth with his, covering her completely with his large body.

Chapter Twenty-Two

"Lizzy, wake up." Darcy pulled the blanket down, revealing the curly head. "Lizzy." He shook her arm.

As there was no visible reaction, he kissed her ear. "Wake up, sleepyhead. Wake up, wake up."

Her eyes opened slowly. "So early," she murmured and glanced at the window. "Still dark." She turned on her side, and pulled the sheet over her head.

Darcy tugged the sheet down to her waist, uncovering her naked upper body. "We are going to Pemberley today." He kissed her creamy arm, "We need to depart as early as possible."

She sat up with a sigh, rubbing her cobwebbed eyes. Involuntarily his gaze was drawn to her exposed breasts, her pink nipples relaxed from sleep

"Come, lift your arms." He reached for a nightgown, and put it on her. "Your maid is waiting with breakfast."

She opened her eyes wider. "You are already dressed."

"Yes, and I have already had breakfast. I did not want to wake you until the very last moment." He put on her slippers and pulled her out of bed and onto her feet. "I need to go down now and see if everything has been done as they should. Remember to eat your breakfast, not just nibble."

"You know that I have no appetite. I feel so sick in the morning," she complained.

"I know, love." He pulled her to him in a comforting embrace. "But we must depart today. Once at home, at Pemberley you will rest."

He strode across the room to open the door. "Martha, Mistress is ready."

The maid entered with a tray with food.

"I shall see you downstairs," he said and left the room.

Three quarters of an hour later, Elizabeth walked out of house. Due to the early morning hour, the street was completely empty. Low mists surrounded the trees in the square on the other side of the road.

Darcy walked to her. "Warm enough?" he asked.

She nodded. "Yes." She had her new coat on, and a green velvet bonnet, which matched her reticule and leather gloves.

Darcy helped her inside the carriage, and without further delay, they departed.

Elizabeth took her place next to the window, as was her custom, but she did not look out of it. Her hands wrapped around her middle, her back slanting. Darcy shifted closer.

"You are not feeling well," he noted with concern.

She nodded, and rested her head on his shoulder.

His arm wrapped protectively around her. "I wish I could take this discomfort away from you somehow."

She chuckled. "You know that you cannot. Women carry babies, not the other way round. Besides, you are so patient, putting up with my constant whining, complaining, and grumping that you should be given a reward for that."

"You are my reward."

She exhaled a long breath and looked up at him. "When you say such things to me, I think that a woman would have to be made of stone not to fall in love with you."

"I do not like to return to those times, but you were quite resistant at first," he pointed out dryly.

She glared at him. "It was your own fault."

Darcy's expression fell and he looked away. He did not like to remember that he had been so close to losing her because of his own arrogance and pride.

"Forgive me." She tugged at his sleeve so he looked at her. "I should not have returned to that."

"You are perfectly right," he said harshly. "I treated you abominably."

"No, you did not," she argued. "I was a bit oversensitive at times." She admitted slowly, "I tend to overreact sometimes, and blew some things out of proportion."

Darcy raised one eyebrow; he did not expect such an honest evaluation of her own character on her part.

"I did not know you at all in the past," she continued. "You can be so hard to read sometimes, to strangers especially, so intimidating."

"Intimidating?" he stared at her in disbelief. "I did not notice that you were particularly intimidated by me."

She rolled her eyes. "I meant to say that now I understand that this stern attitude you tend to display is just your own way of protecting yourself and your family against the outside world."

He gathered her closer. "My wise, Lizzy."

During their conversation, the views outside the window changed, from cobblestoned streets of London to more rural settings.

Elizabeth pushed away from him, suddenly, as her face turned green. "Tell them to stop the carriage," whispered.

One look at her, and he knew what was coming. He hit the roof with a fist, and cried through the window for the driver to stop.

As soon as the carriage came to a halt, Elizabeth pushed the door open and jumped down. Darcy followed close behind her, and wrapped his arms around her as she emptied the content of her stomach straight on the road, bent in half.

The driver climbed down from his place to calm the horses after such a sudden stop. He and the other servant looked at each other, exchanging the knowing glances. They had little doubt that Master had wasted no time, and there would be a baby Darcy in the spring.

Darcy took some water from the servant, wetted his handkerchief and cleaned Elizabeth's mouth. "Can we go? Are you feeling better now?" he asked, looking into her ghostly pale countenance.

She nodded, and even managed a pale smile.

Once in the carriage, he removed her bonnet and soiled dirty gloves, and threw them out the window. He rubbed her cold hands with his warm ones.

"I think it should be better now that I have purged all that I had for breakfast," she moaned.

He kissed her forehead. "I should not have forced food into you."

"Your intentions were good. I know you are worried that I do not eat as I should," she whispered, her eyes dropping.

He tucked her against him, her head under his chin. He put her hands inside his coat to warm them. "I will buy you new warm gloves once we stop to change the horses. Now, try to nap."

***

When close to the evening, they stopped in a small town the size of Meryton, where they planned to spend a night, Elizabeth was on her last legs. The bumps on the road did not agree with her and she felt sick most of the time. She did not complain, but Darcy could not bear to look at her miserable, pale face. He even considered even interrupting their journey, but then he knew that they had to reach Pemberley, the sooner the better. There she would be able to rest in comfort.

He was happy that she ate a bit more for a dinner, though he could see that she did that mostly for him. He left her alone for a moment to check on his people, and when he returned, he found her already dressed in her nightclothes, her hair let free down her back. She stood near the bed, bent down, hand on her stomach.

"Feeling sick again?" he asked with concern, standing behind her.

"No..." She touched her stomach, and lowered down to her knees. "There is something wrong."

"Wrong?" he knelt in front of her.

"I have got cramps." She bit her lip so hard it turned white. "There is something wrong..."

"Come." He scooped her in his arms, and sat her on the bed.

She curled on her side, her face twisted.

Darcy tucked her hair away from her face. "Lizzy, what is going on?"

Her arms wrapped around her middle, she moaned, before her face relaxed, the lines of pain gone. Slowly, she sat up, opened her legs and raised the nightgown. There was some blood, it was dark and thick, with clots here and there.

"What is happening? she whispered, staring at the bloody stains on the white cotton of her nightgown.

Darcy stared at it too, only he did know what happened. He had been ten back then, before Georgiana had been born. He had accompanied his mother on a walk around the lake at Pemberley, when she had sat heavily on the grass, holding her stomach the same as Elizabeth did. She had told him to bring his father as she had felt unwell. He had remembered how scared he had been, running to find him. Father had carried mother to the house, and she had been ill for several days, not leaving the bed. Then he had heard the servants speaking that Mistress lost a baby.

"I will call the doctor." He pulled the nightgown down, and covered her with a blanket.

Her eyes widened. "Doctor?"

"Just to check, love. Stay here and do not move. I will be back soon. The inn's owner surely knows the local doctor."

"William?" She swallowed, looking up at him. "I am scared. What is going on?"

He managed a smile, and kissed the top of her head. "Do not fret." He managed through his tight throat. "I will be right with you. Remember not to move. I love you."

He left the room.

***

Darcy sat in the chair next to the door, his head supported against the wall panel. Thankfully the local doctor was their hosts' relative. He had arrived within half an hour, but now was taking ages in her room.

"Sir."

Darcy lifted his head, seeing the elderly man in front of him. He had not heard the door open. He stood up, looking anxiously inside the bedroom, but the man closed the door quickly before he managed to catch sight of her.

"Let us talk first, sir. Your wife needs some privacy. You shall see her later."

They sat down by the round table. The single lamp on the middle of it lit the room dimly.

"Do you know what happened?" the doctor asked.

Darcy nodded. "Yes, I believe so. I was with her when it started."

"She has lost the baby. I am very sorry."

Darcy stared at the man for a moment, silently. "She has felt fine apart from the morning sickness. She was tired, slept a lot but... She had no pains, no bleeding before, I would have noticed."

"Sometimes there are no prior symptoms to miscarriage," the doctor explained.

"She felt unwell in the morning, was sick, returned her breakfast just as we drove outside London." Darcy ran a hand over his face. "I should not have forced her to travel today."

"You could not have helped that, sir. I dare say that the same would have happened, even had you stayed at home," the man assured.

"How is she?" Darcy asked, his expression strained.

"She is fine, physically I mean. She should recuperate in a few days. Your wife is young and healthy. You both are. You will have many children in the future. I promise it to you, and I promised it to her."

Darcy brought his fist to the mouth and murmured. "But why?"

"We do not know exactly. You may be surprised, but it is quite common and even natural. We believe that sometimes the child simply stops growing , and the mother's body needs to dispose of it, otherwise it could be dangerous for her. I have seen, heard and read about many cases when after miscarriage, a woman gives birth to a healthy baby the very next year."

Darcy nodded. He remembered that soon after his mother's illness, he had gone to boarding school for the first time. When he had returned for the summer, his mother had been big with Georgiana.

"Now, Mr. Darcy, if I am correct?"

"Yes, Fitzwilliam Darcy of Pemberley, Derbyshire."

"Mr. Darcy, do you love your wife?"

"Very much." He smiled through the glossy eyes. "I met her a year ago at an assembly. I was in love before I noticed, not even sure when or how it happened. I did not know what struck me."

"You must show it to her now. She will blame herself. You must take special care of her. Spend a lot of time with her."

"Of course."

"I would advise you to wait a while before resuming your marital relations; two months should be enough."

"I understand. I would never risk her health."

The doctor stood up. "I must go if you have no other questions. I have got a patient with a serious case of pneumonia."

"Of course, I understand."

"Call me tomorrow if anything is wrong, but I do not think that it will be necessary. I talked with her and explained everything, answered all her questions. She should stay in bed tomorrow."

Darcy walked the man to the door. "Thank you, doctor." He pulled out his hand and they shook hands.

Darcy reached to his pocket. "How much do I owe you? I should have money in my coat..." He looked around the room.

"Not now. Leave my pay with the inn keeper when settling the bill. They are my wife's relatives. Good night, sir. I wish you and your wife all the best."

Darcy stood unmoving for a while after the man left. He had to brace himself before going to her.

He opened the door to the bedroom, and saw her curled on the bed. Her trunk was open. She must have changed into a clean nightgown. He could see bits of the blooded cloth burning in the fireplace.

He moved to the bed and sat on the edge. "I am so sorry, sweetheart." He reached his hand and stroked her arm.

It took some time before she looked up at him, her eyes puffy and rimmed red. "Do you hate me?"

He leaned over. "What are you saying?"

"I lost your baby," she whimpered.

He sat down beside her on the bed and pulled her into his arms. "Listen to me. It was not your fault. Such things happen sometimes. You could not stop it."

"I feel horrible," she whispered brokenly into his chest.

His arms squeezed her to him. "I know, love, I know." He kissed her head. "I love you."

She cried silently.

***

Darcy woke up the next morning with a dull pain in his back. He had slept half sitting on the bed, in his clothes, his head supported against the headboard at a strange angle. Elizabeth was snuggled to him. It had been very late when she had stopped weeping and fallen asleep.

Carefully, he removed her arm from his waist, and got out of bed, ignoring the stiffness in his muscles. He covered her with another blanket and quietly walked out of the room.

He hurried with washing, and shaving, and ordered a breakfast for both of them to their private sitting room. As the food was brought, he checked on Elizabeth. She was still dozing. He returned to the sitting room, leaving the door to the bedroom open. Should he wake up her, or let her sleep?

"William?" he heard a weak, raspy voice. "Where are we?"

He hurried to the bedroom. She sat in the middle of the bed, disoriented, her curls sticking in the all directions. Then her hand went down to her stomach and the tears ran down her face.

"No." She sobbed, "No..."

He was beside her in a second. He pulled her to him, trying to soothe her somehow, whispering endearments, though he was, himself, on the verge of breaking down.

When she quietened down a bit, he cupped her swollen, red face. "The breakfast is waiting. I will ask to bring hot tea."

"I am not hungry," she answered in a dead voice, her arms slumping.

"Please, love, you have barely eaten anything for the last days. Do you want to make yourself seriously ill? You must eat, for me. Please," he begged.

She nodded, and tried to get up on her own, but he did not allow it, only scooped her in his arms and carried to the other room.

He sat her down, and put some ham and bread on her plate, making a sandwich.

She began to chew mechanically. As she ate, new tears began forming in her eyes. Darcy felt helpless. It was not Elizabeth, he knew. She was always so lively and enthusiastic, and now he was almost afraid to look in her eyes.

"I ordered a bath. I assumed you would wish to refresh yourself."

She nodded. "I washed myself yesterday after the doctor went to talk with you, and burnt the bloodied nightgown in the fireplace, but a warm bath would be nice." There seemed to be no emotion, no feeling in her voice.

The bathtub was carried to the bedroom and the servants brought the buckets with hot water. He did not want the strangers around, so he sent the maid out. Elizabeth wanted to wash her hair, so he assisted her with it, pouring the water over her head several times to wash down the suds. She trembled the entire time, and he knew it was not because she was cold.

He dried her, helped her into a fresh nightgown, wrapped her hair in a towel, and put her back to bed.

They were silent as the servants took the tab away.

"Tell me now." He took her hand. "Are you in pain?"

"No, not at all. We can go tomorrow." she said, her eyes focused on some nonexistent point in front of her.

"It is too soon, you should stay in bed for a few days."

"The doctor said we could go as soon as I feel well. I do not want to stay here any longer than necessary."

He nodded. "I understand. As you wish."

She looked at him. "I have a favour to ask you."

"Anything, love." He lifted her hand to his mouth. "Anything."

"Do not tell anyone. Anyone." She sat up, her eyes burning. "I do not want them to know what happened."

"Of course. No one will know."

"Your people witnessed me being sick yesterday. Could you tell them that I ate something bad, and that is why we needed to postpone our journey?"

"As you wish."

"Thank you." She dropped back on the pillow. "I will sleep now." She closed her eyes.

Chapter Twenty-Three

Darcy gave his horse to a stable hand and hurried inside the house. He had been away the entire morning, having left early, when the house had been yet asleep. He had ridden to one of the more distant parts of the estate and had a final conversation with a troublesome tenant who had developed an excessive liking for liquor in recent years. His farm was situated on a good plot of land, but had not given any profit for a long time. Darcy had thought of himself a generous and fair Master, but he did not like when somebody tried to abuse his trust and good will. He dreaded situations like these, and even though they happened rarely at Pemberley, it was still his responsibility as a landlord to deal with them as they occurred.

He felt the muscles in his face drawn so tight that it nearly gave him physical pain. He made an effort to relax; he did not want to show his scowl to his family and servants. His true worry was not about the lazy, useless tenant, but only about Elizabeth. Six weeks had passed since they had come from London, and she was far from being her old self.

"Where is Mrs. Darcy?" he questioned the butler from the threshold. When he had been leaving early in the morning, she had been in deep sleep, warm and flushed, buried under numerous blankets.

"She left for a walk about an hour ago," Peters answered as he took his hat and greatcoat.

"Then she should return soon," Darcy murmured more to himself. "When Mrs. Darcy returns, please ask her to come to my study." He spoke formally to the servant.

Peters bowed. "Yes, Master."

In his study, he noticed a fresh pile of correspondence waiting for him. Two letters were for Elizabeth, one from Jane, and the other from Charlotte Collins. Perhaps they would cheer her up.

Involuntarily, his face tensed back into a strained mask. After what had happened six weeks ago on their way to Pemberley, he had expected her to be devastated, to mourn the loss. He was mourning as well. There had not been much evidence of the babe's existence yet when the miscarriage happened. Nevertheless, he had already managed to envision this child in his mind; a bright eyed girl with bouncing curls, just like her mother. He had imagined how he would show her around the park, making small steps, her tiny hand in his large one, or carrying her around in his arms for everyone to admire the little beauty. He did not know why he had thought the child to be a girl, perhaps because his only experience with infants had been with Georgiana.

Elizabeth suffered more than he, it was understandable, she was a woman, and it was her body. At first he had been amazed with her. He had expected her to stay in her rooms, abed for a few days, even longer. But from almost the first day, she had begun her new life as a Mistress of Pemberley, and his wife, as if nothing had happened. Every day she conversed with Mrs. Reynolds, learning the matters of the house. She had asked him if there was some part of the correspondence that she could help him with, answering it as the Mistress instead of him. She admitted guests, who came to Pemberley curious of a new Mrs. Darcy, and visited them in turn. She spent at least some part of the day with Georgiana. All that she did with a constant smile on her face and kindness in her voice, even her light laugh, he could hear from time to time.

Darcy was not fooled with this façade. This was not the Elizabeth he had known and fallen in love with. Her eyes were different, changed, more conscious and, above all, sad. When she thought that nobody was looking, they lost their sparkle, and she stared blankly in front of herself.

What bothered him the most was how their relationship had changed when they were alone, in the privacy of their rooms. She did not avoid him, or shy from his embrace, but she was not the same either. She had become passive and quiet. She could sit for an hour in one place, without speaking a single word to him. Such behaviour on her part would have been unthinkable in the past, when at every opportunity she had climbed on his lap for a kiss, or to tell him something interesting that she had seen, heard or read about in her sweet, uplifted voice.

The worst of all was, however, when she cried, and it happened almost every single day. For instance he would come to their bedroom in the afternoon to check on her, only to see her small body curled on the bed, sobs shaking her. When he tried to talk her into calming down, begging her not to weep, the result was the opposite, as she would wail even harder, nearly turning hysterical. A better way to handle her, he had discovered, was to simply lift her up into his arms and hold her as she gradually cried herself to sleep. At such moments, he wanted to shed tears with her, fighting hard the dampness dangerously itching his eyes. He knew though, that his break down would not help her. She needed him strong and in control, not wallowing in despair.

The knock on the door brought his attention to the present moment. With the back of his palm, he made sure that his eyes were perfectly dry.

"Enter," he said, his voice thicker than usual.

"You wanted to see me?" She stood in the open door; her eyes sparkled and her cheeks were rosy. She always looked like that after a physical exertion.

He put on his best expression. "Yes, love. Please come in."

She closed the door with careful movements and walked forward, stopping in front of his desk. She looked very pretty. He was a lousy bastard to think about it so soon, but he wanted her back, not just sleeping next to him at night, but loving her fully, being inside her.

He handed her the letters.

She took and examined them. "Thank you."

Her lips stretched in a smile and for a change, it seemed genuine, not forced. She played with the envelopes, her small fingers tracing her name, handwritten on the top, Mrs. Fitzwilliam Darcy.

She turned on her feet, making an indication that she wanted to leave. "I promised I would join Georgiana in the music room so we could have tea together. I will read my letters while she plays. If you do not need me..."

"You can read them here," he interrupted her. He hated when she was so formal, so proper with him, and it happened too often nowadays, as if some kind of barrier had grown between them. "The light is better here at this time of the day than in music

225

room," he added lightly. "Georgiana will not mind; you know how engrossed she usually is in her practice. Besides, I thought about having tea as well. I have just returned myself."

An understanding dawned upon her face. "Ah, yes. I should have remembered. How was the meeting with Mr. Kirby? You seemed so worried about it yesterday."

"Not good. I think there is no other way than to terminate the lease the next spring if nothing changes."

She walked closer, her expression of real concern. "I imagine it must be a very unpleasant situation for you."

"Well, yes..." he agreed soberly, staring into her face. His expression changed suddenly and he grinned boyishly. "I think that a cup of tea with my wife will improve my mood vastly."

Her face lit up for a moment, and she stepped to him, brushing lightly against his torso. "I will be back soon."

He looked after her with warmth in his eyes as she strolled out of the room. Her spirits seemed to be higher today, he judged with relief.

As she had promised, she was back with tea before long, just as he finished answering the first letter.

"You may go," Elizabeth said to the maid who carried the tray. "I will call you later to take the dishes away. Thank you." She smiled at the girl, who shyly smiled back and hurried out of the room.

Darcy sat by the small table, as Elizabeth busied herself with the teapot and the cups. He very much enjoyed every time she served tea to him; entirely occupied with his comfort, paying attention only to him.

"Perhaps you would wish something to eat?" she asked as they began to drink.

He shook his head. "No. Thank you. I had a hearty breakfast before I left."

As his eyes locked on her, he noticed her falling into her absent minded mood again. With her half empty cup of tea on the saucer in her hands, she gazed emptily out of the window.

Wanting to distract her, he set his cup on the table and touched her arm. "I am very impressed with you, very proud."

She blinked her eyes repeatedly. "With me?"

"Yes, you are doing excellent as the Mistress of Pemberley."

She blushed. "Thank you."

"I appreciate all your care, work, devotion and effort," he assured.

Her head lowered and she shrugged her shoulders. "At least there is one thing I can do well as your wife."

"Do not say so." He tried not to sound angry. He took the cup away from her hands, and touched her cheek to make her look at him. "Elizabeth, you cannot carry on like this."

She looked away from him. "I did not believe in that child from the beginning." Her voice was no more than a whisper, and a shaky one at that. " There was no joy in me, I did not feel the way I was supposed to feel, so the babe died."

"That is the biggest nonsense I have ever heard," he hissed, ire in his voice palpable. "No good can come from such thinking. On the contrary, you only make yourself more depressed."

She stood up. "That is how I feel about it." She strolled to the window.

He did not allow her to shut him out, and followed her. "Listen to me." He turned her to him. "It was because of natural causes, the doctor said so. This happens to many women. My mother lost children several times before she gave birth to Georgiana."

"But my mother did not!" She pointed to her chest. "Why should I?"

"You must see that we cannot control certain things. You are not your mother. Besides, you cannot be sure whether she never had such experience. Was she never ill when you were little? You can write to her and ask."

She shook her head, her lips pressed tightly. "I do not understand why it happened to us," she muttered.

He pulled her into his arms. "We have so much, Elizabeth. We should appreciate it." He stroked her back. "You cannot expect everything to be perfect."

Slowly, he felt her relax in his arms, the tension leaving her body. She sighed. "You are right; I know that you are. I am immature, selfish and..."

He put his finger on her lips. "Shush... do not. Enough castigating yourself for one day. I do not want to hear any of that. " He lifted her chin, frowning at her. "Do we understand each other on that?"

She nodded and reached her arms up, locking them around his neck. "Let us go upstairs," she whispered.

It was his turn to stiffen.

"I miss you," she whispered, her lips on his neck.

His arms around her tightened. "Oh, Lizzy."

"Shall we go upstairs?"

He shook his head. "The doctor said two months, we should wait two months. It has been only six weeks."

She cupped his cheek. "I feel well. I have just finished my monthly courses, so I think everything has returned to normal."

"I am not sure," he said halfheartedly, at the same time bringing her closer.

She tilted her head to the side. "We can stay here if you do not wish to go upstairs. Lock the door. Unless, you do not want me after what happened."

His eyes glittered furiously. "What, more nonsense?"

She took his hand into hers and began to walk towards the door, pulling him with her.

"Go first." He stopped, preferring no one to see them sneaking together upstairs in the middle of the day, being a bit embarrassed with it. "I will join you in a few minutes."

She lifted on her toes, her hands supported on his chest to maintain balance. "Do not linger." She placed an open kiss on the side of his jaw, and taking her letters, left.

***

Darcy opened his eyes, waking from a nap, feeling every part of his body singing in joy and sensual energy. He stretched and glanced to the side, his eyes locking on Elizabeth's bare back. She was on her side, the sheet only partially covering her.

He reached his arm over her waist and spooned behind. "You are not sleeping?" he murmured into her hair.

"No, I have just woken up." She turned on her back and sat up, supporting herself against the pillows.

Darcy cushioned his head on her bosom. "What does Jane write?" he asked, seeing a letter in her hand.

"This one is from Charlotte Collins." Her free hand played in his hair. "I am leaving Jane's letter for dessert."

"What says Mrs. Collins then?"

"Your aunt bought new stained glass windows for the church. They cost two hundred pounds."

"She tries to buy herself out of her sins."

"William, you should not say that, she is your relative after all, your mother's sister," she reminded gently.

Darcy shrugged. "I doubt my mother truly liked her. I think that the Fitzwilliams were rather relived when she married so far away from home. It is her own fault that her family finds it difficult to keep normal, civilized relations with her."

Elizabeth sighed but did not comment. "The main news, though, is that Charlotte gave birth to a healthy baby girl," she said after a moment. "She named her Catherine, which is not surprising."

Darcy looked up with concern. "It must be uneasy for you to read about it."

"Not really. I knew that Charlotte was expecting yet in Kent when I visited her. I guessed that she should have given birth around this time."

He took the letter from her hand and put it on the bedside. "Let us drop the unattractive subject of the Collinses and my aunt."

"There is still a letter from Jane to read." She tried to protest, the knowing smile playing on her lips.

He shoved her beside him abruptly, making her giggle. "Later."

When they had made love earlier that afternoon, he had taken his time to caress her, make her ready, and satisfied in advance, but now he felt more impatient, more urgent. She had to sense that too, because she opened her legs and invited him in, pulling him on her.

He was about to push himself inside, mindful to be gentle, as she always seemed to need a little while to adjust around him, when she touched his face.

"I love you," she said, looking into his eyes.

He frowned. He did not expect such a confession.

"I know that I do not tell you this as often as I should." She swallowed, her eyes teary. "I love you."

He groaned with a laugh. "I am trying to be gentle here. You are not making it easy."

She laughed too. "Come here." She cupped his bottom with both of her hands, pushing him in.

"Ahhh..." she moaned as he found the rhythm.

"Good?" he asked thickly.

She strained against him. "You cannot imagine."

He smirked. "Oh, I think that I can."

***

"William, wake up. William!" he was nudged firmly.

"Something's wrong?" he murmured, focusing his vision on Elizabeth. She was dressed in her nightgown and robe, her hair strewn down her back and shoulders, the letter in her hand.

He had fallen asleep again after they had made love the second time. He had shamefully spent half of the day in bed with his wife.

"I have just read the letter from Jane." Elizabeth said, her whole expression and body language agitated.

He sat up, running his hand over his face . "What is wrong? Something with your parents?" He dreaded to ask whether another sister had escaped home, giving herself freely into the arms of some rake. He had little fancy for leaving the comfort of his home, family and the company of his beloved wife to rescue another Bennet girl from scandal.

"No, they are fine. It is about Jane herself." Elizabeth paused dramatically. "Mr. Bingely proposed to her."

Darcy dropped back on the pillows. "All is well then. We expected that, did we not?"

"She refused."

"What?" He sat up again. "But..." he shook his head. "I do not understand."

Elizabeth bit her lower lip and stared at the letter in her hand. "I knew that Jane possessed some doubts, but I did not quite expect that..." She sighed.

Darcy stared at her with a frown of his own. "You told me that she was in love with him."

"She was; I am sure she was." Elizabeth cried, her voice defensive in tone. "She must have changed her mind."

"Changed her mind?" he questioned unbelievably. "I had to apologize to Bingley for my interference, convince him to return to her, and now she says no to him. There is no sense to it."

She straightened herself, giving him a slightly offended look. "I am convinced, I know that she had a very good reason to refuse him."

"Does she explain it in her letter?"

Elizabeth nodded.

"What is it then?"

"I cannot tell you, it is private."

"Women." Darcy muttered, as he got out of the bed, looking for his trousers.

She stepped behind him. "Do not be angry."

"I am not, it is just..." He turned to her, buttoning his flap. "I can hardly believe that I nearly lost you because I supposedly separated those two, and now she refuses him."

"Jane is not a person to take such things lightly," Elizabeth spoke with feeling. "I know that she had given much thought and consideration to the matter before she made her decision. She would never harm anyone, or toy with someone's feelings, but it does not mean that she should allow the others to hurt her."

Darcy stared at her incredibly, trying to grip her meaning. "Are you saying that Bingley would hurt her?"

She puffed an exasperated air. "I did not say that... but it is all much more complicated than you may think."

He waved his arms in the gesture of surrender, before strolling to the fireplace. He added a log to the dying fire and sat in his favourite armchair.

Elizabeth quickly invited herself onto his lap.

His arms went around her automatically. "I suppose your mother is not delighted with such a turn of events."

"Jane is very cautious writing about Mama's reaction, but you are right, our mother is not very pleased."

He snorted. "Not very pleased... I can imagine that," he murmured dryly.

She snuggled closer. "I was thinking ... perhaps we could invite Jane here." Before he managed to answer, she was talking again. "I remember how hard it was to deal with Mama's displeasure after I rejected Mr. Collins."

"You cannot compare those two situations," he pointed out reasonably. "There is a vast difference between you saying no to that fool Collins and your sister rejecting Bingley."

"Mr. Collins was a perfectly eligible match for me, according to Mama."

He gave her a disgusted look. "Elizabeth please, do not even suggest that before dinner. It makes me sick to my stomach, thinking you could accept him, or even imagining him proposing to you."

She buried her face into his neck, her hand stroking his flat stomach. "Jane will not be any trouble. Please. May I write the letter with the invitation?"

He sighed. "I shall send the carriage to Hertfordshire."

"Thank you!" She kissed him on the lips. "You are too good."

He had to smile at her enthusiasm. A small prize for making her happy. "Promise me one thing only," he spoke gravely, maintaining her gaze. "You will never, ever involve me in any matchmaking schemes in the future."

Chapter Twenty-Four

Elizabeth expected the country house in which Colonel Fitzwilliam's brother lived with the mother of his child to be rather small, similar in size to the average parsonage. William had referred to it as a modest one several times. What she saw though, looking curiously through the carriage's window, was a manor slightly bigger than Longbourn. She was again struck how wealthy her husband's family was, and how their perspective on such matters differed from hers.

The carriage stopped in front of the one storey, grey stone building. Darcy got out first, handing down first Georgiana and then his wife.

Although the December day was cold, with a touch of frost on the ground, Edward Fitzwilliam, Viscount Cranborne, awaited his guests in front of the house without proper outer wear.

"Welcome. At last! We have been waiting since midday," he cried as he shook hands with Darcy, and they exchanged a short, manly hug. "We began to worry that something must have delayed you."

"There was a fallen log on the road just outside Pemberley. We needed to stop to take care of it," Darcy explained.

"A fallen log?" Edward questioned, his eyebrows raised. "This time of the year?" He frowned. "I do not like the sound of that. It is very unusual."

Darcy nodded, understanding the other man's point without further explanation. "My first thought was also that some highwaymen wanted to set the trap, but nothing like that happened. The spot was quiet and deserted as we removed the obstacle."

"Nevertheless, I will give you some additional people for your return."

"I would appreciate it, cousin." Darcy's voice was grateful. "My men are armed, but one can never take enough precaution when travelling with his family." He looked at Elizabeth and Georgiana, who stood, huddled at his side, hands hidden in identical fur muffs, waiting patiently to be acknowledged.

Edward's eyes spotted the women as well. "Georgiana, you are an adult, young lady!" he exclaimed, "Where is that little girl I remember?"

Georgiana answered his enquiry with a shy smile.

"How tall you are exactly?" Edward wanted to know.

"Almost 5 feet and eight inches."

"Will you be as tall as your brother then?" he teased.

Georgiana shook her head, her expression distressed. "I hope not. I feel that I am already too tall for a lady."

"I would wish to be tall as you are, dear." Elizabeth mentioned kindly. "Imagine being as short as I, and having such a tall husband. We must present quite an odd picture as we stand close together."

"I believe that we are very well suited," Darcy spoke grumpily, glaring at her.

Edward laughed as he glanced at his cousin. "No one dares to doubt that, Darcy." His eyes moved to Elizabeth. "It is a great pleasure to meet you at last, Mrs. Darcy. I have heard so much about you." he assured with a wide smile.

Elizabeth curtseyed. "Surely from Colonel Fitzwilliam," she guessed, smiling back. This gentleman, looking like an older version of Colonel Fitzwilliam, did not give the impression of a sad, broken with life man, as she had imagined him to be.

"Not only, Mrs. Darcy, not only." He shook his head, his eyes twinkling. "But let us go into the house." He made a wide, inviting gesture with his arm. "My Lady will be displeased with me for keeping you in the cold for so long. She could not greet you here herself because the baby is fussy today."

Once in the spacious foyer, the Darcys undressed, servants awaiting to take their warm outer clothes. At first, Elizabeth did not notice an elegant young woman, standing on the first steps of the staircase, with a robust looking child in her arms.

She felt Darcy touching her arm, and only then she glanced in the direction where their host strolled.

Her first thought was that she was seeing the illusion.

"Amy," she whispered, staring with wide eyes at the woman. "Amy Parker, is that you?"

"Lizzy." the pretty blond smiled. "You did not expect me here, did you?"

Elizabeth walked slowly to the staircase. The other woman handed the baby into his father's arms, and stepped closer as well.

Edward Fitzwilliam did not seem surprised, but Georgiana and Darcy's expression were puzzled, as they looked at the two women laughing, talking simultaneously, and holding hands.

"Let us go to the drawing room, Darcy." Edward suggested, turning to his cousins. "I believe that our ladies require some time alone."

Darcy frowned. "They know each other?"

Edward nodded. "From their earliest years, I understand."

Darcy looked at his wife and the other woman who were now entirely oblivious to the others. "Why did you not tell me?"

"Amy wanted it to be a surprise." Edward patted his son's back. The baby was salivating steadily on the fine cloth of his father's light brown coat, his round, blue eyes fixed on his mother over Edward's shoulder. "Come, cousin, let us give them some privacy. I am sure that Georgiana would like some warm tea, or perhaps a hot chocolate after travelling twenty miles on such a cold day."

They were about to enter the room to the right, when the baby uttered an indignant, dramatic cry, twisting in his father's arms, his plump hands reaching in the direction of the stairs.

Amy reacted instantly, her head snapping at the boy's wail. She rushed to the baby, who promptly abandoned his father's arms, clinging to her.

"He is so needy today," she explained, as she rocked the boy and kissed his bald head. "He is teething, poor dear."

She turned the boy to the company, and he stared for a moment at the faces of three strangers, of who, two, Georgiana and Elizabeth, smiled and cooed at him in soft voices, reaching to touch his perfect little fingers, and tiny knit-booted foot. A mild scowl marked Darcy's countenance as he looked at the red, swollen, little face. The baby blinked at the tall, dark man, before erupting into a new cry, his mouth wide open, presenting a single, half grown upper tooth.

Elizabeth elbowed her husband's not so gently. "You are scaring the baby. Smile at him."

Darcy complied instantly, his face stretching into a toothy grin.

The boy chocked back his cry for a second at this display of merriness on Darcy's part, before hiding his face into his mother's neck, new sobs shaking him.

Darcy, perhaps even more scared than the boy, looked helplessly from his cousin to Elizabeth, and later to the mother of the child.

"He is simply tired." Amy tried to calm the baby. "He had little sleep at night because of his emerging teeth."

"You should not take this personal, Darcy." Edward assured. "I was the same with the baby at the beginning. You will quickly learn to interact with the little ones when you have your own."

***

Georgiana, Elizabeth and Amy spent the lovely afternoon in each other's company, sitting by the fire in the drawing room. The two older ladies recalled their childhood memories and acquainted Georgiana with them. The baby allowed himself to be calmed down, but he refused to be taken away by his nanny. The boy clung to Amy the entire time, and did not welcome being held by anyone else. It did not take long, however, till he dozed off in his mother's embrace, clearly out of sheer exhaustion, the knowing smell coming from his nappy. He was carried upstairs by his father.

Darcy seemed to be quite astonished with such attitude; such a small child staying among adults in the drawing room, instead of being closed up in the nursery. He was even more taken aback with his cousin's behaviour, who left the guests to take care of his son.

The early dinner passed in a pleasant atmosphere and without interruptions. Georgiana was asked to play the pianoforte. Close to the end of the song, the maid entered, whispering something quietly to the mistress of the house.

"Excuse me." Amy stood up when Georgiana finished. "I must see to little James."

Elizabeth rose instantly. "May I accompany you?" she asked.

"Of course." Amy nodded, and looked over at Georgiana. "Miss Darcy, would you care to join us?"

Georgiana nodded shyly, leaving her place behind the instrument.

The cousins were left alone, Darcy a bit disoriented.

Edward laughed. "You seem rather surprised, cousin."

"Well, yes." Darcy said dryly, his eyebrow raised as he stared pointedly at the stain on the other man's coat, left earlier by the baby. "Your son seems the centre of attention in here."

"You do not approve of that?"

"I am not sure," Darcy answered sincerely. "I am used to the situation when children are taken care of quietly, and they spend the day with nannies in the nursery. It was like that with Georgiana."

"I do not want to bring up sad memories, but perhaps had your mother lived, it would have been different." Edward suggested.

Darcy gave him a thoughtful look, "Perhaps. Father was not much of a parent after our mother died. It was especially unfair towards Georgiana. He gave an impression as if he could not even bear to look at his daughter."

"Do you blame him?"

"Once I did. However, now when I have Elizabeth, I understand him better." he hesitated, "I cannot imagine how I could manage to live, face every day, would she ever be taken away from me."

"Let us not return to the old, sad times." Edward said with energy. "Come to the library, I have excellent brandy and cigars."

The men walked to the small, but comfortably furnished room full of books, some of them still waiting to be arranged on the shelves. Darcy refused the cigar but accepted a glass ofdrink.

"I have not yet congratulated you personally on the birth of your son," Darcy noted as they sank into the armchairs in front of the fire.

Pride and joy shone in Edward's eyes. "Thank you, Darcy."

Darcy lifted his glass. "A fine boy."

"The finest in the world," Edward agreed with grin and they clinked their glasses.

Darcy smiled at the other man's enthusiasm. "I will not argue that." He paused for a moment, as if trying to formulate the right words. "I know it must be a difficult matter for you to discuss, but have you thought about his future? I am asking because perhaps I could help in some way."

Edward's expression darkened, a deep line appearing between his eyebrows. "I do think about it, every single day, believe me," he acknowledged with a heavy sigh. "Unfortunately, though James has our name, financially his future is secure, and he will be brought up as a gentleman, he has no right to Matlock and the title."

"What about the earl? Is he reconciled?"

Edward's face drew in a reluctant smile. "We are invited to spend Christmas at Matlock."

"Good for you!" Darcy cheered.

"I know that I owe it to my mother, but I am glad that father is ready to meet his grandson. I was rather surprised that they attended your wedding, by the way. No matter how charming your wife is, I doubt that she was someone my father would wish for his only nephew."

"I was surprised as well," Darcy agreed. "When I gave more thought to it, I assumed that it was the uncle's way to show that they wanted to rehabilitate for everything bad that happened in the recent years, your marriage included."

Edward nodded."Possibly. They wanted to prove that they were more tolerant than everyone thought they were, perhaps to show as well that they were not like Aunt Catherine."

"Yes, that is possible. Your father must feel guilty that he pushed you into that marriage." Darcy stared at the fire. "Have you heard from Lady Cranborne?"

"Lady!" Edward snorted, bolting from his place. "*Lady* is the last thing that woman should be called." He raked his hand through his hair. "But yes, I have heard from her brother. She is in good health, he writes. I know how it is possible. She should have died from venereal disease ten times by now. "

"What about divorce?" Darcy prompted. "Did you give consideration to that? It is costly, but in these circumstances... You should not have any trouble, considering her infidelity. "

Edward shook his head. "Not that easy, I am afraid... One of her brothers is a minister in the government now... and they will try everything not to reveal their sister's past and her special interests. Besides, it would kill my father, the scandal. I do not know what to do."

"Perhaps when he sees the boy, uncle will change his mind on this matter." Darcy suggested.

"You think? I hope so." Edward gulped the last drop of his brandy.

Darcy played with the glass in his hands. "Are you not afraid that your wife will become with child?"

"She?" Edward laughed bitterly, giving him an incredible look. "She pretended to be pure and untouched till the wedding night, but I am sure she had got rid of several children before her twentieth birthday. I am certain that she cannot conceive any more."

"That is good. At least you will not be put in a situation when you give your name to someone's else child."

"I would not give my name anyway." Edward cried angrily. "I do not intend to be a fool any more like I once was. I am convinced that even if something like that happens, she will get rid of it like all the others."

Darcy shuddered. "Horrible."

Edward shrugged. "I do not even give her a second thought now that I have Amy and my son. I am happy."

"There must be some way..." Darcy's voice traced, his expression thoughtful. "My opinion is that you should discuss your situation with a good, trusted lawyer, and the uncle of course, now when he is willing to see his grandson. There must be a way to make the things as they should be, the earldom and the title for your first born."

"Could it be done?" Edward asked, new hope burning in his eyes.

"I do not know. Perhaps there is some solution that we are currently not aware of ."

The older man sighed. "It is my dearest wish. I will follow your advice, cousin. Amy and the baby deserve the best."

***

"Does it hurt?" Georgiana asked in awe, as she observed James Fitzwilliam pulling greedily at his mother's breast.

"Not really, sometimes it may be a bit uncomfortable," Amy answered, looking down at the suckling baby.

Elizabeth was equally fascinated as Georgiana. "Do you not have a nursemaid?"

"I have one now, but just before the birth, we were forced to send away the woman that we initially found for this role because she turned ... unreliable." A shadow crossed Amy's face for a moment, but it was enough that she looked down at the baby and her face smoothed in angelic smile. "When Jamie was born, we had no one, so naturally I started to nurse him on my own. Later

Lady Matlock was so kind to send Mrs. Black to us, and she proved to be excellent, but for the first month or so, Jamie had only me. I still nurse him, though not during the nights. Edward insists upon it so I do not have my sleep interrupted."

"That is rather usual," Elizabeth said cautiously.

"I know, but I really do not care what the society thinks about it. It is a wonderful feeling, a great bonding with your child. I have heard as well that women who nurse do not fall with child again so soon. Do not think that I do not want more children." Amy assured quickly, "But I want to enjoy Jamie alone for a little while, before thinking about another one."

The boy's eyelids dropped, but even in his sleep, his tiny mouth was moving, still pulling. Very gently, Amy pulled him from her breasts, and put him on her shoulder, patting his back gently. After a minute, the baby spit up on the white cloth, that covered his mother's shoulder and pronounced a deep, happy sigh in his sleep.

"He should sleep now," Amy whispered, as she gave the baby to his nanny. "I only hope that the teeth will not bother him so much like last night." She buttoned her dress, and wrapped a shawl securely around her bosom. "I want to thank you for the crib, Lizzy. Jamie wants to sleep only in this one."

Elizabeth beamed. "I am glad it is useful."

Before retiring, Georgiana, and Elizabeth accompanied Amy to the nursery, to have a last look at the sleeping baby.

"He is so perfect," Georgiana whispered, staring at the sleeping baby. "I want the same one."

Amy and Elizabeth laughed quietly.

"You must first have a husband, dear." Elizabeth whispered. "However, I am not so sure whether your brother will welcome the news of his sister marrying at sixteen."

"I do not wish a husband," Georgiana explained. "I just want such baby."

"I think you can count on your brother and sister that one will appear at Pemberley in the coming year or two," Amy said, glancing warmly at her friend.

Elizabeth hoped that the semi darkness of the nursery, hid her pained expression. She felt a squeeze in her throat, but she managed to fight back the tears. All was in God's hands. She had to be patient.

***

"How is your sister?" Elizabeth asked the next day as Amy showed her around the park surrounding the manor. Georgiana stayed at home, practicing the pianoforte. The baby was left with his father and Darcy.

"I wanted her to come here, and live with us, but she refused. I think that she dreaded interrupting us. She is such a private person, and does not want to be a burden to anyone," Amy explained. "She is happy for me, and even visited us here. Edward offered to settle her in a cottage not far from here, so she could live comfortably close to us, but she declined this offer too."

Elizabeth stopped walking. "I saw Anne last spring."

Amy turned to her. "I know," she said calmly, "She wrote to me about your meeting in Kent. She explained that she was so humiliated with what you had witnessed there, that she had pretended not to know you or Maria Lucas."

"I thought the same, that she was too ashamed... because I noticed that she recognized us. The family she works for is so horrible. You cannot imagine." Elizabeth shuddered as her hand went to her neck. "I would not wish such a fate to my worst enemy."

Amy touched her arm, to calm her down. "She does not work for them any more. Lady Matlock helped to find a new position for her, as a companion to an older lady, living alone in a grand house in Ireland. She has been there for two months now, and she is delighted with everything. She writes that her employer is very undemanding, and that she has got half the day all to herself. She reads, walks to the beach and she even returned to painting."

"I am so relieved to hear that." Elizabeth assured with feeling.

Amy sighed. "I think that I was much more lucky than she. You may be surprised with what I will say, but after all that Anne and I had been through after Papa's death, when they had taken our house and all the money... It does not bother me what the world thinks of me any more, whether they will call me a whore. Edward is such a decent man; he loves me and I am so happy here. My only worry is about Jamie, and any other children we will have. The world can be so cruel, and they will be always carrying a stigma of being illegitimate.

"Not all is lost." Elizabeth reached for Amy's gloved hand to give it a squeeze. "There must be some way to make everything right."

"Thank you, Lizzy." Amy smiled. "I know how grateful Edward is for your husband's support, that Mr. Darcy did not turn away from him when everyone, even his own father, did."

"My husband is the best of men."

"He is clearly enamoured with you," Amy said more cheerfully as they resumed their walk. "However, I would rather not think of you marrying someone like him. He is so serious."

"There was a time when I did not see myself as his wife either, believe me," Elizabeth admitted.

Amy's eyes shone with curiosity. "Tell me."

"I did not like him at all when we first met. I thought he was rude, unsociable, prideful, arrogant and insensitive to the feelings of others."

The other woman seemed taken back. "You did? Truly? That was your opinion of him? I know little of Mr. Darcy, but apart from being a bit taciturn and reserved, he seems such a decent gentleman."

Elizabeth stared in front of herself. "I was prejudiced toward him, I misjudged him severely," she acknowledged quietly. "There was the matter with Wickham and Jane too..." she sighed. "It is all a rather long and complicated story... The material point is that when I saw your sister at that inn, it came to me that there was hardly anything worse than such a fate, life in poverty, full of loneliness and humiliation. I decided to accept the next man who would propose to me, to ensure myself the security."

"It is very unlike you, Lizzy. You wanted to marry for love," Amy reminded gently.

"I turned out to be a coward," Elizabeth admitted frankly. "I was in Kent, visiting Charlotte Lucas. She married a parson, Mr. Collins, our cousin to whom Longbourn is entailed to, not the most clever man in England to say the least. She seemed very happy though. It was enough for her that she rescued herself from being destitute. I thought that marriage for convenience may not be so bad as I had always believed... What I did not expect was that Mr. Darcy would make me an offer."

Amy clasped her hands. "You agreed."

"Yes, though I regretted it the very next moment. I tried to break up with him, was on the verge of doing it a few times, but he made it very difficult, impossible almost. He was very persistent and pretended not to take any of my hints."

"It sounds very romantic."

Elizabeth gave her a heavy look. "I did not feel like a romantic heroine at all, I assure you. But he was constantly so kind and understanding. I learned to appreciate him..."

"You love him now?"

"I do, very much, and I cannot believe how I could have been so blind about him in the past." She shook her head. "I do not deserve him."

Chapter Twenty-Five

"Was Mr. Bingley very disappointed?" Elizabeth asked.

The two eldest Bennet sisters, dressed in nightclothes, long hair let free, were huddled together on the four poster bed in one of the guest rooms at Pemberley.

Jane hesitated before answering. "I think that he was surprised at first, but then he gave the impression of being quite relieved, which at that very moment convinced me completely that I did well refusing him."

Elizabeth stayed silent for a longer moment. "I expect that Mama was not pleased," she said at last, her expression compassionate.

"I do not remember her ever being so angry with me," Jane admitted, lowering her eyes. I do understand her, though, I truly do. Mr. Bingley was a perfectly acceptable match for me."

"What about Papa?"

"You know him, Lizzy. When Mama demanded from him to voice his opinion he refused. He said that he had been wrong both about you and Lydia and he was not going to get himself involved in the personal life of his daughters any more. In his view, I am of age and can decide for myself."

"That sounds like Papa," Elizabeth admitted, pursing her lips.

"Oh, Lizzy," Jane cried, a heavy sigh escaping her. "I do want to marry, have my own family and children... Mr. Bingley is a good man, he would have given me all that."

"Have you already forgotten how he abandoned you twice, the second time when you most needed him?" Elizabeth reminded.

"What if I am not being realistic?" Jane mused, her expression thoughtful. "Not every person is as decided, devoted and in control as your Mr. Darcy. I must say that Mr. Bingley pales in comparison with your husband. I just want to find someone who would love me the same, not marry me because I am convenient for him. I fear though that I expect too much from life."

"You deserve the best, Jane, someone much better than Mr. Bingley," Elizabeth spoke with conviction.

"I intended to accept him, Lizzy, I really did. I knew that he was a good match. However, when the moment came, and he proposed, I simply could not force myself to say yes."

"You did right." Elizabeth reached to touch her hand and give it a reassuring squeeze. "You should always listen to your heart."

"You did not listen to your heart when you accepted Mr. Darcy, and look how well it ended for you," Jane pointed out. "You are very happy with him, perhaps I would be too with Mr. Bingley, had I given him the chance."

"No, Jane." Elizabeth shook her head. "That was an entirely different situation with me and William. I was blinded with my own prejudice – I misjudged him, I thought that he did things he had not done. It was shortly after I saw Anne Parker with her employers, and I was truly influenced with that picture of her misery and humiliation. Most important is that I did not know William well at all. You knew Mr. Bingley very well when he proposed. He betrayed your trust more than once. You are doing right, Jane. What would you do if he turned his back on you in a situation when you are not his betrothed, or someone he is courting, but his wife, the mother of his children?"

Jane watched her, and her blue eyes, darkened to violet. "Do you really think so?"

Elizabeth looked straight into her eyes. "Yes, I do," she said with force.

Jane sat up and hugged her knees. "I do not know, Lizzy. I am so confused. Perhaps Mama is right and I should have accepted him."

"Mama wants the best for us, but she is not always right. She does not understand everything," Elizabeth said, her voice cautious. "You must remember how furious she was with me when I rejected Mr. Collins; but in the long run I was right and she was wrong. I know that history will repeat itself and you will find your own path in life the same as I did."

Jane's head dropped onto her knees. "I hope so, Lizzy. I really hope so."

Elizabeth hugged her. "Do not think about it now, let us enjoy your visit here."

"Thank you, Lizzy."

"I am so happy you are here."

Jane smiled. "Me too."

The sisters hugged again before Elizabeth slipped from the bed. "I must go. It is late. Sleep late tomorrow, and do not bother to go downstairs for breakfast, I will send a tray to your room. You must rest after the long journey."

A few minutes later, Elizabeth crept into the darkened bedroom, lit only by the fire from the mantelpiece. Fitzwilliam was on his stomach, which was an unusual sleeping position for him. She put the single candle on the bedside on her side of the bed and quickly removed her robe and slippers. She blew out the candle and crawled under the covers, mindful not to disturb him.

"What took you so long?" he murmured, his voice not at all sleepy, as his arm wrapped around her middle.

"I thought you were sleeping," she whispered.

He pulled her to him, as his hand tugged at the top buttons of her gown, and slipped inside, enveloping her breast. "I thought that your sister was tired after the long journey."

"She is tired, but we needed to talk without delay. So much has happened." Elizabeth explained, cuddling closer to him.

"Will you tell me then?" he asked.

"Tell you what?"

"Why did she reject poor Bingley after a year of swaying him back and forth?"

"Poor Bingley?" Elizabeth sat up. "He was not poor when he left her without a word of explanation when the news of Lydia broke. He returned only when the scandal was hushed down, and it was obvious that our wedding would take place."

"So that was the reason." Darcy said calmly, pulling her back to him.

Elizabeth frowned at him. "You tricked me," she accused.

Darcy shrugged, his strong arms winding around her. "I just wanted to know. Jane is so sensible and reasonable. I figured out that Bingley must have done something really stupid if he had alienated her enough to refuse him. She will be better without him."

Elizabeth turned into his arms, looking up at him. "You think so?"

He nodded. "I like Bingley, but he never had a backbone. He should have stood by her, not cowered down and waited to see what happened. It is his own fault that he lost her."

"I said exactly the same to Jane, but she still cannot stop thinking about it. I think that she really liked him."

"I can introduce her to a few acquaintances," Darcy suggested.

She gave him an unbelievable look. "You said that you would never, ever involve yourself in any matchmaking."

"I am not going to," he said quickly, his tone defensive. "I am only saying that I can introduce her to several single men. She is way too attractive not to draw interest."

"She has no dowry."

Darcy smirked. "I assure you that there are men who are wealthy enough to overlook this little detail for having such a beauty by their side; kind and with a sweet disposition too."

Elizabeth scooted closer, and placed her cheek against his warm chest. "William?"

"Yes, love."

"When we met, at the Meryton Assembly…"

"Yes." he prompted, his voice patient.

"Did you find Jane very beautiful?"

"Of course I did. I am not blind, I always considered her very pretty, but perhaps smiling too much."

"You liked her then?"

"Who?"

She rolled her eyes. "Jane, of course."

Darcy was silent for a minute and then he laughed. "You are jealous."

"No, it is just…" she sighed into his nipple. "You speak with such an admiration about her."

He kissed the top of her head. "Do not worry, she never had that effect on me."

"What effect?" she asked innocently.

"I can admire her like a pleasant painting of a beautiful woman, but it never crossed my mind to… you know."

"And you wanted that … with me?"

"Are you blind, woman?" he cried loudly, tugging her on top of him. "Did you forget how I pinned you to the wall in that dark corridor at Longbourn?"

Elizabeth moved to sit on his stomach, straddling him. "And now?" She removed her nightgown, threw it behind and shook her curls.

He grinned. "I am in a lazy mood tonight, I am afraid. It has been a long, exhausting day," he said, his expression turning into a pained one, but his eyes were already devouring her breasts, hands reaching to her hips.

She pouted. "You want me to do all the work then?"

He nodded eagerly, grinning again, his mouth stretched impossibly wide.

"Well..." Elizabeth leaned forward to place a kiss on his shoulder. "I think that I shall manage."

***

"She is so beautiful, Lizzy," Jane cried softly as she stroked Star's soft mane.

The sisters were in the stables, where they wandered after Elizabeth had shown Jane around the gardens.

"A present from William," Elizabeth explained.

"Do you ride her? I remembered Papa giving you lessons last summer."

"Yes, I do ride," Elizabeth announced proudly. "She is so docile that I am not afraid. Georgiana is so kind to bear with my snail's pace as we take a turn around the park every few days, though I know that she likes to ride fast, even riskily, very much like her brother."

They kept talking to the mare in soft voices, giving her carrots and sugar.

"Here you are, ladies," they heard a thick, male voice behind them.

Elizabeth turned, seeing her husband, dressed in his riding outfit, tall boots and beige breeches. Her heartbeat accelerated; he looked so handsome.

"I was showing Jane my mare," she explained shyly.

Darcy strode into the stall, and first narrowed his eyes at the horse's pleased expression, before his gaze turned back to Elizabeth's hand full of white cubes of sugar.

"You will spoil her, Elizabeth, giving her so much sugar every day," he scolded gently, his voice patient. "Her teeth will get rotten and she will gain too much weight to run."

Elizabeth gave Jane an embarrassed look. She knew that horses were expensive. She felt instantly guilty for not taking proper care of the one she had been given. "I did not know that it was harmful for her. She is always so happy when she sees me."

"No wonder," he snorted. "She knows you will bring her sugar."

Darcy stepped to the animal, taking a long look at the mare's legs, and later checking her teeth.

He turned to look at Jane. "Now, I think it is high time to find a mount for Miss Bennet."

"Oh, it is not necessary, sir," Jane assured quickly.

"Do not take offense, Miss Jane, but I saw you riding once back in Hertfordshire." Darcy shot the tall blonde a pointed look. Darcy interchangeably referred to Jane as Miss Bennet and Miss Jane, as if he could not decide which was more appropriate. "I dare say that you and my wife share the same riding style." His smiling yet mischievous eyes locked on Elizabeth for a moment. "I would never forgive myself if you broke your neck riding Georgiana's, or heaven forbid, one of my horses."

"I intended to visit Cowlishaw anyhow," he continued. "If you have no special plans for today, we can go in half an hour."

"Mr. Cowlishaw is our neighbor." Elizabeth explained. "He breeds horses. Star is from him."

"I am sure you will choose something for yourself, Miss Bennet." Darcy said.

Jane shook her head vehemently. "It is not necessary. That is too much trouble. I..."

"I was about to buy a new mare for the stables anyway." Darcy interrupted in a calm, sure voice, but Elizabeth could see that he said that just to ease Jane's guilt over buying a new horse especially for her use.

Jane bit on the corner of her lip, looking at her sister.

"I will show you around the park another day." Elizabeth smiled encouragingly.

"It is settled then," Darcy exclaimed with energy. "I will await you in front of the house in half an hour."

He made a move as if he was about to walk out of the stall, but then he must have changed his mind, because he stepped back to Elizabeth, wound his arm around her and placed a quick kiss on her cheek.

When he was gone, both sisters blushed deeply; Jane because she had involuntarily witnessed the tender moment between the couple, and Elizabeth because the longer she was married, the harder she found it to resist her husband's ways.

***

Before taking the direct road to the Cowlishaw's farm, Elizabeth insisted on stopping by the store in Lambton, where she wanted to buy small trinkets for the girls. Together with Jane, they decided on the bright ribbons for the two eldest girls and a doll for the youngest.

Jane was very curious about the orphaned girls, and she asked a lot of questions about them during the few mile drive. Elizabeth answered the best she could, describing her last visit, when she had met the girls.

The day was almost sunny and rather warm, so despite it being the middle of January, they took an open carriage so that Jane could see more of the countryside. Darcy drove himself, and stopped the carriage in front of the house first, but when it appeared to be quiet, with no sight of the host or his daughters, he drove right to the stables.

Darcy handed the women down, and went to look for Mr. Cowlishaw. Before he managed that, three little red haired girls ran out of the stable, gathering around Elizabeth and Jane. Elizabeth introduced Jane to them, and distributed the presents.

"They are so sweet." Jane whispered to her sister as the girls were occupied with admiring their ribbons. The youngest one, Mary, tugged on Jane's skirt and lifted her small arms to her. Without hesitation, Jane picked her up.

The child watched her with wide green eyes before placing her head on Jane's shoulder.

"Papa!" Becky, the middle girl cried, and together with her elder sister they ran to their father approaching at a fast pace.

The girls tried to show their father their gifts, but he seemed to ignore them, his eyes drawn to Jane, still holding Mary in her arms.

"Mr. Cowlishaw thinks he has something appropriate for us," Darcy said as he reached Elizabeth.

"Pray forgive us this unannounced visit, sir," Elizabeth said with smile.

Cowlishaw, however, did not answer the Darcys enquiries. His full attention was on Jane, who held his gaze boldly.

Elizabeth looked up at Darcy, who answered her with a frown of his own.

"This is my sister-in-law, I told you about, Cowlishaw, Miss Bennet," he said formally. " We would like to buy a horse for her stay here."

Cowlishaw bowed at last. "Tis a great honour to meet you, Miss Bennet."

Jane smiled sweetly, showing the row of perfectly even, snow white teeth, and two dimples in rosy cheeks.

"Sir." She curtseyed with much politeness.

"I see that my youngest has already claimed you," he spoke as he took his daughter from Jane's arms. Mary tucked her head on his chest, wrapping around him like a little monkey. "Forgive her. She is very clingy."

Jane smiled gently. "She was not a burden. On the contrary, I like children."

"We were to see the horse," Darcy reminded, his voice matter of fact.

Cowlishaw acknowledged Darcy with a short glance before his eyes returned to Jane. "What kind of horse would you prefer, Miss Bennet?" he asked, his voice almost soft in tone.

"A gentle mare. I am not much of a horsewoman, very much like my sister." Jane acknowledged, all blushes.

"Let us go then." Darcy grunted.

In the spacious stables, Jane followed her brother-in-law, who pointed to a brown mare with gentle eyes. It was bigger than Elizabeth's Star, but as Jane was much taller than her sister, it seemed appropriate for her. The animal was brought outside, so Darcy could see how it walked.

"Would you like to try her, Miss Bennet?" Cowlishaw asked, as he stepped behind Jane, when she stroked the horse's black mane.

Jane's eyelashes fluttered. "Yes."

Cowlishaw cried to bring the tack. When the horse was saddled, Jane looked around. "There is no mounting block."

Darcy moved forward, ready to help Jane, but their host was quicker. "Allow me," he said, and without further asking, put his gloved hands around Jane's waist and lifted her on the horse without much visible effort.

A small gasp escaped the lady's lips as she took the hold of the reins. She kicked the mare gently with her heel, and the animal obediently went into a slow trot.

Cowlishaw followed the horse and the rider, leaving the Darcys behind.

"What is he thinking?" Darcy muttered furiously, puffing. "Staring at her like that. Taking liberties, when lifting her on the horse. It is unacceptable."

"If I remember correctly, you did exactly the same for the first weeks of our acquaintance. You constantly stared at me." Elizabeth reminded him sweetly.

Darcy gave her his worst scowl. "You cannot compare those two situations. He is a farmer."

Elizabeth shrugged. "You are a farmer too, strictly speaking."

He shot her an outraged look. "You know very well what I mean," he insisted. "It is not his business to look like that at a gentlewoman, and closely related to Darcys too."

"You admitted yourself that Jane was a beautiful woman. Can you blame that a man can admire my sister?"

"Elizabeth, do not try my patience, pretending you do not take my meaning…" he started, but she interrupted him.

"Hush. They are coming back. Besides, you do exaggerate. He was only looking."

***

The rest of January passed peacefully at Pemberley. Jane was so quiet and unassuming, that Darcy most of the time barely noticed her presence, and soon treated her as another family member. Elizabeth seemed most happy with having her beloved sister so close, and Darcy thought about asking Jane to stay with them permanently. Knowing his mother-in-law, the poor girl had no home to go back to, after she had rejected Bingley. More important, it would make Elizabeth happy to have her beloved sister so close. Darcy also thought that in time he would find Jane a suitable husband so she could settle nearby.

By the end of the month, the letter came from Viscount Cranborne. Edward shared the happy news that his father had reconciled himself completely with the thought of his son getting a divorce from his current wife. The earl had accepted both little James and his mother, calling her his daughter. The Matlocks planned to go together to London to start the legal procedure as soon as could be. Lady Matlock was about to join them as well, to show her support for the matter of her son's divorce, and use her influence in the town's social circles to draw the public opinion to their side. The viscount asked in his letter whether Amy and the baby could not stay for a few months with the Darcys, as he dreaded to leave her in an empty house for so long.

The answer to the letter from Pemberley was promptly sent back, inviting Edward's family for a prolonged stay. To Elizabeth, Jane, and Georgiana's joy, Amy and the baby were expected in the first days of February to stay till the summer.

Ola Wegner

Chapter Twenty-Six

"Amy, he is so adorable!" Jane exclaimed, as his picked up little James Fitzwilliam from the floor just as the baby tried to crawl busily across the room to the pianoforte where Georgiana was playing a merry melody especially for him.

"Can you imagine that he is already trying to lift himself up, and constantly attempts to get out of his crib?" Amy announced proudly. "And he is only eight months old."

"A brave boy. Brave boy." Jane bounced the baby in her arms, lifting him up higher and higher till James squeaked in joy, his legs kicking in the air, his blue eyes widening.

The first days of the boy's stay at Pemberley, when he had been shy of the new surroundings and people, clinging to his mother and often crying, had passed slowly. Now he felt more than comfortable with all the attention he was given daily by the four women in the house, his mother, Elizabeth, Georgiana and Jane. There were always awaiting arms ready to carry him around, bring him toys and play with him.

Darcy tried to interject, suggesting that the baby would become impossibly spoiled with all that attention, but he was mostly ignored. Elizabeth left the boy on his lap a few times, and the child seemed to accept his company and did not cry, but only stared at him, unblinking. All Darcy knew was that once the boy was carried into the room, he, the Master of the place, was instantly forgotten.

***

"Lizzy, who is the gentleman Jane is talking to?" Amy asked, adjusting the cap around James's head so he would not get cold. They were taking their walk with the baby as they had every day. The boy was well bundled against the cold, so that only part of his face was uncovered.

Elizabeth turned her head in the pointed direction to see her sister on the other side of the gulley, talking with a well built, bulky man.

"It is Mr. Cowlishaw."

"Who is he?"

"Our neighbor, he breeds horses."

"A farmer?"

Elizabeth nodded. "Yes, and a very prosperous one, I hear. He is a widower, and has the three most adorable little daughters. His wife died in childbirth."

Amy shifted the baby on her arm to see the couple better and narrowed her eyes. "Jane smiles at him a lot."

Elizabeth lowered her voice. "I think that she likes him. She is usually rather reserved with men, not showing her true feelings to them."

"She gives him an encouragement then?"

"I believe so. I saw how she smiled quite openly at him the other day when we saw him in Lambton."

"I wonder if he would be bold enough to ask for her hand," Amy mused. "Jane is the daughter of a gentleman, after all."

Elizabeth peered at her sister and Mr. Cowlishaw who were walking towards them unhurriedly. "Mr. Cowlishaw is a mature man who knows what he wants, and it seems to me that is exactly why my sister likes him."

"I hope that she realizes that a farmer may expect more from her as far as household duties are concerned than someone from her own social background," Amy noted.

Elizabeth frowned. "Do you think so?" she hesitated, "He hires a housekeeper, and other servants, so I do not expect he would want her to actually clean or cook. Besides, Jane knows her own mind at this point. She is of age, and though she would wish for our parents' blessing, she will act in the way she considers the best for her future happiness."

The conversation was stopped because Mr. Cowlishaw and Jane approached them.

"Mrs. Darcy." He bowed. He must have heard who Amy was, because he placed another deep bow in front of her. "I came to see your husband. I have some news from Lambton which I think should interest him."

"He is in the study," Elizabeth explained with kind smile. "Jane, would you be so kind as to show Mr. Cowlishaw the way."

***

Elizabeth ran the brush through her hair a few last times, put the brush away on her vanity and walked to the bed. She removed her robe and slippers and slipped under the covers.

William sat silently, his back supported against the pillows, his dark brow furrowed.

"You have been distracted the entire evening," Elizabeth said as she snuggled against her husband's side.

Darcy brought her closer, his arm tightening around her, and he kissed the top of her head.

"What is troubling you?" she asked after a moment.

His only response was a sigh.

"Tell me," She stroked his stomach, knowing he liked that. "You will feel better."

"Do you remember how I told you about that tenant who neglected his farm because of heavy drinking? I considered terminating his lease and finding someone different for his place."

Elizabeth frowned in recollection. "Yes, I do remember. Kirby is his name, am I correct?"

"Yes, that is him."

"Was he the reason for Mr. Cowlishaw's visit today?"

Darcy nodded. "Cowlishaw heard him to speak loudly of how I mistreated him. Kirby threatened me, us, the Darcys, in the public house in Lambton. "

Elizabeth lifted on her arm. "What sort of threats?"

"I should not have told you that," he said regretfully. "I only scared you."

She shook her head. "Of course you should, and I am not scared, just worried. What came into that man to tell such tales in the public place in Lambton? Do you think he intents to act on this?"

"No, of course not, sweetheart. " Darcy's voice was calm as he hugged her closer. "He would have to be mad, and he has no means to fulfill his threats, but still it requires my taking some decided actions towards him. I hear that his wife left him, returned to her family, but still I do not want to throw him out of the house in the middle of the winter." A frustrated groan escaped him, his fingers tightening on her rounded arm, "I do not understand, I was always fair to him, same as the others."

"Some people are just not willing to work hard and live a good life," Elizabeth pointed out, her voice calm. "You cannot change him. Even worse, trying to help him you can only harm yourself."

Darcy sighed. "This situation reminds me of Wickham."

"I believe that in dealing with such people, the most important rule is to protect yourself, and the others as well, from their bad influence. You did talk to him, and wanted to give him a chance on the condition he would stop drinking."

"You are right," he agreed, his voice firmer. "I need to be more decisive about this. I cannot show weakness now."

"What will you do?"

He hesitated, "I do not know yet. Perhaps I will need to remove him from the cottage using force. I just need a few days to prepare everything."

"Nobody will think that you are doing wrong or any injustice to him." Elizabeth assured, "Everyone here knows you as a compassionate and fair Master."

Darcy was still tense, so she shifted her position and drew him to her, cradling him in her arms. "Do not think about it now. Your worrying cannot change anything, and it will only add to your overall exhaustion. Just close your eyes." She touched his face gently. "Try to rest."

He buried his head into her midsection, his eyes closed. "My Lizzy," he whispered, as she kept stroking him.

***

Joseph Cowlishaw was on his way back home from Lambton where he had unsuccessfully tried to hire new servants . He was again left without a housekeeper. The one sent from Pemberley last summer had left a few days ago, taking along her niece, who had served as both maid and nanny to the girls. He was well aware that he could not go on like that for much longer without help. Girls required attention, and the right upbringing, and he was too busy to take proper care of them. He needed to remarry soon. A very young girl was out of question, he wanted a more mature woman, sensible, and with experience running a household and bringing up children.

He had been looking around the neighborhood for the right candidate, and there were two stately, childless widows who he knew would accept his offer. They seemed decent enough, but he dreaded to trust them with the girls. Neither did he feel attracted to either of them; he could not imagine taking those women to his bed.

Mrs. Darcy's sister was a totally different matter. With her, he would have no trouble fulfilling his marital duties. On the contrary, he would have been barely able to hold till the nighttime to bed her. She would have very little sleep as his wife. What a woman she was. He had never in his life seen such a beauty. She could pose as an angel. He was surprised that Darcy had chosen the little dark-haired woman of his instead of her elder sister, but love was blind, they said, and the Master of Pemberley was certainly in love with his wife, any man could see that.

Joe was not a fool, and he knew that Darcy's sister-in-law was far beyond his reach. Although, he had heard from a good source that Mrs. Darcy, though the daughter of the landed gentleman, had no dowry to speak of. It explained why Jane Bennet had not married so far, because he could not believe that there had not been at least several men who had been seriously interested in her. He had talked to her twice so far, and had seen her once in Lambton where she had been with her sister and Miss Darcy. She had smiled at him across the street that day, and he had felt her favour for him; he had no doubt about that. However, he knew her too little to be sure of the sincerity of her intentions, and he had to be cautious. There was always a possibility that she simply toyed with him. Darcy could easily acquaint her with his well connected and wealthy friends. Why should such a beautiful woman, almost a goddess, have any reason to choose him, a farmer, over some landlord, perhaps even a titled one? Such things did not happen.

Contrary to his private life, his business had done surprisingly well in recent years. Financially, he could certainly afford to marry Miss Bennet, and even ensure her all the comforts she was used to, like nice clothes and home servants so she did not have to cook, wash and scrub the floors like his first wife had done at the beginning when he had been less affluent. His first marriage had been for practical reasons - his parents had chosen his wife, and he had cared for Janet in his own way and mourned her loss. It seemed that his second union would be very much the same, only worse, because how could he develop feeling for this or that widow with the embodiment of his dreams and desires living a few miles away? He shook his head. He had to be realistic; he had three daughters to raise, and that should be his goal. On the other hand, Jane Bennet was perfect for the girls, as she would have made real ladies out of them. Who could teach them better how to behave and speak in polite society than a gentleman's daughter?

He was so deeply lost in his thoughts that he barely noticed that it became almost completely dark. His horse knew the way home so well that he did not have to direct him. It had been snowing lightly for the last days, and the thin layer of white down covered the ground. Breathing the cold, northern wind, he was sure that this night they would have a snow storm. In the morning, the girls would be delighted with the snow banks around the house to play in.

He kicked the animal into a faster pace when he thought to see something that moved, across the pasture. A figure of a rider... galloping? He narrowed his eyes and lifted in the saddle to see better. Abruptly, the horse stopped before the stone wall which bordered Pemberley from his land. He could see little through the thick snowfall, but the rider must have been thrown down.

He turned off the road and rode hard across the pasture, in the direction where he thought the man should lay, as there was no sign of the his horse, that had probably run away. After half a mile, he thought to see a shape on the ground. It was barely visible, because it was already covered with a fresh layer of snow.

When he was close enough, he could see the it was a definitely a woman. He dismounted in one practiced movement and ran to the unmoving figure. She was lying with her face to the ground, no head covering, long hair cascading down her back. When he turned her gently, his heart froze.

"What are you doing here?" He touched her face. It was bruised around the lips as if someone had slapped her, and she had a large bump just emerging on her forehead, probably acquired from the fall from the horse. "Miss Bennet, do you hear me?"

She did not answer, and the next words he murmured more to himself. "You should be at Pemberley... I do not understand. What happened? Who hurt you?"

He put his head to her breasts, feeling her heart beat, slow but steady. He put her back on the ground to examine whether she had anything broken. But no, her strong, slim limbs seemed sound.

He gave a low whistle, and his horse stepped closer. He removed his overcoat and wrapped it around her. He picked her up and lifted her on the horse, mounting quickly behind her before she managed to slip to the ground.

He checked whether she was well bundled and kicked his horse hard. "Hold on." he whispered as they rode through the blizzard.

At first Joe thought to take her to Pemberley, but then he reconsidered and turned to his own home. His farm was much closer, just a mile or so, while Pemberley more than eight miles from the place where he found her. She should be in the warmth as soon as possible, besides he would have her at his home for a few hours at least, and judging by the worsening weather, till tomorrow morning.

When he entered the house, carrying his foundling in his arms, the girls, waiting for his return downstairs, surrounded them, asking dozens of questions. He hushed them quiet and ran up the stairs straight to his bedroom.

He shut the door behind, and very gently put her on his bed, which was the only furniture in the spacious chamber. In a minute, he had built up the big fire. He lit the candles and returned to her. She had not moved, she lay as he had left her.

He knew that he needed to remove her clothes to check whether she was not in danger of frostbite, or had not experienced something worse than slapping on the face. Not to mention that staying in those numerous wet skirts would surely give her a serious cold, or even worse, pneumonia.

It took him some time to remove all the layers, his overcoat, her own perhaps fashionable, but rather thin coat, her long sleeved dress. He was surprised to see that underneath she was nearly completely covered. To be sure a lady's undergarments much differed from what his late wife had donned. She had several white skirts, and a sort of girdle hugging her midsection, which was, at first, tricky to remove. He gulped when she was left just in a half transparent chemise, giving him a perfect view of her full breasts. He touched the material. It was damp too, so he lifted her up, supporting her on his arm to remove it. Her lovely upper body was completely naked, and for a long moment, he just stared at her. It was hard to force his attention down. When her shoes and stockings were off, he freed her from three skirts, and to his astonishment, he found one more unusual garment, the knee length white pants decorated with pink ribbons. He had never heard about anything like these on a woman, probably it was some new fashion to wear on colder days. They were perfectly dry, and there was no sign of tearing or blood on them, which meant that she had not been worse degraded. There was plainly visible a triangle of soft looking curls in the front of the garment. He lifted her leg gently to the side, and gasped; the pants were crotchless. Who the devil had invented something like that for a woman to wear? He felt himself growing very hot; the hair over her womanhood seemed a few tones darker than the pale, sunny blonde on her head.

His eyes swept over her lovely body one last time, and he threw the covers over her, up to her chin. He was a low man that all he could think about were her sweet places when her life could be threatened as the result of the fall at this very moment.

He put another thick blanket over her and picked up all her clothes, strewing them on the floor, in front of the fire so they would dry through the night.

The girls very much wanted to see the guest, so he let them stay with Jane for the time he needed to check whether his people had properly closed the stables for the night. When he returned half an hour later, Jane had still not moved, and his daughters were perched around her on the bed, watching her quietly. He hoped she would wake up in the morning without any permanent damage. The bump on her head did not look serious, as he put a cold rag with snow on it to help the swelling.

It was difficult to put the girls to bed, as they were so curious about the unexpected guest. When he managed that at last, after sitting for nearly half an hour beside Mary till she dozed off, he put a few additional logs on the fire in the girls' room and left.

As he entered his bedroom, he noticed that Jane was turned on her side. He thought it a good sign. Her face was peaceful, as if she was sleeping soundly. He looked longingly at the big bed. It had been a long day, and he was tired. He could go downstairs to sleep on a sofa that was too small for him in the first place. That would be the right thing to do. He could not imagine leaving her alone here though. She might need him during the night. He stared at the bare hard wood floor. Had he been gentleman, he would have chosen sleeping there, next to the bed.

"She will never know," he whispered as he removed his own clothes. "I will keep her warm and safe through the night."

He checked the fire and climbed into the bed. He did not dare to move closer and touch her. He was afraid not only of disturbing her, but also his own reaction at having her snuggled against him, almost skin to skin.

***

Joe woke up at his usual early hour, when the sky was yet gray. He felt a warm, soft shape next to him. Somehow during the night, he had shifted closer, and now he spooned behind her, her bottom nestled against his morning erection.

He wished to stay like that forever, but it would be no good if she had woken up and found herself in bed with him. With reluctance, he got up and shrugged into the clothes he had worn yesterday. Her clothes were dry, so he gathered them together, placing them on the bottom of the bed. He put new logs on the dying fire so she would stay warm.

With one last look at her calm form buried under the covers in his own bed, he left the room.

***

Jane opened her eyes and gazed about the unfamiliar room. She was naked apart from her undergarments, and all her clothes were placed neatly on the foot of the big bed she was in. Then the recollection of what happened to her yesterday came and she screamed.

Loud, heavy steps were heard outside the room and the next instant, the door fell open and a man stepped in.

Her heart stopped, but then when she recognized his face, she closed her eyes in relief.

"Do not be afraid," he said slowly.

"I am not." She opened her eyes.

He sat on the edge of the bed, his eyes searching her face. "How are you feeling?"

"Well, though my head hurts." She touched her forehead, feeling the bump.

"No other pains?" he asked, almost tenderly.

She shook her head and gazed around the room. "Where am I?"

"At my home. I found you yesterday, late in the afternoon in the snow on my pasture. What were you doing so far away from Pemberley? "

Jane stared at him for a moment, silently.

"Do your remember what happened to you?"

She nodded. "I went on a walk around the park. My sister was busy with Mrs. Reynolds, Georgiana stayed with Amy and the baby, because the boy seemed to have developed a slight cold. I was all alone. I walked perhaps too far, almost to the end of the park, where it turns into a forest behind the manor. I only noticed how far I walked when two men appeared out of nowhere. They put a sack on my head, and though I struggled, they put me on a horse and we rode somewhere."

"Do you know who they were?" he asked urgently.

"I do not know them, but from I what I heard of their conversation, I think that they wanted to capture Georgiana and not me. They must have mistaken me for her because we are of the same height, similar figures and both blondes. They brought me to some place, and when they removed the sack, I could see that it was a cottage, old, dirty and shabby. It could not be that far from Pemberley because we did not ride for a very long time."

"You say they mistook you for Miss Darcy."

"I heard them speaking that now when they had his little sister, Darcy would pay them for all the wrong he had done to them. They sounded very proud of themselves."

"It must be Kirby."

"Who?"

"Your brother-in-law's tenant. Darcy decided to terminate his lease on the farm because of his drinking and overall uselessness. Kirby must have gone completely mad to attempt something like this. Darcy will tear him apart. But somebody must have helped him. There were two of them, you say?"

Jane nodded.

"How did you escape?" he wanted to know.

"It was not that difficult. They did not even tie me down. I think that they were quite a bit drunk, because their speech slurred, they did not smell nice, and to the very end they thought that I was Georgiana. Besides, they drank more after they had brought me in. I used the moment when one of them left the cottage, and the other turned to build the fire. I hit him with the chair and ran outside. There was a horse in the front yard, so I mounted it somehow. As you know, I cannot ride well, and I had never ridden astride like a man, so it was very difficult to keep myself in the saddle, but I knew I had to run away as far as I could. The last thing that I remember was that the horse threw me down and I hit the ground. Then I woke up here."

"Thank you, God, nothing worse happened to you."

"I am only surprised they did not follow me. After all, they had two horses... I took one, but the other was left."

"They could have followed you, I think they did, one of them at least," he explained. "But then they saw me coming to you, and they preferred not to risk, or they were already too drunk to follow you."

Jane shook her head, her eyes wide. "How very strange. I can hardly believe all that."

Joe reached instinctively to her cheek, cupping it with his rough hand. "Thank you, God, that nothing worse happened. You were very brave."

She allowed their eyes to meet for a long moment, before breaking the contact and leaning away from his touch

Jane took a peek beneath the covers. "Who removed my clothes?" she asked very quietly.

"I."

She gasped. "You should not have."

"I had to. They were wet. You could have become very sick had I not taken them off."

"You could ask a servant."

"I have no servant in the house at the moment. I was on my way back from Lambton where I tried to hire one without success when I found you lying there in the snow."

Jane bit her lower lip, lifting the sheet higher, her eyes averted.

"I cannot say I did not look at you," he admitted, "You are the finest woman I have ever seen. But I did not harm you."

Jane's face bloomed in intense blushes. "I did not want to imply that you hurt me. It is just..."

"I am of a lower class than you, but I am a man," he grunted. "And I think that you are lovely. You can slap me for that." He sounded rebellious.

Jane looked up and smiled. "Thank you for rescuing my life."

"I will leave you now." He moved from the bed to the door, his expression all businesslike, his voice firm. "I must see to the horses, later I will send someone to Pemberley. They must be dead worried about you."

***

When Joe returned upstairs after nearly an hour, he found his bedroom empty, and most of her clothes gone, apart from her coat and gloves.

"She could not have gone far," he murmured, running down the stairs. She must have thought him some brute, no better than the ones who had abducted her. He cried for the girls. Perhaps they had seen her.

"We are in the kitchen, Papa." Abigail's voice answered.

As he stormed into the big kitchen, he saw Jane was by the stove, dressed in her very own, now very wrinkled dress, her pale, straight hair let free, hanging down her back.

"What are you doing?" he barked, frowning at the skillet in her hand.

Her pink mouth fell open. "I…" she stammered, "The girls were hungry," she explained. "They said they did not have anything for dinner yesterday, and I thought it was because all that fuss with me, so when I saw those eggs..."

He looked at his daughters. They were eating scrambled eggs and bacon. He felt hot in the face; he was ashamed he had forgotten to give them dinner last night. What kind of father was he; keeping them hungry through the night? What was worse was that it had not been the first time it had happened.

"Sit down, you must be hungry too," she added shyly.

"You should be in bed," he grunted, his expression almost hostile.

Jane shrugged. "I am feeling well. Just a slight headache."

He looked at the girls, who seemed not to pay attention to them, only munching their food noisily, their forks moving busily.

He moved onto his usual place behind the large table. "I did not know that a woman of your station could cook, Miss Bennet."

"Our mother was rather thorough in our education," Jane explained with ease, putting a plate with food in front of him. "We did not have to prepare meals of course, but I observed our cook many times."

Joseph tasted the food. "It is good." He could not remove the surprise from his voice.

Jane smiled.

He frowned at her in response. "Sit down and eat too," he ordered.

After the meal, he wanted her to return to bed, but she refused. He sent her with Mary to the front room, and he started to clean up after the breakfast. Becky and Abigail stayed to help him to dry the dishes and put them into the cupboard, as they always did when they had no servant at home. Jane asked whether she could help, but he spat at her brusquely in response, showing her out of the kitchen. Darcy should be here soon, and the last thing Joe wanted him to see was his sister-in-law washing the plates and scrubbing the pans in the cold water.

Chapter Twenty-Seven

Elizabeth sat next to the fireplace, her back limp. She had spent the last several hours in the smaller drawing room, which was the closest to the main entrance to the manor. At last she heard the anticipated noise in the foyer.

"Jane!" she cried breathlessly as she ran out of the doorway, her feet slipping on the marble mosaic.

Darcy, standing with his back to her, his dark outwear dusted with snow, talked with the chief footman. There was no sign of Jane.

"Where is she? Where is Jane?"

Her husband turned very slowly, and she read the answer on his face. "We have not found her. We shall start the search again tomorrow at first light."

"But what could have happened?" Elizabeth's eyes pled. "She has been gone for so many hours. Something must have happened. She said she would take a turn around the park."

Once out of his coat and hat, Darcy put his cold hands on her shoulders. "We found only this." He looked at the servant behind him, who took out a navy blue bonnet from behind his cloak.

Elizabeth reached for it and examined carefully. The ribbon on one side was torn. "Someone took her, abducted her?" she whispered, as she searched the faces of Darcy and the footman.

"It is our only explanation, I am afraid," Darcy agreed gravely. "Unfortunately there are no traces, as the snow covered everything. We barely noticed the bonnet. But if someone took her by force, it means that now she has at least some shelter for the night, that she is not lost somewhere in the woods."

Tears stood in Elizabeth's eyes. "But why... who...?" she asked, her eyes shifting hopelessly from her husband to the servant.

"We have some suspicions," the servant said, his voice cautious.

"We cannot look for her now," Darcy explained, his concerned gaze on Elizabeth. "We must wait till it stops snowing, till the morning. It is ▌pitch dark right now."

Elizabeth swayed, and stepped back awkwardly. Darcy was beside her in a second.

"She is all alone out there," she croaked. "What if she freezes to death somewhere in the woods?"

"We cannot think the worst," Darcy tried to soothe her. "If someone kidnapped her for ransom, and in my view it is the only logical explanation, then he will not hurt her; she is too precious."

Elizabeth's face went white, her pupils dilated and she began breathing heavily, as if wheezing.

"Come, my love, you should retire." Darcy directed her towards the stairs, his voice quiet. "We shall start to look again in the morning."

"I will not able to sleep." She grounded herself in place. "I want to stay here and wait."

"You will make yourself ill." He lowered his voice even more. "You do not want to harm the babe, do you? This cannot be good for it. Jane would not want that."

Elizabeth looked up at him, and nodded slowly. "You are right. I will go to my room."

Darcy looked over her head at Mrs. Reynolds, who instantly rushed to their side. "Let us go, Mistress." She took Elizabeth's arm. "I will have you made a cup of nice herbs so you could sleep well through the night."

Darcy watched as Elizabeth ascended the staircase slowly, Georgiana and Amy, who stood on the landing, giving her sympathetic looks.

Darcy heard the clock strike ten o'clock. Wherever Jane was now, they would find her tomorrow.

***

Elizabeth felt her head to be impossibly heavy. William was calling her name, but it was so difficult to open her eyelids. Then she remembered the events of yesterday, and forced herself to sit up and look at him.

"She is fine, safe and sound," Darcy spoke without preamble, his face a picture of relief.

She blinked at him, her eyelids still as if glued together.

"Jane is well," he repeated.

"Where is she?" she murmured, still sleepy.

"On the Cowlishaw's farm."

"Why?"

"Cowlishaw's stable boy came half an hour ago," Darcy explained. "He said that his Master found her yesterday evening on his pasture. She escaped from Kirby's farm, but the horse threw her down and she lost consciousness. I have already sent people to Kirby's place. Cowlishaw saved her life, taking her to his home, there is no doubt about it."

"But is she well now?" Elizabeth prompted, her expression still concerned.

"The boy did not see her, but he was told to say that she was in good health."

Elizabeth threw the covers aside, getting out of bed. "I want to talk with that lad."

Darcy smiled. "He is in the kitchen now, cook has something special for him."

She slipped on her feet and locked her arms around her husband's chest. "I am so relieved that Jane has been found and nothing worse happened. I was so frightened."

Darcy exhaled. "I was quite worried myself. I hate knowing that harm could come to anyone under my roof. What is worse, I did not dare to think what would have happened to you if she had, heaven forbid, not survived, or been seriously hurt."

Elizabeth shuddered. "We should not even think of that."

He brought her closer. "Are you well?" his hand went to her midsection.

She nodded. "Yes, I am well, though..." She gave him a troubled look. "William, I am not sure whether I am with child again. I do not want to raise your hopes only to have them shattered later on like the last time."

"You have missed your monthly bleeding for three months now. Is that not proof enough?" he asked.

"I have no morning sickness like the last time, my appetite is steady," she pointed out.

"You are more tired. You sleep longer."

"That is true," she agreed.

"There is more of you too." He palmed her breast very gently through the fine cotton of her nightgown before his hand tugged at the opening of it, loosening the ribbon at the front. "They are so much darker, you see, not pale pink as usual, but almost brown now." His finger gently traced her nipple. "I have read that it happens so that the baby could see better where to suckle."

Elizabeth's expression fell. "I do not dare to hope that we could have been blessed so soon after..."

He put his finger on her lips. "Shush."

She looked up into his eyes, and bit her lower lip. "I am afraid, if again..."

He cupped her face and kissed her temple. "All will be well this time."

"How can you be so sure?"

He smiled. "I have a good feeling about this one." His hand went down to her midsection. "Trust me. Have I ever lied to you?"

She shook her head.

He squeezed her to him, palming her round bottom. "Run to dress yourself and have breakfast. You do want to go to see Jane as soon as possible, I gather."

Elizabeth smiled, sighed and listened to him.

***

Jane sat on the sofa in the large front room in Mr. Cowlishaw's home. Mary was snuggled into her side, her plump arms wrapped tightly around Jane's waist. The girl did not talk, just held on to her. Jane's heart tore at the sight of the little one. The child was so needy; perhaps her father did not hug her often enough. Mr. Bennet had been the same, he had been perhaps more affectionate with Lizzy, as his favourite, but he had rarely touched any of the daughters or sat them on his lap, even when they had been toddlers. Jane believed that children, both girls and boys, needed physical contact to be perfectly happy. She could best see it in the example of the little Gardiners, who though often cuddled by their parents, were not in the least spoilt with their affection, only well loved.

Jane took the opportunity of being alone just with the youngest girl, and let her eyes wander about the room. Mr. Cowlishaw's house was new, sturdy looking and truly spacious for a farmhouse. It could have been such a lovely house with the right wallpapers, curtains, carpets and furniture; and first of all, a good cleaning. She could even see a pianoforte, covered with a fine layer of dust, which indicated it was not used often. It was a shame, because if there was the instrument, the girls could start to learn how to play.

She heard footsteps, and brought her eyes back to Mary. She did not want Mr. Cowlishaw to see her staring. She did not want to be rude.

The two elder girls entered, holding the door for their father, who carried a tray with what seemed to be tea.

Jane was about to stand up and help, but Cowlishaw grounded her with his pale green gaze.

"We thought you would like some tea," he said. He sounded a bit grumpy, as if displeased, but strangely Jane did not feel troubled or offended with his tone.

"Yes, thank you," she said sweetly.

He grunted something under his breath, and his heavy gaze laid on his youngest daughter, who still clung to Jane's side. The scowl on his face deepened.

As no one made a move to help her, Jane poured herself a cup and added some sugar.

She took a sip. "It is very good."

"I imagine Darcy should be here any minute," Cowlishaw ensured.

Abigail looked at her father and then at Jane. "Will you leave us?" she asked as she stepped closer to the woman.

"Yes, I have to, I am afraid. My sister must be very worried," Jane explained, but then added quickly, "But I can visit you, or you can come to Pemberley to see me."

Becky took a place on her other side. "You could stay with us."

Jane blushed, and forced a nervous smile. "I cannot, I am afraid."

"Why not?" Abigail asked. "You have not got a husband."

"No, I have not."

"You could marry Papa," the girl suggested.

"Abigail, that it is quite enough," her father spoke sharply.

The child frowned, her chin stubborn. "Our last cook said that you would have to marry anyway, and that we would have a new Mama. Miss Bennet is nice, and we like her. We do not want some horrible, nasty, old lady from Lambton!" she cried out.

Cowlishaw stood up, muttering, "Abigail, go to your room, but first you will apologize to Miss Bennet."

The girl's chin trembled, and she lowered her eyes. Jane pulled her closer in a compassionate gesture. "There is no need to apologize," she said, her voice gentle as she stroked the child's skinny back. "All is well."

The girl let a quiet sigh, and hid her troubled face in Jane's shoulder.

The clamor outside caught everyone's attention, putting the end to an awkward situation. Jane followed the girls to the window to see the carriage from Pemberley. Cowlishaw hurried to open the front door.

"Jane!" Elizabeth cried as she burst inside before the others.

"Lizzy, I am here." Jane said, her voice relatively calm.

"We were so worried." Elizabeth fell into her open arms.

"I am well, sister. Entirely thanks to Mr. Cowlishaw." She looked at the man who now stood with Darcy at the door. He found me. Had he not, I do not know what would have happened."

***

Despite Jane's assurances that she was well, the doctor was sent for as soon as they returned to Pemberley. The man announced her that she fared well indeed after such an ordeal, and seemed to think that the bump on her forehead would slowly disappear without any serious repercussions.

However, the same day, closer to the evening, Jane began to feel feverish, and when the next day the doctor was summoned once again, he said what her sister had already guessed. The patient had developed a cold, and she should stay for the next days abed, so as not to turn it into something more serious.

Jane was completely recovered in a week's time, and very anxious to join the family life downstairs. Darcy assured her that she should not have any fears now as Kirby, and another drunkard who had helped him, were now far away on a ship on to Australia, where they would likely stay till the end of their days.

***

"What is the matter, Jane?" Elizabeth enquired as she gazed at her elder sister.

They were taking their walk, making the best use of the warm, March afternoon, looking for the first signs of spring time.

"I am well, Lizzy." Jane assured with an instant smile.

Elizabeth watched her intently for a long minute. "You do not fool me, sister. Is it about that Kirby man who abducted you? Do you think about it still?"

"No, of course, not."

"William feels so guilty that something like that happened to you here at Pemberley. He is worried that you cannot forget about it."

"I am not sad because of that accident; all ended well, and Mr. Darcy is the last person who should be blamed."

"Then what is it, Jane?" Elizabeth stopped. "I can see that something is troubling you."

Jane faltered for a while, then sighed. "It is about Mr. Cowlishaw."

Elizabeth moved closer, her expression stunned. "Mr. Cowlishaw?"

"Yes, about him," Jane confirmed and looked to the side. "We have not heard from him since that day. Almost four weeks ago."

"William mentioned to me that Mr. Cowlishaw asked about you when they met in Lambton last time."

Jane's face lit up. "He did?"

Elizabeth nodded. "Yes, he heard about your cold. Such news spread fast."

Jane resumed their walk, and Elizabeth followed her, her expression confused.

"Lizzy, could I take a phaeton for a few hours?" Jane asked, turning abruptly. "I will drive myself."

"Where do you want to go?"

"I need to talk with him."

"With Mr. Cowlishaw?" Elizabeth guessed.

The other woman nodded.

"Jane..." Elizabeth searched her sister's face. "You like him, am I right?"

Jane blushed prettily. "Yes... and I thought that he liked me too, but now he does not want to see me... so I am not sure any more."

"I am certain he admires you."

"You do?" Jane asked in a small voice, a new hope lingering in her tone.

"I saw the way he looked at you, even William noticed, and you know how oblivious to such matters he can be."

Jane's expression sulked. "I fear that he thinks that I am so above him socially that there is no point in even trying to get closer to me."

Elizabeth watched her sister for a moment, her expression thoughtful. "William will be away for the most of the day tomorrow. We shall take a carriage, and I will go with you. It is ten miles to Mr. Cowlishaw's farm, I do not think that you should drive on your own."

"What about Mr. Darcy? What will he say?"

Elizabeth shrugged, and spoke with confidence. "He does not have to know about everything, for now at least."

***

Joe scoured the mare's side with more force than necessary. Usually he was not involved in grooming horses personally, not any more. He had people for that, but today he wanted to distract himself. He had been worried when he had heard she was sick, but when he had talked with Darcy the last time, the man had ensured him that his sister-in-law had been on her way to recovery. Joe wanted to see her, but he knew that there was no point in trying to approach her. She was out of his reach. He had repeated it many times in the last weeks. That night when she had slept in his bed was already too much, and had to be enough. In time he would get her out of his head. Perhaps it was time to start looking seriously for someone he could accept, someone suitable for him.

He stilled, hearing a female voice asking for him. He strolled out of the stall, a frown on his face.

"Miss Bennet?" he gulped.

She walked closer. The day was warm for March, and she only wore a light blue dress and matching spenser. Again he was struck with her beauty.

Her face brightened as she stood in front of him. "Good morning, sir."

"Good morning," he murmured. "What brings you here, Miss Bennet?"

His cold tone seemed not to deter her, because she kept smiling. "I hoped to see you after what happened to me, but there has been no opportunity so far, so I decided to come here. I want to thank you for your help that day, and for saving my life."

He watched her. "You have already thanked me, if I recall. Mr. Darcy was also most generous."

That was true; as a token of gratitude, Darcy had gifted Joe with one of his best stallions, which was certainly a valuable addition to his stable.

"Are you here alone?" he questioned.

She shook her head. "My sister brought me. She is with the girls now."

"I am glad to see you in good health," he said after a moment, not being sure what else there was to say.

Her eyes were lowered to the ground for a while before she asked, quietly, "Mr. Cowlishaw, could we talk in private?"

Without a word, he gestured the way.

He led her through the whole length of the stable, to the other end of the building, till they emerged on the back pasture.

"No one will interrupt us here." He stood with his back to the fence. "How can I help you, Miss Bennet?"

She smiled, nervously. "You do not make it easy for me."

"I do not understand."

She hesitated. "It is not customary that women propose to men."

He could not help his heartbeat accelerating. "Do you know what are you saying?"

"Yes." She looked in his eyes. "Yes, I do."

He stepped to her, grasping her forearms. "It is not some fancy game? You are not toying with me?"

She shook her head, her blue eyes unblinking.

"I can ensure you a good living, not worse than you are used to, but I cannot ever give you what your sister has with Darcy. Never. Do you understand?" he shook her gently. "There will be no balls, parties and fancy trips."

"Do you care for me?" she asked only.

"I told you once that I cared. Should I repeat it?"

She smiled sweetly. "Yes."

Joe took a deep breath. "I think that you are lovely, you being mine is more than I could have ever dreamt of," he murmured softly. "I did not dare to come to you because I knew you were out of my reach…"

Jane clung to him, her arms tightly wrapped around his neck.

His arm went around her waist securely, his other hand placed on her delicate nape. "Jane Bennet, will you marry me?"

"Yes," she whispered into his ear.

He pulled her away from him, to look into her eyes. "I can hardly believe it." He inhaled happily, his eyes admiring her pretty features. "What did I do to deserve you?"

She smiled and scooted back into his arms. He cupped her face, and kissed her, gently at first, but when she pressed to him with trust, he deepened the kiss. He could tell that she had no experience. Had all the men in the south of England been eunuchs, or what?

He drew back to see her lovely face flushed, her expression dreamy. "I should go to Hertfordshire to ask your father for your hand; though I rather expect him to run his dogs after me. After you sister's marriage to someone like Darcy, your parents would expect nothing less from you."

Jane shook her head, her gloved hands supported on his chest. "Do not worry about Papa. I will give you a letter to him, explaining everything. The last time we talked, he said himself that I was of age, and I could decide for myself as I chose. He will not oppose us, but even if he did, I would not step back, though of course I wish for his blessing. As for my mother..." her voice trailed away and she sighed, "I have come to terms with the fact that she will never accept any choice of mine after I rejected Mr. Bingley. Unless I married at least a Duke, or some cousin of the Prince Regent, tenth in the line to the throne," she laughed.

Joe grinned. "So you have rejected some poor fellow, huh? I knew there must have been someone in your past, you are way too beautiful and sweet not to fall for you. Who was that Bingley?"

"A friend of Mr. Darcy."

"Rich?" he guessed.

"Not like Mr. Darcy but...yes, rather wealthy," Jane agreed reluctantly.

Joe's expression fell, and he searched her eyes. "Jane, are you sure of this? It is not too late yet for you to change your mind?"

She gave him a steady look. "I have never been so sure of anything in my life. I want you, and I want to take care of the girls. I will be good to them, and I know they will grow to trust me, if you only liked me enough to tolerate me around you..."

He laughed. "Tolerate you? You silly girl." He squeezed her tightly to him. "I am so dumbstruck that you have come to me and want me. I cannot believe my own luck."

Jane placed her head on his shoulder, a happy sigh escaping. He liked that she was tall. His chin was about at the height of her forehead. He could still look down at her when necessary, but there was no need to bend in half to kiss her.

Reluctantly, he freed her from his arms. "Let us return. Your sister must be worried about you."

She nodded, but did not release him instead taking his arm.

As they were passing by one of the empty stalls, Joe glanced to check if it was clean enough, and without asking, pulled her inside. She gasped in surprise, but did not protest when he pressed her against the wall and took her mouth. She was sweet, willing and trusting as he kissed her.

"You do not want a very long engagement, tell me you do not," he murmured thickly.

"As you wish," she breathed into his mouth.

They began to kiss again, but soon Jane stiffened, and pushed away from him as she heard her sister's voice.

"Jane... Jane, are you there?" Elizabeth Darcy's soprano carried in the air.

Jane checked her appearance, adjusting her bonnet which he had pushed back to be able to nibble on her neck.

Joe smiled smugly. Jane looked well kissed, and she could do nothing to change that. Her sister would have no difficulty in guessing what they had been doing for such a long time alone.

***

Darcy walked through the halls of Pemberley, his movements energetic. He had answered all the correspondence for today, and there was still a good part of the day left that he intended to devote to his wife.

Elizabeth had seemed to be so happy in the last weeks. They kept the news of the baby a secret, without making any official announcements. Elizabeth had been so scared for the first months that the history would repeat itself and she would miscarry again. At this point, however, in a matter of weeks, her state would be visible to everyone. He felt as proud as a peacock that soon her body would grow heavy with his child. He was more than certain that this time everything was well. He could even already see and feel the hard bump once he undressed her in bed. He anticipated the moment when the child would start to move. He even started to spend more time with Edward's boy to gain some practice while he had a chance.

Darcy had a feeling that Edward would return soon for a visit, or decide to bring his family to London. His cousin sent letters almost every day, not only to Amy, but to him as well. He constantly asked about her and the baby. Darcy understood him well, for he could not imagine separating from Elizabeth for such a long time.

Elizabeth was not in any of her usual places, so he decided to check upstairs. Perhaps she had taken a nap.

To his surprise, he found his wife together with Jane in the main foyer. They stood there with three little girls, helping them to remove their caps.

He strode to the small group. "We have guests, I see."

Elizabeth turned to him slowly. As he saw her face, he knew that something was wrong. She was up to some mischief, he knew that look all too well. "I did not expect you here. I thought you were busy with your correspondence."

"I have already finished," he explained.

Elizabeth moved to step behind the girls, in which she succeeded only partially because the youngest one hid behind her skirts. "Do you remember Mr. Cowlishaw's daughters?"

Darcy leaned forward and smiled. "Of course I remember. Welcome to Pemberley, ladies. Why do we own the honour of your visit?"

Elizabeth rolled her eyes at him, while the eldest girl stepped forward, and dropped an awkward curtsey. "Good afternoon, sir," tiny voice spoke from near the floor.

Darcy smiled at the red haired child, but then frowned as his gaze rested on his wife and her sister. Jane would not look at him. They were plotting something behind his back. He had no doubt.

Elizabeth gathered the children to herself and then pushed them towards the other woman. "Jane, please, take the girls upstairs and show them their room."

Jane picked up the youngest, and hurried up the stairs. The other two girls followed her closely, their eyes widening as they looked around the white marble hallway, the golden banister and the steps covered with red carpet.

When they were out of the earshot, Darcy gave her his second most serious glare. "Elizabeth, what is the meaning of this? Are these children staying with us?"

She smiled brightly. "For a few days."

"Does their father have some problems so he cannot take care of them?"

"In a way. He must travel to the south of England, and there is no one he can leave them with."

His eyes narrowed; she sounded too innocent. "I do not understand why you did not tell me about this earlier. Why did Cowlishaw not come to me with that? I would not refuse him any help after what he has done for us. Still, I think that there is no reason for his daughters to stay in a guest room upstairs. That is an exaggeration, Elizabeth, although I do understand that you are grateful to Cowlishaw for rescuing your sister. My opinion is that you should have asked Mrs. Reynolds to put them in the servants quarters in the attic."

"Servants quarters!" she huffed at him.

"What else would you expect? They are the daughters of our tenant, whom I like and respect but still…"

"Mr. Cowlishaw is not your tenant." Elizabeth interrupted him furiously, and looked around cautiously, lowering her voice. "He is an independent and wealthy farmer in his own right." She straightened her back and lifted her chin up. "Let us go somewhere where we can talk."

She did not wait for him, but strode away first.

"Will you tell me now, what is going on here?" Darcy asked as he closed the door to his study.

"I will not beat around the bush," she said, standing in front of him her arms crossed on her chest. "Mr. Cowlishaw proposed to Jane last week. He has gone to Hertfordshire to ask my father for her hand. Someone has to take care of the girls during his absence, so I thought it natural to invite them here. Jane will be their mother, after all, and quite soon I believe, because they do not wish to wait with the wedding."

Darcy stared at her, muted.

"Are you well?" she asked, searching his shocked features. "William?" she probed.

"How… what…" he stammered at last.

"Shall I repeat?" she proposed kindly.

"How dare he?" Darcy choked at last.

Elizabeth walked to the sofa and settled herself on it comfortably. "I expected that you would have some difficulty when it came to accepting this situation," she noted calmly.

"Difficulty! What is that man thinking?! He should have come to me first."

Elizabeth raised one eyebrow. "To you? You are not Jane's father."

"But she is under my care, living in my home for the time being. I would refuse him her hand on behalf of your father. He would not have to travel so far, saving time and money."

"Papa will not refuse him," Elizabeth said.

"Elizabeth, your father tried to refuse me! Me!" he cried, gesturing to his chest. "Fitzwilliam Darcy of Pemberley! Do you think that he would accept his daughter marrying a farmer?"

"My father felt apprehensive about our union because he thought that I did not return your affection," Elizabeth pointed out. "He did not want a loveless marriage for me. Jane loves Mr. Cowlishaw, she is happy, willing to marry him and be the mother to his girls. I can assure you that Papa will not oppose."

He gave her an unbelievable look. "You do not know what are you saying."

"No, it is you who does not understand the facts." She stood up, her tone losing its calm tones. "My sister is three and twenty, she is of age and she can decide for herself. She will marry Mr. Cowlishaw even without our parents' blessing. It was Mr. Cowlishaw himself who insisted on going to our father and asking for her hand."

Darcy raked his hand through his already tousled hair. "I cannot believe that. It seems now that the only reasonable person in your family will be your mother. Oh, I am sure that Mrs. Bennet will not welcome with open arms a farmer as her son-in-law."

Elizabeth gritted her teeth, watching him, but said nothing.

Darcy walked to the window, his facial expression strained. "I can imagine it, what a laugh, in front of my friends and acquaintances... This is my sister-in-law, Mrs. Wickham, her husband is the son of my late father's steward. And that is my other sister, Mrs. Cowlishaw. She is married to my tenant." He let out a mocking laugh. "Has your sister gone completely out of her senses? What happened to her? She rejected Bingley to marry a farmer. Perhaps she suffered from her accident more than we thought?"

The room went silent for a few minutes. Very slowly, Elizabeth walked to him. "You have not changed at all. My first impression of you was correct. Deep inside you are the same cold, arrogant, and prideful man I knew in Kent. Why all the pretense for the last year?"

He turned to look at her. "Why? Do you not know?" He leaned to her, and spoke his voice lowered. "To have you. And it worked."

Her expression softened. "You do not mean it."

"Do I not? I am cold, arrogant and prideful, after all."

Elizabeth lowered her head, looking to the side.

"You push my patience and good will too far with this, Elizabeth," he said, his voice calmer.

"If you expect me to turn my back on Jane because she can find her happiness with a good man...I will not do that. You can send me back if you wish. I can raise the baby alone," she announced defiantly.

Darcy flinched, as if she had slapped him.

"Do not talk nonsense," he muttered impatiently. "Be serious for once. I am not pleased with the news about Jane, and I have my reasons. You will not convince me that this is all normal and acceptable. How can you even use such arguments against me? You are mine, my wife. Your first loyalty is to me and what I decide, and not to your sister."

A single tear ran down her cheek, and then another.

His face tightened even more at the sight of her crying in front of him. He stepped closer to her.

"This is the last time I will hear from you that you want to leave me, or that I could send you away with our child. Do not ever threaten me with that. I do not deserve it. Do you understand?" he demanded sharply, his expression pained.

She choked back a sob, tears running freely down her cheeks.

Darcy exhaled, before pulling her roughly into his arms. "Do not cry, please sweetheart, I beg you," he whispered, kissing the top of her head. "No matter what, I love you."

"I love you too," she whispered shakily.

"I will try..." he sighed. "You must see that it is not easy for me."

"I know," she whispered and clung to him.

Epilogue

Darcy woke up to find the place beside himself empty. Worry tugged at his heart. "Elizabeth!" he cried, his hoarse from sleep voice with an edge to it.

"I am here," her calm voice answered from the other side of the bed.

He snapped his head in the direction. The window was wide open, and she sat on a chair in front of it, the early morning air blowing on her face.

He dropped back on the pillows. "That warm, love?"

She turned her head to look at him, her hand placed on her extended stomach. "This baby makes me so hot inside. Next time I want to go to confinement in the middle of the winter, and not in July."

He smiled. "I shall see what I can do about that."

She raised herself very slowly and waddled back to him.

With his help, she climbed onto the bed. She tried to settle on her back, but quickly she turned on her side.

Darcy sat up, and began messaging her lower back.

"Do you think that we will have a girl this time?" he could not remove the excitement from his tone.

She moaned unenthusiastically in response. "I know that I want this child out." The tone of her voice told him that she was close to tears. "I am so exhausted."

His arm wrapped about her. "It will not last long. A week or two more. Stay in your rooms today."

She nodded. "I think I will. Could you please ask Martha to draw me a cool bath?"

He kissed her neck. "Perhaps some ice-cream for breakfast?"

She turned her face to him and smiled for the first time this morning. "Yes, please. And send Thomas to me later. I want to see how his knee is healing."

Darcy kissed her face, whispered *I love you,* and got out of the bed.

When he returned to her two hours later, Elizabeth sat in her private sitting room in her robe, the tea and a saucer with slowly melting ice-cream on the side table in her reach.

Five year old Thomas had his uncommonly skinny, long limb stretched in front of her. The boy had taken his body build from his father, there was no doubt to it.

Elizabeth examined the scraped knee carefully, blowing gently on the wound.

"Does it hurt still, darling?" she asked.

The boy shook his head. "No, Mama."

Past Darcy's legs ran three year old Henry, crying loudly. "Mama, Mama!"

The youngest boy tried to climb on Elizabeth, which was rather difficult, due to his much taller brother who fiercely guarded his own space around their mother, refusing to move an inch, and another obstacle in Elizabeth's large stomach.

"Boys, stop at once!" Darcy ordered, and the children froze. "I told you many times, and asked repeatedly that you not bother your mother now."

The boys expressions sulked, and they stepped back obediently.

Elizabeth smiled at them warmly, reaching her hand to stroke the dark curls of the younger one. "Run downstairs, darlings, and tell Mrs. Peters that you can have some ice-cream."

The boys squeaked in joy, and in a matter of seconds they were out of the room, their excited voices heard in the hall.

She lifted her dark eyes at him. "It was not necessary to snap at them like that."

"You spoil them, love, and what is worse, they use your own kindness against you, and tire you down."

She smiled calmly. "I want them to be sure one day that they had a mother who loved them, so they would know how to show affection to their own children. Besides you are always there to put them in line when they get out of control."

He sat with her while she ate her ice-cream and drank her tea. She seemed in a better mood than in the morning.

"Go to your duties, do not worry about me," she said when she noticed that he was stealing glances at the clock. "I shall be fine. I have a new novel to read." She pointed with her eyes to a thick book nearby. "Besides Jane promised to come, and I expect Amy any day, perhaps even today."

"Will Lady Matlock stay for a longer time?" Darcy asked formally.

Elizabeth's childhood friend had married Darcy's cousin three years ago, but she had not witnessed her husband finalizing the divorce with his first wife. The woman had been stabbed to the death by one of her lovers during a ball, freeing Edward from his misery, and causing the greatest scandal of the decade in the higher circles of London society.

"Yes, she promised to stay till the birth, and some time after. I cannot burden Jane now, especially when Mr. Cowlishaw is so busy now with that new farm they acquired."

Darcy nodded. Jane Cowlishaw was with child as well, her husband was always working stubbornly to ensure her and all their children a comfortable living. He had truly admired both of them, and the family that they had created.

As he was descending the staircase, he saw his sister-in-law, surrounded by the brood of red haired children. Jane looked as beautiful and elegant as ever, even the small bump on her front did not ruin the graceful line of her figure. The sisters carried their pregnancies very differently; while Jane was always able to disguise her state for a long time, Elizabeth was as big as a house from the fifth month.

"Jane, so good you came," Darcy spoke as he approached her. After years of referring to her Mrs. Cowlishaw, he finally began using her first name. "Elizabeth is very restless."

She smiled at him. "I cannot stay for long, I am afraid, just two hours before Joe comes to take us back. I am sorry for bringing them all with me." She gave him an apologetic look as he stared at the five bouncing children. "There was no other way."

"The more, the merrier, as Elizabeth says," he assured politely. "Do not worry, sister, our boys are always pleased with the company."

"Thomas, Henry!" he cried loudly. "Your cousins are here."

Soon there was heard the speedy tapping of the little feet and two dark haired boys ran to them.

Jane left, going upstairs to Elizabeth, and Darcy lined all the children against the wall. "Now," he gave them his most stern look. "You will go to the smaller dining room where you will get some ice-cream." The Cowlishaws heavily freckled little faces lit up at the news. "And you two," he glared at his sons. "Milk and cookies, because you have already had a portion of ice-cream today. But!" He lifted his finger. "We sit in our seats, we listen to the nanny, and we do not touch anything with our hands."

The boys' nanny, Mrs. Peters, was already standing behind him, waiting to take over the children.

Darcy gave her a serious look. "You should call someone to help you today, Mrs. Peters."

The woman shook her head with a smile. "I shall manage, Master. I had it worse once when Lord and Lady Matlock came with their children at the same time when Mrs. Cowlishaw was in confinement with her youngest one and the other four stayed with us." The woman glanced at thirteen year-old Abigail Cowlishaw, who held her two year - old sister by her hand.

Darcy nodded and turned to the children again. "Now, you will walk, I repeat, walk to the smaller dining room, after the nanny."

Mrs. Peters pulled out her hand. "Come children."

The End

Ola Wegner